PART 1

Dedication

To the people who create entire worlds in their heads to escape the fuckery of ours, this is for you.

Cover art by: Mary Dublin

Character art by: Fairchild Art

This is the rewritten and republished version of Paxtyn Ferdelman's 2023 novel—**Her Last Kingdom and Her Last War. This duet is now combined into one book, with parts one and two.**

This book contains time jumps that are necessary for the story's plot.

TRIGGER WARNINGS

This novel contains graphic death, gore, and sexual situations that are not appropriate for readers under the age of seventeen. If you are a sensitive reader, do not go any further.

There will be depictions of a child's death, family death, bloodshed, violence, and war. Please do not continue if any of those subjects will cause you harm of any kind.

Your mental health matters.

AGAIN—PLEASE DO NOT READ IF YOU ARE A SENSI-TIVE READER.

Contents

Prologue

The air that passes through my lungs is crisp and cool, the silence around me deafening.

I keep my eyes cast forward, as if no one else exists but me and this next terrifying, inevitable moment. These next moments—moments that will define how I go down in history.

All I wanted was peace.

All I wanted was a life I was never meant to bear.

A life of solitude while the people of the continents rejoiced in prosperity and joy.

A serenity that I was never meant to bear.

My steps falter the closer I get to the cabin ahead, and the absence of nature's noise is a thunderous crash against my eardrums as I reach the abandoned cabin. The rustle of leaves and snapping twigs is the only indication that I am not completely alone.

I can feel him behind me, silently pleading with me not to enter.

It is only now, all these years later, that I wish I had listened.

1

Elaudia

Elaudia Sonella Eudomean.

A mouthful of a name and general pain in my ass.

Nevertheless, here I am.

Hair as black as midnight, with almond-shaped white eyes that I inherited from neither my mother, nor my father. It is only my seventeenth summer—yet I feel as if I have lived a hundred lifetimes. My uncle, Jaharis, laughs lightly as he blocks my blow and strikes back with his foot. I growl under my breath, trying to avoid the bruise coming my way. I'm mostly unsuccessful.

"Feet apart, young princess. Keep them that close together and you are just **asking** to be knocked on your ass."

"Ahem!"

Jaharis and I glance over at my governess, who watches our sparring with a keen eye and disgruntled frown.

I roll my eyes and giggle.

"Thou shall not use such language with the young princess, old man."

Jaharis grins widely.

"Old you say!"

His outraged cry comes right before another sweep of his sword, and I find myself face-to-face with his boot in the next instant. The breath leaves my lungs, and I wince, pushing myself up and out of the dirt. A huff of disbelief echoes from my governess and the few guards who have stopped to watch our sparring, chuckle at my expense. I blow a strand of silken hair out of my face and grin at my trainer and uncle.

"Couldn't you have spared me the bath I will now have to take before dinner tonight?"

Jaharis reaches down and offers me his hand. I take it lightly as he hoists me up as if I weigh no more than a feather.

"Now then, niece, I fought against your father for the right to train you in the art of battle. I did not challenge him so fiercely just to take it easy on you. You get faster with each day that passes. You've come far these past few years. Another twenty and you might be almost as good as me."

I growl his way and shove him off of me playfully. His hair is as bright as the summer cornfields—though strands of gray are beginning to work themselves in—and his eyes match everyone else of our lineage, a dark stormy blue.

Everyone but me, that is.

Unlike my mother and father, Jaharis has never treated me differently because of the creamy-white haze that seems to cover my vision. I can see almost as well as everyone else can save for a few colors here and there.

I cannot say that the same treatment extends from the Queen and King.

My father treats my eye color as if it is something that hinders our bloodline, and my mother prefers to stare at bland walls than look my way if I'm present.

Even still, they keep their disdain behind closed doors.

Thankfully.

It's embarrassing enough to hear their remarks late into the night, I could not imagine if I had to be subject to them in public.

That would make my already small friend group even smaller.

Governess Theadora pushes an invisible strand of grey hair behind a sharply pointed ear and ushers me forward.

"We shall have luck if we arrive on time! There's filth sticking to your knees."

I smirk at her frown, deciding to kill her with kindness, like usual.

"Better from training than rutting with the—"

Theadora shrieks her outrage.

"Young lady!!! The Queen shall hear of these insinuations!"

Her face is red as she reaches her hands out, grabbing my shoulders before turning me around roughly and ushering me towards the castle's side entrance. I high-five a young guard—Natonak—on the way, while Theadora is distracted with her ranting. Natonak is a close friend from my childhood, and I was saddened to hear that he would be leaving next week to go study across the seas.

I make a face at him—mocking Theadora behind her back—as we continue on past him. She's going over a list of all the things we will have to do to get me ready for tonight's dinner.

I have been told there is important news, rumors that royals from our neighboring kingdom, Lashforn, will be in attendance.

Lashforn is known as the golden kingdom of our lands, seeing as their kingdom trains Bellator's, an ancient line of warriors that protect the integrity of the lands and keep dark forces from invading. As a royal, I am privy to this secret information taught to me by my private tutors. The Bellator's location is not something that is well-known throughout the continents.

Though there hasn't been a Bellator born in many years, and their current numbers are low.

I have never seen a Bellator in person, but I'm told they are tall women with strong features and are charismatic by nature. My height is one of my biggest insecurities. I've always wished to take after Jaharis or his wife, Nyreen, who stands tall and willowy.

Everyone in my family is tall.

I seem to have drawn the short end of the stick—pun intended.

Lashforn is the reason that the current tyranny has not usurped the thrones of our Eastern continent. A war has been raging for almost twenty years, ever since the war general of Mykena set the Kingdom of Dornman ablaze, along with the royal family that slept within, the Syraxes—an ancient bloodline known to be blessed by the Gods.

I pass under the brick archway that leads inside, following Theadora up to my bedrooms. She barks orders at the passing maids, insisting a tub be filled immediately and the finest oils to be ready for use.

Great.

She's going to make me smell like one of those girls from the brothels if she keeps it up.

I clamber up the stairway, shooting a grin at the elderly cook on my way. He tosses me a wink, letting me know he will have one of the servant girls sneak me a cookie at dinner time.

While my parents could have been more at-tentive, I received what they lacked from the castle workers.

Love.

"The Queen insists that you wear the red gown, the one imported from the Free Cities. Savage beasts, but they do create the finest silks and gowns I have ever set my eyes on."

I look up at her with an eyebrow raised.

"How do you know they are truly savage, Theadora? Have you been to the Free Cities?"

Theadora huffs with flapping hands.

"You know as well as I do, child, no one is permitted entrance to the Free Cities. That's how I know they must be uncivilized. Why else would they hide away from the proper king-doms? They must truly be animals."

I roll my eyes at her superiority and scrunch my nose.

"Maybe because they know there's a war go-ing on? I don't know...just an idea."

I giggle at her sneer—a permanent fixture on her face and something I have grown quite used to over the past seventeen years. Theadora has never quite appreciated my sense of humor.

We arrive at my chambers, and I push the door open, heading straight for the tub that has already been filled with steaming water.

Cora and Adelaide—my ladies' maids—wait on the side of the tub, their forms practically overflowing with excitement. I much prefer to be washed by them than Theadora, who scrubs my scalp until I feel as if it's bleeding. When Theadora walks off, I blow out a breath of relief and begin stripping my training clothes off.

"I've heard through the cooks that tonight's feast will be cause for celebration."

Adelaide murmurs to me as she runs an expensive oil throughout my waist-length black strands.

"A Bellator is rumored to be present at the feast."

My eyes widen in disbelief as I whirl toward her voice, blinking away the water that falls into my eyes.

"A Bellator! Are you sure this rumor is true?"

She bites her lip and nods vehemently as she twists my hair dry.

"I heard from my husband himself, they said she is to be revealed tonight and sent to training in Lashforn by first light."

I sit back in the tub as both astonishment and excitement run course through my veins. Nothing exhilarating has ever happened here, though I wish it would. The Kingdom of Aland is the richest on the Eastern continent, in large thanks to our gemstone mines.

The only thing present here are ladies dressed in gold finery, extravagant parties that run late into the night, and watchful eyes that never let me more than a mile from the castle.

I crave adventure and adrenaline.

The closest to an adrenaline rush I ever get is when my cousin Cadmus and I go horseback riding through the cliffs of Edyn. The jagged rocks and constant ledges provide a blood-pumping thrill. Sometimes while riding, I close my eyes and pretend I have a life half as thrilling as a Bellator.

Bellator's are the last of the full-blooded immortals, ever since the Fae and those of their lore were killed off in the great war of Shamonhide a thousand years ago. The only reason the Bellator's did not perish completely was because there was no pattern to when and where a Bellator would be born.

While their magic could be detected at birth by a mage, their warrior abilities did not kick in until their first blood.

The war of Shamonhide was a bloody war, one that brought the wrath of the Gods and concluded with many lives lost. It is something I have always wished I could have helped to stave off.

Perhaps if I had been born at a different time, I might have prevented their extinction.

People feared the Fae—feared what they could do.

They were magical beings, capable of magic greater than anything this world had ever seen. Some lived on land, some in the water. Some had the faces of creatures, but the intellect of scribes. And the Northland Fae...they were so powerful that one could feel their aura from miles away. They contained so much raw magic that it had to be unleashed in small waves, so that it would not overwhelm the Fae who carried it and kill them.

Humans became afraid of what they could do and prayed for the Gods to put an end to their species. I was taught that some of the God's agreed and acted, but most of that information was lost after Shamonhide.

And so, the humans fear destroyed entire races.

I'm pulled from my musings as my hand-maidens help me to stand and step out of the tub. I offer Cora a smile in thanks as she drapes a warm robe upon my body.

They set about getting me ready, not stopping until my hair is covered in ruby gems and braided into two crowns around my head. I slip into the blood-red gown that Theadora insisted upon, wincing when they start on the corset.

These dresses should count as torture devices.

Theadora bursts into the room with a shrewd look, her gaze lowering from my hair to the shoes Adelaide has me step into.

"Good work."

That's all the praise my maids receive before Theadora grabs my wrist and ushers me towards the door. I follow her hasty steps, shooting a smile at my friends on my way out. I'm not so keen to miss out on this dinner now that I know what awaits.

A Bellator in the flesh!

My heels echo throughout the halls, and I can feel the speed of my heart pick up as we descend upon the great dining hall. There are a few important lords and ladies of our court who stand waiting for the arrival of the King and Queen.

They bow as I pass by, acknowledging me with lowered heads. The room is lit with thousands of candles and our royal stamp—a burning golden sea serpent—takes up the entire North wall. I head straight for my seat, two chairs to the right of my mother, and wait for their arrival. I wait no longer than three seconds before the grand doors open once more, and my father's name is called.

"Presenting His Majesty, King Waylin and Her Majesty, the Queen Helena of Aland!"

The squire announcing them steps aside as they enter, and I peek around the room, watching as everyone stands still, admiring the beauty of my parents. Golden-haired and bronze-skinned, they are everything I am not.

The people of Aland adore them—something they never let me forget it. I would adore my regents as well if I had evaded war for so very long—though the jagged cliffs that surround our kingdom are what truly have kept us safe.

My mother wears her signature red smile for the people, and I watch as more than one young woman blushes as my father passes by before glancing towards the ground submissively.

My father married into the family, meaning my mother is the last pure-blooded royal of her bloodline. Her parents were brother and sister—gross—but Jaharis was produced through infidelity, meaning his blood was dirty.

Everyone else has died out.

Or been killed.

I wouldn't think of putting it past them. The only thing my mother cares about more than her vanity is her shiny crown.

I nod politely at my parents as they pass by me and my mother reaches out, placing a slender hand on my shoulder. Her tight squeeze lets me know that Theadora ran straight to her and informed her of my potty mouth.

The snitch.

I bite my lip and keep my eyes cast down until they reach their places at the dinner table. When the squire bangs his staff down to announce more guests, I dare to take my eyes off the ground.

"King Henry and Queen Sofia of Lashforn."

They enter the room slowly, their eyes taking in the scene before them as their guards keep close.

They are dressed simply for royals, and that alone makes me warm toward them. They both have light brown hair and soft eyes as they approach, and I quickly take notice that no one else follows in their wake.

The disappointment hits me hard, and I can feel my shoulders slump down.

Adelaide must have been misinformed.

I see no signs of a Bellator.

I wait for my parents to sit, then follow suit. My eye catches King Henry holding the chair out for His Queen, and it makes me like him even more. He must feel my gaze on my face because he looks up and shoots me a quick wink.

My surprise is a hard thing to tamper down. My cheeks heat with embarrassment and I look to the side, trying to ensure that no one witnessed our encounter.

"Elaudia, quit with the slouching!" My mother hisses.

I sit up straighter and look down as conversation begins at the table begins, droning out when I hear nothing but the boring politics of royal life. My mind drifts to the dessert that is coming my way, when I suddenly hear my name leave my mother's lips.

"As promised, Elaudia has been kept pure and was raised by our best Governess. Her training started at ten summers...a little early, but we were persuaded it would be best for the child. Jaharis had taken a special interest in the girl and as my half-brother, we decided to humor him."

She chuckles as if her relations with him were something to joke about.

"She should be well and able for her trials this coming summer, as we agreed."

Wait, what?

Unbeknownst to me, my outburst was said out loud and I glance around in shock as the table descends into a silence. Queen Sofia tosses an accusing glare toward my mother.

"You did not tell the child?"

My father shrugs a hefty shoulder and takes a hearty drink of his wine.

"It did not seem important to inform the girl. Her knowing would have changed nothing of the future, and we did not wish for word to spread, lest the General be alerted to her survival."

A fist slams down on the table, causing the dishes and my heart to rattle. King Henry's face is red in anger.

"Do not play the fool with me, Waylin! You stole the child from Dornman as leverage against the General—should you have needed it."

He sneers the words, and I can almost taste the contempt he has for my father from where I sit.

"We allowed you to leave with her that night, only for the protection your kingdom could bring her once he retreated. We agreed! You mean to sit there and tell me the girl knows nothing of what she is!?"

My father does not answer.

So, I speak up in his stead.

"You speak of me...do you not?"

Four sets of eyes swivel my way, but I resist the urge to shrink back even further into my seat. Queen Sofia leans her body closer to mine as she rests her arms on the table.

My eyes fall on the velvet green lining of her gown and the golden designs that decorate her sleeves.

"Yes, child...we speak of you. Can you tell me your name? Your full name?"

I purse my lips in confusion.

"Princess Elaudia Sonella Eudomean, of Al and...your Majesty."

Her husband shouts again in disbelief.

"An outrage!"

The Queen shushes her husband, soothing his anger like balm on an open wound.

She turns her attention back to me and I notice that my parents sit stiffly in their chairs.

"Child—your name is Elaudia Sonella Syraxes—Queen of the Syraxes bloodline, and the only surviving Bellator of The Kingdom of Dornman."

I know logically, it's not the best time to faint. But when have I ever followed through on anything logical?

So faint is exactly what I do.

2

Elaudia

I let out a decidedly unfeminine groan when I open my eyes.

My bedroom ceiling greets my eyes, its blue and golden swirls offering a small comfort for the nightmare I just had. I sit up in my bed and catch sight of the rising sun, groaning when a knock sounds at my door the very next moment.

I haven't even opened my mouth before my uncle—Jaharis—and his son, Cadmus, come charging into my room.

I shoot them a scolding look.

"You know you're supposed to wait for me to allow you entrance, right? I have barely opened my eyes, what if I had been indecent? In addition to that, I have just had the most *dreadful* nightmare!"

Uncle Jaharis rests a hand on his sword and looks at me with sad eyes as though he has just killed my favorite puppy.

Not that I've ever had one.

Cadmus frowns, shooting a glance at his father before he steps forward, his hands resting on his belt.

"It was no nightmare, Elaudia. You are the last royal blood of the Syraxes line. A Bellato r...as well."

I swing my legs over the side of my bed and land on the floor softly, crossing my arms over my chest protectively. My brain feels as if it has turned to mush as I regard them both for a moment.

"Well...that cannot be. Because if I am a Bellator and Syraxes...that means that my parents are not my parents. And you, Cadmus... you're not my cousin. And Jaharis..."

My voice weakens and trails off when the solemn looks on their faces do not change. I step back as if I have been punched in the gut.

That is exactly what it feels like.

I look between my favorite two people in the world, begging for this truth they speak of to be a terrible lie.

My white eyes scan their blue.

My hair...*black.*

Theirs...the color of the moon and corn-flower.

A whimper that I cannot trap escapes my lips.

Jaharis steps forward in alarm as he out-stretches his arms to my own.

"Sweet girl..."

I can feel my lips tremble as I step back and fall back onto my bed.

"How long?"

A grim understanding dawns in their eyes and I close my own in despair. Salty tears track down my face.

"Since the day you arrived...Princess."

A sob leaves my mouth, and I cover it to stifle my cries.

"Please, Elaudia. We do not have much time. I managed to secure Cadmus a position as your guard for your travels, but you are leaving by the end of the hour. You must know we truly love you as our own. Blood changes nothing."

Jaharis sweeps forward and engulfs me in his arms, and I let him, simply for the fact that if he had not—I might have crashed to the floor. His battle-scarred hands lift my face until he is looking into my eyes.

"You will face more heartbreak in these next few months than I can bear to think, but I have trained you well, little flower. You will survive the trials to come, and you will become the Bellator you were always meant to be—the *Queen* you were always meant to be. General Neem of Mykena still enforces the roles of the dark rebels and searches for remaining Bellator's. Kingdoms are falling. We have tried to shelter you from the war to come, but now the time has arrived for you to take your place."

His fingers gently wipe the tears from my face.

"My entire life has been a lie," I whispered brokenly.

He shakes his head in denial.

"Your entire life has a *purpose*. Tell me, little flower...what will you yearn for here at home?

The façade of substitute parents who do not truly love you and aimlessly wandering these halls until your mind grows weary from boredom? You are meant for so much more than this life—this kingdom."

Cadmus steps forward and places a heavy hand on my slim shoulder. I look up at my elder cousin, the boy who has grown up with me and never left me to face a single day alone.

"He's right, sweetheart. But our affection for you transcends bloodlines. You are my best friend and *my family*. I will not abandon you now. I swear it, I am yours to command."

I can tell that he means the vow he speaks, and I burrow my head into his chest, snuggling close. Another knock sounds at the door and we break from our embrace. This time, my visitor waits for my acknowledgment.

"Enter."

Queen Sofia enters alone, regarding the three of us with gentle eyes. Her voice is soft when she speaks.

"May I have a moment alone with the young queen?"

Jaharis and Cadmus both promptly bow with respect before departing from me.

"Of course, Your Majesty."

They leave the room swiftly, but not before Cadmus assures me that he will be ready and waiting by the carriage. The door shuts with a click as I bow my head and drop into a small curtsey as I channel every etiquette lesson Governess Theadora has ever taught me.

"Your Highness, I apologize for my episode at the dining table. It was unlike my character, and I assure you it will never happen again."

I keep my chin pointed towards the floor and only raise it when a hand pulls it up.

"Do not apologize for the mistakes of others, because that is exactly what last night was. The Queen knew she was being malicious when she kept your true identity a secret from you. Helena has always had a mean streak."

A small smile lights up her eyes and I relax, sensing that Sofia is nothing like the woman I have called mother all these years.

"Please, have a seat."

She guides me to the tea table in the corner of my room, pouring us both a fresh cup.

"When General Neem originally declared war on the four continents, the Bellator's rallied together to defeat him—or at the very least—hold him off. When he enlisted the help of the civilians who wanted Fae and immortality gone from the world, our fight became more difficult. You see, Bellator's are restricted from killing outside their jurisdictions. It is something in the old magic that created them to ensure no one woman would seek a path of destruction across the lands. A way to ensure order, if you will."

I sit forward, trying to keep up.

"There is a reason that the Syraxes line was exempt from this magic—and why General Neem ambushed The Kingdom of Dornman. Many centuries ago, your great ancestor came across the Demi Goddess who created the Bellator's, Freydis. She was facing an attack from men who were angry with her, for she chose woman to inherit enhanced battle skills and strength—and not man. They were four hundred to her one, and though she fought bravely, she was losing, for they had the help of a black magic witch from the western city of Myke-na."

Sofia takes a sip of her tea before continuing.

"Your ancestor, Eriny, defended her valiantly, at the risk of her own life. She was no Bellator, for the Syraxes line was a new bloodline from across the dark seas. The ancient scrolls state that Freydis was cast down by The Gods for failing to abide by their rules. She was in a weakened state and stumbled upon the town of Vianijn—not too far from the Northland's—a magicless place where a Bellator's abilities became completely null."

I sit forward; my eyes wide as I listen with absolute rapture.

"While the witch was distracted by Freydis, Eriny plunged a knife into the heart of the witch, killing her."

My brows furrow together as I try to piece this story into one.

"So, when Eriny defended Freydis...she was made into a Bellator and granted the privilege of defending wherever she went?"

Sofia nods solemnly.

"Freydis saw how pure her soul was, and so the Syraxes line was blessed by Freydis, for every first–born daughter could defend the people, wherever she may be in the world. She would be blessed with magic, increased agility and strength. Advanced knowledge of weaponry and its uses. She may kill those who wield black magic—the one magic invincible against all others. And she has *courage.* Bellator's are the bravest of the brave. More so than any man on the four continents."

She states it proudly and it suddenly dawns on me.

"You're a Bellator, aren't you?"

Her laugh is infectious and genuine, surprising me.

"No, my dear one. But I have the privilege of being related to one—*you. "*

I must have heard her wrong. I wait a second more for her to correct herself, but she does no such thing. I shake my head back and forth.

"You're the Queen of Lashforn...the Syraxes came from across the dark seas...?" She nods in agreement.

"This is true. But my brother, Griffin, married your mother, Fridella. You are my niece by blood."

I can hear my heartbeat in my ears at this point as the blood drains from my face. The Queen must sense that I am on information overload because she takes pity on me.

"There is no reason to try and dissect everything today, dear one. We leave for Lashforn now and when we arrive, you will have a few days to adjust before your true training and trials start."

"My *true* training?" I breathe.

Her hand pats my own.

"With your sisters in arms. Come now, I was told your belongings will follow us shortly, but we *are* in a bit of a time crunch."

I sense there is something that she is not telling me but quickly decide that I have absorbed too much information for the moment. Anymore and I might just have a mental breakdown. She takes my hands into her own and studies me for a moment.

"I know I am a stranger to you now, dear one, but I hope that in the future you might come to think of me as true family. I know you have not had the best exposure to the word here, but believe me, if we had any other options at the time, we would have taken them. Lashforn was not as formidable at the time as Aland was."

I nod up at her and smile softly.

"You said this was the safest place for me to be raised last night, you truly meant that?"

Sofia frowns.

"Unfortunately, yes…Aland is one of the last three great kingdoms that has yet to be invaded by the General Neem's forces. I grew up with Helena…we used to be dear friends before she was ruined by her father. Though the anger in her heart is justified, her disregard for you is not. But, because of their own selfish reasons, I knew they would protect you until you came of age."

She allows me a few moments to change out of the sleeping gown that my maids must have helped me into while I was unconscious. I quickly change into fresh clothes—a pair of black training pants, a white tunic, and a half corset. Once I have emerged from my changing

screen, prepared for travel, she ushers me towards the door. Just before we step out, I turn
her way and place a hand on her arm.

"You mentioned Lashforn and Aland were
the last of *three* kingdoms untouched by the
war. What is the remaining one?"

"The Kingdom of Atarah in the Northlands.
On the same lands as the Wild Woods."

I freeze in my tracks.

"But...aren't the Wild Woods on the same
lands as The Free Cities?"

The Free Cities have rejected our hierarchies
for centuries, instead choosing to lean on their
own tools and knowledge for survival.

"Indeed, they are. King Axel of Atarah has
just signed a treaty with the rulers of The Free
Cities. In exchange for his protection from the
coming war, he is now their ruling monarch."

Holy Fuck.

3
Elaudia

The carriage ride grows less bumpy the further away from Aland that we travel.

The Queen and King ride in a separate carriage, much to my dismay.

I wanted to pick my aunt for more information. Cadmus sits silently beside me, and I know he must be waiting for my anger to escape now that we are finally alone.

I find I can only muster one emotion—grim acceptance.

I am a Bellator.

Me.

Boring old Elaudia who reads naughty romance novels in her chambers and prefers the smell of the horse stables over dining with the wealthiest of our ladies.

I fiddle with the ends of my hair in my lap before casting a glance at Cadmus.

"Did you truly fight to come with me?"

He glances down at me with surprise, his deep voice making the carriage seem smaller when he answers.

"I meant what I said back in your room, little flower. You might have just learned who you are, but I have always known. And against my father's judgment and my mother's, I became your closest friend because of your pure heart and kind soul. Because you are an *amazing* person. I knew when this day came for you, that you would need someone by your side. And I determined it would be me."

I raise an eyebrow.

"Jaharis and Nyreen did not want you to grow close to me?"

A sheepish look takes over his broad features.

"They knew you would not stay forever. I think they were trying to protect us both from the eventual separation. When I made it clear that I had declared you my favorite cousin in the entire world, they changed their minds."

I laugh lightly and smack his armor covered chest.

"You made that decree when we were eight and I stomped on your foot because you ruined my mud castle. You were nonsensical."

His laugh echoes my own as he tosses his head back.

"Indeed, I was, cousin. Indeed, I was."

My heart lightens at the easy banter between us, and I relax knowing that one thing will stay the same on this new journey.

I sit back and lean into Cadmus, closing my eyes. I was told the journey is just over a day's travel, and despite my full night of rest, I find that my mind is exhausted in a way I didn't know it could be. Cadmus pulls out a scroll for his never-ending studies and I nudge his shoulder with my own.

"Wake me up if you see anything interesting."

A grin tilts the corners of his lips.

"Sure thing, little flower."

I fall asleep the sound of rustling paper and hoofbeats taking me to my new home.

***

I must have slept the day away, because the sky is dark when I open my eyes.

I shake away my odd dream and glance to my left, smiling at the sight of Cadmus slumped against the carriage wall, taking me with him. The steady rocking of the carriage soothes me, and I let out a wide yawn, shivering at the temperature drop.

The Kingdom of Lashforn is closer to the Northlands than any other land I know of.

I pull the curtains to the side and see nothing but trees, though the frost-bitten sight of everything on the ground lets me know we are much further north than I have ever been.

I reach under my feet for the blankets I know to be stacked there, pulling two out and covering Cadmus and then myself. The sky is so dark it looks black, with thousands of twinkling stars winking back at me as if they are attempting to show off.

I used to wonder how many people were staring back at the very same stars.

How many people yearned for the same peace and tranquility I did?

I lean out and whisper to the guards riding beside our carriage.

"How much further is Lashforn, Sir?"

The older man in armor glances my way, smiling softly.

"About a quarter of the night, Princess."

I nod at him in thanks and sit back once more, snuggling in.

With one more glance at the stars, I close my eyes and hope that I fall back into my dream. A dream where a burning pair of eyes watched me from the shadows—waiting for me.

4
Axel

"Was there anything else you needed, My King?"

Bador's voice pulls me from my reveries, and I glance over at my Hand and longest ally.

"That is all for the night, Bador. Enjoy your evening."

He bows deeply, his thinning red hair falling into his face.

"Your Majesty."

The doors to my private chambers click shut, and I turn my head back to the sky, swirling the amber liquid in my glass.

Something called out to me tonight.

Though I don't know what.

Today's events were cause for celebration—for I am the first ruling monarch to not only enter the Free Cities—but induct them into my lands, making them my own. Seeing as I do not let just anyone into Atarah, the leaders of the Free Cities related to me in a way. When they realized the war that General Neem would soon bring to their doorstep, they were quick to sign the treaty with my Kingdom.

I look out, still hearing the sounds of music and the cheering of my people.

I run a thick hand through my black hair, and then the growing stubble on my jawline, trying to pinpoint the cause for my restlessness.

I think for a moment to send for Vivienne, the very rare concubine I will take to bed, but then remember she had disappeared last full moon.

It is for the best.

She had grown too forward with her touch lately, attempting to connect with me outside of the bedroom.

Something I do not tolerate.

I have no need for a queen, nor do I want a wife.

The only thing my soul craves for is a mate—someone I will now never know with the extinction of magic and my people. Usually, the women who bring my release understand it is an act of physicality and nothing more.

They come to the guest suite the floor below my room for the night of pleasure I give them, and then I send them on their way.

Being raised by a woman as pure as my mother has turned me off to the women that roam this castle.

Only after wealth and power.

No...my father's line will end with me.

I could not subject a child to a lifetime of loneliness like mine.

But still...

Something is calling out to me.

I can feel it.

5
Elaudia

The trill of trumpets sounding wake me up before Cadmus's grumbling does.

I sit up and stretch, arching my back until pleasure tingles up my spine.

Those make for the very best stretches.

Sunlight glints through the closed window shades and I lift them up before Cadmus can stop me. He grumbles a shout of dismay, covering his eyes.

"Cadmus wake up! We're here!"

For the first time since the revelation of my true nature, excitement courses through my veins at the sight of Lashforn. We travel down cobblestone roads, and I catch sight of the townspeople out and about, bartering for goods and calling out greetings while they brandish fur coats and bright smiles.

There are multiple ponds frozen over, and I grin with delight at the sight of the ice.

I have always wanted to try ice skating.

Aland's weather never dips below a cool breeze in the winter, so the season has never touched me until now. Cadmus wipes the sleep from his eyes, blinking at me wearily.

"You spent most of the night going over those scrolls, didn't you?"

He grins at me sheepishly.

"Women love a man with knowledge."

I roll my eyes and chuck one of the very scrolls I spoke of at his head.

"Come here and look at all of this frozen ice!"

He slides over on the bench and leans out, letting out a whistle.

"They definitely have a hard time hunting around these parts, that's for sure."

"Lashforn is a kingdom of great wealth and food because of their trade ships that brave the dark seas. I doubt they hunt to survive...more than likely it is just for the pleasure of it."

Cadmus nods in agreement as we watch the passing kingdom in silence for the next few moments.

It is at the end of the road that we begin the final ascension to the castle.

Rough cobblestone turns to smooth brick lay, and I grin at the relief it brings my back. I adjust myself in my seat and attempt to calm my racing heart and mind. A faint noise transforms into the roaring sound of thunder, and I peek out, catching sight of more people than I have ever seen in my life. They cheer as my carriage passes by, throwing favors our way onto the ice-slicked roads.

"Cadmus..."

He witnesses what I do and begins running a soothing hand up and down my back.

"Well, it could be worse...they could be sharpening their pitchforks for you..." He jokes.

I elbow him in the ribs and grin as he lets out a grunt. My breath releases in a whoosh.

"I don't think I will ever be ready for *this...*"

I sit back as the carriage rolls to a stop in front of the grand castle steps. Cadmus leans down so that he's kneeling in front of me. I look into his blue eyes for the reassurance I know he is trying to offer me.

"No matter what challenges face us outside these doors, no matter what is asked of you from this moment on, *I will be here.* We will do this together, Laudi, I swear it on my life."

A tear that I cannot stop trails down my cheek, and I close both of my eyes and nod.

"Okay."

"Are you ready?"

I sigh and stand as they begin to announce my arrival.

"As I'll ever be."

The door swings open and Cadmus steps out in front of me. I can hear the hush of the crowd at the sight of him and know that I can prolong my arrival no longer. I take the first step into the light slowly, keeping my head down.

I look nothing like a Bellator.

I'm short and small, with white eyes.

Surely the people of Lashforn will see this and be disappointed in what their monarchs have brought them.

I look up, holding my breath.

I can feel a hundred different pairs of eyes on my body, examining me and what I have to offer. I brace myself for their rejection, but as soon as my white eyes meet theirs, the crowd erupts in screams that pound against my eardrums. My name begins as a chant across the grounds as Cadmus takes my hand and leads me forward to where the King and Queen stand tall and proud with smiles adorning their faces.

The Queen pulls me into her arms.

"I told you that you had nothing to worry about. Our people have long known of you. You are royalty in their eyes. Come now, let us get inside and out of the chill."

I follow my aunt up the steps and take notice of the immediate guard that surrounds us completely. The door to the castle is twice as large as Aland's and it takes twice as many men to push it open.

The guards wear black gear, with green and gold crusted emblems crossing through their chest plates, representing The Kingdom of Lashforn. They place a hand across their chest and bow their heads with respect as we walk by.

My eyes take in the bodies that are bustling back and forth throughout the castle halls, and I look at my aunt with a raised eyebrow.

"Tonight, we celebrate your arrival and welcome you properly."

I point outside with a confused look.

"That wasn't a proper welcome?"

Cadmus stifles a laugh behind his hand and ruffles my hair.

The queen smiles.

"That was simply a hello." She murmurs.

I open my mouth to question her further, but two women appear out of the fray and rush forward with beaming smiles.

"Hello!" They echo each other.

Queen Sofia giggles and extends a hand toward the beaming ladies.

"Elaudia, these are your ladies' maids, Nelly and Bria. Anything you may need—they can see to it. I hand-picked them myself."

I can see by the redness that takes over their cheeks that being hand chosen by The Queen herself is a great honor to them. I smile softly and go to shake their hands.

"It's a pleasure to meet you two."

Their eyes widen briefly in shock at the sight of my outstretched hand before they recover and grab for it, shaking it gently. Nelly has beautiful curly strawberry–blonde hair and a freckled face, while Bria has hair as golden as the sun and the brightest green eyes I've ever seen.

Eyes that I've noticed keep straying to Cadmus and the hand he has placed around my shoulder.

I smile to myself.

Looks like there might be hope for him yet.

"Well now, I think Nelly and Bria should show you to your bedchambers and help you settle before the feast tonight, yes?"

I nod at my aunt and uncle.

"What about Cadmus?"

The King steps forward and places an arm around my cousin.

"Don't you worry about this young man here. I've heard The Captain of our royal guard wishes to meet with him. He wants to ensure he's the proper man to protect the last royal blood of Dornman."

I watch as Cadmus puffs his chest with pride before he plants a kiss on my forehead.

"I'll come to find you later, alright? Go settle and rest."

I nod and say goodbye, then turn as Nelly and Bria usher me towards the staircase.

Nelly speaks first.

"You'll love your bedchambers, Your Highness. There are grand windows that overlook the frozen seas, but in the summertime, you can witness all creatures of the ocean at play!"

I smile her way softly.

"That sounds lovely, Nelly. But please, call me Laudi."

They both stumble and glance at each other, exchanging shocked looks, before smiling my way.

"Whatever you wish, Your—um, Laudi." Nelly stutters my name out.

We reach my bedrooms quickly and although I'm eager to make new friends, the pressure from today's events hits me all at once.

"Do you both think it would be alright if I settled in by myself? I'm afraid my travels have left me exhausted."

"Of course!"

Bria hustles over to the large armoire, opening its large black doors.

"There are gowns here for you to wear during your stay. The Queen has had them fitted just for you, as well as trousers and blouses for training. They have stocked your bathing room with every necessity you could need, but if something has run out or if you prefer something different, just let Nelly or I know, and we will bring it right to you."

I force a grin her way and wait for them to both exit my room completely before I let out a heavy sigh and slump against the bed behind me.

I'm a Bellator.

An actual warrior.

Not just another princess doomed to serve my kingdom by being wed into a marriage I do not want and made to produce the next generation. I have...freedom.

Real freedom.

For the first time in my life.

I place my hands on my sides and lay back into the soft bedding, sighing at the comfort it brings me.

I have been trained my entire life in the art of the dagger and sword, but never have I ever accessed any of the powers that Bellator's are rumored to possess.

The more I think about it, the more my heart races in my chest as I think of failing. As the last of the Syraxes line, it is my duty to carry on the name.

My duty is to make my ancestors proud.

The only problem?

I have no idea where to even begin.

6

Elaudia

Three months later

The sound of metal crashing against one another is a familiar noise in my ears, bringing me a strange sense of comfort.

I twirl away from Clarice, a fellow Bellator, and my closest fighting companion. Her brown eyes light up with challenge as she charges me once more, lashing out with her whip. Its end is barbed with metal spikes, her chosen weapon in battle, though she is just as spectacular with a bow and arrow.

She's so tall that she can reach an ungodly number of places with her whip, including spies resting in trees.

My own weapon, a polearm fastened to my short height but as deadly and sharp as any sword, glints in the sunlight.

I block her attack once more and then swoop down low, throwing her legs out from underneath her. She lets out a sound akin to an animal choking as I press my polearm into her neck before she has the chance to regain her breath. Sweat beads on our foreheads heavily, and my limbs ache from the intense training we've subjected ourselves to for the past six hours, but still, I smile down at her and offer my arm.

She smiles back and takes it, heaving herself up. I crane my neck to look up at her as she readjusts her fiery red hair into a bun.

My first week here is when I learned what I knew would be obvious, I'm the smallest Bellator to ever exist, but that didn't stop them from treating me as equally as any other.

They trained me hard but were just as kind and welcoming.

For once in my life, I had a *true* meaning of family—of sisters.

"You know I almost had you in the first half." Clarice chuckles.

I roll my eyes and playfully shove at her as we make our way to the castle.

"You would need to actually *get* me to defeat me, Clarice."

She makes a noncommittal sound while she places her whip back onto her belt.

"It will happen one of these days princess."

I was the best yet by no means, but the others quickly learned that my small stature was to be used to my advantage.

And use it I did.

I learned to be the most agile Bellator on the training fields, deflecting blow after blow. I was rarely put down and I know it made my aunt proud. Between training physically on the fields and training magically with the best scribe Lashforn could employ, I have begun my journey to becoming exactly what the world needs right now.

The General's rebels have gained more power these past few months, causing more destruction and chaos than I care to admit. Bombs have ignited and cities have burned, all because of a man that became so power-hungry, he lost all sense of his morality.

Atarah and Lashforn remain the only Kingdoms completely untouched.

Just last month, Aland was finally infiltrated.

I immediately sent word to Jaharis and Nyreen and was assured of their safety. I sent another letter, begging for them to come to Lashforn where we could all be together, but communications cut off as soon as it was sent. I know that Cadmus worries, even if he has hardened since coming here, determined to reach the status of my royal guard when I step up and inherit my throne.

The only time I see him smile is when we are eating a ridiculous number of sweets at the end of the night in my chambers and gossiping about his commanding officers—very few who think him worthy of protecting me.

Clarice and I exit the gates, and I catch sight of my cousin up ahead, looking for me. He immediately spots me and joins my side. his expression fierce.

"Come with me."

His abruptness catches me off guard, and I shoot a quizzical glance at Clarice. She shrugs lightly as I follow after him. He leads me through the front corridor and down the hall, ducking under the low-hanging bricks. His steps have hastened, and I can feel my heart start to beat faster.

"Cadmus, what's happening? Is everyone okay? Is it your parents?"

He shoots a quick glance back and squeezes my hand gently.

"Everyone is fine, Laudi. This is about you."

Now I'm really confused. We reach the end and enter the forest surrounding the castle walls. It's very rare that I'm allowed to go so far without a full guard, but I trust Cadmus. Aunt Sofia fears for my safety, insisting that until it is announced that the last of the Syraxes line sits on the throne, I'm to lay low.

Once General Neem learns of my existence, he will stop at nothing to kill the one person who can put an end to his madness.

Me.

Cadmus paces for a moment under the great oak as I untie my braid, my black hair trailing down to my ass. I run my hands through it, soothing away the sweat clinging to my forehead.

If I know anything about Cadmus, he thinks his next words are about to hurt me.

He always paces in agitation before he breaks the bad news to me.

I bite my lip in anticipation.

"Just spit it out already!"

He stumbles, as if he forgot I was present, and rubs a hand down his face and through his thickening golden beard. Something I don't know how he gets away with.

Every warrior I've seen in Lashforn is clean-shaven.

"They plan to wed you. By the next full moon."

My heart stops in my chest. I blink hazy white eyes his way and tilt my head in confusion.

"What?" I breathe.

I watch his throat work to swallow.

"I heard Sofia and Henry...I was with Yumin in their private quarters."

Yumin is the Captain of the Royal Guard.

"A Lord of Misit has learned of your existence. He threatens to take the information to

General Neem himself if we do not meet his demands."

Misit sits close to Atarah's boarders. I cannot fathom why anyone would want to assist General Neem in any way—marriage or not.

Cadmus must read my mind because he steps forward.

"Power. The Lord has discovered your bloodline. He knows that a Queen of the Syraxes bloodline lives."

The breath I had been holding escapes as this reality falls over me.

Cadmus places his large hands on my shoulders and looks down at me, rage for the Lord and love for me in his eyes.

"He plans to become The King."

7
Elaudia

I have yet to ever see Sofia shed a tear in my presence, not since the first day they came for me.

She cries now though, great big tears that soak her face.

"I'm sorry my child, we tried to stall him, we've offered him everything we could think of. He wants nothing short of you. I don't know what else to do. You're not ready to face General Neem and his army."

I stare blankly ahead, as I have done ever since Cadmus brought me back to the castle to meet with Sofia and Henry.

I know that Yumin is angry with Cadmus for exposing this truth to me too soon, but one sharp glare from me and he glances away in respect.

Henry steps forward, a solemn look on his face.

"General Neem cannot gain access to you, my dear. If we lose you, this world is lost forever."

He says nothing that I don't already know, though it doesn't lessen the pain that pierces my heart. I hadn't given much thought to the future apart from fighting alongside my sisters. Marriage always seemed just out of reach, something of an afterthought.

I haven't heard much of this Lord, though that doesn't mean anything. Misit is a very small city—with little to offer other lands. I didn't study it much during my schooling.

"What is this Lord's name?" I question my uncle.

His hands continuously run through his graying beard.

"Lord Krevosh. I've asked my advisors, and they know little of him, other than the grand home he keeps on a piece of land close to Atarah's borders."

I stand and begin pacing, my mind grasping for ways out of this.

My aunt clears her throat delicately and steps towards me with a hand on my shoulder.

"He'll be here tonight."

I whip towards her, my black hair flying into my face.

"*Tonight!?*"

She nods once more, lowering her head in shame. I look at her a moment longer before turning my gaze to Cadmus. I can see the rage in his eyes threatening to erupt, but with the thin ice he is already on with Yumin, I know if I break here, it might further hinder his progress with his captain.

Cadmus would steal me away in the night if I ever asked.

He would fight anyone or anything to protect me.

I take a slow, steady breath.

"Okay."

I can hear their intake of breath, the surprise evident on their faces. I glance down at my attire, my clothes filthy and covered in mud.

"I guess I should make myself presentable then."

I don't give anyone another word before I head for the doors, keeping my head high. I can have a moment in my chambers, alone.

Aunt Sofia tries to say something, but Henry silences her.

"Let her go, she needs a moment alone to come to terms with this information, and we need to try to think of a way out of it."

I thank him silently for stopping her as I rush towards my rooms, passing Nelly and Bria on the way. Tears threaten to fall down my cheeks, so I ignore their attempts to stop me.

I reach the doors and throw them open before immediately slamming them shut as I collapse against them.

The sobs I've been holding back finally break loose. I can hear a shuffle of footsteps and dresses rustling.

Nelly and Bria.

"My lady? Are you quite alright?"

"Did she seem alright to you, Bria?" I can hear Nelly snap.

"What should we do? Should we call for The Queen, perhaps?"

"That won't be necessary girls."

Cadmus.

"Please, leave us. Laudi has just gotten some bad news. If you could please prepare her a dress for the engagement dinner tonight. I'll take care of her, I promise."

Gasps ring out through the hallways, and I take comfort in the fact that my ladies' maids and friends did not know of this news.

"Right away, Lieutenant," Nelly whispers before they leave.

My sobs lessen as Cadmus attempts to open the door. I sit where I am, pushing him back out.

"Please just leave me be."

His deep voice rings out in reply.

"I'm giving you one more chance to move that big behind of yours before I move it for you."

I sit where I am, trying to prove I am more stubborn than he is.

He huffs once before shoving it open and shoving *me* onto my hands.

"Hey!"

I glare up at him and stop at the sight of his slight grin.

One moment later and we both burst into laughter.

Well—my version is more of a laugh-and-cry. His eyes soften as he leans down, grabbing my hands and holding them within his own.

"Oh, Laudi."

I whimper at his soft tone and rush forward, wrapping my arms around his waist and inhaling the familiar comfort of my cousin and best friend. His chin rests upon my head as he strokes my hair.

"Say the word." He whispers. "Say the word and we will be gone before nightfall, and they will never see us again."

I sigh before looking up at him.

"I know. But we *both* know that's the coward's way out. I am to be a Queen, am I not?"

He smiles gently before nodding.

"You will forever be my family before royalty, and I will do whatever it takes to see you smile. You deserve happiness Laudi...you deserve true love."

Cadmus wipes the tears from my eyes.

"We will go through with this farce of a dinner, but you say the word, and I will end his very life if I must. Blackmail is not the best way to start a marriage. I can already imagine the type of man he is, this Lord, and it's making me want to punch his lights out."

I agree with him.

Lord Krevosh made it abundantly clear that he cares not for me as a person, but only for the power my status will bring him. I nod and step back, pulling from within myself for my Bellator's courage.

"Okay then. Send Nelly and Bria back to me. I'll get ready."

Cadmus nods and opens the door, glancing back.

"Remember, say the word and it will be done."

I nod solemnly and step back as I wait for Nelly and Bria to return and begin.

8

Elaudia

"I cannot fathom how word of your existence has been let known, Your Grace. It's an absolute act of treason!"

Skirts ruffle and flutter as my very *angry* handmaidens work around me.

"The castle staff was made aware before your arrival that we were to mention nothing of your Syraxes bloodline! The people were only told that a new Bellator had come to join our ranks! We were sworn to protect this secret in front of the very Gods themselves!"

Nelly has been on a constant rant since the moment she entered my room, and her rage comforts me.

She's acting how I wish I could, and it brings me solace to know that even if someone in this castle betrayed the kingdom and myself, it wasn't my friends.

Cadmus and the royal guard have been making rounds, turning the castle inside in an attempt to sniff out the traitor. They are convinced they will find them by the early morning.

I sit still as Bria softly braids my hair into an elegant updo, adding roses and blades to the sections closest to my scalp.

The roses were her idea, the blades, mine.

I will forever be a warrior before a princess, and having a weapon hidden on me brings me comfort. The dress I adorn is made of the finest silk and is of the darkest red I could imagine.

My aunt cared not to make me look like a delicate flower, but a powerful woman, and I'm grateful to her for it.

Just as I think of her, she enters my room. I stand as Bria finishes with my hair and turn to face Sofia. She herself has donned her finest gown, a deep emerald color that matches the color of the jewels in her crown.

"My child...you are simply breathtaking." She breathes.

Nelly and Bria have both stepped back, their heads bowed.

I step forward and curtsey, lowering my head until she commands me otherwise.

A hand under my chin pulls me up and her eyes glisten with tears. I swallow the lump in my throat before speaking.

"I will make you proud."

Aunt Sofia has given me everything.

She gave me a future and freedom.

Something I thought I would never have.

She laughs softly before her own eyes harden.

"No child. *You will give him hell.*"

The girls behind me gasp at the queen's language, and I can feel my own lips—painted blood red—widen into a smile.

She offers me her arm.

"Shall we?"

I take her offered arm and as we make our way to the dining room, my heart feels lighter than it has all day. Nelly and Bria trail behind us, prepared to grab our skirts at the staircase. The castle workers are all dressed in their finest dresses and vests. The clothing they adorn only for very important guests.

I hope he's flattered because he sure as shit isn't worthy.

The doors open and I sigh in relief to see that Cadmus has been positioned close by.

The King sits at the head of the table with two men on the opposite side of him to the left. One with hair the color of dying fire, and the other a sandy blonde. Usually, when we dine together as a family, Henry and Sofia sit next to each other and I sit where the newcomers lounge.

It seems we are in full royal effect for the night.

Sofia parts from me at the bottom of the stairs, heading for the chair at the opposite end of the table.

My uncle nods to the chair next to her and I relax, sitting next to my aunt. I'm grateful Henry is keeping the men far away from me.

"You're late."

It's the blonde man who speaks; his tone void of any kindness for the princess *he has just met.*

I open my mouth to respond, but my aunt cuts me off, her glare cold.

"Elaudia is never late." She speaks clearly, daring him to defy her words.

His square jaw clenches with annoyance and I can tell he did not think that my aunt and uncle would be so close with me.

Gods how he was wrong.

Henry nods towards the staff and they rush forward with glasses and plates full of meats and vegetables. A throat clears before Henry speaks.

"Lord Krevosh, my niece, Elaudia Sonella Syraxes, Queen to the Syraxes line. I apologize for the informal meeting, but I'm sure you can understand, these are very informal and last-minute circumstances."

I study Krevosh's face at my uncle's words, watching for any emotions that might pass over his face. He would be slightly good-looking if not for the flat nose and non-existent chin. I'm sure he is all the rage to the young and impressionable women of his lands.

Personally, I prefer my men dark-haired and rugged. Men with calloused hands, a fighter's build, and an aura that screams *danger.*

This Lord is thin, clean-shaven and weak.

Add in his absolute snobbish attitude and I can hardly hold back the vomit that builds in my throat. He picks up another glass of wine, chugging it down, before gesturing for the servants to refill it.

"It's fine, *Your Majesty*. Though her tardiness is a sure thing to be corrected soon, I'm sure she will be easy enough to break."

My aunt chokes on her sip of wine, and I can hear a growl break loose from Cadmus' throat.

My own eyes widen in shock at his casual words and Henry's face reddens in anger. He opens his mouth to defend me, but Krevosh cuts him off with a finger wag.

"Ah ah ah...let's not sit here and pretend to be nice. You made it well enough known how you feel about my marriage to your niece, but we shouldn't pretend that I care. Your desperation to keep General Neem out of your kingdom is the price you paid to give me the princess."

His attention turns to me as he downs another glass.

It seems my future husband is a drunk.

I might be able to work with this.

"Now, I don't particularly care for you or your feelings, I do however care for the throne I'm promised for being wed to your disfigured body."

Disfigured? I'm just short!

I screech in my mind.

The red-haired man watches everything with quiet eyes and an even more silent mouth.

I decide he must be just as bad as Lord Krevosh.

"What is your name, sir?" I ask the man next to Krevosh.

Krevosh waves his hand in dismissal.

"Sir Bador, *Princess*. He has been a messenger for me for many years and is of no consequence to you. Now I am tired of these pleasantries, when will you have the preparations ready?"

Henry grips his dinner spoon, his gaze deadly.

"Everything will be in order by the end of the week. We still wait for word of Aland's arrival."

Word that I'm not sure will ever come. I catch sight of Cadmus at the mention of his parent's home and my heart breaks for him. I know he aches to hear of their continued safety.

Krevosh laughs loudly.

"Aland? Surely you jest! General Neem has invaded too far inland. We will wait for no one; the wedding shall come by the morning."

He slams down the fifth cup of wine he just ingested, and stands abruptly, tilting slightly towards the left before correcting himself with the help of one of his soldiers.

"You there, maid, show me to my quarters."

He snaps his fingers toward Bria, and I grow wary of the way he leers at her.

Cadmus clenches his own jaw at the sight, and I stand quickly, stepping in front of her.

"Allow me, My Lord," I said demurely. "It would be an honor to be so close to a man of your stature."

He grins lewdly at me.

"There's a good whore, already learning your place."

Gasps ring out in the dining room, but I show no reaction, pushing Bria back towards Cadmus until she stands behind him, protected from the wolf in sheep's clothing. Uncle Henry has risen in outrage, but I shake my head, letting him know I will handle this.

It's Lord Krevosh's own mistake, believing he could come into our kingdom, *our home*, and think we would let him get away with his outrageous comments and unsavory attitude.

I watch as Krevosh stumbles forward, only standing upright because of the guard that keeps him from face-planting. Cadmus makes a move to follow us, but I shake my head, gesturing for him to stay with Bria. I'm sure the night has frightened her nerves.

I lead the way, only glancing back once to make sure the nasty bastard is following me. His gaze runs down the length of my body as we walk and while my skin shivers in disgust, my lips curl into a secret smile.

He'll learn soon enough.

"You know, you little whore, you might as well show me to your private chambers. We will be wed before the week is over, after all, and I never have been...traditional."

He slurs as he speaks, spittle dripping from his thin and chapped lips. This is what happens when men make one small clever move in chess and believe they've instantly won the game.

I climb the staircase and reach the landing, turning left. I open the brass knob to the servants' quarters and smile.

His glazed eyes look up and down the bland room and I can see the confusion working its way through his alcohol–riddled mind.

"Your rooms, my Lord." I smile demurely.

"You little *bitch*!"

His lips curl down into a sneer as he steps forward with his hand raised. I anticipate the move, grabbing his wrist and twisting it back until I hear the satisfying crunch of his radius snap. I lift my own hand and plow it into the side of his nose, grinning enthusiastically at the sight of the blood that immediately flows from it.

He cries out, exactly how I imagine newborn babes cry when they first taste the air.

All high–pitched and wailing.

There is confusion in his eyes.

"You're not from these lands! You should not be able to lay a hand on me, you vile creature!"

A laugh escapes my lips before I can stop it. He doesn't know then...doesn't know that the Syraxes line is immune to the rules of a Bellator's blessing.

Idiot.

He should have learned everything he could about my bloodline before coming and attempting to blackmail me.

I push him back into the room, watching as he collides with the wall. He's a sniveling and pathetic mess and I hardly touched him.

I could never be wed to such a coward.

"This was just a warning, *Lord Krevosh,* of the future that awaits you. I will *never* bow down to you or your will. I will never bow to any man. I will give you this one chance to leave Lashforn tonight with your dignity intact. You will go home, you will not mention me to *anyone* else, including General Neem. If you do not take this act of mercy, I will hunt you down and I will end your miserable life where you stand. Are we clear?"

He nods slowly, his tears drying up, though I can see the rage in his eyes.

He has never been bested by a female before, and I can tell before I leave the room that this will not the end of it.

I turn quickly and exit the room, taking note of the red–haired male that stands passively by the entry, his eyes appraising.

He lowers his head in respect as I pass by.

"Princess."

I nod in return before addressing him with my hands folded together and my head held high.

"Be sure he takes my warning seriously, Sir Bador. I only give them once."

9

Axel

"You are positive, Bador?"

My hand nods, having just returned from the mission I had sent him on. He speaks from behind me as I watch the waves crash against the large black rocks in front of me. The wind blows through my hair, and I sigh at the relief the fresh air brings me.

"I'm positive, your grace. It happened in front of my very eyes. The princess is the last of the Syraxes bloodline—the last Syraxes Bellator. I witnessed them training together this morning before I departed. She's..."

I raise an eyebrow and turn his way as he trails off.

"She is...?"

He clears his throat before stepping closer, dropping his voice so that my guards cannot hear.

"She is breathtaking, Your Majesty. Though she looks nothing like a Bellator woman usually does. By the Gods, she only reaches my chest in height! And her eyes...I've never seen eyes as hers! Fully white, Your Grace, with no pupil. I thought she was blind at first glance, but she proved me wrong with the left hook she threw at Lord Krevosh!"

Bador chuckles nervously at the recollection, and I find myself smiling as I think of the tiny creature who put a grown man on his ass.

I've met the vile Lord—which is why I have Bador spy on him. He cannot be trusted.

I have no doubt he deserved the justice she served him.

Taking the free cities into Atarah has served me with months of stress, endless paperwork, and negotiations that have made me question my desire to rule. General Neem's progression has not affected my lands yet, but I have no doubt that if Lashforn falls, he will grow stronger and march my way.

I've sent assassins after him and have only received their heads back in warning.

Apparently, General Neem had met a powerful black witch years ago and tortured her until she placed a protection spell on him.

A spell only one person could break through.

A Syraxes Bellator.

Someone who, until very recently, was thought to no longer even exist.

"Did Lord Krevosh leave before you?"

Bador shakes his head.

"He claimed to have a last-minute business meeting to attend to within the city and demanded my leave...I figured since you needed me to return as well, I would leave him to his affairs. I must confess, Your Grace...I grow tired of this charade."

I look at my oldest friend.

"Not much longer. I cannot leave these lands with Neem so close. I will not lower myself to the level of Krevosh, threatening the princess's will."

I tap my fingers against my thigh, trying to conjure an image of what this stunning creature looks like.

"Perhaps a ball will draw her in?"

I mull over the thought, ignoring the choking sound Bador releases.

"A ball, your majesty? But you've never opened the castle doors to anyone outside of this city...and with the newest members of our kingdom still being introduced, are you sure it is the safest time to host a party?"

I scoff, throwing him a side-eye. Bador has always been the more paranoid of the two of us, which is why I made him the hand of the King. He forgets sometimes that I have powers of my own. I remind him before making my way back to the castle.

I will unearth any assassination attempt before it even makes its way through my castle doors.

Bador startles quickly, as he always does when my mind infiltrates his own. Mind walkers were very rare before the war of Shamonhide, and most keep their identity hidden.

They essentially became extinct as the magic slowly faded from all bloodlines.

There are so very few magical creatures left—one being the damn black witch.

Men such as the general would only exploit them, so I don't blame those who went underground. Bador nods as he follows after me, his eyebrows raised.

"Shall I make the preparations then, your grace?"

I nod.

"Make sure Lashforn is the first to receive an invitation. I'm curious to meet the acquaintance of Princess Elaudia. Very curious indeed."

10

Elaudia

Sweat drips from my temples in small, salty drops.

I use the black scarf wrapped around my head to wipe it away as I roll away from another strike from Cadmus.

Clarice and Aunt Sofia stand close by, watching our duel with keen eyes. I always fight harder when my aunt is watching, wishing to make her proud. She has been a mother to me in so many ways this past year.

I catch sight of a letter in her hand, and my curiosity gets the best of me.

We haven't received a letter in months.

Cadmus must not realize I've become distracted as he swipes his sword across my stomach.

Damn.

Any other time, I would have dodged.

Guess he's getting two gold prilne tokens from my stash.

Sofia's eyes widen with a shout as she rushes over, her ladies' maids hot on her heels.

I feel the blood before I feel the pain, and Cadmus swears. My body is thrown to the left from his force, and I steady myself, looking down. The cut is not deep at all. I wince slightly at the burning sensation making its way through my body.

"Laudi! Forgive me...please. I didn't realize you had looked away."

Cadmus pants heavily as he speaks, and I know it's from the panic of the situation and not exertion.

He stands in better physical condition than most soldiers I know.

My aunt grabs an offered shawl from one of her maids, pressing the fabric tightly to my stomach to staunch the bleeding. Clarice holds me up by the arms and begins shouting orders.

"Call for the healer at once!"

Her voice is sharp and commanding, and I catch sight of multiple guards rushing for the doctor. I look up into her light brown eyes, taking in the worry they shed.

I smile at her lightly.

"You guys…I'm alright, I promise. It is just a graze."

Cadmus wraps an arm around my waist—replacing Clarice—to support my weight. I thank him in my head because as soon as I open my mouth, dizziness crashes over me.

Maybe it's not just a graze…

I chance a look down and take sight of my blood rapidly soaking through the shawl and wince.

Not just a graze.

I try to say something, but the ground rushes up to meet my face faster than I can blink. The last thing I remember is the feeling of being swooped up into a strong pair of arms and the sound of my blood hitting the dirt beneath me.

***

"Have you lost your mind, boy!? Our one last chance of survival against this blasted army, and you almost take her out in a *sparring match*!"

Voices hush and rise as I open my eyes slowly and take in the sight of my bedroom. The door is shut, but I can hear Captain Yumin on the other side, no doubt berating Cadmus for my unfortunate incident.

Aunt Sofia rests by my bed, and I can hear my uncle hushing the captain.

"You know as well as I do that the boy would never intentionally hurt Elaudia. You heard my wife, Elaudia became distracted. It was nothing more than an accident. The healer insists she'll make a full recovery!"

The captain huffs, and I sit up in bed, startling my resting aunt.

"It should never have happened in the first place! I have trained him harder than any other man that has ever been under my command, as you ordered me to. To be smarter, to be faster. He should have halted the moment the princess looked away, but to follow through with his attack. Pathetic! He should be whipped at the post for this!"

Rage wars within me at his words, and a fire lights itself in my blood.

Aunt Sofia soothes my hair back away from my head.

"Elaudia dearest, please, you mustn't strain your abdomen. Your magic is at work."

Feet scuffle on the other side of the door, but I do not wait any longer to hear what else Yumin might throw at Cadmus.

I glance at my aunt.

"Help me."

She sighs heavily, but to her credit, she does not protest. She gathers me into her arms and helps me descend the tall bed frame. My hair covers my body and dressing gown in an inky waterfall as I shuffle towards the door.

I throw it open, startling all three men on the other side.

The captain and my uncle look as if they are ready to duel themselves and I must hand it to the captain for not fearing the monarchs in front of him.

Cadmus stands as still as stone with blood-shot eyes, and I know he must be beating himself up tremendously.

"As unfortunate as my accident was, Captain, it was no one's fault but my own. I am a Syraxes Bellator, am I not? I am the one who is naturally faster, stronger...smarter. Cadmus is but a normal man who has chosen to fight by my side and protect me, never mind the threat that may befall his own life one day. He left his home...his family, for me."

He opens his mouth to speak, but I cut him off just as quickly.

"You are well respected here, sir, and I thank you for everything you have done."

I stand up taller as I say this and leave my aunt's side, limping over to stand in front of him.

"But if you *ever* threaten harm to Cadmus in such a way again, I will kill you myself."

Silence echoes throughout the sitting room, and the maids have stopped their tidying. I can feel every eye on me, but I do not back down. The captain's jaw clenches. I can see the panic in his eyes—the fear he must have felt.

A sigh leaves my chest.

"I know you care for this kingdom and its people...and me. I assure you; I am unharmed and will remain so until the threat of General Neem is only a page in our history books."

I place a hand on his shoulder in a gesture of goodwill, and he closes his eyes briefly before nodding in respect.

"Your Highness."

He bows and takes his leave, nodding towards Cadmus, who I face next. I open my arms and arch an eyebrow, ignoring the pulling sensation in my abdomen.

"Come here, you big oaf."

He approaches me slowly as if he might hurt me by just walking. I wrap my arms around him and relax with the feeling of family.

True, beloved family.

His chest rattles with the breath he releases.

"Never again." He rasps.

I chuckle at his words, wincing a little.

"Never again shall we duel? I should hope not, good sir. I owe you an ass-kicking that you shall receive as soon as this wound is healed.

Which, with my healing rate, will be by next eve's sundown."

My aunt stifles a laugh as she ushers me out of Cadmus's arms and back into my room. Once I'm settled back in bed, I turn my head towards my aunt.

"I was distracted by the sight of the letter in your hands."

Her eyes widen, and she nods.

"It wasn't from Aland...it was from King Axel of Atarah himself. He is to host a ball in hopes to unite the last-standing kingdoms against General Neem. It shall take place in a week's time."

My mouth drops open at the thought of the elusive king hosting an actual ball in his lands—something I've been told has never happened. Cadmus seems just as surprised as I am, and he sits forward, resting his elbows on his knees.

"You're sure?"

Aunt Sofia nods.

"I am. Though I have yet to send back an answer. He requests the entire family attend, but the kingdoms all know it's just Henry and me."

A heartbroken look enters her eye briefly as she looks at me, but it disappears as quickly as it came. She must be hinting at the fact that my existence is still being kept under the radar. I reach over and place one of my hands in her own.

"Maybe it is time. If King Axel is finally opening his gates, finally stepping out of his comfort zone, maybe it is time we do the same. You know I am ready, I have been for quite some time, today's unfortunate incident aside."

My aunt throws a glance at my uncle, who nods.

I look into her eyes and smile.

"I can do this. It's time for everyone to know about me. And if—no, *when*—word reaches General Neem, we will be ready to end him and his invasion...together."

My aunt squeezes my hand and nods.

"Together then."

II

Elaudia

I was correct.

My wound had closed completely by the next night, only leaving a pink scar in its wake, in addition to the many scars marring my stomach and back. Many women may suffer the curse of vanity, but I wear my past wounds with pride and honor.

They tell the story of my life.

I press my hands into the bedframe as Bria fastens the black corset tightly against my waist. I chose to wear a billowy beige colored shirt underneath the half corset with my favorite black pants, a uniform fit for fighting.

One thing I've learned since coming to Lashforn is to always be on your guard.

Seeing as this is the first time we are to leave the kingdom in a year—venturing into unknown territory—I want to be ready for anything. My waist jerks back once more before Bria begins winding the laces through each other.

"All done, Laudi."

I turn to face my maid and friend, shooting a smile her way.

"You had too much fun dressing me today, and you spent extra time on my hair. Is there a reason for that?"

She ducks her head and blushes. She stutters as she starts to speak.

"I–I've heard rumors of King Axel, princess. Rumors of his striking features and abundant...attributes."

I arch an eyebrow her way. By the blush staining her cheeks, I would dare to say she's fantasized about these attributes more than once.

"But the King has never left his kingdom...pray to tell, who have you heard these rumors from?"

Nelly chooses that moment to burst through the doors in a flourish.

"There is a horse attendant in the stables. She came from Atarah when the General had first begun his invasions. Her mother felt Lashforn to be the safest place, and at the time, it was. But now that King Axel has united with the free cities and their savage forces, it seems that we may be the ones seeking out his protection in the end."

Bria rests her arms on the frame of my bed, sitting and looking me over with appreciation.

"And if Nelly and I have anything to say about it, the dark-haired king and his infamous stoic demeanor will crumble at the sight of you, princess."

Bria smiles at me with a smug glint, and I toss her an eye roll. I am here to prevent the war from further breaking out across our lands, not to ensure a love match.

My ladies' maids seem to think otherwise.

I do not correct them.

Let them have their fantasies of the dark king. I have my own fantasies, and they include killing the general and halting his reign. I run a hand through my long hair, ignoring Bria's protests as I grab my polearm on my way to the door. I glance back quickly at the two women who have become close friends and smile their way as they gaze longingly at my packed trunks.

"Well? Hurry and pack, you two are coming with me."

Their squeals of shocked delight echo throughout my room as I shut the door, and a deep chuckle breaks out to my right. Cadmus is dressed for war—as am I—with his long sword strapped to his back.

"You finally told them, eh?"

He joins my side as we head down to the carriage that will take us to Atarah. The castle has been bustling with movement ever since news leaked that we would soon be traveling to meet King Axel. My sisters in arms haven't stopped with their incessant chattering and questions since the morning I told them.

And they continued on when we said our goodbyes to each other.

I'd do anything to take them with me but seeing as the majority of the remaining Bellators were born on this land, they're needed to stay and protect it.

My farewell to Clarice was more difficult than I expected it to be, but she only smiled and held me tight, whispering that she would never be far. As soon as she let me go, Bria and Nelly burst through with heaving chests and packed bags.

Cadmus nudges my arm with a snort, and I smile.

"Yes, I wanted to keep them in suspense a little longer. I honestly cannot believe they thought I would leave them behind. Who else would give me all the hot gossip?"

The castle door creaks as it is opened for us, and we step outside into the light. The breeze is blowing swiftly, and I grin up at Cadmus.

"How far did Aunt Sofia say the trip is again?"

Cadmus searches the grounds as we walk, keeping his eyes peeled.

"A day's ride if there are no unexpected surprises. We pass through Bandit territory by the Fresia River. Other than that, we should have a pretty uneventful trip."

Un-eventful, my ass.

This is the first time I get to see the roads that lead to the great city of Atarah.

It will be anything but uneventful for me.

I keep my eyes trained on the roaming horses, noticing that Celeste, my speckled white Appaloosa, is not hooked up to the carriage I'm supposed to ride in. There is also a saddle upon her back.

A grin sneaks up my lips right as Captain Yumin steps into my line of sight.

"It wasn't my idea—but well deserved all the same. It took all night for Cadmus to convince the Queen. So long as you stay by me and Cadmus, you're free to ride with the guards."

I can barely contain my excitement as I throw my arms around them both before running after Celeste. I let out a shout of excitement that causes her ears to perk up, and then she runs full speed towards me. She reaches me in record time, and I run my hands up and down her snout.

"You ready for an adventure, girl?"

She lets out a whinny and trots in place, letting me on to just how excited she is. I mount her quickly, making sure to keep my polearm strapped in place behind my back. I wait only seconds for Cadmus and the Captain to ready their own horses before giving Celeste a gentle kick in the side, urging her forward.

I wave at Aunt Sofia as she enters the royal carriage, blowing her a kiss.

"Be careful!" She calls after me.

My hair blows away from my face as I look back.

"I'll meet you there! I love you!" She smiles in response, shaking her head.

I can hear the beat of hooves at my back, but I don't waste another moment as I head for the gates that are held open in front of me. My grin widens at the thought of finally leaving the castle grounds.

We ride in peace for the next few hours, my eyes open and enjoying every bit of the country-side that I can. It is only when the sky begins to change its hue that I realize nightfall is coming.

"Your hair looks as if you've had a tumble in the sheets, cousin."

I look to my left at Cadmus's chuckling face, reaching out to punch his shoulder.

"A better tumble than you've ever provided, I'm sure."

He gasps in mock outrage, and leans towards me on his own horse.

"I'll have you know I have never once left a lady disappointed. I'm sure Bria could calm your wandering mind." He drawls.

My eyes widen in shock, and I let out a startled chuckle.

"So...who finally made the first move? Bria or yourself?"

Celeste jostles me on a particularly rocky hill downwards and I tighten my hand grip on the saddle.

"Well...she's been making those bedroom eyes at me for so long now, and with this new adventure that we're going on—I didn't want to have any regrets."

Hmmm.

"So last night then?"

His mouth flattens but his eyes show humor.

"Yes, just last night."

I look up, catching sight of the great golden walls before us.

Atarah.

"That explains why she was in such a glorious mood this morning; usually she breaks my ribs getting me into my corsets, today she only bruised them."

We both glance at each other before breaking out into laughter.

"What about you? Are you ready to meet King Axel? I'm sure someone will bring up the grand idea of marrying you to the man. Uniting the Kingdoms and all that nonsense."

"I'm prepared to do what I must for the good of the lands and its people. Aunt Sofia and I talked about it earlier. I'm going to stay back, let him meet the King and Queen first. I want to get a good idea of the man before he has to fake an introduction."

Cadmus purses his lips.

"A smart idea." He murmurs thoughtfully.

Yes, I thought it was very clever. I suppose we will find out soon enough. Our riding party comes up to the gates and I have to crane my head all the way back to see the top of them. These gates are a sure reason this Kingdom has never been invaded. The weather outside has a bite to it from the dying winter, but the last of the snow is almost gone.

Though since we're in the Northlands, I doubt it will get any warmer than this.

"Who goes there!" A guard shouts.

"The royal family of Lashforn. We have arrived at the request of your King."

I can see the two men in heavy metal helmets converse amongst themselves before he sends a hand signal down to someone on the other side of the wall. Within seconds, a great groaning begins to sound, and I watch in awe as the large golden wall parts ways.

I wait until it's opened completely before nudging Celeste forward. I've barely entered before I gasp at the sight of the city before me, in all its glorious wonders.

Cadmus grins at my delight.

"Welcome to Atarah, Princess. The greatest city in the world."

12

Elaudia

I let the biggest chunk of our group go ahead, falling back with Cadmus at my side.

The captain passes by us with the royal carriage, and he sends us both a warning look.

"Stay alert and be at the castle within the hour. Keep your eyes low, Princess Elaudia."

I toss an enchanting smile his way before nudging Celeste towards the horse stalls at my right. Cadmus dismounts before me, coming to my side and helping me down. I thank the merchant who begins tying off our horses' reins as I thread my arm with Cadmus.

"Where to first?" I'm practically jumping up and down.

He chuckles at my excitement before responding.

"Everywhere."

We spend the next hour enjoying every bit of food that we can—from fried delicacies to freshly picked fruit. The night sky is bright with a thousand stars, and music ripples throughout every stall we walk by.

I catch sight of both the dark-skinned, scantily clad people of the free cities and the emblem-covered people of Atarah, all joined in laughter and peace. Though I'm shocked at the sight of the Wild Woods folk wearing so little, Cadmus reminds me that their people have survived centuries in such conditions, meaning their bodies have adapted well.

I'm reminded of what the entire realm was like before General Neem began his invasions.

Any king who could do this—who would *want* to do this—could not be a bad man. I catch sight of a little girl no older than eight summers, watching a sparkling purple scarf in a stall as it waves in the midnight breeze.

By the look of her, they were of the Free Cities before coming here.

She tugs on her mother's short skirt, who glances over with sad, tired eyes and shakes her head no.

The child's shoulders drop, and my heart clenches. I urge Cadmus to go on without me.

"I'll catch up in just a moment. Grab one of those lemon tarts for me."

I leave his side and walk over to the silk stall.

"How much for this purple scarf?"

The stall attendant spins my way with a happy grin.

"Some of my best work, isn't it!"

Her smile falters slightly when she catches sight of my royal emblem that has slipped out from underneath my cloak.

"My Lady!" She gasps and begins to drop herself into a deep curtsy.

My arm shoots out, stalling her.

"Please! There is no need."

My voice drops to a whisper.

"I wish to remain unknown for the night if you please."

Her eyes stay wide, but she returns to her normal height.

"As you wish, my L-...miss. Take it, please—my gift to you."

I smile softly.

"I could not...it truly is fine work. Should fifty cover it then?"

The attendant looks as if she is going to have a heart attack at any moment.

"Fifty tallies!? I couldn't possibly."

Tallies are the paper currency they use here in Atarah, and I'm suddenly grateful that Captain Yumin ensured we had some.

Out of the corner of my eye, I watch as the little girl begins to follow her mother away, her shoulders still slumped in sadness.

"I insist."

The attendant wraps the scarf gently before placing it in my hands with a grateful smile.

"May the Gods bless you, My Lady." She speaks softly.

I return her smile and follow after the little girl and her mother while unwrapping the scarf. They head for a cluster of cabins off to the west, a slightly more beaten area of the town, and I watch the mother consoling the crying child. I imagine taking in so many new citizens would present some struggles, but the home look sturdy enough and have proper windows and doors.

I realize the young mother couldn't afford the scarf, so I wait a few moments until they are safely tucked within their home before knocking on the wooden door. I duck into the dark alcove on the side of the house and wait. It is only a moment before the door opens and the curious mother peers out, looking around, before looking down.

She startles in delight at the sight of the shimmering fabric, kneeling down as tears gather in her eyes.

"Ravenni! Come quickly, my darling!"

The little girl appears once more.

"What is it, Mommy?"

The mother gathers the silk in her hands before placing the fabric around the child's shoulders. Ravenni squeals with delight, and her happiness radiates throughout my own body. They giggle and laugh even after the thin wooden door is shut, and as I slip away from the darkness, my soul quiets with joy.

And yet still yearns for the love of a small child.

13
Axel

Magnificent did her no justice.

She was majestic and admirable.

A striking beauty with a heart that could be compared to only the Gods. I gather my black cloak closer to my lithe body as I stalk her throughout Atarah's streets. When I catch sight of her watching the little girl with tender eyes, my balls tighten with anticipation as the primal being inside me snarls with possessiveness. This bond, I feel, will drive me to madness.

I'll give you one of your own, my little warrior.

I stay back, far enough that I know she won't notice me as I watch her exchange with the stall attendant.

Then I watch as she follows the young mother and her babe home. I can feel my soul yearn-ing for hers and I shiver as feelings take hold of me that I have never before experienced.

My father always told me that I would know my mate when I saw her. The instincts built into us rear violently at the first sight of our female, not settling until we claim her.

My wife.

My love.

The other half of my soul.

I always thought he was talking out of his ass.

He wasn't.

This beautiful creature with hair as dark as midnight and white eyes will be my Queen.

It wasn't until I caught sight of her strange eyes that I realized she was the hidden princess. I stay close as she heads back toward the festivities of the town, and I step over a fallen log, prepared to watch her wander for the rest of the night.

A primal need tells me not to let her out of my sight.

I'm about to clear the forest, so enraptured by her, when the smell of metal reaches my nose, and I find a sword pressed against my neck.

"Move and I will slit your throat."

The voice is clear and male, but I'm so en-thralled by my mate's departure that I do as he says and still myself.

I arch an eyebrow.

"You do know who I am, don't you?"

The sword comes closer to my skin.

"I don't care if you're the King himself. Why are you following Laudi?"

Oh, the irony.

"I am the King, boy."

A breath leaves his chest, and he spins me around, sword still raised.

I can tell he truly does not care who I am. He only cares for her life.

That makes him a friend to me.

I grin at him as we study each other.

"Politics bore me...do they not bore you? I figured my courtiers could greet the King and Queen of Lashforn. I was intrigued by Princess Elaudia. Can you blame me?"

His stance calms slightly as he lowers his sword, his eyes flashing to the royal seal upon my armor that I show him.

"She was intrigued by you as well. How did you know we stayed behind?"

I walk forward, taking my gloves off and gesturing towards his sword.

He hands it over reluctantly as I study the fine metalwork.

"I have my ways..." I trail off, waiting for a name.

"Cadmus—I'm Laudi's Queens Guard, as well as her cousin. Speaking of, I should probably catch up to her. She never stays out of trouble for long."

I grin at his words and hand him his sword back.

"Do me a favor, Cadmus...and I will owe you one of my own. I was never here."

He watches me closely, studying me, before nodding his head. He turns away and steps out of the forest's line, but not before tossing one last remark over his shoulder.

"She likes lemon tarts."

My lips widen into a feral grin.

I knew I liked the boy.

14
Elaudia

"There you are!"

Aunt Sofia rushes over to me, a distraught look on her face. I sink into her embrace and laugh.

"I'm perfectly fine. No—I am *more* than fine."

I've never been so thrilled in my life. This city is like none I've ever seen before, and seeing how happy the citizens here are warms my heart.

She pulls away.

"I am absolutely *wonderful.* I have imagined plenty of things over the years, but nothing could have prepared me for the sight of this city. It was absolutely breathtaking! And you should have tasted the fresh-baked goods at the baker's stall, he had the most delicious—um—"

I toss a look over my shoulder to a grinning Cadmus, who has just emerged from the side hallways.

"What were those yellow bars called again?" I ask.

Cadmus lets out a snort.

"Lemon tarts."

"Lemon tarts!"

I grin up at my aunt as she rolls her eyes and ruffles my hair lovingly.

"Yes, well, you truly did not miss much. According to the courtiers who stayed to greet us, King Axel was feeling under the weather. We are to dine with him in the morning, should he feel well enough. Not that we need to stay up late discussing war matters anyhow, I'm sure you're quite tired from such a long day."

A group of older men who hover nearby watch me closely, and the one with a head full of silver hair clears his throat and steps forward.

"We have prepared the east wing for you and your family, Your Majesty. As you requested, there are three spare rooms waiting for your entourage and guard. His Highness understands your need to keep your people close to you."

Sofia graces him with a blinding white smile, and I giggle as he flushes and steps back. He lifts a robed arm and gestures for the castle's handmaidens to lead the way. I admire everything about the grand black castle on my way, as well as memorizing escape routes along the way.

I split off from everyone else, saying my goodnights before the handmaiden leads me into a grand room, where I see Nelly and Bria are already waiting for me.

The quiet handmaiden bows her head and goes to exit, leaving me alone with my maids. I take a seat as they begin to undo my loosely braided hair and ready me for bed.

I look around at my surroundings with rapture.

The room I've been placed in is fit for a Queen, with beige-colored walls that shimmer against the firelight. The bed itself is bigger than any I have ever slept on, and as my eyes slowly wander the length of the room, I take note of a second door, one that has a plush couch in front of it.

"Nelly, did anyone mention that door to you when they brought you here?"

Bria and Nelly both follow my gaze to the heavy wooden door and shake their heads.

"We tried to open it, but it is locked. We barricaded it, though. If you ask me, it's completely outrageous! To put the princess of the neighboring kingdom in a room that cannot be completely secured. Madness indeed!" Nelly growls.

She brushes through my hair with quick strokes, pulling harder the more she talks. I steady her hand with my own and look at her in the mirror.

"I'll be fine, Nelly."

Bria hums her agreement as she takes over for Nelly.

"The Princess is more than capable of taking care of herself, and you know it."

She finishes with my hair and rubs a lotion into my skin, working her way up and down my arms, then onto my shoulders. The first week they tried doing this, I was appalled.

When I asked them why they wouldn't let me ready myself for bed alone, *they* looked downright appalled, explaining that they were the first ladies to be chosen for such a prestigious position in Lashforn, and it would be seen as a disgrace to their families should they not follow through with their tasks.

After a month of arguing and debating, I finally relented, if only to save myself the headache.

I gaze out onto the balcony, the white gossamer drapes blowing with the pace of the breeze.

"You can go get some rest, my friends. I'll change myself."

They both bow together before wishing me sweet dreams, and I sigh in relief as the silence echoes around me.

I peek into the wardrobe, wondering if King Axel has decided to provide me with any clothing.

I am not disappointed at the sight that greets me.

I change into a green dressing gown that is a similar shade of the Jade gemstone, smiling at the feel of the silk against my skin. Not even Lashforn has silks this luscious.

I wrap a matching shawl around my shoulders and make my way to the balcony.

The night sky greets me with a thousand blinking kisses, and I grin up at it. This castle is by far the highest up on land, meaning I am closer to the sky here than I ever have been before.

My white eyes catch the burning shape of shooting stars, something apparently only I can see. I once asked Cadmus if he could see the bright yellow color shooting throughout the sky, and he told me all he could see was a streak of light. I close my eyes as I lean against the railing, breathing in the fresh air of pine and lemon. Pine from the trees that surround the lands, and lemon from the tarts that Cadmus snuck back in with him.

I unwrap the dessert I carried out here with me and bite into it, moaning at the still-warm taste of vanilla and melted citrus.

So fucking good.

"You know, a man might mistake that sound as an invitation."

My heart stutters in my chest as I whirl around, facing a man larger than any I have ever seen at court.

The only men I know of to be that tall are the wild folk of the Free Cities.

My eyes dart past his to my polearm that I left resting against the armoire and my mind takes a calculating turn.

The strange man in front of me has hair as black as mine, but his eyes shine the color of melted honey. He's wearing armor—obviously to me—but to a normal person it would just appear as multiple layers of clothing. The two ancient-looking broadswords crossed behind his back let me know this man is as every bit fighter as I am.

Only the strongest of warriors can wield such a heavy weapon, let alone two. He grins as he watches me inch closer to my room.

"There's no need for that, little warrior. I mean you no harm, I just wanted to meet you...formally."

His deep voice causes a shiver to break across my spine as something ancient sparks inside my belly, but I pay him no mind, feinting left and rolling right as soon as he moves in the direction I anticipated.

I dart for my polearm, twirling it around so the pointed end is faced his way, my shawl forgotten on the ground as I take a stance against him. His eyes are amused, and he still has his hands held up as if in surrender.

"Who are you?" I demand.

His head tilts with curiosity and something else I don't feel comfortable exploring.

He's looking at me with something akin to *desperation*.

"I like your accent...it's beautiful."

I step closer, weapon still aimed at him.

"Answer me now, or you will die."

His eyes look me up and down, assessing me and the threat I pose to him, which is a lot.

"King Axel of Atarah and The Free Cities...at your service, My Lady."

He bows his head low as he speaks, and I'm slightly stunned, though no less wary.

I raise my chin, standing a little straighter.

"And I suppose being the King of this great kingdom allows you the freedom to just march into any lady's bedchambers? Unwelcome and unannounced?"

The King bites his lip as if he finds me amusing.

I growl at the thought and lash out with a warning strike. He ducks to the side, avoiding my strike. I expect him to become enraged, but all he does is grin that stupid, infuriating grin.

He must be mad.

The insane kind of mad.

"Forgive me, princess. I wanted to meet you without the pressure of your family around. I wanted to see you as you truly are when you are alone."

"That is why you put me in this room, with the door."

A statement, not a question.

"Where does it lead to?"

A large hand reaches up to brush the hair away from his face, and I fight the urge to drool. I love a man with large hands.

I shake my head.

Focus Elaudia.

"My bedchambers."

My eyes widen at the confession and what could be assumed of it, and I strike out again with a snarl—this time, nicking his cheek. The cut is shallow, and I watch as blood begins to dribble from underneath it.

The King seems as shocked as I should be, and he looks at me with wonder in his eyes as he wipes the blood away. I glance at the couch that seems to have moved itself across the floor. How did I not hear anything?

"I never intended any insult, My Lady. Here."

He reaches into his coat pocket and pulls out a golden key.

"There is a hidden lock on your side." He smirks. "One that I can show you, in a gesture of good faith."

He strides toward the door, his muscled thighs eating up the distance, and I follow him, weapon still raised. He lifts an eyebrow.

"You're still threatening me." He muses.

"You're still pissing me off." I throw back at him.

He chuckles at my retort and lifts a latch, showing me a hidden keyhole underneath.

"If you are to lock it from this side, it cannot be undone from mine."

My mind whirls as I think about this.

"Why does this exist?"

He hands me the key gently, as if I were a wounded animal he might frighten.

"My father made this room for my mother. She had trouble adjusting when she was first brought from across the seas of Soundra. It was an arranged marriage, and though he fell head over heels in *love* with her, she was...reserved. From across the world, hell, she did not even speak the common tongue."

Axel opens the door to a staircase.

"He had his best stone masons create this, a way for her to have her privacy and time alone. A way that she would not be questioned and pressured by the people if they found out she was not immediately sharing his bed."

I listen quietly as my body becomes more relaxed and I lower my weapon.

"He sounds like a kind man."

A smile touches his full lips, surrounded by a thick beard.

"He was...and my mother...she could swoon a man with just her smile alone. It took a little time, but she fell in love with him, just as deeply as he loved her."

He looks down at me with an intensity that causes my heart to stutter, and I look away.

"I'll let you rest, little warrior. I hope you can forgive me for the way I went about our introductions. You'll be at breakfast?"

He sounds hopeful, and it almost makes me laugh.

This great, strong king, looking like a child in a candy shop at the mere thought of me dining with him.

I nod softly, my eyes still taking him in.

Gods...he takes up so much space.

He walks to the door, calling out softly as he shuts it.

"Sweet dreams, little warrior."

15
Axel

Leaving out the part about my father building that secret stairwell almost a thousand years ago stung a bit, but as I leave her alone for the night, I reassure myself.

One day, she will know everything.

My mate...

I have a mate!

A chuckle escapes my lips as I think back on our meeting with delight.

By the Gods, she is *everything*.

I cloaked myself for longer than I care to admit, watching her in her most fragile and unguarded moments. The look of pure bliss that crossed her face when she bit into that lemon tart made my cock harden with desire, and I had to bite the fangs that wanted to appear and sink into her flesh—claiming her as mine forever.

I stop in the hallway to the left of the kitchens, adjusting myself.

Once I'm sure that Sarabeth—my head cook—will not see the evidence of my arousal, I enter the kitchens. Sarabeth is the last one here, an aging woman who has been in my service for the past sixty years.

She startles when she spots me, her wrinkled hands kneading dough just as efficiently as the day she started.

"Ah! Young King! What can I do for you, boy?"

I grin at our inside joke and make my way over to the table.

When the war of Shamonhide struck, my father knew that for our line to survive, we would have to live the rest of our days in secret. By protecting the inner-most city of Atarah, our last standing court, my citizens knew what it meant.

They knew we would close our walls and never open them again.

It was a great commitment to make, and an intense sacrifice.

Though our outlying citizens did not think twice to protect me and my lineage.

This is why I guard them so fiercely, ensuring they live their mortal lives outside the grips of poverty and sickness.

It will be an adjustment getting all of the folk from The Free Cities intergraded with our own, but my council has assured me the transition will be swift, and the once abandoned cabins updated completely in a timely manner.

Now with General Neem on the rise, it seems my time in hiding may be coming to a quick end.

I take the offered glass of water from Sarabeth, cooling the temperature until the crystal frosts over.

I look up, my eyes bright as I address her.

"I found her."

Sarabeth's eyes search my own for a moment—her head tilted to the side in confusion.

I give her a few moments to think my words over, and she does not disappoint. A shriek leaves her, and she rushes to me, squeezing me harder than a woman of her age should be able to. She pats my back and pulls away, wiping at the tears that leave her eyes.

"How is it possible? I thought Fae mated with Fae?"

I nod my head, agreeing with the words that never leave her mouth.

"I did too. I don't know how, but I could feel it snap into place, the moment I saw her."

"Who is she, Axel?"

"The Princess who has just arrived from Lashforn."

Her eyes widen.

"You don't mean-"

"Yes...she's a Bellator." Sarabeth covers her mouth.

"She must be quite intimidating! What does she look like? I've heard rumors of them—is she as tall as they say?"

Her excitement makes me laugh, and I shake my head, urging her to close all of the doors and come sit.

Once I'm sure no one is eavesdropping, I shake my head.

"She looks nothing like a Bellator. She hardly comes to my chest, Sarabeth. She's so delicate,

I would almost be afraid to touch her, if not for her temper."

That earns me a raised eyebrow.

"Temper?"

I wince slightly, preparing myself to be knocked in the side of the head by this old lady.

"I may have put her in mother's old rooms..."

Sarabeth gasps in shock.

"And snuck in once she was in her night-clothes..."

There it is.

I rub the side of my head where Sarabeth has just struck me hard and grimace. She's the only one in the world who could raise a hand to me and remain unharmed, and she knows it.

Now there are two of them. I dread the day my little mate realizes she can come for my balls without retribution for me.

Actually...now that I think about it...

Sarabeth raises her hand with another threat, and I raise my hands in surrender for the second time tonight.

"Get your mind out of the gutter, boy."

We both settle down and I drain the last of my water.

"Aside from barely escaping with my man-hood intact, she has agreed to dine with me in the morning."

My head cook claps her hands together in delight.

"Don't you worry, child! I'll have the girls up and ready before first light, we'll prepare a breakfast so tempting, she will never want to leave."

I stand up, reaching down to hug the woman who has been a mother to me in the absence of my own.

"Can you make sure there are a few platters of lemon tarts? Apparently, she's a fan."

Sarabeth's eyes wrinkle in delight.

"Just my specialty! Go on then, and get some beauty rest. You need it."

It's not until I head back to my own chambers and climb into bed that I notice a glinting piece of metal sitting on my bedside table.

A quick inhale causes me to relax and other parts of me to tense at the same time.

Not only did my little warrior not lock her door—she gave me back the key.

I breathe in her scent, trying to ignore the precum that leaks from my cock at the smell of her.

I fall asleep with dreams of tiny feet running through my castle halls and a mate with eyes as white as snow.

16
Elaudia

Giving the key back to King Axel wasn't something I did lightly.

Though having a male enter my domain so freely is something I am not used to, I can defend myself just fine. I try not to examine my decision too closely, lest I discover something I'm not quite ready to study.

His room was just as grand as I imagined it would be, but at the same time, completely different from what I imagined.

Black plants covered every inch of his furniture, some even winding through the wooden design of his headboard. Vines ran across the walls, and the bathroom had a completely open concept, with a shower fit for ten people and a waterfall slowly spilling down the tile.

I have played with multiple scenarios in my head, and magic is the only one that could create a *waterfall* out of nowhere, even if it is a smaller one.

But how could King Axel have magic?

There are so few magical beings left in our world.

And why—if it was to be a secret—did he trust me with access to his rooms?

He surely cannot trust *me*.

I ponder over the strange man as I get out of bed and stretch, groaning at how stiff and sore my muscles are from yesterday's traveling. I think back to last night and touch my lips when I realize a smile has formed.

I'm to dine with him this morning.

"You're to dine with His Majesty this morning!"

I wince at Nelly's echoing, shrill tone as she and Bria stumble into my room with a gown and a platter of ground coffee with cream. It's almost as if the two are in a race to see who can get to me first.

Nelly wins by a hair, and my eyes widen at the sight of the dress.

I raise an eyebrow, and she winces.

"Queen Sofia's idea."

The dress is beautiful, if not a little...risqué.

I can hardly believe she picked this one until I realize she would have caught first sight of King Axel this morning.

I huff out a sigh.

What a matchmaker my aunt has suddenly become.

"Well, I've never said no to her styling choices before..."

The girls giggle together like schoolgirls.

"But—"

Simultaneous groans reach my ears, and I laugh.

"There's no way. I'm here to make allies to prevent another great war, not seduce King Axel."

I reach for my coffee and pour some cream into it until it's a light toffee color and mumble into my cup, mentally preparing myself for their reaction to my next words.

"Besides, I already met him last night."

Twin shrieks reach my ears, and I roll my eyes, already regretting my words. I spend the next ten minutes recapping last night's events whilst Bria tightens my corset around my fighting clothes.

The girls are absolutely delighted when I mention how the king snuck in and his first words ever to me were an innuendo. I frown, wondering if their lack of common sense when it comes to my privacy should concern me.

Bria ties off my hair into a long braid, much to her distaste.

"Have you seen Cadmus this morning? He usually beats me to breakfast."

The question is directed at both of my maids, but my eyes stay on Bria, whose cheeks turn a deep crimson color.

"I believe he's still asleep, Laudi."

"Hmm...do you think you could have the cooks here brew something for that snoring of his? I don't think I could last another carriage ride with it?"

Bria smooths out the nightclothes she has put into drawers and shakes her head.

"Oh no, he doesn't snore."

Nelly and I both whirl her way, waiting for her to realize what she's said. I smirk when Bria looks up, gaping in shock.

We spend a moment looking in every direction at each other before bursting into laughter like schoolgirls. Nelly bats Bria's arm and scoffs.

"When were you going to tell me?? The future captain of the Queens Guard! And *you*?"

She spins my way, pointing an accusing finger.

"When did you find out?"

I smirk as she feigns betrayal.

"He let it slip yesterday after I pestered him," I explain.

Nelly rolls her eyes as she finishes cleaning up our breakfast, and I smile at Bria, who keeps looking at me as if I might explode.

"I'm happy for both of you, really. You are two of the truest friends I have ever had, and you deserve love."

Bria hugs me gently and reaches for my polearm.

"I figure if you're eating in your warrior attire, you'll be armed like one as well."

"You know me well."

I strap my polearm so that it rests diagonally across my back and open the door, letting them lead the path they have already familiarized themselves with. Now that dawn has risen, the castle is bustling with bodies moving in every direction.

I catch sight of decorations and dishes being hoisted from door to door and breathe a sigh of relief as a sleepy Cadmus emerges from his rooms—fully dressed. I can be happy for my cousin and friend, but I still *never* need to see him unclothed.

He joins me as I pass his room, shooting a secret wink toward Bria.

"The cat is out of the bag now, cousin. No need to try and hide your lady lover." I snort.

Cadmus's eyes widen, and he shoots a look at Bria, who turns, hiding her face behind a hand, and nods.

Our boots echo on the stone floors as we make our way to breakfast, and we come to a door that has four guards standing watch.

Though none are as intimidating as the monarch I met last night.

"The Princess may enter—alone. All others should report to the main dining hall."

Cadmus opens his mouth to speak, but I cut him off.

"All others will remain right here with me, or your King will dine alone."

Their eyes widen at the sight of someone openly challenging orders given to them, and I almost laugh at the sight of distress on the face of the guard who spoke.

"Let them in, Samuel. There is plenty of food here to go around."

King Axel's voice rings out from behind the guards, and I hate that my stomach tingles in response to his deep voice. The guards move aside, allowing us entrance, and I barely refrain from gasping at the lazy sprawl of him.

His broad chest reclines in a chair big enough to fit three of me, while his legs lie open and spread.

"*My goodness.*" Nelly chokes, her tan face flushing red.

Axel stands as I approach, his eyes never once leaving my own.

"I hope you slept well, princess."

He reaches out for my hands, aiming to place a kiss on the back of them. For some strange reason, I let him.

"I did, thank you. Where are my aunt and uncle?"

"Here, darling."

Aunt Sofia enters with a flourish that only she could ever accomplish, with uncle Henry walking close behind her—like always.

"Queen Sofia, King Henry."

Axel nods his head in respect.

Sofia regards him for a moment before smiling.

"King Axel. Thank you for inviting us to your beautiful home. While we are shocked you have decided to open your gates, we understand it is for a bigger reason than to host a *ball*."

Axel grins but does not bother trying to hide it.

"Bador! Could you come in here, please?"

We all look at the door to the left, and my chest rattles with rage at the sight of the male who exits the doors.

"You!" Sofia hisses.

Cadmus draws his sword, coming to stand in front of me protectively while I push Nelly and Bria toward the doors.

"Now now—there's no reason for that. Cadmus, if you could lower your weapon and allow me to explain."

Axel doesn't seem worried about the sight of the man who traveled with Lord Krevosh to blackmail me, and for some reason, my temper soothes.

How he knows Cadmus, though, is an entirely different story.

"I planted Bador years ago, to act as a spy for me on Lord Krevosh. His actions, his allies, and his extracurricular activities. Word reached me that he was thinking of allying himself to General Neem and he was my best chance at getting inside information. You have my word that he has always worked for me. He is Hand of the King."

I eye him as he speaks, his tone stable as he introduces Bador.

"Which is completely believable, seeing as no subject outside of this kingdom knows what you or your hand looks like." I finish for him.

He sighs and nods his thanks.

"Exactly. It was the best way for me to get information on the outside while still protecting Atarah and its people. I have soldiers that occasionally leave to speak to civilians to get word on General Neem's whereabouts—but no one who could get so close to a Lord."

Aunt Sofia rubs her temples and lets out a sigh.

"So, you know then. You know what she is. Bador witnessed it when she beat Lord Krevosh, and I know the Hand of the King would not keep such information from you."

Axel's eyes study me for what seems like a lifetime, then his eyes roam the people in the room—my *family*—before he answers my aunt.

"I know that she is my fated mate."

What the fuck did he just say?

My own thoughts are echoed with a train of expletives from the others, and I look over at the seat closest to me before huffing and throwing myself down.

Everyone watches me as I move, their forms frozen while they wait for my reaction to this news.

I lean up—catching sight of all the lemon tarts—and grab one, biting into its gooey center.

I sigh at the taste and lean my head back, closing my eyes.

"It's too goddamn early for this."

17
Elaudia

I hear a scoff from Cadmus at my nonchalant attitude.

Twelve pairs of eyes stay trained on me as Axel drops this bomb of information.

I wave a hand, indicating that we should at least get on with our breakfast.

I'm playing it cool on the outside.

My insides—not so much.

Mate?

He thinks I'm his mate?

Very few people in today's world even remember the true meaning of the word. It was something that existed when magic was still flourishing in our world.

When the Fae freely roamed, the mermaids took over the seas, and rumors of Dragons, Sprites, and Gryffin's were alive and well. Only two of my sisters-in-arms have found mates in other men, and they both have muted Sprite bloodlines, almost thrice removed.

My eyes squint as I take in the powerful male before me.

He is almost larger than he was last night in my bedroom, thicker somehow, and I have to shake my head to clear it of the filthy thoughts that come to my mind.

I see Bador nod at Axel as if he had been asked something I didn't hear, before he ushers Nelly and Bria out of the dining hall, leaving only my family and King Axel.

Aunt Sofia and Uncle Henry sit next to me on either side, while Cadmus stands behind me, forever on the watch.

"What bloodline do you hail from? Sprite...? Werewolf?" She gasps and eyes his mouth.

He says nothing.

"Vampire?" She whispers. "I've not heard of a Vampire's descendant in many, many years."

My Aunt voices the question as if it's the most scandalous creature she can come up with, and I wait to see if he will answer.

A shake of his head is all he grants her.

I start to wonder if he is going to outright refuse her, when his eyes swing to mine, and an unfamiliar presence enters my mind.

"My secret is an old one, and imperative to Atarah's continued survival. Do you trust them?"

My eyes widen in shock at the invasion of his voice within my mind. The deep baritone feels as if it bounces off of my brain, and it causes me to startle, sitting up. I choke on my lemon tart—to my dismay—looking into his eyes.

"Laudi?"

Cadmus places a concerned hand on my shoulder, which I cover with my own.

"I'm fine."

My gaze swings back to Axel, who has yet to take his eyes off the hand on my shoulder.

It shouldn't be possible. Mind walkers were extremely rare, and only blessed to the line of the...

Fae.

I whisper in my mind.

He must hear me because he nods slightly.

I swallow the lump in my throat at the knowledge that I am sitting in front of a real and very *alive* Fae male.

"I trust them with my life."

I say to him in my mind.

Axel nods, and I swear I can see the tension radiating off of him as he addresses my family.

"My father was King Aeacus Volith of Atarah. My mother, Queen Cheche Gaila, from the land of Minegrost."

My Aunt lets out a startled laugh and sets her teacup down gently.

"That's impossible. King Aeacus ruled over a thousand years ago. He fought in the Great War, alongside his Fae brethren and the dragons."

A wistful expression enters her eyes as she remembers the great creatures that we have only ever known in the storybooks told to us before bedtime. Light beams through her eyes as a thought comes to her mind, and she sits forward.

"Fae? A full-blooded Fae." She breathes. "They had a son!"

Axel nods.

"My parents knew that war was imminent. They knew the humans were building an army, though they did not expect it to be of the magnitude it was. They did not expect the Gods to answer their fury-fueled prayers."

Axel's eyes are sad as he speaks, though his face remains impassive.

"When my mother became pregnant with me, they decided to keep it from the world, knowing I would be targeted as the Heir of Atarah. When the human council invaded with their troops in my seventeenth year, I was sent away to the temple of Yallendoy to learn how to conceal my Fae nature. The holy temples were common ground and deemed not a threat by the council, though their highest masters were loyal to my family. When the masters of Yallendoy were satisfied, I was to be sent back here, to take over as a human king implanted by the council, or so they believed."

I lean forward; my brows scrunched.

"But it's been a thousand years! How have they not learned of your true nature?"

Axel studies me for a moment before replying.

"I killed them all. All of the original founding members and their families. I searched for years for any surviving creatures of my lore. Dragons, Sprites, Merfolk, and Trolls. Though my search was not bountiful, it was successful."

"That's why the council refuses to be seen." I laugh. "It's because they're not human!"

Excitement drips from my every word.

"Do you know what this means? We can bring magic back to this world! General Neem has the help of the black magic witch, but with you and your armies by my side, we *can* defeat them."

I thought I would have to plead.

Get on my knees, perhaps, and beg the foreign king who had never opened his gates.

But I don't.

As the rest of the table sits silently, eyes wide and brains absorbing this new information, the man who calls me mate only nods, his eyes softening.

"Exactly my thoughts, little warrior."

A cup slamming down breaks my line of sight, and my aunt claps her hands together.

"This is splendid! We must start war plans immediately."

A throat clears to my left as Bador has returns. How he snuck up on all of us remains a mystery to me.

"Pardon, Your Grace. There is still the matter of the Ball in two days' time. Invitations have reached the households already—there is simply no way to cancel them."

I watch as Axel runs a hand through the scruff on his face, his eyes still on me.

"Let them come. Call for my council of elders immediately. Tell them we are to begin discussions on a first attack on General Neem. One night of dancing will not interfere with what we plan, General Neem has no knowledge of Atarah's involvement with the Princess."

I wince.

"No, but he knows what I am. I'm sure that's why he invaded Aland, as revenge for them hosting me all of those years. Which means..."

Cadmus speaks up.

"Lashforn is next."

A few swear words reach my ears, and I place my head in my hands. I heave a sigh and sit back up.

"It's my fault. If I had not done what I did to Lord Krevosh, maybe all of this could have been prevented."

"If I ever hear you blame yourself for the actions of others again, I will put you over my knee, royalty or not."

I choke as Axel speaks to my mind, pressing my thighs together at the uncomfortable feeling that burns between them. I shoot him a glare, which he promptly ignores by sending me an actual *image* of me bent over his muscled thighs, my bare ass marked red with his handprints.

I hate how red my face feels.

I'm about to introduce him to several swear words I learned from a pirate captain last year who was visiting Lashforn, but I'm cut off as Bador responds.

"At once, Your Grace. I'll inform them immediately. Shall the meeting take place this evening?"

Axel nods, smirking at me.

"Sounds delightful." He hums.

I stand abruptly, leaving my half-eaten lemon tarts on the table as I whirl, followed by Cadmus.

"I'm going for a walk."

I sound like a child who has been told no, but I find I do not even care. I make it halfway to the door before I whirl back around and snatch my cookies off the table.

Screw him for getting inside my mind and causing these strange feelings to take root inside me.

"They could use more cream."

I've barely crossed the threshold when I suddenly hear my aunt murmur.

"What in the heavens was that about?"

A deep chuckle resonates behind me.

"I believe that was my beautiful mate throwing a tantrum."

I growl in return. Cadmus follows behind me silently, which irks me even more for some unknown reason.

"You don't have anything to say about that—that unseemly man?!"

A chuckle reaches my ears, and I refrain from whirling around and kicking him in the shin.

"You know, I actually think he is pretty cool. I mean—you have to admit, we have not only just met a full-fledged Fae—but sat and *conversed* with him. He is over a thousand years old, Laudi! Think of the knowledge he possesses, the things he has seen."

We have reached the garden maze that stands by the kitchens, and I throw my hands up in exasperation.

"He is still an *ass*!"

My chest heaves, and I blow out a piece of hair that had flown into my face at my outburst.

"A handsome ass, apparently." Cadmus laughs.

"Ugh. Leave me be, you *traitor*. I wish to think." I pout unprettily.

"Not going to happen, princess. We are in unknown territory. Can't leave you alone."

"She won't be alone."

We both turn away from the rose bushes I caress to face the newcomer.

Him.

"You know, when I said I was going for a walk, I meant so I could get away from you."

King Axel only smirks and addresses Cadmus with a nod, to which he nods back and turns—

Oh no, he is NOT.

"Excuse me! Where do you think you're going!?"

Cadmus doesn't even turn back around, only calling over his shoulder with a smirk.

"You did tell me you wanted me to leave."

I let out an un–princess–like shriek, pointing an accusing finger at Axel.

"What did you say to him? What did you do?"

His thick fingers play with a blue rose that he has picked from the bushes, twirling it in his hands gently.

"We met briefly, Cadmus and I. When you and your entourage first arrived at my city's gates. He seems like a good soldier, and an even better friend."

"You won't find better. Now, if you'll excuse me."

I turn away but don't make it one step before a hand is grabbing my arm and pulling me back. I collide with a tall chest and look up at the king.

I should neuter him—I think angrily to myself.

"I would prefer you didn't, I quite enjoy my balls right where they are. Who knows, maybe one day soon you'll like them—"

"Ah! That's enough!"

I shout out loud, clapping my hands to my ears. His eyes are full of mirth as I scowl up at him.

"You know, for royalty, you're very crass. It's no wonder you haven't yet found a bride."

He steps even closer so that his body heat is radiating into mine, and I can smell his woodsy scent. Pine and cinnamon.

"I have yet to take a bride, little warrior, because I was waiting for you." He purrs.

His left hand reaches up to stroke away a stray strand of hair that has fallen into my face, and I think to myself that he must have an *enormous* pair hanging between his legs to think he can just touch me whenever he wants to. I raise my fist—prepared to strike—when warm lips crash down onto my own, and I'm sucked into a kiss that takes my breath away.

His tongue seeks my own, claiming me in a way I have never been claimed before. I lose myself, completely. He must have dropped the rose he held because both of his hands reach up to cradle my face as he tilts my head up.

I think I moan.

I cannot be entirely sure because of the rushing sound in my ears. The feel of him against my skin is nothing short of utter bliss and I find myself praying that it never ends.

As quickly as it begins, it ends, and he steps back.

"You know about mates, Elaudia. You know what they are to each other, what they become to each other. And though the male does feel the bond first, make no mistake. You are *mine*. I will wait for however long it is necessary for you to see that. But know this, no one else aside from me will ever touch you again. No one else will kiss these perfect lips, or feel that warm, wet heat you hide between your thighs."

I try to control my panting as he speaks, straightening my clothes.

I can still taste him on my tongue.

My brain is so muddled by our interaction—and my very first kiss—that I can only get a few quick words out before I do something I have never done in my life before.

"I will see you at the meeting."

And then I flee.

18

Elaudia

I've been pacing my rooms for the past hour, my body vibrating with a need that I cannot identify—*only I can.*

It wants him.

The King.

I want him.

Only, there are far too many more important things to be worried about.

Like the war. We need to determine how to infiltrate spies into the rebel camps. This means we will need to find individuals prepared to fight for our side—willing to die for it. Not likely. My bedroom door opens as Nelly races inside.

"Sorry, I'm late, Laudi. The headmistress was showing me a new technique for that baked bread you like. I figured it was too good to pass up."

I flash my friend a genuine smile.

"That was thoughtful of you, Nelly. Thank you. And you're hardly late. The council should be arriving soon. I just need to look slightly more like the Bellator I am, and not a whimpering princess."

I gesture to the gown Bria insisted I try on after breakfast. It is beautiful—if not a bit exposing. A devious glint enters her eyes.

"Warrior Princess?"

I laugh and nod in agreement.

"Warrior Princess."

Nelly works her magic quickly, pulling clothing from drawers I did not even know I had. It's simple enough, but as she goes to pull the final pieces from a large, embroidered box, I realize it's—

"Nahirian Armor," I whisper.

Armor that was worn by the Fae in the last great war. Armor that has not been seen or heard of in centuries. My eyes flash to hers in absolute surprise, and she grins back at me.

"Your Aunt and I—along with Bria—have been working on this for quite some time. It

took ages of negotiations and secret measure-
ments, but they have finally all arrived."

I shake my head in confusion.

This doesn't make any sense. Nahirian armor is made of dragon flesh. The only thing
almost as strong as their scales. Nelly sees the
questions in my eyes as she places the black
and white armored clothing on me.

"Queen Sofia said she began her search
when you were taken as a babe to Aland. She
always knew the day would come when you
would lead us into war. She found a dragon's
descendant across the black seas, one who hat-
ed the humans. She begged him to hear her
story. His name is Graven."

She whispers as if the walls have ears.

"He had dragon skin in his possession and
used a seamstress of his own findings to put
it together. She has been sworn to secrecy
by Graven. He gives this willingly, with the
promise that you would make all those who
target the innocents suffer."

She finishes lacing together my boots and
looks up.

"I know you will not let him down." She smiles.

I cannot even respond. To say that I am honored would be an understatement. I look down at the fine armor, taking in the very distinct pattern of dragon skin—its coloring white.

"Where is Graven now?"

Nelly works to braid my hair and answers.

"The last I had heard, he was packing his things and heading to the southern cities of Javert. He hopes to find people willing to fight for Atarah and Lashforn. Queen Sofia paid him quite handsomely."

I open my mouth to ask more questions about this mysterious male, but Bria clambers through the doors, her face flushed as she pants through her exertion.

She holds a metal box in her hands, pushed close to her chest.

"I've got them! They have finally arrived!"

What has?

Bria grins brightly, hustling us both over to the vanity and urging me to sit. Nelly lets out a squeal of excitement, and she tries to take the box out of Bria's hands. Bria backs away, shaking her head.

"Uh uh uh! You got to show her the Nahirian armor! Now it's my turn."

I arch an eyebrow.

"I'm having a hard time imagining what could possibly be more amazing than armor made of a dragon's skin."

Nelly grumbles at Bria but waves her hands over at me with a wide smile.

"Turn away and close your eyes. Do not peek until we tell you to."

I sigh softly as I turn slightly and close my eyes, my ears immediately focusing in on every sound in the room.

"How will you know if I peek or not if you're going to be focused on whatever is in that mystery box?"

Nelly and Bria share a look and purse their lips. Bria heaves a sigh and makes a hand gesture.

"Blindfold her."

The laugh that leaves me is contagious, and my friends join in.

I roll my eyes but allow Nelly to place a scrap of silk around my eyes, blinding me to the world.

I hear a rustling sound, concluding that it cannot be any more fabric if the zinging sound of metal is anything to go by. Cool hands touch the area closer to my chest, and I feel the fabric at my breast and rib cage pull tighter so that the dragon's skin is one with my own. It pulls tight before weaving around my throat, where one of the girls secures it at my nape. Hmmm. This is interesting.

But that's not all.

A weight is settled upon my head, and my eyes widen beneath the blindfold. I exhale a sigh as the blindfold is lifted away so that my own reflection is the first thing I see.

By the Gods.

A golden breastplate adorns my chest, engraved with not Lashforn's sigil—nor Aland's or even Atarah's—but the Syraxes Sigil. It has been carved into my breastplate, the depiction of a feminine hand holding a short sword, surrounded by the many hands and claws of every lore creature to ever exist.

A Bellator's hand.

The defender of all.

My eyes burn with tears I refuse to release as I catch sight of the golden crown upon my head—bright blue gemstones decorating the spines that curve upwards. Nothing dainty and easily destroyed.

But solid.

Its design is simple and sturdy. Worthy of a warrior.

I will be worthy.

I swear to myself.

"You look like a Queen." Bria breathes out, her hands clasped together.

Nelly snorts and smacks her playfully.

"She *is* a Queen. And once General Neem has been defeated, you can claim your throne."

I turn to face them both and stand. "Dornman's throne?"

"King Axel's, of course. I'm sure he would let you sit right on his—"

Now I'm the one doing the smacking, my face flushed scarlet.

"Do not even think about it! You're such a harlot!"

"I was just going to say his throne," Nelly says innocently, her eyes wide and doe-like.

"Yes, I'm sure you were." I laugh.

I take one more look at myself in the mirror as Bria hands me my polearm. I wasn't sure if weapons were allowed in a meeting like this, but it's about time that I start making rules of my own instead of following others.

My first rule would be to always be armed in the presence of others, no matter what. I add two daggers to the holsters on my thighs and nod.

"I'm ready. You've been told where this meeting is to be held?"

They both nod.

"Nelly is going to stay here and prepare your rooms for bed, and I will escort you. As well as Cadmus, of course."

A blush arises on her cheeks, and I grin.

"You're in love with him," I state.

We exit the door into the halls, giggling as Cadmus joins us silently. He must have been waiting for us. Bria does not answer verbally at the sight of Cadmus, but her nod is an affirmation.

My smile in return is genuine.

They both deserve to be happy.

We walk in silence to the third floor, arriving at a solid oak door by the end of the hall, manned by two Atarahirian guards.

"Well, this is where I leave you," Bria says, turning and grabbing my hands. "You'll be great. Just...be yourself, and they will love you."

Cadmus snorts and I glare at him. He tries to recover by complimenting my new wardrobe, but I just roll my eyes and ignore him. I arch an eyebrow at him and nod.

"You ready for this?"

He smiles lightly, "Are you?" He retorts.

Not really. But I need to be, so I nod and face the guards, who step aside.

"Princess." They murmur.

Cadmus stays close to my back as we enter, and I try to keep my breathing stable at the sight that greets my eyes. A large war table sits in the middle of the room, with various bobbles and miniature statues decorating it.

The cities and their defenses.

And sitting around the table are seven people-

No. Not people. Creatures of our lore.

They stand as I enter, all eyes on me.

It's impossible to make out who is what exactly, as I have never seen a pure-blooded lore creature in the flesh before. My eyes trail around, noting three women and four males. They all appear in their older years if the wrinkles around their eyes are any indication.

They are elders. Older than King Axel, even.

Speaking of Axel, I catch sight of him sitting at the opposite end of the table, watching me observe all those in the room.

His eyes drift up and down my body seductively, but I refuse to give him the satisfaction of a response. I look down and see a chair sitting empty, presumably for me. Before I take a step further, the King's deep voice fills the room.

"Council, I would like to introduce to you, Princess Elaudia Sonella of the Syraxes line. The Last Syraxes Bellator of our world."

Murmurs break out through the room, and I take a deep breath, making eye contact with each elder as I speak.

"It's an honor to meet you all. I hope you know I will do everything in my power to bring General Neem's invasion to an end. Whatever the risk, whatever the sacrifice."

The murmurs turn to a hush as a woman with black hair and slanted eyes turns back to me.

"You are someone that we have waited for—for what seems like a very long time, Princess. I hope you know what it will take to truly defeat General Neem?"

I keep her stare and nod solemnly.

I'll have to kill him.

Her name is Hydrandra. She is an Elf, little warrior.

Axel's voice echoes throughout my mind, and I thank him silently before looking around. They seem to know what I'm asking, because the male closest to me steps forward and bows his thick forehead.

"Niho, Troll."

A woman with white hair and tired eyes speaks next.

"Lynola, Voydanoy."

A water sprite?

Their introductions continue on until I have met a Druid, two Shape Shifters, and Ballon—the son of the blood dragon—Vilathem—who razed the battlefield of the Great War after his mate was killed.

I glance black at Hydrandra.

"General Neem will die. We will free these lands to the magic that once belonged. Your lines will continue on, I swear it."

Niho releases a hearty grumble and smiles my way.

"Well then, little Princess, let us begin."

He gestures for me to sit in the chair opposite Axel, and as I do, the rest follow. Axel smiles in approval, and I try to tamp down the butterflies that seem to want to erupt at his approval. I try to focus on the man who speaks, but as I look over, I take notice of Axel's eyes on me, as they roam up and down my body in appreciation.

When a few moments pass and he continues on as if we are not in what could be the most important meeting of our lives, I sit up and begin to unfasten the buttons that hold my top up.

Everyone grows still as Niho trails off, and right as I unclick the second button, Axel snarls in warning, his lips pulled back over his teeth as a streak of bloody violence flashes through his eyes.

That's what I thought.

"Pay attention." I chide into his mind, knowing he is listening.

Axel smirks at me but says nothing, only offering me a warning glance as I button myself once more.

Niho clears his throat as Axel speaks.

"General Neem's dark rebels have taken Aland. His supporters continue to grow out of fear, not support. My sources have brought to my attention that he gathers survivors in groups before threatening the remaining children. As long as the adults cooperate, the children are spared."

Fire lights through my chest as my rage burns.

He is threatening fucking children?

Axel continues.

"I sent five men on a mission before the last moon's crescent, and they have reported to me that with the help of the Bellator's, we may be able to extract the children from their holding cells in Aland."

"Any word on my sisters in arms?"

There were only twenty of them left in Aland by the time I received my last letter from Clarice. The rest have separated and gone to their own territories. Knowing they can defend themselves does nothing to stop the ache in my chest.

They can be killed far easier when they're alone.

Axel shakes his head.

"As far as my resources could tell, no Bellators remained in Aland. But that's not to say they're not there."

I can tell by the reservation in his eyes that he did not wish to tell me about this news in front of all of these strangers. I swallow the devastation in my throat and blink.

This is war, Elaudia. Focus.

"Cadmus and I can rally a small group of rebels from Javiort. Queen Sofia has sent someone to bring them here."

I turn away and speak to the guard closest to me.

"Ask for the Queen's presence immediately. Tell her to make haste."

The guard looks down at me impassively, making no move to follow my orders. For a moment, I think he'll ignore me completely, but then Axel speaks, his voice like death.

This look is one I have yet to have seen.

"Your future Queen has ordered you to do something. I suggest you do as she has asked."

The guard's eye snap to Axel's, as do mine.

"Yes, Your Majesties."

The guard almost trips hurrying out of the war room.

The council spares a few looks my way, but they say nothing as we wait for Sofia to arrive. I'll dwell on his insistence on me being his Queen tonight.

My aunt must have been close, because five minutes later, she walks into the room as gracefully as ever. Her brightly colored eyes scan the room with keen intelligence, before settling on me.

"You called for me, my dearest?"

I smile gently at her before standing and offering her a bowed head. Gods, do I love her.

"The girls have told me of Graven just this evening. Have you heard any word of him and any success he might have had?"

Sofia nods and clasps her hands together.

"He should be arriving within a week's time. He has informed me of sixty-five rebels, both men and women, who have chosen to fight with us. All of Lore's descendants."

Lynola speaks up, her eyes are bright with excitement.

"If that many escaped to the southern seas, then there is hope indeed that our magic might once again flourish in this world. We must begin our search once more, my brothers and sisters."

I watch the varying looks of hope wash over the council, thinking of how lonely they must have been this past century. Thinking that they were the last full bloods of their entire species. Yunic, the Werewolf Shifter, runs a hand over his tired face. I can tell he does not wish to diminish the hope in Lynola's eyes.

Hope that has been gone for so long and is now a fresh seed at the word of so many survivors. I walk closer to him and place a hand over his much larger one.

"If I had the chance to even get a glance at any of my people—even if it was for just one day, I would risk that heartache. I would risk the fact that it would soon be gone. Just to know, for *one moment*, that I was not alone."

Yunic stares at me for what seems a very long time before his eyes fall shut, and he nods his head.

"Once we have decided on the details of our next course of offense, we shall begin the next defense and scour the four corners of our world to find any lasting survivors."

Murmurs of excitement ripple throughout the room, and I smile, sitting back down.

My movements are interrupted, however, by the mental image that flashes across my mind.

Of me.

Bent over the very table I stand in front of.

Axel stands behind me, running a thick hand over my naked breasts, his fingers deftly pulling at my hardened nipples.

My whimpers seem to bounce throughout my head as he pushes the thick length of his cock into my—

I gasp, pulling myself out of my head.

Before I can even think of what I'm doing, my hand is reacting, throwing one of my daggers straight at his face.

As I knew he would, the bastard catches it.

The room has fallen into a hushed silence, and I try to ignore the heat of my face while I snarl at him.

"You missed." He winks.

I hiss.

"Stay out of my goddamn head!" I shriek.

Not very becoming of a princess—I know. But at this moment. I *really* do not give a fuck.

I huff out a breath and stand as tall as I can.

"We will wait for our own fighters to arrive, at which time, we will assess who belongs where. Only then will we take back Aland from the General's clutches."

A hearty rumble of 'ayes' echoes through the room and I nod, satisfied with our course of action.

Axel smirks at me with those deliciously full lips and licks the end of the dagger.

My dagger.

I roll my eyes and go to exit, Cadmus and Sofia by my side—when the door slams open, forcing us back. Cadmus has his sword drawn in a second and pushes me behind him.

But it's not a threat.

It is Bador, panting heavily with panicked eyes. Axel stands quickly, and if I thought the look on his face when he addressed the guard earlier was deadly—this look makes it seem like child's play.

When no one speaks, I step towards Axel.

"What is it?" I ask Axel, as my heart beats slightly faster than normal.

"Lord Krevosh is at Atarah's gates. He has given me an ultimatum. Give the Princess up to be wed to him by tomorrow's eve, or he will take the information of her survival straight to General Neem."

An uproar erupts in the war room, but I stay silent.

Motherfucker.

19

Elaudia

A xel clenches his jaw at the news of our unwanted visitor.

"Everyone out. I will handle Lord Krevosh."

I watch as the council of elders bow their heads in respect before filing out of the room until it is only the three of us left.

I look over my shoulder.

"You can wait outside Cadmus; I will be perfectly fine."

My eyes do not leave Axel as I speak, and I wait for the shuffle of footsteps to recede before I open my mouth to make him see reason.

"I know we have agreed to go into this war together, but not with General Neem's knowledge of my existence. It's the only advantage we have."

Axel's lips pull back into a smirk.

"Not the *only* advantage." He growls.

My eyes widen at his implication. I don't know what comes over me, but I find myself placing a hand on his arm.

"You can't mean to expose yourself to the world. If the wrong people find out a true-blooded Fae is alive—"

He cuts me off, twisting his arm so that his hand holds both of my own above my head as he pushes me against the wall. My breath catches in my throat at the move, and I tilt my chin, looking up.

"If the wrong people come after me or *anyone I love*, I will slaughter them where they stand. The time of hiding is over, do you not agree, Princess?"

He arches an eyebrow, and I know it's a challenge. I wiggle my wrists slightly, but they don't give. Warmth builds in my stomach at his proximity and though I hate to admit it, I whimper when he pushes his muscled thigh between my legs.

"I agree." I'm breathless and I hate it. I've never been touched like this before, and it's messing with my senses completely.

Axel's eyes burn with desire, and I don't want to imagine what he will do if we stay in this position much longer.

Or maybe I do.

I curse my throbbing lady parts that seem to be in some kind of heat.

I notch my foot behind his thigh, twisting until my body weight is thrown into him as I pull him over my shoulder and onto the ground. He goes with ease, and I frown down at the bastard who grins up at me from his place on the stone.

"You know touching me is punishable by death." He chuckles.

I sneer, which only causes him to laugh harder.

He let me do that.

My ire grows even more at that. I look down at the great king who seems perfectly content to lounge on the floor beneath my feet, and I huff out a breath of ire before sliding down the wall to sit next to him.

I do not know why camaraderie with him seems to come so easily, but I find myself growing softer with every word he speaks to me.

"We need to give him what he wants."

I look over to see that Axel is watching me with soft eyes.

"We will. We will give him a wedding grander than one he could have ever dreamed of. But as soon as he enters these castle walls, he will not ever leave them again. Threatening me was one thing. Threatening you? Well, little warrior. He's all but signed his execution."

I ignore the feeling that wells up in my chest at his words.

No one aside from my family has shown me so much care.

It's new, and if I'm being honest with myself, not completely unwelcome from him.

"Let it be before the ball. We will have a ceremony, with all of his guards present. Cadmus and his soldiers will stand ready. Lord Krevosh thinks that because I am royalty that I follow the rules. "

I nod my head as I listen to his plan.

"Here's what we're going to do."

And as he continues, my smile grows.

And so do these new feelings for him.

By the time he's done talking, a tiny voice in the back of my head is running over a list of why he is so perfect for me, and I have to stop it before it gets to the physical aspects of what he offers. He bumps my shoulder with his own and grins, his lips peeking out from beneath his beard.

"What do you think, little warrior? Is my plan foolproof, or do you see anything that needs to be corrected?"

I purse my lips and sigh.

"Well..."

His eyes light up as I draw the word out. I grin lightly.

"It should work. But we will have to make sure only Cadmus is aware. We can't risk any spies, from my side or yours. If he catches wind of anything rotten before he walks down the aisle, we might as well hand over the information to General Neem himself."

Axel nods and stands, offering me his hand.

"Let's go welcome him to Our Kingdom then, little warrior."

I look down at my armored body and sigh.

"I should probably change into something more amenable to his Lordship. Perhaps one of those frilly gowns my ladies' maids seem so fond of?"

Axel's eyes darken as he pulls me up from my sitting position and looks down at me.

"You will let him see you exactly as you are."

His voice is as sharp as glass, and it causes a shiver to work its way down my spine. These intimate moments we seem to share are becoming more frequent, invoking feelings of warmth and safety—safety I have never felt within the presence of another man.

Not even Cadmus.

"You are the safest person in this Kingdom when you are in my company, little warrior. Never doubt that."

I huff out a breath and pull away from him, breaking our contact.

"You really should learn to keep to your own head."

Amusement twinkles in his eyes as he grins.

"But if I kept to my own head, how in the world would I know that you would like to look up at me while you suck—"

I shriek.

"That is quite enough!"

I shove his arm in exasperation.

Whether or not it is real, I could not say.

Axel chuckles and opens the door, gesturing for me to go first. I roll my eyes as I leave, catching sight of Cadmus not far off. His eyes look worried and I'm sure I know the reason for it.

"We have a plan," I whisper into his ear as he joins me.

I take note that Axel stays close to me the entire time, though he walks in front of us as we head for the foyer. I watch as Cadmus's shoulders slump with relief.

"Just follow our lead and say nothing to Sofia or Henry. This must look as real as possible."

His eyebrows furrow together.

"Just what do you two have in mind for him?"

Axel slows his pace as we reach the entrance, and he looks back at Cadmus with an evil glint in his eyes.

"We're going to give him exactly what he wants."

The foyer is alive with whispers, and I catch sight of more than one maid with an apprehensive, stricken face. Nelly and Bria are among them. The girls rush to me as soon as they catch sight of me, almost tripping over their skirts in their haste. I keep my face perfectly blank, offering them a stiff smile.

Axel nods to the guards who stand sentry at the castle doors, and they turn to open them. I hush Nelly and Bria, moving so that I stand in front of them, but still behind Cadmus, as is his job.

The evening air is cool as it blows into the room, and I look up at the stars who have come out to play in the darkening sky. Gods give me the strength to not kill him where he stands.

The vile man.

He looks exactly as I remember him, disgustingly skinny with a nose that would rival the sharpness of a bird's beak. He smiles widely as he enters, throwing his hands up as if he owns the place.

"King Axel himself. What a pleasure it is to meet a man of such *intelligence.*"

It seems we are skipping out on the pleasantries. I look over his shoulder at the soldiers who stand behind him, all wearing the color of his house. He must have bribed and threatened everyone near to have amassed such a small army.

"Lord Krevosh." Axel purrs. "As is my honor to have such a formidable ally in my kingdom."

I choke on my spit, not expecting Axel to play act so well. Lord Krevosh's eyes swing to me, and I fight the sneer that tries to arise.

"Ah! Here she is. My greatest disgrace and triumph all in one. I cannot say I've missed the pleasure of your...stimulating company."

His tone lets me know that he has yet to forget being bested not only by a woman—but by a Princess. I grin as I remember our last encounter, stepping out from behind Cadmus.

"How is your nose, Lord Krevosh?"

His face reddens in anger, but surprisingly, he holds his tongue.

"Easy tiger."

Axel might be warning me in my head, but I can sense his pride and amusement. A scuffle by the hall draws my attention as Aunt Sofia rushes in, only to be held back by my uncle. The wrath on her face hurts me, but I know this will play in perfectly to our plans.

"You filthy swine! You will not have her! You cannot!"

I look over my shoulder with tears burning my eyes, playing into the part of a damsel surprisingly well.

"At least there is one monarch left to rule who is not a complete fool. I shall make sure General Neem is aware of how well you have accommodated me."

Axel inclines his head.

"My staff has prepared your rooms, just a few minutes down the path off of my gardens."

Lord Krevosh chokes, his smile turning into a sneer.

"We are not to stay in the castle? I wish to be close to my bride-to-be." He croons while looking me up and down.

Axel takes a protective step to my left.

"With treaties signed not that long ago, there are still many dangers presenting themselves to us. The house I shall host you in is safer, as it is off the path and secluded. But I welcome you to join my ball tomorrow evening—after your nuptials—of course."

The Lord's eyes widen.

"You will wed us tomorrow?"

Axel nods and hums. "As soon as possible, I think is best. I will do whatever is necessary to protect Atarah. My war general will show you the way to your beds, as I'm sure you are quite famished after such a long journey."

Aunt Sofia lunges once more, still held back by Henry.

Lord Krevosh offers a nasty smile.

"Of course, King Axel." He steps forward, walking around Axel, until he is only a step away from me.

Cadmus growls and puts his hand on his sword, only halting when I place a hand on his arm. I step out from around him, making sure my face shows the solemness I would surely feel if this was real. He lifts a hand, placing it onto my hair.

"I so look forward to our wedding night...I should finally be able to teach you those manners you so yet lack."

And then he squeezes.

And screeches.

I smile.

He pulls his bleeding hand away, the one that was just impaled on the blades I keep in my hair.

"Oops." I smile.

His mouth opens, spit flying my way.

"You vile whore!"

He raises his hand towards my face, prepared to backhand me.

To keep our cover, I'm prepared to take it, but in the very next second, Axel is there. His hand twists Lord Krevosh's at an odd angle, and I try to hide my smirk at the joy his screams bring me.

Axel's face remains composed, but I can see the tension radiating off of him. Everyone silences, except for Lord Krevosh's guards, who have drawn their weapons.

Axel's eyes flash with violence as he addresses him.

"She will be your wife very soon, Lord Krevosh. But she is not yet. She is still a Princess at this very moment, and you would be very wise never to strike her or attempt to strike her in my presence again. Am I clear?"

Krevosh grimaces when his arm is pulled tighter.

Axel leans in, whispering in his ear.

"Keep in mind, you are in *my kingdom*, only receiving what you want because of *my will*."

Krevosh nods and takes a cloth from one of his men, wrapping his bleeding hand.

"I understand. Allow me and my men our leave. We will see you tomorrow."

Axel lets him go with a shove, standing tall in front of me like a sentinel. We wait until they have all left the entrance and the doors are shut before speaking.

"I would say that was very convincing, wouldn't you?" I huff out a breath.

Aunt Sofia rushes me.

"Convincing?"

She's an intelligent woman, and I only raise my eyebrow at her before it dawns on her face.

She turns and launches herself into Axel's arms, tears trailing down her face.

"You won't let him have her." She breathes.

Axel seems shocked at the display of affection, but slowly wraps his arm around her, returning her embrace. His eyes stay on me, hard and unflinching.

"I will not."

20

Elaudia

The breeze ruffles my undone hair as I take a moment to breathe in the fresh air, relaxing after the night's events.

My white cotton dress is simple, fluttering around my ankles gently. I feel like every touch against my skin is a fire just waiting to be lit.

The sky has darkened, leaving pale shades of purple and blue to splash across the horizon, and I look down to take in the crashing waves below. Not too dangerous—indeed, nothing that would kill the likes of me.

After Nelly and Bria helped me to change and took the blades from my hair, I had the urge for fresh air and the salt sea.

Luckily for me, Axel's castle sits near a cliff, which they use as their training grounds. It is also the furthest away from the disgusting Lord Krevosh.

Axel...

I purse my lips as I think about the Fae male who has dug himself so deeply under my skin in such a short time. I never gave much thought to any kind of marriage—let alone mating. It did not seem possible at the time.

But now, with all of this new information that has come to light about the magic that is indeed still left in our world, I feel...

Lust.

Hope.

Intrigue.

All for a king who looks at me as if I am the answer to all of his prayers and the object of his latest obsession. A king who has proven he will do what he must to keep me from harm, though I have yet to actually need it.

The wind picks up, blasting through my hair and blowing against me until I am forced to take a step back. As powerful as I may be, I am still nothing against Mother Nature herself, and I smile at the thought.

"I hope you're not thinking of jumping. I have yet to use all of my clever innuendos on you."

I whirl around, keeping my smile in place. It's not the first time he has caught me off guard, but I find that I do not really care.

"Surely the king of such a vast and great kingdom has more important things to do than stalk a mere princess."

I face Axel completely and look my fill. His black hair is windblown, and the beard on his sharp jawline has been shaved down just a bit. He has changed his clothing as well and now wears something simple. A black tunic and pants adorn his legs, with booted feet. There is an impressive bulge that catches my eye, and lust surges forward at the sight.

His swords stay strapped to his back. Gods...he's such a magnificent creature.

I have yet to study the male body so intensely, even though Clarice and the other's secretly hired males to entertain us on the night of my eighteenth summer. I chickened out as soon as they began unbuttoning their pants to dance for us, claiming I had to be up early for training.

But I cannot lie and say I haven't wondered.

Wondered what it would feel like to feel a male's calloused fingers run across my breasts, using their thumbs to work the sensitive peaks until I'm squirming with pleasure.

Wondered what it would be like to feel their hot breath against my neck while they rut between my legs—

"Stalking a princess seems so criminal. I prefer protecting my mate. You never know what dangers may lurk in the trees."

He gestures behind him to where the forest lies. I roll my eyes, pulling myself out of my burning fantasies. There's a wicked gleam in Axel's eyes, as if he knows exactly what I was thinking about, but he has mercy on me and says nothing while I look at the trees.

I'm a Bellator, and I damn sure fight like one. I have nothing to fear from whatever could be hiding in those trees.

Now the mating part—I most definitely want to circle back to.

"Why can't I feel it?"

I don't need to explain myself. He knows what I mean.

Axel steps forward until he is within a mere foot of me, and he looks down, his eyes softening.

"Fae mate with Fae. I have never heard of this happening in all the years I have lived. While it is common for the male to feel the bond first, mating with a Bellator would be a first."

He takes another step.

His muscled stomach brushes against my breasts as he places a hand below my chin, tilting my face up until my pure white eyes stare into his warm, honey ones. I let out a breath at the feel of his skin against mine.

It's almost as if my very core is vibrating while a beast under my skin thrashes for the male in front of me.

"I promise you this, though. I am full-blooded Fae, and I have made no mistake. You are my mate, Elaudia Syraxes. That is something I take with the utmost seriousness. It is why I am going to war, why I have protected you from Krevosh—A Lord who has a surprising amount of pull with the citizens of Misit. It's why I'm prepared to sacrifice the security of my people to end General Neem's conquest."

I place a hand on his chest.

"It will not come to that."

My heart is fluttering faster than it ever has before, and I try to swallow—but I cannot breathe. Not when Axel continues to look at me as if he wishes to devour me.

He lowers his head slightly, keeping eye contact with me.

I'm panting softly now, my chest heaving.

I take a step back, backtracking until I am once again standing near the edge of the cliff. His eyes widen when my steps do not halt. He starts chasing after me as I strip myself of my outer robes.

Once I'm left in nothing but my thin white nightdress, I start jogging faster.

He won't chase me.

He's a King.

"Elaudia! You reckless creature—come away from there before I put you over my knee for this disobedience."

I can only laugh as he drops his two broadswords.

My eyes widen as he takes off toward me.

"Come and punish me then."

He won't jump. But seeing the look on his face was priceless. I open my arms and close my eyes as I tip back and free-fall into the water below.

21

Axel

If I were not Fae, Elaudia would surely be the reason I begin to grow gray hair twenty years too early.

Her small body drops off the edge of the cliff in front of us, and I rush forward, dropping my ancient swords to the ground without a second thought.

I lunge over the edge, but instead of feeling panic, I begin to chuckle mid-fall. She is everything I have ever wanted and everything I believed I would never have.

I have seen her kindness firsthand to the lower-class people of my kingdom.

Her true and pure friendship with those in her employ.

Her devotion to her family and theirs to her.

I have quickly become acquainted with her beautiful soul—her pure heart—and could think of no other woman I would rather be mated to. My father and mother must have been looking down at me in this moment because I swear, I can feel the stars brighten in joy as I crash into the water and immediately begin my search for my little warrior.

It doesn't take long, my enhanced strength powering me through the waves as I allow my mating bond to search her out. I wrap my arms around her waist, pulling her up and out of the sea.

Her eyes widen in shock as I pull her to my chest.

"You jumped." She whispers.

I push back until we are underneath the small waterfall to the left, and we tip our heads down as we duck under it, settling in the small alcove.

My body is alive with a need so strong, I'm surprised I have managed to keep my power tampered down.

I hold her tight, pulling her legs apart until she straddles my waist as we float. Such a beautiful, headstrong, wonderful woman.

And all mine.

Possessiveness courses violently through my body.

"I jumped."

And then I crash my lips down onto hers, tasting the salt water and her honeyed tongue.

She whimpers into my mouth, the sound causing a feral growl to leave my chest as I tighten my hold on her. My tongue tangles with hers, dancing together as if we have been doing this for years. Her hands slide up my chest, feeling the muscle that lies beneath.

My cock has hardened into granite, and I know the exact moment she takes notice because she starts to grind her sweet little pussy against me, taking her pleasure.

"Axel." She moans.

I kiss my way down her neck.

"That's it, princess...take what you need from me. Rub that swollen little clit on me until you're screaming my name."

I reach the shallow end of the alcove, clamping my hands down onto her hips.

"No one can hear you, Elaudia...keep going...ah, that's my good girl."

I toss my head back as pressure begins to build in my balls and I clench my jaw, knowing I won't get any relief.

I find I don't care.

Not as long as my mate is crying out so beautifully against me.

"Axel! I've never—ah! I've never done this."

If I thought I had been possessive before, it was nothing compared to the present, knowing I was the first male to ever touch her—to ever have the privilege of settling between these perfect creamy thighs. I hook a hand under her pert little ass and push us tighter against the smooth rock.

"Don't let go," I growl.

I place her hands around my neck and begin thrusting, ramming my hard cock into her throbbing clit faster and faster.

The feeling of our soaked bodies working in tandem beneath the lapping waves is a memory I will etch into my very essence for as long as I remain alive. Her breathy little cries become more frequent as I move her body on top of me, and I can feel the moment she comes apart in my arms.

She tenses up and cries out, chanting my name over and over again.

I feel like a God, knowing I have brought my mate such pleasure.

I pull her closer—if that's possible—and place a kiss on her wet forehead, brushing her coal-colored hair away from her temple.

She sighs happily, returning my affection and nuzzling into my neck.

"Axel?"

I look down at her orgasm-induced smile and arch an eyebrow.

Something so happy and soft is new to see on her face.

Nothing like that bloodthirsty and frightening warrior I have come to know.

"Can I be the one to kill Lord Krevosh? I owe him for that hair-pulling stunt."

I chuckle.

And there she is.

22

Elaudia

Axel kisses me softly in the glow of the candle-lit room, growling into my mouth.

He was worried I would catch a cold after our night swim, and I was all too happy to roll my eyes and inform him that I don't really catch human sickness.

But I indulged the muscled Fae who touches me as if I am spun glass beneath his calloused hands and followed him into his room without complaint. I watched as he drew a warm bath for us, oils and candles included.

I do love a good soak in the tub.

My nipples tighten as he lathers my hair, his hands moving through the thick threads gently. My first male-induced orgasm seemed to have reduced me into a puddle of nothingness, and I soak up the feeling, knowing it will not last forever.

Hell...it won't last through the night.

I convinced Axel that we need to rest after our bath, and he agreed.

We have a long day ahead of us tomorrow.

Balls to host, people to kill.

I look up from my resting place against his strong chest. A part of me feels so strangely at how the events of the week have turned out, but the other part of me feels as if this is so right.

Like it was fate.

I suppose it was.

I just need to stop fighting it.

"Were you lonely?" I ask him softly.

Thankfully, I don't need to elaborate. He knows exactly what I'm speaking of.

"Every single day. I was young by Fae standards when the war broke out. Though my parents did not just send me away for my safety. I was at the age where it was normal for most fae to be schooled for the next twenty years—though never in the temples. I needed to become better, and more controlled. I was too powerful at that age, more so than I should have been, and it worried my mother. It wasn't until my fourth week of training that I got the news that they had all been killed."

His voice has grown deeper the more he speaks, his eyes growing somber.

"So many fled—apparently more than I thought even survived. I accepted decades ago that I would live this life alone. Never to marry. Never to mate. Never to have a child."

He clears his throat.

I turn around and cup his face with my hands.

"I have known that loneliness since the day I was brought to Aland. I have lived, breathed, and accepted it."

My thumbs run across his sharp cheekbones and the growing beard beneath.

"But we are no longer alone. The Gods have given us this gift...and I am honored to accept my place by your side. If–If you will have me, that is?"

I feel uncertain for the first time in a long time.

Of rejection.

Of being *truly* alone.

"Your uncertainty is unwarranted, little warrior. I would be proud to have you by my side. I *will* have you by my side." He vows.

His rough hands slide up and down my naked back and I close my eyes, soaking in the feeling of him against me.

My lips lift up into a soft smile as he gentling strokes my skin, his touch gentle and adoring.

"Forever then."

He places a chaste kiss on my cheeks, then my forehead, and then my lips.

"Forever then."

***

I roll my eyes as Bria and Nelly fuss over my hair as if preparing me for my funeral and not my wedding.

I wish I could tell them the truth of what will occur today, but it is already risky enough with Sofia and Henry in on it.

We cannot risk anyone else learning the truth.

The gown that was sent to me this morning is beautiful, smooth, and simple—with a veil that is longer than anything I have ever seen. The sleeves end at a cuff, with fine pearl buttons.

My white eyes study my reflection, watching as Nelly fastens the veil to my new hairstyle, left half up in an intricate bun. I wish I could say I feel bad about what is about to happen, but I hold no pity for thieves and blackmailers.

"You're sure there is nothing to be done, Laudi?" Bria whispers, her eyes downcast.

I close my eyes and prepare myself for another lie to my friends. I frown and pull her close, acting the part.

"There's only one way to defeat General Neem. He must remain unaware of my existence for now."

Nelly wipes a few tears that trail down her face and shakes her head.

"Allow us to help you, Princess. I will carry your veil. Bria, grab her weapons and keep them close."

I smile at Nelly, who has always been the tougher of the two.

A knock on the door signals it is time for us to make our way to the great hall that will serve as the wedding ceremony. The girls get ready behind me, and I give them a reassuring nod.

"We are ready," I call out.

Cadmus opens the door, his face grim. I hate that he has to keep this from Bria, but hopefully, all will be forgiven come first light.

We make our way down the hall, and I watch as The King's Guard stays close to us, making sure we are not disturbed on the way. My heart yearns to see Axel, but I know that for this to look real, he must not seem to fancy me in any kind of way.

Trumpets begin to roll as we approach, and I kiss Nelly and Bria on the cheek as they depart me, making their way to their seats by Sofia.

I reach up, straightening my long veil, before looking up at Cadmus.

He offers a smile for me alone.

"Make him suffer." He whispers into my ear.

I grin up at him.

Not the grin of a woman in love who is about to marry the love of her life—but a woman who is about to make a man suffer for all of his wrongdoings against her.

The doors open swiftly, and I watch as the crowd stands, waiting for me to begin my walk. I see many faces I do not know, yet they look on with sympathy in their eyes.

Sympathy for me.

The music is slow, and I try to match pace with Cadmus, who tightens his grip on my arm the closer we get to Krevosh. He stands there with an evil smile, prepared to make my life a living hell, all because I rejected and out-witted him.

I keep my emotions in check as we arrive at the end of the aisle. Cadmus hands me off with a kiss on the cheek and I smile at him, though it looks more like a grimace.

I face Lord Krevosh with dead eyes, waiting for the officiate to begin speaking as my eyes start to look around for Axel.

As I take in the room, I notice that for each Guard of Misit, there stands a Royal Guard of Atarah next to him.

When I allow my eyes trail up, I finally catch sight of Axel, watching the entire thing with a poker face that could rival that of a seasoned gambler.

"You are doing well, little warrior."

Peace washes over me at the sound of his voice in my head, and I zone in on the old man speaking, asking us to love and cherish each other.

Yuck.

Yeah right.

Just a little longer.

Lord Krevosh leans in and whispers softly.

"You're ours now."

My eyes widen.

I play with the plan in my head, knowing Axel will use his Fae gifts to kill Krevosh. But what if Lord Krevosh lied when he said he would keep my existence from General Neem? What if he has already sent a messenger to his camp?

If he learns of both me and Axel at the same time, we will have no upper hand against him in this war.

My lips lift into a snarl as Lord Krevosh says, 'I do'.

And then I reach for the dagger hidden beneath the belt of my dress and slit his throat while his mouth is still open in a vow.

Screams sound throughout the halls as his blood spurts out, coating the front of my white gown. I don't have to wait for anything else, because as soon as I moved, each guard of Atarah thrusts their own sword into the unsuspecting stomachs of Misit's guards. The people stand once more but make no move to exit.

Nelly and Bria have clutched onto to each other, watching with wide eyes next to Queen Sofia, who smiles softly.

I never thought my aunt to be so bloodthirsty. I look down at Lord Krevosh, whose body has slumped and lies on the staircase, face down. Blood drips from my hand and onto the stone floor beneath.

My first kill.

And I feel nothing but relief.

Before I can become too lost in my head, Axel is there, grabbing the weapon from my hands.

I let him take it and embrace me softly, breathing in his scent as he rests his forehead against my own.

"Vicious little thing. I should have known you would stray from the plan. You'll never be one to wait for me, will you, little warrior?"

I smile softly and look up, ignoring the officiate behind us who has gone white as a ghost.

"He said I was *theirs* now, Axel. I don't think he kept his word. I don't think he was ever going to. General Neem will soon receive word of my existence."

Axel's face transforms into something dark and deadly as I speak, and I glance over to the waiting crowd. I lift my hand, soothing his brow.

"Not here."

His eyes clear up as he remembers where he is, and he turns to face his court.

"Let this be a lesson to all who come into my kingdom and attempt to blackmail me. I am King Axel of Atarah and the Free Cities, and I will take orders from no man! This Lord got exactly what he deserved as he has aligned himself with the tyrant General, and I applaud The Princess for her bravery to seek out what I already planned to do. Rest assured, you are safe and will remain so under my rule. This ceremony is over. I ask you to join the festivities of the royal ball immediately."

No one speaks out; they only bow to King Axel and exit swiftly.

I wait until the room is empty and then turn to my family, all who have approached me with cautious looks.

"I'm fine," I assure them with a smile.

I hug the girls first—who cry openly now with relief—and then Sofia and Henry, who both snuggle me close.

"I'm proud of you, Elaudia." Aunt Sofia says.

I grin up at her and roll my eyes.

"This family is so dysfunctional."

Laughter greets me in return, and they exit the hall, heading towards the party on the other side of the castle. Nelly and Bria stand a few paces away, waiting for me. I'm assuming so that they can change me out of this bloody gown before I join the ball.

Axel kisses my lips softly, ignoring our small audience and their gasps of surprise. His big hand brushes a curl away from my face, and I lean into his palm with a sigh.

"Go get changed. My people will clean this mess. Tonight, we will enjoy the victory of this battle. And tomorrow, we prepare for war."

***

The blood came off my skin with ease—much to my surprise—though the gown was ruined.

Not that I cared, I would be happy to never see it again. Nelly and Bria work quickly to change me into a gown of soft green, with silk sleeves that caress my skin like a lover would.

They also won't stop asking me questions about everything that has just occurred. I shoot them both a gentle look and they stop, finally allowing me to speak.

"We needed the element of surprise. It needed to look real, and we needed him to believe that Axel has no inclination towards me or my safety."

Nelly nods while Bria continues on.

"But he kissed you!"

I wince, forgetting they bore witness to that little part of the night.

"We might have feelings for each other."

I leave out the part about us being eternal mates. Bador escorted them from breakfast before that piece of information was revealed.

The girls squeal at this new information and start fluttering around me even more than before, making sure everything about me is perfect.

"I knew it, I knew it! Didn't I tell you, Nelly?! Soon she will sit on his throne and his co—"

"Bria!" I scold her.

It only lasts a minute before I'm laughing alongside their giggles. I shift in front of the mirror, watching as the gown glitters when I move. The girls have left my hair down and curled against my naked back.

At least the front covers everything it needs to.

"You look beautiful, Laudi." They say in unison.

Before Axel, I did not give much thought to fashion or my appearance.

Now, though, I find myself wanting to appease him. I wait for the girls to get ready and then as one group, we head for the ball—surrounded by guards of course. I find myself wondering what it will look like, what the people will act like.

I've never attended a ball in a different kingdom before, and my heart beats slightly faster in my chest. Nelly nudges me with her elbow and shoots me a playful smile.

"You'll be fine." My shoulders relax at her reassurance.

We arrive at the large staircase that leads to the ballroom, and I thank Cadmus as he grabs my hand and helps me up. I ignore the searing gazes of the guards standing watch on either side, wondering if they are starting to catch on to how their King feels about me.

"Presenting Princess Elaudia, and Her Royal Guard Cadmus of Aland."

Cadmus chokes at the introduction and looks down at me. I only shrug.

"Aunt Sofia must have decided it was time to promote you."

He stands taller at this, his watch turning into a full scan of the premises.

"I will not fail you, Elaudia."

I roll my eyes but let him have his manly moment. I know it is important for the ego of the opposite sex.

My eyes scan the sea of people dancing before us, the ladies with flowing gowns and the men with perfectly tailored waistcoats. I push Nelly and Bria along, urging them to join in on the festivities for the night.

They giggle and run along, but not before Bria shoots a coy smile at Cadmus, who returns the sentiment with a wink of his own.

"I'll be with you shortly." He says softly.

And then we are lost in a sea of strangers, dancing and drinking and forgetting that to-morrow we will begin our war plans. Music plays loudly from all corners, the musicians matching each other's tempo.

Exotic women of The Free Cities dance bare-ly clad, which I have come to learn is just their style of clothing.

I have time for one dance with Cadmus, smiling as he twirls me, before the trumpets sound once more, causing everyone who was dancing to halt.

"His Royal Highness, King Axel of Atarah!"

My breath leaves me at the sight of him, standing tall and proud and daring anyone to go against him. His black hair is combed away from his face, leaving his strong jawline on for show.

He's shaved.

I see more than one lady fan herself at the sight of him, but as I look back up, his eyes are on mine. I gasp softly at the intensity of his stare and feel my body come alive as he slowly makes his way down the staircase.

Cadmus leans down to murmur in my ear as he slowly approaches us.

"That is my cue, Princess. Enjoy the night."

As he exits my space, Axel enters mine.

He keeps walking until his breath begins to mingle with my own and he whispers lowly so that no one can hear us.

"You can have my lands, my armies, and my throne. All that I ask is you give me your next thousand climaxes...along with your heart, little warrior."

My breath hitches at the vehemence in his tone, and I look around, watching everyone watch us. Axel seems to pick up on my train of thought.

"Dance." He commands softly but with power.

Just like that, the music begins once more, and the people resume, twirling and laughing, though I'm sure still trying to watch us and see what we will do next.

I look over to the gardens on the left and smile before grabbing his hand and pulling him to the exit.

"You know it's considered rude for the king to exit as soon as he arrives?" He says with amusement.

I raise an eyebrow.

"I don't see you trying to stop me."

He pulls me back into his chest as soon as we arrive between two hedges.

"That's because I am your willing victim. Please do whatever you will with me." He purrs against my shoulder before dropping a kiss on the naked spot.

He groans at the warmth of my skin.

"This gown...you look ravishing, little mate."

His eyes turn completely black for a moment, and I watch as he struggles to control his other side.

It's the first time he has let his guard down enough for me to see his Fae nature, and I find myself honored at his show of trust.

"Marry me," I say softly. If it were any other moment, I would laugh at the look of disbelief on his face.

"I don't want to wait. Tomorrow, we start planning a war. I know it's fast, and I don't know what the future holds for us, but I know that I want to face this war and everything else in this life together. With you by my side."

His hand reaches up to cup my face as he grins.

"I know a place."

23
Elaudia

The place he knew turned out to be a hole-in-the-wall church down a very questionable alley.

I laughed as he helped me over broken glass and discarded reading paper that I'm sure was used for something other than knowledge. I was starting to become skeptical of this being a place for a sacred ceremony, but as soon as he opened the door, it was as if we were transported into an entirely different world.

"Yarlon is a descendant of the Elves. His power is limited, but what he *does* have is strong."

Strong indeed.

It looks like a magical oasis with vines hanging from the ceiling and a glowing blue pool centered under a skylight.

"Wow..."

"Beautiful, isn't it?"

I nod and look over, expecting him to be taking in the warm view before us, but he's not.

He's looking at me.

I can feel my face heat up, but before I can say anything, a skinny man wearing silk robes and a bright smile emerges from the door to the right.

"My King!"

He walks up, embracing Axel as the two chuckle with each other.

"Hello, old friend. I'd like to introduce you to my mate, Princess Elaudia."

I take note of how he leaves out my true last name, but I say nothing. The elf before me shouts jovially, bringing me in for a hug. I laugh at his excitement and hug him back.

"I assume this means you can only be here for one thing! It certainly isn't so I can make friends with a creature so pleasing to my eyes." He jokes.

Axel pulls me closer and chuckles.

"I need you to wed us, old friend."

Yarlon grins brightly and bows.

"It would be the highest privilege, Your Majesty. Girls!"

I look over, shock adorning my face as two women seem to materialize before us. They reach for me, urging me into a back room. Axel laughs at my look of disbelief before nudging me along.

"Go on, love. You'll be fine. His daughters will prepare you. I'll be right here when you're done."

I shoot a silly smile his way, my heart fluttering when he calls me *love*, but I follow the two tall women with slightly pointed ears. They murmur in soft-pitched voices about my beauty and the length of my hair, and I smile in thanks.

They work quickly once we are shut in the room, fluttering about and undressing me. They hand me a silken silver gown that leaves little to the imagination and shimmers in the sparkling light of this magical cavern.

I've never seen a gown so beautiful.

I open my mouth to ask for undergarments but think better of it. I probably won't need them.

They undo the corset of the gown Nelly and Bria helped me into, clucking their tongues as it finally falls away and allows me to breathe.

"Too tight, princess." She murmurs with a beautiful accent as she helps me into the new gown.

I grin and nod.

"The life of royalty," I say.

The one in front of me rubs a soft metallic glitter on my cheekbones with a brush, tracing it to the tip of my nose.

"To compliment your eyes, Princess."

I wait a moment longer, and then she spins me gently so that I can see myself in the reflection.

Holy shit.

Gone is Elaudia the Bellator. In her place stands someone who looks as if they could be a Goddess of the Moon.

My skin glows, and my face has been made to look like perfection itself—my hair left in ringlets down my back.

I grin brightly at the two elves before me, a teary smile touching my painted lips.

"Thank you."

They bow before me and hurry out.

I look at myself once more and heave out a breath.

This is it.

I'm about to marry Axel.

A Fae.

The last full-blooded Fae in this world.

A King.

I'm getting married. To my fated mate.

I stop myself from thinking too much and glide over to the door, my dress sliding across the stone floor as I move. Axel and Yarlon wait by the edge of the pool, the former taking in every inch of my body. His eyes have flared with a desire that makes my knees weak, and I take a deep breath as I walk over and place my hand into his extended one.

"Please, enter the sacred pool of Ethilomean," Yarlon says quietly.

Axel smiles down at me, waiting for me to make the first move. He's making sure this is what I really want. My heart warms as I nod at him to go ahead, and then I follow him into the warm waters below us. He walks us to the middle of the pool, and I note that it stops at my thighs and his calves. I look up, gasping at the beauty above. The moon is at its crescent phase, with thousands of stars glittering around it like a comforting blanket.

"Axel, you have requested that I wed you in the ancient ways of the Fae, to which I happily oblige, My King. Please, take your beloved's hands into your own."

Axel reaches for my other hand and brings them closer to him, running his fingers over my knuckles. And then he begins to speak in the language of his people.

"I votum amatum, servire et tueri, et mori. Aeternum."

His voice whispers the translation in my mind, and I find tears stinging my eyes as he speaks.

To love. To serve. To protect. To die by my side. For eternity and all the lives that come after.

I repeat the vow to him, doing my best to copy his words. If we are going to honor his people, I'm going to do it right.

A tear streaks down my left cheek, but I let it fall. I let him see how utterly enraptured I am with him.

Yarlon grins as I finish speaking, and he raises his hands to the side as water begins to trickle from the open cavern above our heads as the pleasant feeling of magic washes over us. I gasp softly.

"And so it will be, from this day, until your last. Fated mates. Axel, the Gods have blessed this union. You may kiss her."

Axel doesn't wait, pulling me into him before Yarlon has finished speaking. He crushes his mouth to mine with a fever that matches the fire lit inside my veins, his tongue clashing with mine gently as he makes love to my mouth.

And then I feel it.

A pull like nothing I have ever felt before snapping into place as I moan into the heat of his mouth. I gasp and fall back, my words a sob.

"I can feel it," I whisper.

He doesn't ask me what.

He knows.

He shouts his excitement while twirling me, and I swear it's as if the waters below us come alive, glowing with our elation.

"My mate." He whispers reverently.

I grin at him.

"My husband."

***

Axel pulls my silver gown to the side, letting it fall off my shoulders, and onto the floor below us.

We made a hasty retreat to his rooms as soon as we returned to the castle, sneaking through the hallways like giggling schoolchildren. He leans down, placing gentle kisses along my collarbone and I sigh as goosebumps break out along my arms.

"My beautiful mate..." He murmurs, biting the spot where my neck meets my shoulder.

I gasp at the bite of pain.

"My beast wants to come out and play, little warrior...will you let him?"

I tilt my head back into his chest as he wraps his hands around my front and pinches my nipples.

The thought of seeing his other side, the side of him that he has kept locked away from others for centuries, awakens something inside of me.

"Always..." I whimper breathlessly.

I'm whirled around faster than I can blink and look up, expecting to see my husband's dark, caramel eyes.

Instead, I'm greeted with black, pupilless eyes. I place my hand on his cheek gently, assuring him that I am not a threat.

The creature that looks back at me is ancient, and I can feel the power radiating off of his frame, which seems to have grown two sizes larger as his ancient magic seeps from every single pore he possesses.

"You are exquisite." His voice is a soft hiss, reflecting the beast that he is.

He moves his hand down my front gently, watching as my nipples pebble under his touch.

"We thought it was useless. Life after the war. We were alone...so alone."

I can hear the agony in his voice, and I place a kiss on his chest before looking up.

"You will never be alone again...not either of you."

I continue my trail of kisses, leading down his stomach and onto the rock-hard length that is fighting to break free of his pants. I lower myself onto my knees—wanting to wrap my lips around his cock—but just as I hit the floor, his hands are under my arms, hoisting me up.

"You bow before no one." He snarls.

And then he is on me, ravishing my mouth with fangs that pierce my lips.

He walks us over to the king-sized bed and follows me onto my back. I whimper as he positions himself between my naked thighs and I lift my hips, trying to create any kind of friction to ease the ache that continues to build in my lower stomach.

"Mate! Please!"

His lips leave mine, but before I can ask where he's going, his mouth is on my pussy, licking and feasting as if he has been starved for decades. His tongue slides between my folds, and I can feel my back leave the mattress at the pleasure that is wreaking havoc through my body. I run my hands through his dark locks, admiring the way his muscles bulge between my legs.

The thought of having such a powerful male pleasure me like this sends me over the edge, and I come around his thick tongue, crying out as my release coats his lips.

"I'll be back soon, little mate. I'll never again be parted from you." He growls again, licking my pussy once more. Two moments later, I watch as the beast recedes, leaving Axel in his place.

He grins as he crawls up my body, and I watch with hooded eyes as his large cock bobs against my stomach.

"You should feel proud—my beast hates everyone."

I arch an eyebrow and giggle as he peppers kisses all over my flushed face.

"Everyone?" I question.

"Except you." He confirms.

And then he is thrusting inside my virgin walls, using my release to part my tight pussy.

"Mine."

He snarls and bites into my shoulder, pulling his long cock out once before thrusting back in again. Over and over, he repeats this process as I hold onto his shoulders tightly, soaking in the feel of his teeth claiming me as his own.

"Axel!"

I shout as my orgasm builds with each rub of his cock. He tilts my hips up with the palm of his hand and this new angle hits something deeper inside of me than I ever could have imagined.

He moves quickly now, and my eyes roll back at the intensity of the new position. I can feel myself cresting higher and higher as he pounds me into the bed, the frame moving with us.

"Open yourself up for me, wife. I'm going to coat this pretty little cunt with my seed."

That does it for me.

A wave of pleasure consumes me as I cry out, whimpering when I feel his hot seed shoot out, coating my walls.

"Laudi..." He groans, continuing to gently pump into me.

"Don't move, little warrior. Let my seed take...my beast needs it."

If I weren't so consumed by the pleasure, I would have argued that now is most definitely not the time to become pregnant.

But the pleasure of my mate will forever outweigh my brain trying to be reasonable, so I close my eyes and breathe in the scent of my mate as sleep takes me under.

24

Elaudia

I went to bed yesterday as Elaudia Sonella Syraxes.

A Bellator.

But as I stretch my arms lazily in the morning sun and my hand hits a warm chest, it all comes rushing back to me.

"Good morning, wife."

Axel purrs into my ear as he pulls me closer into his body, and I sink into his warmth with a delighted sigh. I look up with sleepy eyes, enjoying our moment of contentment before we're forced to brave the chaos of the day.

I press a kiss to his chest and lay my cheek there, breathing in his scent.

"Good morning, husband."

His thick hands run through my hair—still tousled from our rigorous activities the night before. I bite my lower lip and wince at the soreness. Axel notices, rubbing it between his forefinger and thumb.

"Have I ever told you how much I love your eyes? They are magic themselves."

Axel traces my eyelids as he speaks, and I can feel my lips pull into a grin.

"I don't know why they're like this; no one does. When I left Aland for Lashforn, Aunt Sofia spent hours with me alone in the library looking for answers, but there has never been another Bellator with eyes like mine."

Axel rolls over, pulling me on top of him as he goes.

"My ancestors have written scrolls. I read once when I was a boy that certain individuals with a physical tell might be blessed with greater gifts than the normal Fae. A scarred face. A blind eye, or a missing voice. Legend says that when the Gods decided to bless them with one of their gifts, they took something in return. Perhaps you are one of these individuals, and the Gods took the color of your eyes."

I soak in his story, grinning as he speaks. Out of all the ancient scrolls we found in the small library back home, this one is by far the most exciting story I've heard.

"Maybe..." I say, blowing a piece of my hair out of my face. A knock on the door interrupts our blissful morning as newlyweds, not that anyone else knows yet.

"My King, the Council is waiting in the war room, but we cannot find the Princess, sire."

His voice is slightly panicked, and I muffle my laugh with my hand, hiding my face in my husband's chest. Axel stretches back, tossing his hands behind his neck.

"I'm sure she'll turn up, Kirigan. Make sure Sarabeth has breakfast waiting for her in the war room. The princess becomes quite irate when she's hungry."

I glare at him with fake outrage as Kirigan answers, assuring Axel that he will seek out Sarabeth immediately.

"You're going to give me a food complex at this rate." I deadpan. Axel's chest lifts as he laughs, placing a kiss on my forehead—and then my lips—before rolling us out of bed.

"Let's not keep them waiting, wife." I push his chest away from me so I can stand and wrap my silk robe around my shoulders.

"I don't see that getting old anytime soon." I murmur as Axel's strong arms wrap around my waist, hugging me to his chest.

"Mhmm. I don't either. Go get changed. I'll wait for you." I turn in his arms and lift an eyebrow.

"Are you sure you want to tell them now? We know Kreovsh must have already sent word of my existence, but you're still the secret weapon."

"My Fae heritage is the secret weapon, not my union to you. I would have walked through my Kingdom's streets singing about our wedding last night if I hadn't been so consumed by your beautiful scent." He nuzzles his nose into my neck, and I giggle.

"I never knew you were such a romantic."

"Only for you, my sweet mate."

After kissing him again, I leave his arms and head for the door that connects to my room.

"I'll be just a minute." Axel smiles and opens the door for me, smacking my ass as I walk through.

"Heathen."

"My Queen." He answers.

The word rattles my chest and I smile the entire walk to my room. I guess I finally am.

***

Aside from The Council, both Cadmus and Aunt Sofia attend the meeting by my side, eyes shrewd as they take in the plans the Council has come up with.

To say everyone in the room was shocked by our surprise wedding would be an under-statement. It took about fifteen minutes for the room to settle before congratulations were of-fered, but everyone seemed genuinely happy for our mating—Cadmus more than anyone else.

I think knowing that someone else will care for my safety as much as he does has taken a weight off his shoulders.

"Our scouts have reported more rebel activity near the borders of Misit. They seem to have caught on that Lord Krevosh was offering information to General Neem in exchange for protection as he makes his way west."

Niho points to the borders of Misit, circling a cluster of trees that is housing a group of rebels—the kind of rebels we *need* to make a difference in the coming war.

I cross my arms, my eyes roaming over the table of figurines. I can feel Axel's eyes on my face as I think.

"If I can convince them to move, we can solidify our borders between Lashforn and Atarah. We know he's going for Lashforn next, it's the only thing that makes sense, seeing as Atarah is now bigger than any other Kingdom there ever was. He'll save Atarah for last as he builds his armies. If we strike his first battalion the fortnight before they arrive, then Lashforn's army can pick off any survivors."

The room is quiet as I speak, and I don't know if it is out of respect for me as a Bellator or the new queen.

I'm hoping it's the former.

Hydrandra smiles softly and leans forward.

"If they truly have as many rebels as the scouts have reported, then your plan is fool-proof, young queen."

I shoot her a genuine grin and nod in respect. I look around the room, noting Lynola, and her keen eye for detail. She's already caught four mistakes on the table since we began. I wait a second more before she nods as well, and I breathe a sigh of relief.

For some reason, earning the respect of these ancient creatures means something to me. I don't want to let them down—not when I've finally presented them with hope. Axel's warm hand rubs the center of my lower back as he pulls me closer.

"You're a natural, little warrior. I am so proud of you."

His voice is a whisper across my mind, and it soothes my mating bond. Cadmus leans forward, placing his closed fists on the table.

"They won't know who we are, though. Who is to say they won't fire first, and ask questions later? We can't risk Elaudia on a retrieval."

Aunt Sofia smiles softly as Cadmus's worry shines through, and she places a hand on his arm.

"We must trust that they will see our colors and listen. General Neem did right by claiming black and gold. They are depressing colors to be sure, compared to ours. I have sent two riders ahead to deliver the message of your arrival. They will be successful in their endeavors, I am certain."

"You always do think ahead." I murmur with a grin.

Aunt Sofia smiles at my compliment before winking my way. She walks over until she stands between Axel and me, and she looks down with a motherly smile on her face.

"You will prevail, as the good in the world always does. Graven shall arrive soon with the others, and once we have so many bloodlines in one place again, General Neem and his witch will not stand a chance."

She kisses my cheek before she turns to leave, her ladies' maids waiting by the door for her.

Axel pulls me closer and nods his dismissal to the Council, who all bow to both of us as they exit.

That will take some getting used to.

Cadmus walks over, his eyes on the table.

"Our horses are being fed and watered as we speak. The sooner we leave, the sooner we can intercept the first battalion. I'd like to thank you for the forces you have provided us with." He speaks to Axel, who only raises his eyebrow. Cadmus clears his throat.

"I know you have never left the castle...I assumed you would stay behind...as King..." He trails off, uncertainty in his eyes. I nod and look up at Axel.

"He's right, you know. Atarah cannot be left undefended. Graven and his soldiers are not set to arrive for another fortnight."

Axel's eyes darken and he growls.

"You expect me to sit back while my *mate* walks into a rebel camp that has not made itself known in ten years?"

I shake my head, putting a bit of sternness into my voice.

"I expect you to trust that your mate is a trained Bellator and can handle herself. As soon as we negotiate terms with the rebel leader, we will return here to reconvene. If all goes well, as it should, I will be back just in time for Graven's arrival." Cadmus backs away awkwardly and raises his hands.

"I can see this is a marital matter...I'll meet you at the horse stables, Laudi." I laugh as he books it out of the war room, rolling my eyes.

"He's not ready for marriage." I laugh. Axel sighs through his nose and pulls me close, closing his eyes.

"Is anyone ever truly ready for the trials of marriage? Never in my wildest dreams did I think I would be blessed with such a headstrong and intelligent mate. It seems the fates are laughing at me one last time for all of the trouble I gave my parents growing up."

I smile up at him and place a kiss on his cheek. That's a story I'd like to hear.

"I'll share my childhood wiles with you as soon as you return to me, then." I sigh at his presence in my mind and look into his eyes.

"I'll be fine. Cadmus will stay by my side, and we will return before you even have time to miss me."

He lets out a low hum but does not answer. He pushes me back until the middle of my back hits the edge of the table and I moan into his mouth as he kisses me breathless, devouring my next words.

I lift my legs, wrapping them around his waist as he shoves himself between my thighs. I whimper at the feeling of his thick length and use my booted feet to shove his pants down, working them around his ankles.

He growls with urgency, and I hear a ripping sound. I have no time to think about the damage done to my preferred comfy cotton pants though, because my husband wastes no time thrusting inside my damp heat, claiming that new favorite place as his own.

I toss my head back as he stretches me, relishing in the pleasant burn.

"My beautiful little warrior. Do you think to leave me on our honeymoon? I should turn this perfect little ass red for the torture you inflict upon me."

I grind my hips into him, matching the eagerness of his thrusts. He growls low, his jaw clenched tight as he moves.

"I'm not just your wife, you know? I am Queen of Atarah now. I must do whatever possible to protect these people. They are mine as much as you are."

His answering growl reaches my ear once more as he thrusts harder, hitting my cervix with every blow.

"I knew you would be perfect. From the first night I saw you, wandering the city streets. I saw what you did for that little girl, my sweet-hearted mate."

My eyes widen at his confession, and I look up, my hands clenched onto his muscled shoulders, crescent moons forming where my nails dig in.

"You were following me the entire time." I pant as waves of pleasure wreak havoc on my body.

He nods and nuzzles my neck, his length thickening inside of me.

"I saw the way you watched that precious little girl. Don't worry, my sweet wife. I'll give you one of your own babes. I'll watch this lit-tle belly swell with my child, watch as your breasts grow heavy with milk and whenever they become too full, I will drain them for you as you squirt your release all over my cock."

I cry out at his words, feeling a wave of wetness coat his cock as he shoots inside me, marking me deeper than he had the night be-fore.

Something I did not think was possible.

We're a panting, sweaty mess against the table, and I sigh in bliss. Axel lifts my chin with his finger, kissing me once more, deep and hard.

"Be smart and keep your guard up. Kill any-one who is a threat to you and return to me swiftly."

I nod and kiss him once more before stand-ing.

"I'll be fine," I promise him. I only hope as I exit the war room to change my clothes that I'm not lying to my mate.

25
Axel

I haven't stopped pacing in the hours since Elaudia departed with Cadmus and the soldiers I ordered to go with them.

The soldiers I sent are first rank, the only ones who have been on the outer walls in the past and are seasoned to the threats outside of this Kingdom. I run a hand through my unruly hair once more before a smaller hand gently settles on my arm.

I look over into a pair of soft green eyes.

Sofia.

I'm surprised she did not rush back with them—considering Lashforn is her Kingdom—but her faith in Elaudia's continued success is something she never hides.

"She will be fine. She is fiercer than you know."

I smile softly at my wife's aunt before following her to the tea table.

"You're sure the men you had planted will recognize her?"

May the Gods help any creature who harms my mate.

Queen Sofia sips her green tea and nods, the jewels in her crown glinting in the afternoon light.

"They are loyal to me and know their mission. They will ensure she meets with the leader safely." I blow out a breath and rest my elbows on my knees.

"It is strange, I know. Feeling something so intense for someone you have just met. When Sorrir died..."

Her eyes mist over as she trails off, and my head shoots up as I stare at the queen who proven to be a formiddable ally.

"I thought Henry...?" I begin to ask, but she cuts me off, shaking her head.

"I met my fated mate when I was just seventeen years. He was only two years older, visiting from a neighboring city. A descendant of the water sprites."

Sofia's eyes glaze over as her memories work through her mind.

"My parents were not too pleased—but you cannot argue with fate—lest it strike back for your ungratefulness. We had a daughter. And we had five amazing years together. Before he was lost to one of General Neem's attacks while visiting Elaudia's father—my brother. I lost my daughter as well, Odette. We were secretive at the time because of the uncertainty that General Neem presented...and then once they were gone, I could not bear to even speak their names."

Her lip trembles as she recalls her family, and I reach out, grabbing her hand.

"It is the worst pain you can imagine, losing a true mate. But losing your true mate *and* your child? I was ready to meet my death and join them. But then I realized...Odette had an entire life ahead of her. One that she was so excited for. What kind of mother would I be if I did not wake up every morning and live that life for her? And then two years later, just as I had begun to pave a way for myself once more, I was introduced to a beautiful little girl with white eyes and a penchant for putting grown men on their asses, even at such a young age. Elaudia was a precious child—so headstrong and mischievous."

Sofia giggles as she thinks of Elaudia, and I can feel my own lips lift into a grin.

"Odette and Sorrir gave me a reason to stay alive, but Elaudia gave me a reason to begin living again. The memory of her is what got me through these past eighteen years. She is brilliant, brave, and kind. She will persuade the rebels successfully before returning back to us safely."

I smile and nod as I sit back. My brows furrow as I begin to think and I turn my head to Sofia.

"Does Henry know? About Odette and Sorrir?"

Sofia clasps her hands together and smiles.

"The one and only time I tried to join my family on the other side, I was discovered by Henry. He is the one who convinced me to stay."

My Fae hearing picks up on a slight shuffle of feet.

"And I thank the Gods every day that I did."

We both whirl in our seats to King Henry, who leans against the wall, smiling at his wife. Sofia grins brightly and glides over to him, resting in his embrace as he places a kiss on her forehead. I can see the acceptance in his eyes. The purest form of it.

"Love comes in too many ways, boy. But the greatest love of all does not judge, nor condemn. It just accepts what is. It is a sacrifice, but it is well worth it."

Sofia nuzzles her nose into Henry's greying beard, and together, they leave me to my thoughts. I'm only alone for a mere two minutes before I make the choice.

I call for my guards, ordering them to prepare my horse. I'm strapping on my cross swords and chest plate when Bador bursts through the door, chest heaving in panic.

"Krevosh's spies have alerted General Neem. His first Battalion is two days ahead and he has sent a swarm of his second towards the forest to intercept the Queen before she can reach Lashforn!"

With his words, I can feel my own world shrink as I make a choice that could sabotage the war.

Love is about sacrifice indeed.

26

Elaudia

"What is it like?"

I look over at Cadmus as he speaks, and I arch an eyebrow, urging Selvita along.

"Marriage." He clarifies.

I laugh and shake my head as I look at our surroundings, taking in all of the trees that tower over us. Our party moves swiftly and quietly throughout the forest, doing our best not to disturb the trail too much.

According to the scouts, we should make it to the rebel camp just before dusk.

I'm tempted to tell him to ask me once again in five years when I'm slightly more experienced, but I know he asks me because of his longing for a life with Bria.

I ponder his question and tilt my head to the side, just as an arrow zips through the air, slicing my cheek open. Selvita jerks to the side, and Cadmus shouts to alert the guards.

I twist around and let my dagger fly, hoping its aim stays true through the foliage of the trees. I watch as a body falls from the tall oak, and a body hits the ground. A bell rings out and men scream, drawing their weapons as they rush out from the bushes in a swarm of shouts and metal.

Our own guards race forward on their horses to meet our attackers head-on. I reach behind my head and grab my labrys, a two-headed ax that Axel gifted me with before I departed.

"Its length is similar to your polearm, but the end is much deadlier. Once you adjust to the weight of it, you'll wield it as if you have done it your entire life."

He explained to me as he strapped it to my back.

It was made just for my size, balancing perfectly in my hands. I had to swallow back the lump in my throat as he presented it to me. No one had ever given me such a precious gift before.

I swing it to the left, beheading the man behind Cadmus's horse and I kick Selvita forward.

"You take the right!" I order Cadmus.

He thrusts his sword down and into the chest of another man. Cadmus growls in anger.

"You've lost your goddamn mind! I'm on your ass! Now go!"

We rush forward, into the fray of the attack, which looks to be forty to our twenty. We're just barely inside the lines of Lashforn. I get a look at the black armor and curse. That son of a bitch Lord Krevosh was more two-faced than I had previously thought. I hop off of Selvita, not willing to risk her in the midst of the fight.

"Elaudia! Get back on your *fucking* horse!"

I ignore Cadmus's shout and begin sprinting, taking down each soldier in my way. Blood sprays out and splashes against my cheekbones, but I don't blink. The Bellator inside of me has taken over completely, and the only thing on my mind is defeating the evil in front of me.

Two men launch forward at the same time and narrowly miss striking my side as I spin on my knees, avoiding their swords.

I launch up, slicing my weapon towards their necks, watching as the delicate skin breaks open and their bodies drop lifelessly to the forest ground.

Cadmus has dismounted his own horse in his panic to get closer to me, and I watch as he disarms another soldier. Men shout and grunt as they fight for their lives on the dirt road, and I catch sight of one of our own go down as an arrow appears once more, lodging itself in his chest.

"Archers!" I shout out, hoping to alert Axel's men.

My men.

I deflect another arrow as an archer turns his focus to me, hiding my face behind my labrys. Cadmus shouts his fury as another arrow is aimed my way, and he races for the trees to take the archers down.

"Cadmus stay low!"

I lose sight of him as three more men descend upon me and I strike out, deflecting their blows. Another man in gold falls and I breathe through my nose, finishing off the three in front of me. I make it five steps before I am surrounded once more and I growl my frustration, just as an arrow flies once more.

But this time, it is not toward me. The arrow finds its home in the eye of one of my attackers and his arms drop as he sinks to the ground, dead. More shouts ring out, but this time, they are feminine.

My eyes widen and I look up, just in time to see them galloping down the small hill on their horses, a fierce brown-eyed warrior racing straight for me.

Clarice.

My heart rejoices at the sight of my fellow Bellator sisters and I twist, slicing open the guard approaching me from behind. Clarice bellows out as she fires another arrow into the heart of a man on my left, and I watch as the General's men slowly start to fall.

Clarice is the only one born of Lashforn's land, so she's the only one with the ability to kill the men we fight against.

Our numbers have evened out as Clarice hops from her horse and backs up against me until we are moving as one, taking them down. The rest of my sisters fight the men, wearing them down for us to finish off.

"You always do know how to make a grand entrance!" I huff, blowing hair from my eyes as I strike again.

Her laugh greets me as I duck and roll, watching her arrow strike true. She lets out a huff of breath, speaking louder so that I can hear her over the roar of battle.

"Yes well, I've perfected the art, seeing as *you* always know how to find trouble!"

We laugh as we fight, and I slow my breath as the enemy dwindles until there are only a few men left.

I watch as they are surrounded, waiting until I know it is safe before I turn to Clarice and pull her to me, hugging her tight.

"I have missed you, sister." Tears sting my eyes as the muffled words meet my hair and she hugs me tight.

I'm about to reply when a glint of light reflects off the sun and I push her to the side as a man still hidden attacks, throwing himself on top of me. I fall back and hit the ground as he raises his sword, prepared for a killing blow.

Just as his weapon descends, a form materializes out of nowhere, striking a sword into the neck of my attacker. Black mist fades as I look up, blinking through the blood that has sprayed my face.

"Axel." I breathe.

My mate grins and roughly kicks the body to the side with disgust written on his face. He places his hands under my arms and hauls me up, keeping his hold on me.

"You didn't actually think I would choose my Kingdom over you, little warrior...did you?"

***

I finally manage to pull myself out of Axel's embrace and head over to the remaining soldiers who have been restrained by Cadmus.

Clarice and Axel stick close to my sides, the former who has not stopped questioning me on why I hugged the reclusive King Axel. Even more so, why he was reluctant to let me go. I sigh as everyone collects our horses and begins cleaning their weapons, turning to my closest friend.

"We might be married." I wince at the look on her face, her features turning so red I fear she might explode any minute.

Her mouth hangs open as the shock sinks in and she begins stuttering.

"But you–I don't–when did–" I chuckle and close her mouth before patting her cheeks.

"I'll explain tonight. And you can explain to me how you knew we were coming."

She's about to respond when I hear a choking sound coming from Cadmus, and I whirl around, on my guard. I watch as he takes off, sprinting towards three more people arriving through the thicket. My heart stutters in my chest, and I can feel tears begin to sting my eyes at the sight before me.

"Jaharis! Nyreen!" I run after him, running as fast as I can towards the man who raised us.

Cadmus hugs his mother tight to his chest as I barrel into Jaharis, burying my face into his familiar scent as tears leak from my eyes. His form is still as sturdy as it's always been, and he hardly budges from the impact of my body.

"You're alive...you're okay." I sob my statement as the other two come closer, and we turn into one big group hug.

Jaharis pulls away and taps me under the chin before placing a hand on Cadmus's shoulder.

"Look how grown you both have become. So fierce. We are so proud of the two of you."

I laugh through my cries and start to wipe my tears, but Axel beats me to it, cleaning the salt from my face. I smile at him in thanks before squeezing Nyreen. The gentle and kind woman smells just as I remember, and I know Cadmus must be feeling the greatest relief in the world right now.

"When communications went silent, we thought the worst." I murmur.

Jaharis nods, his white hair falling forward.

"General Neem's first battalion attacked at night, when we were least expecting it. They

raged through the castle and took no survivors. It was only because of Queen Sofia's
spies that we escaped in time. The King and
Queen, however, refused to leave. In the confusion of our retreat...many lives were lost. Elaudia...I am so sorry. Aland has fallen."

His words ring out in my ears, and I think of
the kingdom, the *people* I grew up with. I sigh
shakily and run a hand down his arm. They
weren't my true family.

"It's not your fault. This is Neem's fault. This
is a war that he started. But we're going to
finish it. *I'm* going to finish it."

"I'm glad to hear you say that."

I peek around my foster parent's forms and
into the eyes of a new arrival, one I had dis-
missed before. The man standing before me is
tall, almost as tall as Axel, with red hair and
bright green eyes. He looks to be a little older
than me, and his voice lilts with an accent that
I have never heard.

I walk over, putting my arm out. He looks
down at me with curious eyes before grinning
brightly and clasping my arm with his hand.

"Bristol Hayard. Leader of the South Wall rebels."

This is the leader?

I expected someone older, and more seasoned for battle. I take in the intelligence in his eyes, realizing that brawn is not all it will take to win this war.

"Elaudia Sonella Syraxes."

I watch as the truth dawns on him before he begins to laugh like a maniac, pulling me forward and tossing an arm around my shoulders.

"Oh shit! We're gonna have some fun together little lady."

A deep growl sounds from behind us and Bristol's arm is thrown to the side as Axel bares his teeth at the man, his black eyes showing the beast at the surface.

Bristol raises his eyebrows and surrenders his hands, hiding his head between his shoulders.

"Mated pair. I got it. I meant fun with the General. *Bad* spooky King. Get your mind out of the gutter."

He does a fake shudder, and I try to hide my laugh, as do Clarice and Nyreen. Axel bares his teeth in annoyance.

"I am not to be described as spooky." He huffs his annoyance, and I pat his chest, giggling.

Bristol lets a low whistle out between his teeth and turns his back, throwing another comment over his shoulder as he motions for us to follow him.

"*Sexy* spooky King, then?" I watch the realization arise on Axel's face.

Oh...

***

The rebel camp isn't on the ground.

That's why the General's men never found it. We walk about a mile west before Bristol kicks a rock with his toed boot. I watch as it skips across the dirt before a metallic sound rings out.

He walks over and kicks the toe of his boot down three times before stomping once. I squint my eyes, trying to see through the mess of dirt and leaves. And then the ground opens up, two doors falling open into the ground below.

Bristol winks at my shocked face and squats before jumping down and *disappearing* into the ground below.

We all gather around the opening, waiting to hear the telltale signs of his landing.

We don't.

I glance up at my mate and shrug my shoulders. I have dry blood caking my face, so the sooner I can get this meeting over with, the sooner I can bathe. Cadmus and Clarice urge me back, jumping first.

When I don't hear anything suspicious, Axel nods, but he doesn't help me forward or act like he's going to jump. He lets the rest of our party go first before wrapping his strong arms around me, looking down.

Excitement flutters through me and I grin.

I was so caught up in the battle that I had forgotten how he arrived.

He used his Fae powers.

For the first time in my presence, other than his mind talk, I saw his Fae gifts. He grins at my elation and then we are blinking out of existence and arriving in an underground bunker.

A *huge* underground bunker.

With a lot of gaping mouths and shocked eyes. Bristol smiles and shakes his head.

"Maybe we aren't as secure as I thought." He mumbles to himself.

As I look around, I calculate that this cannot be everyone, and Axel answers me, his voice a warm caress against my mind.

"They keep the women and children three stories below. The sick are above them, and two of the wings in the west are for fighters."

My mind can't comprehend something so large underground, but they have been hiding successfully for ten years. They would have expanded and learned to survive like this. Bristol points to a large table that has dried meats and vegetables waiting for us, along with a few men and women who watch us closely.

He sits down across from us and twines his hands together, leaning forward.

"You must ensure Axel's gifts remain known only to the soldiers in this room." I say firmly.

Bristol nods with a seriousness I have yet to see on him before he turns his back to us and relays my request to the guard behind him. I watch as he moves about the room, speaking to the people who still stare at us with wide-open eyes.

A few more guards take the prisoners we captured down the hall, and I watch as they disappear. Bristol follows my line of sight.

"They will be questioned and then hanged for their crimes. Our magistrate will ensure it is swift, which is more than I can say for their wrongdoings against our continent."

I nod my head but say nothing. I am a stranger to these people right now—they don't need me coming in and telling them how to run their operations.

"We have water sprites here, half-blooded. They keep the water systems flowing smoothly, providing us with drinking and bathing water. The dragon descendants offer fire in the winter, and our two snow mages use their ice to keep us cool during the summer. I was still a child when my father, Branol, brought the half-bloods to us. He smuggled them in from across the seas, offering them protection in exchange for their services. Since then, we have been flooded with creatures of the lore, with powers we long thought extinct. My father passed a few months ago, leaving me in charge. By vote, of course." He finishes wryly.

"Why did your father not seek my protection? I had the space for him and his people." Axel asks the question, but I find myself pondering the same thing.

Bristol purses his lips and looks around, leaning in closer.

"There were rumors that you had magic, but no one was sure what you were. You had great protection to offer, yes, but if you turned out to be in on General Neem's plans, you could help him wipe us out. We never went in search of help...but...if the help came to us..."

I break in as he trails off.

"So when Jaharis and Nyreen brought the escapees here, they told you about me. You've been expecting us."

Bristol smiles, delighted that I am able to piece the story together. He leans back and tosses his hands up.

"Precisely! Though I had no idea you were bringing the King of Atarah as well, you over-achiever!"

I hide my laugh with a cough at his care-free attitude while Axel rolls his eyes. Jaharis nudges me from the left and leans down to whisper into my ear.

"He takes some getting used to, but he is a really good lad. He's intelligent, that one."

If Jaharis trusts him, then I trust him. I tell Axel as much once we've been given a bedroom to sleep in and fresh clothes. I put my weapons down next to Axel's broadswords, grinning as I feel two strong arms wrap around me from behind.

"If we can convince the rebels by tomorrow to ride for Lashforn, we might be able to con-vince them to come back to Atarah with us once we have defeated the first battalion. I mean...*ten years*, Axel. They must have chil-dren who were born here, who don't know what it is like out there in the world. All of the good that it still has to offer."

Axel places a kiss on my forehead and turns me around in his arms.

"They've been here for ten years, my love. This is what they know; it is how they survive. We will offer them the chance, but you must prepare yourself for their denial. People will choose a certainty of safety over a possibility."

I sigh and follow him to the standard queen-size bed we have been given for the night. It is not anything close to what we have been raised with as royalty, but I find, as my husband wraps me into his arms, that I don't even care.

"As long as they have the option." I snuggle into Axel's chest and breathe in his scent, one that has become so familiar to me in such a short time.

"First, we must win this next battle. We will worry about the rest later."

As he trails off, lulling me to sleep with stories of his childhood, I find myself hoping that we win the battle—and then quickly—the war.

Because no child deserves a life without the sun.

27

Elaudia

B ristol's voice projects throughout the room, his passion for the people here completely clear as he addresses them the next morning.

"We have been hidden in this bunker for ten years, my friends. Watching as our homes, our livestock, and our families have been destroyed. Torn down by General Neem and his black witch. I know we have found comfort in our stone walls, but today, for the first time since my father has ruled, I offer you more than hope!" He shouts.

"I offer you a chance to take back what was stolen from us! I offer you a chance for revenge upon the men who raped our women! Slaughtered our fathers! I offer you the last Syraxes Bellator of the world! The Princess who is destined to exact justice upon the tyrant who has been allowed to live for far too long!"

Cheers roar out across the common area, which is really a large hunk of space with a small staircase to a wooden stage.

I watch as Bristol paces back and forth, his arms swinging as he hypes the crowd up for my introduction.

I can see why they chose him.

I can see the rage and devastation in his eyes as he recalls the horrors inflicted upon all of us by the General.

Bristol turns and holds his hand out, urging me forward. I glance up at Axel, who holds tight to my hand, and he nods, following me out onto the stage. A hush falls across the crowd as they catch sight of us, dressed in our armor and weapons, two golden crowns upon our heads.

I look out at the men and women before us, their eyes shining with hope. Their clothes are plain, devoid of color, their faces pale.

"My name is Elaudia Sonella Syraxes, daughter of Queen Fridella and King Griffin, heir to the Syraxes throne. And I offer you my deepest regrets that it has taken me this long to come."

I take a deep breath, watching as they stay silent, allowing me to continue.

"Please know, that if I had any idea of how bad things truly were, I would have come immediately. I was hidden against my knowledge, and I've only recently learned my true heritage. I have been training ever since to become the protector I know this continent needs."

Murmurs break out as they begin whispering amongst themselves about the bomb of information I just dropped. I let go of Axel's hand and walk down the steps. I can feel my mate a step behind me, not willing to allow me to get any closer without additional protection.

My eyes scan the tired faces.

So very tired.

"My husband, King Axel of Atarah, has come with me to not only offer you a chance at life above ground, but revenge upon General Neem. By tomorrow's first light, his first battalion will attack the Kingdom of Lashforn. We have sent word for them to evacuate, but as you know, his spies are everywhere. King Axel and

I will ride tonight to hold them off before they can overthrow the castle. If you wish to join us in this fight, please, speak now. If you wish to stay, then know that I do not judge you, and our offer of protection will still stand."

My voice echoes off the walls as I try to speak loud enough so that the mass of people before me can hear every word.

I can feel Axel's eyes roaming the crowd, taking in the people. His lips lift into a tiny smirk, just as a voice rings out, deep and loud.

"I will fight by your side, Princess!"

"Aye, so will I!"

"We will fight as well!"

More and more voices ring out, reaching my ears, until everyone is shouting and smiling. I sigh a breath of relief as arms raise and they begin to chant as one.

"Long live the Queen! Long live the Syraxes line! "

I walk forward and hold my hands out, touching the lost and forgotten rebels of the war.

Men and women alike cheer and shout and as I look over my shoulder, I catch Axel's eyes beaming with pride. I smile when his voice whispers across my mind.

"Long live indeed, little warrior."

***

"You must rest the arm, Charlie, or you won't be playing jaopole with the other boys anytime soon. I may have healed the broken arm, but the tendons will still be sore."

I hear a small child whine in disappointment before the curtain is pushed over and an older woman with black hair appears, urging the little boy forward with his mother.

"Bring him back in two days, Jenia, and I will check on him then."

I step out of the way as the boy and his mother pass by, but I'm stopped by a tug on my pants. I look down at the boy, who can't be older than six. I crouch down so that I am eye-to-eye with him. His mother balks at him as she eyes my crown, but I offer her a gentle smile.

"Have you ever had a broken bone, shiny lady?"

I laugh as he asks me the question, realizing the 'shiny' comment must be because of all the armor and weapons.

"I have, sweet boy. But they healed very fast because I listened to my healer. And I had to eat some vegetables too, but they aren't as bad as you think. My favorite was broccoli with cheese balls." I whisper the end of my sentence to him and his eyes light up as he looks up to his mom.

"Can we have broccoli tonight, Mama?! I want to get my arm better quickly, so Himor doesn't take my spot as guardian of the net!"

The young mother tosses her head back and laughs, winking my way as she urges to boy out.

"Of course, Charlie. My Queen." She curtsy's quickly with a grateful smile.

I grin and stand up, returning her smile as she leaves with her son.

"You have quite a way with words, young queen. With the masses, and with the young. I'm impressed. I'm Kaleen."

My face heats up at the healer's compliment, but I only shrug and shake her hand. She finishes writing something in her notebook before she takes her glasses off and turns to me, taking me in. Her eyes widen as she smiles.

"Well, I suppose I know why. Congratulations are in order, it seems. Though I must express my concern at your fighting in this condition."

My heart stutters as I tilt my head.

"I'm sorry...what condition?"

Realization dawns on the mage's face, and she places a hand on her mouth.

"I'm so sorry...you are very early...it is a part of my gift. I can see the workings of the body, on the inside...you are pregnant, young queen. The babe has just taken."

My hearing goes out as she speaks, and my eyesight goes fuzzy until I can see the world around me, but it is all a blur.

My body has frozen up, though I can hear the muffled sounds of the mage healer as she tries to get me to sit down.

My hair blows to the right as a force enters the room in a whirlwind of magic and wind and then my mate's arms are around me, carrying me to the closest medical bed.

"What happened?"

His voice is as sharp as ice, and I wince at the rage he is directing upon the sweet healer, who has yet to speak. I take a deep breath in, struggling as if I have been submerged underwater for too long. I raise my hand and grab Axel's hand, pulling it away from my face.

"I'm pregnant," I whisper.

It's not supposed to be possible. Not with the herbal teas I take religiously.

Axel's face pales as he looks down at my stomach, and a flash of desire crosses through his eyes. He leans his head down and rests it against my flat stomach, murmuring in a language I'm not familiar with.

Once he has finished, he goes silent, his eyes far away. It feels as if the world is moving in slow motion and I take a deep breath, trying to calm my racing heartbeat.

Five seconds later, Cadmus and Jaharis are bursting through the doors, their faces serious, with only a slight hint of panic.

Axel leans up and captures my mouth with a kiss, shocking me, before pulling back. His eyes are dark, like he's made up his mind about something important.

"Take the Queen back to Atarah immediately. She is to be protected at all costs."

Excuse the fuck out of me?

I watch as they both anxiously look back and forth between me—the Queen, and Axel—the King.

It dawns on me that he must have used his gift and called for them, informing them of what has transpired.

My lips curl back into a snarl, and I roll off the bed as Cadmus reaches for me, drawing my weapon. They will not take away my choice.

"*Try it* and you'll be getting your due for opening up my stomach." I hiss.

Axel growls, his beast briefly flashing in his eyes, but doesn't ask what I'm talking about. I look at my husband, more pissed off than I have ever been with him. Not that it says much, considering we have only been married for about a week.

"You want to talk about this, then we will talk. But if you think you're going to order me around just because I'm carrying your babe, you're going to find out why the soldiers back home never want to train with me."

The men surrounding me have backed up, their arms raised. The healer is screeching her distress in the background.

"This is not good for the mother or the baby! Back up you fiends!"

A scroll flies out and smacks Jaharis in the head and I grin.

I knew I liked her.

Axel sighs and tries to approach me once more.

"Little warrior...*please*...do not ask me to watch you ride into battle tomorrow knowing you are carrying our heir inside of you. Our *child*." I can hear the plea in his voice, but I ignore it.

"You're not going to watch me, you're going to be by my side. I will not abandon these people, not when they have just placed their trust in me. I am a Syraxes Bellator, Axel. I will be fine, I am meant for this life, this war!"

I lower my weapon when they stop advancing and try to ignore the sting of disappointment. He doesn't think I can do this. He reads my mind and shakes his head vehemently.

"It's not that and you *know* it. I just don't want to risk the babe. You should be resting in a condition such as this, not fighting a battle."

I roll my eyes and toss back at him, urging him to listen.

"The battle, not the war. I will be fine, Axel. Once we secure Lashforn and the rebel's safety, I promise you, I will go back to the castle and remain there until I have this child. But you cannot ask me to abandon the people now. Not *now*."

I see the exact moment the fight leaves him, and his head lowers until it's hanging in defeat. I nod for Cadmus and Jaharis to exit and they leave, followed by the mage. I place my hands on my husband's cheeks and lift his head until he looks at me.

"My love...I will be fine. I wear dragon armor and am well-prepared for this fight."

His eyes soften at the dragon armor comment, and he huffs, pulling me close. I can feel his own heart thumping in his chest, and I have to wonder when the last time the ancient Fae male had been this worked up. His lips skim my forehead, and I feel him inhale, breathing me in.

"Promise me. This battle and then no others until our little boy is born." I raise my eyebrow and grin, looking up.

"A boy, huh?" Axel's lips meet my own and he sighs.

"I know these things...like how I just *knew* you were going to resist me...which is why I called for backup."

I step back and point a finger at him.

"Try to play it smarter next then. Because I was very serious about the fighting part."

He grins and taps my nose.

"I know you were, little warrior. I know you were."

28

Elaudia

We had to send urgent messengers back to Atarah the night we arrived in the rebel camp.

We could only hope that they came back with the five hundred men and horses we needed, in addition to another two hundred horses to carry the rebel men fighting. When they arrived at the meeting point before the break of dawn, I could feel myself breathing a little easier.

"Make sure the horses are watered once more before we leave! Timony, grab the last of the swords from the armory and meet me back here!"

Bristol was shouting out orders to his men as Axel and I saddled our horses, preparing for the ride to Lashforn. I pull at the strap wrapped around Selvita's underbelly and pat her hind as she lets out a whinny and trots in place. I giggle and look up at her.

"You ready for some action, girl?"

Her head shakes, and she nudges my shoulder, huffing. It's moments like this that I swear she understands everything I say. Axel comes up behind me and pats her snout, murmuring soft words to her.

"Protect our girl today, Selvita. You'll be carrying twice as much precious cargo."

Selvita stares into my husband's eyes for a few moments before bowing her head and blinking. I watch the exchange with wide and curious eyes. Axel's lips lift mischievously and then it dawns on me.

"They understand you."

He grins and nods, wrapping his hands gently around my waist and lifting me until I am sitting on Selvita's back properly.

"The Fae had many different gifts, depending on the bloodline. Amongst the line of my father was the gift to communicate with animals."

I stroke Selvita's mane and gaze at her tenderly with wonder.

"She's been with me for so long, on all of my new journeys," I say softly.

Axel smiles and reaches up to hold my hand.

"She adores you, Elaudia."

I laugh, tossing my head back.

"I adore you too, girl."

Bristol's shouts reach my ears once more, and I look over as Axel mounts his black war horse, who comes up on the side of me. I look around at our army, all with serious faces and weapons, their shields ready.

Axel's royal guard moves to surround us—along with Cadmus and Jaharis—the former of whom winks at me.

I grin.

He always knows how to make me laugh. I grab the reins and turn Selvita to the side, facing the army.

"Today, we finally take back some of our freedom from General Neem. We cause a hindrance for him in the form of an entire lost battalion! We stop his oppression from furthering into our lands even more. Let it be known that while this may not yet be the war we will face against him, this fight is not over!

It may last weeks, months, or even years...but we will *not* back down! Not until he and his black witch are rotting in the pits of the underworld where they belong!"

A roar erupts amongst the crowd as spears and swords raise high. I watch as birds fly out from their perches on the trees above, startled by the war cries.

And then we move.

***

I notice the exact moment the scenery becomes familiar to me, catching sight of the pale-yellow flowers that line the trees, my favorite flower to pick in the fields behind the castle on the summer days.

The ground thunders underneath us with the force of our army, and I keep my eyes peeled for any movement. We make it another two miles before I see the rolling hills that surround Queen Sofia's castle. And just behind the third tower, I see a crest of black, like an oil mine that has burst free from its broken dam.

I reach back, releasing my labrys from its sheath, the metal slicing through the air. I steady Selvita as the rest of the army follows suit, their weapons emerging like a wave of the great sea.

I turn to Cadmus and Jaharis.

We've *barely* caught them.

"Take the first line to warn the castle occupants! You and Jaharis know these streets like the back of your hands. The field by the lake has enough shrubbery. Take them there and have them stay low until the fighting is done."

Cadmus and Jaharis bow their heads and kick, their horses leaping into action toward the back alleyway that exits the city. The General's army has made it over the hill, their weapons shining in the early morning light.

I wait for Cadmus and Jaharis to reach the gates before I look over at my husband. The male who has become everything to me in such a short time. His face is stoic as he watches me, his weapons still strapped to his back.

I know he wishes I had returned to the castle and stayed hidden away, but my love for him grows because of his choice to listen to me and trust my abilities.

His voice is hard as he speaks to me, willing me to understand what he is about to say.

"I will not hold back. I know we decided it was better that he not learn of us both, but with my child in your belly, I cannot."

I look around at all of the men who are in the dark about my husband's *true* nature, including Bristol, who is listening to our conversation. Bristol nods at my look of unease and he grins, turning around and raising his sword.

"Long live the King and Queen!"

The army echoes Bristol, and I grin, looking at my husband. My labrys is above my head as I nudge Selvita and then we are charging forward, into the sea of black.

Hoofbeats thundering.

Metal clanging.

Sweat dripping down my back.

We cut off their descent into the gates, meeting them by the stone walls. Horses collide and screams begin ringing out—both in rage and pain. My weapon is dripping blood as I behead another soldier dressed in the enemy's colors.

There's no time to think, no time to watch for the others.

I am running on pure instinct right now, my Bellator nature taking over. Axel cuts down a man coming at me from behind and I grin at my mate, who has long abandoned his facade. His eyes have a black glow to them as he turns and rams his sword into the ground.

I watch as a shockwave of earth blows up, taking the enemy with it.

He snarls at a man as big as him in height and raises one of his cross swords before parrying and shoving it clean through the man's stomach. He's an absolute machine, killing everything in his path.

I shouldn't be turned on, but I am.

Axel glances my way and smirks, knowing exactly what I'm thinking.

I look to the hills, hoping to see Cadmus evacuating the cattle servants and the city's people. Bristol is holding his own, surprisingly, as he guards the gate's entrance with his rebels.

Small explosions set off as they throw bags of blue.

Bombs.

Huh.

Never thought of that.

Selvita gallops forward, narrowly avoiding a man's axe and I turn, cutting his arm off. He bellows out with rage—roaring at me—and in the next moment, he falls, an arrow sticking out from his left eye.

Clarice.

"What is it with you and eyeballs!?" I shout over to her.

She laughs viciously, her amusement drowned out by the sound of battle.

"Quickest kill! Fun target!"

I roll my eyes but dive back in, just as Axel disappears from his current spot and reappears behind a man holding Bristol by the neck, about to slit his throat. Axel reaches out and twists, breaking the man's neck with a vicious glint in his eyes.

Movement catches my eye, and I look over and up, my chest filling with relief at the line of people rushing out of the castle like a swarm, Cadmus at their lead. The fight in the trench of the hills in is full effect, people falling left and right. Blood coats my face and body.

Even Selvita's white coat is drenched with red.

A few soldiers notice the city's evacuation in process, and they roar their anger, charging forward. I cut them off with Selvita, but the smallest man carries a Kusarigama, and he launches it into the air, straight towards my side.

I wait for the impact, but it doesn't strike.

Because Selvita lifts up on her back two legs, and the weapon embeds itself into her stomach. She screeches and stumbles as I try to hold on, but the weapon lodged in her side causes her to fall, taking me with her.

I cry out as I am thrown from her back and turn over, trying to crawl on my knees.

No no no.

I look up, Selvita's eyes meeting my own as she takes her last breath, struggling to breathe. My lips tremble as I watch the life leave her eyes and I yell out, my heart clenching at the sight of her dying in front of me, her side split wide open.

I scramble forward on my knees as tears trail down my face, clearing a bloody path.

The men above me grin in delight, their ugly faces stretching into smiles that I want to rip off. I stand and grab my labrys, my face wet. I'm about to rush forward when they stop in their tracks, their eyes widening in fear.

Black veins take over their faces as they fight for oxygen, their mouths gaping like fish. They stumble back, falling, and I watch as they die the same way Selvita just did, their stomachs splitting open from an invisible force.

I look around until my eyes meet Axel's, and I can see the anger on his face.

"I told you I wouldn't hold back." He growls lowly.

I deflect another blow before turning back to Selvita with sorrow.

"Focus, little warrior! We will not leave her, but you must focus! This battle is not yet won!"

I know he's right—even though it hurts—so I tighten my grip and lunge at the next attacker, taking him down with a spray of blood. I twist to my left and kill a man who was on top of one of the rebels, allowing him to stand up once more. Hoofbeats sound once more as the soldiers dwindle and I look over to see Cadmus returning to my side, his armor showing only a hint of blood.

"They had spies waiting to let them in." He explains.

"Are they safe?" He nods and hops down, sword drawn.

"They're all safe." I open my mouth to respond, but a voice cuts me off, high-pitched and oily.

"Not for long. Did you actually think daddy wouldn't see all of the possible outcomes with a black witch on his side? Karisma sees all."

I'm still on the daddy part of that sentence.

We whirl around and face a woman much taller than I am, with black hair and brown eyes. Her face has just started to show signs of aging, though her body looks like it has been prepared for battle her entire life. Too bad for her, I was made for this.

"Go make sure they stay that way, Cadmus. I can handle this." He looks at me and stalls, letting me know that's he's going to try and refuse.

"I'm not leaving you alone."

"She's not alone." Axel's voice is dark—his beast at the surface—as he watches the newest addition's arrival with a sneer. Her lips tilt up into a smile and she stalks forward.

"Axel..." She purrs. I hiss at the look on her face, but it's not until he responds that confusion hits.

"Vivienne." His voice is like death, waiting to strike. I watch them face off, my body still.

"An old concubine of mine, little warrior. She means nothing."

Logically, I know that a thousand-year-old male did not go without pussy for that long. It's not exactly something I would have expected him to do. Still, I raise my eyebrow and look at him, but he only sighs.

I'm more interested in how she snuck into your kingdom and got into your bed.

My husband is not exactly stupid.

"Thanks." He says drily.

"Quit reading my mind if you don't want to hear everything then," I respond in my head.

"It was actually very easy, considering I was born in Atarah. You see, mommy had a thing for the bad boys. So, she snuck out one night and met daddy, who was all too eager to spread his seed into a woman of the capital of the greatest kingdom to ever stand. He left, of course, only returning once I was old enough to be of use to him. He gave me some wonder-ful...gifts, in exchange for my service."

Her lips curl into a grin, and I watch as her fingernails lengthen, growing into points. When we remain unimpressed, her face grows red with rage.

"He'll give me more once I've brought him your heads!" She lunges forward, slicing out with her claws. I twist away, avoiding the blunt force of the impact, but when I look down, I see two small rivets in my dragon armor.

I curse.

Black magic.

"Axel..." I warn.

My mate immediately understands what I'm getting at when he catches sight of my armor. He growls, his eyes going black once more as he shouts and charges Vivienne. They parry back and forth, his swords and her metal-infused claws. He blocks her blow as she turns her attention back to me, attempting to get through him. Axel roars and then shouts out, his words feral.

"*Kettuna, venire!*"

The dirt begins to lift and swirl, forcing the circle of soldiers fighting to back away. I cover my eyes from the dirt storm as Axel attacks Vivienne and when I look up, a beast of lore stands in front of me, its chest purring happily, while its large head looks down at me expectantly.

A fucking Chimera.

Vivienne growls and blocks a blow, trying to charge for me. The Chimera before me roars and turns, blocking her path to me with an angry lion's hiss. Her eyes widen and she backs up.

"Impossible!" She screeches.

"*Kettuna, protect!*"

A blade slices through the air towards my head, but before I can even move, a scaled tail lashes out and flicks it to the ground. Kettuna roars and lunges for the man who tried to kill me, ripping his head off.

Axel's arm wraps around Vivienne from behind and he pulls her tight, sword at her throat. She watches the ancient beast with hesitant eyes as it approaches her, keeping me tucked to its side with its snake-like tail. This creature is thrice the size of a horse, and I find myself completely enraptured by its presence.

The battle has dwindled, and I try to ignore the beast that protects me, focusing on the general's daughter and my husband.

"You cannot win this." She hisses before continuing on, ignoring the sword at her neck.

"His army is too great, and Karisma is too strong. They have been planning for this war for *decades!*"

"And they will fail," I tell her quietly as the last guard falls until there is nothing but a sea of red and black on the ground. Bristol pulls his sword out from a chest and he stalks forward.

"Let us be finished, my Queen. Kill her and let the General know the pain we have all known for thirty years!"

His chest heaves from the battle and I soothe my hand over the tail of the ancient creature that tenderly holds me, requesting to be released. Kettuna rumbles softly but let's go, allowing me to walk over to my husband. I can feel her eyes watching everything, prepared to strike at any moment.

Vivienne watches me closely, her head held high.

"His succession is not written in the stars, his name is not told in any prophecies. He is a vile man who wanted too much and took without a thought for innocence or life. A part of me grieves for the little girl you once were, knowing you did not have a choice."

She laughs at that, the sound wicked and grating.

"Oh, I had a choice, *little Bellator*. I chose power over a lifetime of being a nobody. A seamstress's daughter. An orphan on the streets. I have been given more than I ever could have wanted."

"And it has cost you your life," I say softly, looking at Bristol who nods and grabs the rope from his horse.

"She will be hung in front of them all, a statement to those who serve the General."

Axel holds her tight while Bristol approaches, his eyes watching her with a wariness that

I haven't seen from him yet. I can understand why.

Black magic oozes from her pores.

Forbidden.

Wrong.

"I am no one's prisoner." Vivienne declares.

Her voice is fierce as she speaks and she slashes out, allowing Axel's sword to dig into her neck. Blood begins to flow but it's not enough to kill her—yet.

She doesn't get to escape this by suicide.

I rush forward, pushing Bristol out of the way as I cut off her hands and plunge my labrys into her stomach. Blood spurts out of her mouth and onto my face, sliding down my cheeks like a rivet of tears.

I hear the thud of her hands hitting the ground and Axel releases her, allowing her body to fall. Soldiers and rebels have gathered, watching silently. Jaharis stand behind me and is the first to speak as he places a hand on my shoulder.

"The citizens of Lashforn are safe. You did it, Elaudia...we won."

His voice is soft as he speaks, and I offer him a wry smile.

Not yet we haven't.

"This war has just begun."

29

Elaudia

A voice clears as I turn my attention to the rebel leader.

"Aye...it has. But that war will not be fought today." Bristol says, sinking to his knee.

"My Queen. My King." He declares his fealty for us in front of his people, letting them see his deference to us.

The soldiers and rebels slowly follow suit, clutching their wounds but bending the knee. I look around at what is left of our army. It is more than I thought we would have.

"You fought bravely, my friends. You protected the innocent and destroyed those who would see them dead. Now let us rest. Because the real war is heading our way...and we must be prepared."

The men nod their heads and stand, helping their fellow brethren. I look up at Axel, who has placed his hands on the nape of my neck.

"Send her hands to his war camp in Aland. Allow the soldiers there to deliver the news of his daughter's defeat. A warning for what is coming. Burn what is left of her."

Bristol nods with a vengeful grin. With his hair slicked back, I cannot tell where the color begins, and the blood of our enemies ends. The crowd disperses as they load the wounded onto the remaining horses and head for the citizens whom we have hidden in the forest.

"We will rest here for the night and then head back to Atarah come first light."

I nod into Axel's chest as he speaks, soaking in my husband's strength. I made it through my first true battle, but not without loss. I look out across the war field to Selvita's still and lifeless body, and my eyes sting with tears once again.

"She was a good horse." He says softly, placing a kiss on my forehead.

I had almost forgotten about the beast of legend behind me until its soft purr reaches my ears and it licks my cheek, its tongue rough against my skin. I look at it with a hint of wonder and pet its coarse fur.

"My wedding gift to you."

I look up in disbelief at my husband who seems to have more secrets than I ever could have guessed. He offers me a wink and strokes Kettuna.

"She was one of our castle pets growing up. She's been with me since I was a boy. One of the fiercest protectors I have ever known. I sent her across the dark sea when the war was at its climax, fearing for her safety. She'd been roaming freely...until I met you. I knew there was no other creature I could trust to watch over you in my absence, so she is yours."

I look at Kettuna with a question in my eyes, one she responds to.

"Hello, small female."

Her voice is soft in my head, with a feminine trill that is pleasant to my ears. If she was Axel's pet when he was a boy, then she must be ancient. A serpent's tail flicks gently on the ground below as she watches me with wide brown eyes, her lion nose twitching.

I raise my hand, smoothing it over the coarse skin on her ribcage.

"You're beautiful," I say softly.

Kettuna's chest puffs out with pride, and she shakes her large mane as if soaking in my admiration. I look over at Cadmus, who has returned and begins ushering the injured into the castle walls with the help of the citizens and healers. I sheath my labrys at the same time that Kettuna's body begins to glow. In the next second, a small fox stands in her place, its lithe body running across the field, jumping and leaping. And then I do something I never thought I would be able to do whilst standing on a bloodied battlefield.

I giggle.

Two rebels from the outer rings catch sight of her and chase her, clamping their hands down on her neck. Axel snarls and stalks over, but I beat him to it.

"Release her immediately!" I shout as I race over, watching as Kettuna's fox-like mouth curls away from her teeth and she takes a chunk of meat out of the man's hand. He curses and yelps, releasing her. Kettuna charges for me, twining up my legs and resting on my shoulders. I look down at the bags of weapons they were bringing us before they caught sight of her.

I raise an eyebrow as the man clutches his bleeding hand with a wince.

"Weapons to take home with us." The man with black curly hair explains. The one standing next to him appears younger, a little too green for war. His eyes are wide as they take in the animal that just shifted onto my shoulders.

"Thank you. Have the blacksmith from Lashforn clean them tonight and ensure they are reinforced. Then rest. We head back tomorrow. Do not try to capture her again. She is not yours to touch."

I turn away with Axel's hand in mine when a voice rings out, panicked.

"You cannot bring that beast back to the rebel camp! It is dangerous!" I sigh and turn back, ready to rest and be done with this, when Axel's dark voice speaks over my own.

"Tell my mate what she can or cannot do ever again, and I will show you the Fae power you so long to see."

The men before us audibly gulp, grasping the back of their heads as Bristol approaches and slaps them silly.

"Go on then boys. You heard our Regents." They both mumble but nod, bowing their heads slightly toward us before hauling the bags away. I throw a grateful glance towards Bristol, who only winks and stalks off.

"He needs to stop with the winking," Axel grumbles. I let out a giggle and shove his arm.

"Jealous, husband?" Axel scoffs and pulls me tight to his chest, looking down with tender eyes.

"No...territorial though? Perhaps." He grins lightly; blood smeared on his forehead.

And then he kisses me.

Soundly.

Deeply.

Until I realize I have been holding my breath as long as possible to make sure I feel every slide of his tongue. Every press of his lips against mine. It feels like the night has passed when we finally pull away, panting.

"I am so very proud of you, little warrior."

And for the second time that day, tears sting my eyes. Only this time, they're from happiness.

30

Elaudia

"Oh my God, Henry! Come quick! They have returned!"

Aunt Sofia's shouts echo in my ears as she rushes down the flight of stairs before her, hands gripping the skirts of her olive-green dress. The ride to the rebel camp and then home was long, filled with more people than I have ever seen in one gathering.

We kept the sick from the camp front and center so they might reach the healer faster.

Bristol rides behind Axel and me, next to Cadmus and Jaharis, and has not stopped whistling a battle tune for the past two hours. He casts roguish grins at every maid we pass.

I'm ready to never hear the song again.

Kettuna has flown off, staying hidden within the castle walls, but enjoying a stretch of her wings. I still cannot believe she exists. That she has chosen to fight by me—it's nothing short of a blessing from the Gods.

I'm pulled from my musings as Axel dismounts first, his Kingdom cheering so loudly I am afraid my eardrums will burst.

He reaches up, gently clasping his hands around my waist and pulling me down as if I am made of glass. I suppose I will have to start thinking that way, considering my way of life and my current condition. As soon as my feet touch the ground, I am enveloped in a pair of thin, but strong arms.

I inhale the familiar scent of Sofia, relaxing into her hold.

"I am so happy you have returned to us in the same condition you left! I was so worried!" Henry approaches us and smiles, bringing me into his chest and squeezing.

"She sure was, couldn't shut up about it."

I grin as Sofia rolls her eyes and places her hands on my cheeks, raising my face. Axel clears his throat as we walk up the castle stairs and I sigh, knowing where this is heading.

"I'm not exactly in the same condition as I was when we left."

Aunt Sofia halts abruptly and turns, gripping me tighter. Her eyes are wide with panic.

"What do you mean? What has happened?"

Her hands roam over my body, feeling for anything that might be amiss. I laugh and stop her roving hands, gripping them within my own and sliding them to my flat stomach.

I sigh softly.

"I'm pregnant," I whisper.

She goes stock still and I am afraid I have permanently damaged her mind.

She doesn't move.

Doesn't breathe.

But Henry does. He shouts and smiles, pulling me out of her arms and into his once more, twirling me around. Aunt Sofia finally moves, her mouth wide open.

"A baby." She breathes.

Tears fill her eyes and fall down her cheeks. "A little baby." She repeats once more, hugging me close.

I laugh into her hair and nod.

"Not exactly the timing I was hoping for..." I trail off, not knowing what to say next.

Axel smoothes a hand over the back of my hair in an attempt to soothe me. But Sofia remains ecstatic.

"A baby is a blessing at any time! Oh, the child will be loved by all! Just as you are."

I sniffle and shake my head, pulling away.

"By all?"

She ignores me and ushers me forward, her mouth racing.

"Oh, there's so much to do! So much to pre-pare." We enter the hall, and she shouts in a most un–queenly like way.

"Bria!! Nelly!! Come at once!"

My lady's maids rush out and reach for me as Sofia keeps talking. I grin at their relieved faces and hug them both. I look back to Axel for help as they direct me toward the king's room, but he only smirks and bows his head to me.

"I told you; you are going to rest. I keep my word, little mate."

I can't do anything other than stick my tongue out and follow the flighty girls who each have a hold on me, rolling my eyes.

"I love you."

His lips lift into a genuine smile.

"I love you too, my little mate."

***

Five Years Later

"You can't catch me!" His voice rings out, loud and piercing.

I grin as I chase him through the woods, my feet flying. I embrace the feeling of the summer breeze against my skin, laughing with joy. The skirts of my cream-colored dress whisper around my ankles as I crouch between two trees, searching for my prey.

I close my eyes, listening. In the last few years since we have locked the castle down, I have trained every day to attune my senses to something similar to a feral jungle cat.

Kettuna has helped me immensely with that.

There.

To my left.

A rustle of leaves sounds out, followed by a thud on the ground, and a curse that I know came from hanging out with Bristol too much. I launch off my knees, rushing forward and catching him just in time.

We roll on the ground, and I turn my back so that his body lies on top of mine. Giggles sound as he thrashes about, trying to break free.

"You got me, Mama!"

I roll on my side, brushing dirt and leaves from his curly black hair as we lie on the forest floor.

"How many times have I told you! You must pick up your feet, little fish."

Oliver rolls his eyes—or at least he attempts to—before standing up and brushing off his small knees.

"Mama..." He groans. "If you keep calling me little fish, then everyone is going to know about the lake."

He puts his hands on his hips in an attempt to be serious, and I grin, lifting my hands up.

"But you swim just like a little fish...flopping around...flopping to the side..." I trail off and attack, tickling his sides.

He screeches and laughs, falling to his bottom. The sound of my son's laughter heals something inside of me. I continue my tickling until a deep voice rings out, and I look up, watching my husband approach in all of his magnificent glory.

His Fae features have been known to me for years, but they still take my breath away.

Once Oliver was born, Axel's fear for his safety unfolded a thousand times over, and his Fae nature took over so that his Fae senses are in full force at all times. His face is more angular, his jawline so sharp it does not look real. His eyes are almost black, with only a hint of honeyed green in the center, and his frame is almost twice as big as it was when he was in his human form.

It took me and everyone else some getting used to, but I have never been more attracted to my husband than when he is in this form.

A form that can give me twice as many orgasms when we are lying in bed early in the morning, lounging in our passions from the night before.

I smile and help Ollie up, my lips widening as he rushes for his father.

"Papa! You're back!" Axel laughs and lifts Ollie into his arms, hugging him close.

"I told you I would only be gone a day, little fish."

Ollie's little hands cup his father's cheeks as he strokes the beard that has since been trimmed close to his face.

"Did you find the bad man yet?" Axel raises an eyebrow at me, and I can only shrug.

"He was getting bored with the books that Cadmus was bringing home. He's ready to hear some of our history, don't you think?"

Axels lets out a sigh before nodding and walking over, pulling me into his arms.

"It is not yet history, little warrior. But I understand." He turns his attention back to our precious son.

"I have not found him yet. But I will soon, I promise. Then we might have hope to move on from this threat and live in peace."

General Neem disappeared with his black witch after the retrieval of his daughter's hands. His camps remained in place, holding the cities they have already taken, but he has made no move to encroach on Atarah or Lash- forn again. Aunt Sofia and Henry come back and forth between Kingdoms.

I believe it is only because they cannot bear to be far from Ollie for long, and I never complain. I love having them all here, where everyone is protected behind Atarah's walls.

I press a kiss on Ollie's forehead and Axel releases him.

"Run along and tell Grandma we will be there soon."

His little legs carry him towards the castle in sight, and I fall into my husband's side, looking up.

"Where could he have gone?"

Surely Karisma's power is not that strong? To keep them hidden from our scouts for so long...from Graven and his people?

Axel watches our son until he reaches the soldiers awaiting to bring him home. He high-fives the men by his side, and I smile.

He is so loved by this Kingdom. I press a hand against my stomach. Though once again flat, I feel as if the biggest connection to my son is still present when I press a hand against the place that housed him for nine long months.

Axel's eyes turn down, and he smiles gently, cupping my hand with his own.

"We will find him. He has to resurface some-time. The rebels are close to taking back Misit, and Neem's men grow tired of waging a war with no leader. It won't be long now."

We walk back to the castle in blissful silence, soaking each other's strength up.

Though if I had known what his resurfacing would bring, I would have wished him into hiding for another hundred years.

31
Elaudia

"Mama says that broccoli heals broken bones, isn't that right mama?"

I laugh at Ollie, who continues to tease Cadmus with his antics. He lifts a fork with broccoli on it and flies it in circles to Cadmus's mouth, which only makes him grin and open, eating the green vegetable.

Cadmus returned from sparring with Bristol this evening, and unfortunately, suffered from a broken wrist.

Most likely because Bristol was showing off for Nelly and fighting *dirty*.

Nelly has been giving Bristol the cold shoulder ever since, and I have to admit, I am enjoying the glum look on Bristol's face. The former playboy of both men and women has not been able to get the look of a kicked puppy off his face at her rejection.

The table is alight with joy and laughter, and I soak in my family's happiness. This is where I am my most relaxed, my worries forgotten. When we all come together as one and share a meal.

Nelly and Bria have long since left behind the title of my lady's maids. Now, they run the castle together, with the help of Axel's cook, Sarabeth. Everyone laughs and jokes, enjoying each other's company.

Axel's hand reaches over and teases my thigh, his thick palm creeping up my skirt. My belly warms at my husband's touch, and I raise an eyebrow, daring him further. He grins and stands, holding out his hand for my own.

"The Queen and I are going to retire for the night. Ollie, mama will be in to tuck you in for bed after dessert."

We each place a gentle kiss on our son's head before saying our goodnights to everyone else. Nelly offers me a grin, but doesn't say anything, only winking my way. We only make it to the hall outside before we are latching on to each other. I moan as Axel pushes me against the wall, pawing at my breasts.

He pushes us into a dark alcove behind the kitchens, and brings my dress down, his mouth descending upon the pebbled skin and sucking hard. I cry out as he sucks hard, biting my sensitive nipple. Two guards stand watch at the entrance to the dining hall, and I know they can make out our forms.

"Axel...please..." He hums but doesn't answer, only gripping my thigh and pulling it up around his waist.

His eyes have darkened with lust and his movements are feral, the way he has been for the past few years.

"Turn around and face the wall. I cannot wait any longer." He grits out.

I turn with his help and then I'm pushed tight against the wall as he places a shield of protection around us, his magic glimmering and hiding us from plain view. My dress is pushed up—my panties yanked down—and then he is sliding home, shoving deep inside of me until the tip of his cock reaches my cervix.

"Such a naughty girl...letting my guards watch me fuck this tight cunt. I can feel your juices spilling down my balls."

He snarls into my ear, biting the lobe. His form blocks mine from view completely, but knowing there are eyes on us, knowing that they know what is transpiring in this dark alcove, is almost too much for me to bear.

"Should I put another babe inside this womb, little mate? I love the sight of your belly swollen with my child."

He growls low and thrusts harder, hitting me at my deepest depth with every plunge of his long cock. I cry out and push back, begging for more.

"God, but you cry so beautifully for me Elaudia."

His hands are rough on my hip bones, and he uses me like a doll, taking his pleasure.

I fucking love it.

Every minute of his touch, of him owning me so completely. I can feel my release approaching quickly, and I throw my head back, begging for his mouth. He doesn't make me wait long as he presses his lips to my own as my pussy clamps down on his cock, bringing a wave of wetness.

He snarls and thrusts once more, unloading his seed inside me, making me take it all. The only sound within the shield is our panting, low and unsteady.

My thighs are slick with our combined release, and I smile at the feeling. He pulls out gently—still half hard—before using his cloak to wipe me gently between the thighs.

"Once this war is won, I am going to keep you pregnant for years to come." I raise an eyebrow and look up.

"Is that so?" Axel only grins and places a gentle kiss on my temple.

"It is so, wife. I love the sight of your belly big with my child."

I think about it for a moment, remembering the pure joy I felt when Ollie was born.

"I think I could get behind that...but for now, I need to go put our child that is here now, to bed."

I kiss him once more as he rights my clothing, making sure that I am completely covered before I head to our son's room. I walk in and catch sight of Ollie already curled up in bed, chocolate still rimming his lips. Kettuna rests in her fox form, perfectly at ease.

I smile and lower myself to the edge of the bed, reaching for a warm and wet towel that sits beside his bed. Nelly probably brought him to bed and knew I would need it.

"Bristol let you sneak two extra cookies into your pockets, didn't he?"

Oliver's eyes widen in shock, and he sits up, cuddling Kettuna closer.

"He told you!?" He sounds betrayed and I laugh, shaking my head at his open mouth before lifting the towel and wiping the chocolate from his lips. I pull it away, showing him the evidence, and he grins at me sheepishly as he strokes Kettuna's soft fur. She chirps and snuggles closer into her favorite human.

"Lie down then, little fish. Try to rest well with all of that extra sugar in your system."

I say it softly as his eyes shut, my hand stroking his hair. I watch for a few moments as sleep takes him under, and I smile.

My precious boy.

The glow of the lamp beside his bed causes an illumination of light against his little face and I stroke his cheeks softly before rising and heading for the door quietly. I look back once more and watch his chest rise and fall slowly.

"Protect, Kettuna."

The chimera's fox fur shifts as she moves closer and her voice rings out in my head.

"Always, little female." She chirps.

***

"Your Majesty, have you seen the little Prince?"

I turn away from my musings at the window that overlooks the west side of the lake, facing Sarabeth. Axel left yesterday to head for the shores of the Dark Sea to welcome more refugees.

My brows furrow and I step closer to the older woman.

"No...he was supposed to come to see you this morning after his world lesson. Did he not arrive in the kitchens?"

The look on her face tells me all I need to know. I grab my labrys, stalking for the door.

"Axel!"

My shout reaches my husband's head instantly, and he materializes in front of me, his arms stopping me in my tracks. He looks down with curiosity but quickly reads the panic in my eyes.

"Find Oliver, *now*!"

He takes me into his arms, and we disappear as horns begin blaring out throughout the castle. We appear back in his room, to a sight that causes my blood to run cold.

Kettuna is entrapped in a cage in her fox form as she thrashes about, snarling in rage. Axel rushes forward, attempting to break her free.

It doesn't work.

That's not possible. Simple metal could not contain a chimera. Unless it's...

No.

I rush over, my Syraxes blood humming into my weapon as I swing my labrys against the lock. I watch as it breaks, freeing Kettuna. My blood runs cold.

No, no, no.

My heart stops as Kettuna shifts into her chimera form, her eyes black with rage.

"Black witch!"

She shrieks and shoots for the window, the window bursting and falling to the ground in a rainstorm of shimmering glass. I look at Axel right before he grabs me and we vanish, disappearing and reappearing to follow the path of her flight.

Footsteps thunder behind us as the soldiers of the castle run after us, weapons drawn. I only catch sight of Bristol and Cadmus briefly, but I can read the pure terror on their faces as well as I can *feel* my own. Axel inhales the scent of our son at each spot, following his trail.

We travel for what seems like miles before we finally arrive at a break of trees, the land cleared. A cabin sits in the middle, abandoned and old. I break free from Axel as Kettuna lands and shrieks, shaking her head as her wings flap furiously.

Black magic oozes from every square inch of the cabin in front of me and I keep walking, reaching for the door.

No, no, no, no.

Please God no.

I cannot hear. I cannot see anything but the path in front of me.

Kettuna's roar shakes the ground as I open the door, stopping me in my tracks. Static explodes from my body as my husband wraps his arms around me, holding me still.

"Elaudia...my love..." His voice is broken, cracking as he speaks. My chest breaks open at the sight before me, and I can feel the tears falling freely from my eyes.

"Oliver!"

I'm screaming. I'm screaming and I cannot stop. Power surges into my body, and I can hear Axel grunt as more static lifts my hair away from my body and flows into him.

"My baby!!"

My face feels as if I have washed it in the salt of the sea for a year, burning and stinging. I welcome the pain. My legs fall out from under me.

I can faintly hear guards shouting, ordering a retreat.

Get back.... they shout.

Get back.

It is as if a fog has separated me from their world, whipping me up, away from everything I have ever known. I know if I don't stop—if I don't control it, I will kill everyone here.

But I can't stop as I look into the open eyes of my little boy.

My little Oliver.

My little fish.

He hangs by a rope in the entryway, his eyes open but remaining forever unseeing. His body is still. His chest doesn't rise. My heart does not beat as I look at his little face, gray with death. His mouth...

Oh gods his mouth–

His cheeks.

His little knees.

My baby. My baby. My baby.

I scream once more and I do not stop. I scream my anguish and rage and sorrow as my power surges. A new and deadly power, blowing leaves from trees and causing dirt to swirl into tornados.

They did this, they took everything from me.

I bellow out another scream as my knees crumple completely to the ground as my sight goes out.

The last thought I have before I am rendered unconscious is that they will pay.

If it's the last thing I ever do, they will pay.

32

Elaudia

The tears fall freely from my face as I watch them lower his body to the ground below. His casket is simple. And small.

It's so small.

I keep looking at it, studying the details, but all that registers is that it is so small.

It's so small.

I don't feel the wind that rages against my cheek.

I don't feel Axel's hand in my own.

I don't hear the wails of my loved ones.

I just see the casket. The *small* casket. It's too small.

It has been two days. Two days since my world ended. And three days since the General made his move to start the beginning of the ending of this war.

I take a breath, willing myself back into a reality I no longer wish for.

Everyone has come to say goodbye to our little prince. I catch sight of Graven briefly, the stoic dragon standing off to the side of the hill, his face scarred viciously.

He has only met Ollie a few times throughout the years, but I saw the look of endearment he often gave my son. When he arrived with the other rebels from across the sea, he revealed his true form to us.

I understood why he kept his dragon a secret from the world and will be forever grateful for the gift of his scales. Clarice stands by Nelly and Bria, their faces all puffy with the tears they have cried.

Sofia...Henry...Jaharis....Nyreen.

Their names spin around in my head, and I have to close my eyes to make it stop. I lose the fight with reality, crawling back into the depths of my mind.

I turn my face back to my son—back to his *casket*—as it finally rests underneath the ground. I falter, but hold steady, ignoring Axel's hand that shoots out as if to stop me from falling to the wet ground. Stops me from crawling into my son's grave so that I might always be with him.

The sky has not stopped crying for days.

It is a royal funeral, with nothing withheld. All soldiers are present. All flags are flying. All faces are wet with tears and bodies are soaked with rain. Kettuna stands firm at the edge of Oliver's grave, her eyes defeated. She wailed throughout the first night, the cries matching my own.

The ancient female took to Oliver as if he were her own cub, staying by his side from the moment my belly bulged with him. Axel has remained stoic, betraying nothing.

But I can feel it...I can feel his beast thrashing inside of him to be let free from its cage. I tighten my hold on his hand as we attempt to ground each other in our sorrow.

My hair hangs limply to my waist, the skin below my eyes black from lack of sleep. I lashed out at my ladies' maids when they tried to touch me, only settling when Nelly and Bria sent them away and left me to my broken heart.

I dawned on a simple black gown, pinning Ollie's favorite flower to my breast.

And I showed up.

To say a final goodbye to my little fish.

They did this. The General and his black witch. They have taken my life, my *love.*

And now they had better prepare for this war, and prepare well.

I move my fingers together softly, alighting the static energy between my fingers against the rain, watching as blue fire alights between the two digits. My stare is blank, but my mind is on one thing. His casket is so small.

Axel was right. The Gods took something from us at birth when we were born different from the humans.

Blue eyes.

So small.

But they gave us something in return.

So small.

Blue fire.

So small.

I'm going to burn them all.

Her Last Kingdom

PART 2

Prologue

My vision blurs from the spattering of blood.

I thought that by now I would be used to it.

The bloodshed.

The cries of sorrow and the rage of their screams.

Maybe I am.

Maybe I have split myself into two, in an attempt to survive what has been wrought upon me unwillingly. The younger version of myself that was carefree and happy. Truly happy. Before the truth. Before the training. Before the heartache and the death.

My glowing weapon strikes out, its blade alight with my power.

I can't see him.

My heart beats faster in my chest as I look around the hills of bodies before deflecting General Neem's returning strike.

I can't see him.

The only reason I still breathe.

I can't see him.

I steel my spine and calm myself. I'll find him.

But I can't see him.

33
Elaudia

Whispers of feet.

Ruffles of dresses.

That is the extent of what I can see or hear. My body has frozen itself, locking me inside my mind.

I can't move.

I can't breathe.

I don't think anyone has managed to force food down my throat in three days, which is what they had to resort to these past few weeks, seeing as I didn't want to *live*, let alone eat. All I can see in my mind is my little fish.

My little baby.

Hanging in that damn doorway, his precious life gone. I went back to the forest after his funeral and razed the cabin to the ground, along with the trees and animals surrounding it. My anguish was unleashed, and I could not control it. My rage though?

It's still there. Waiting to strike.

But I can't move.

The door opens again as Bria and Nelly exit, trading places with Sofia. They all take turns. Everyone has cemented a perfect routine of sitting and speaking to me as if I were conscious. I suppose, technically, I am. Everyone comes and goes, everyone except for Axel. He has not left my side since I returned from the destruction I caused and collapsed into myself on our bathroom floor.

Sofia is talking to me, I believe. But I can't hear a word she's saying. But Axel can. His calloused hand tightens around mine as Sofia turns around abruptly before changing her mind and stalking back towards me.

Something in her eyes is different right now.

It's crueler.

No longer holding a grim resignation.

Axel stiffens and sits forward, his eyebrows angling down towards his eyes. He opens his mouth to speak firmly.

"Sofia, *don't.*"

It's too late, though. My Aunt has marched straight up to the chair I have not left, and she slaps me across the face viciously.

It happens before I can blink, and for the first time since I lost my little Ollie, I can feel something other than black emptiness. My head whips to the side with her burning handprint flaring to life on my cheek. Axel roars, and in a flash, he is on his feet, pushing her away from me as his beast snarls a warning. His primal instincts are at the surface—wanting to attack—but then Henry's voice reaches my ears.

I can hear him pleading with Axel not to retaliate.

"She's mourning as well, you know this, Axel," Henry begs him not to harm her.

He never would. He knows how much they mean to me—knows that I see them as the parents I never had. My face is still turned when he begins to speak, his voice as cold as death.

"If you *ever* strike my mate again, it will be the last time you ever enter our lands."

She ignores him, though, looking straight through him to me. I almost come to life to admire her balls of steel.

Until she speaks.

"This is pathetic. *You* are being pathetic. You are the strongest Bellator in the world, Gods be damned! So, get up and *fight*! Take revenge for Oliver. Take revenge against the General and his whore of a witch! Do *anything*! But get up out of that fucking chair!"

Sofia's chest heaves with her rant, and I turn my head slowly, taking in her anger. Her finger remains pointed at me as if she's trying to cast a spell—one that will ensure I do as she says. I almost wish she could. Maybe if she had magic, she could take away this endless agony.

I blink slowly at her. Her lips clench together as she pushes Henry off of her, shoving her way through a still-raging Axel.

Warm hands grip my cold wrists, and she leans down, perched on her knees.

"You think you are the only one to have ever lost a child? The only one that has had to watch as their body was lowered into the ground for an eternity?"

"Sofia..."

Now, Henry is the one warning her.

"The General killed my husband, Claude. And my daughter, Odette...my little Odie. My *little girl*. She was five...just like Oliver." Tears gather in her eyes.

I look down. She never told me.

"I could have wasted away into nothing like you are choosing to do now. But you know what that is, right...?" Her beautiful face lifts into a sneer.

"It's a big *fuck you* to your child, and the life they could have lived."

I hiss at her words, coming alive for the first time in weeks. Axel and Henry look at me, their faces showing the extent of their shock.

I'm trying.

I wish I had said it out loud. But I didn't. I can't force my mouth to open, even though I'm clawing for release on the inside. Sofia doesn't look shocked, though. She looks me up and down with disdain.

"I guess Oliver didn't mean that much to you after all."

I screech in my mind at her words, and blue fire alights over my hands and legs as I stand, burning away the chair I was sitting in. She backs away from my power.

"Get *out*!!"

My screams hurt my ears, and I know the rest of my family, who are waiting to come in, can hear me. But still, Sofia only looks at me with soft anger and a hint of relief. She lifts her head and turns around as if she were victorious in some way by coming in here and making me re-live my son's death all over again.

Henry and Sofia reach the door, and the former leaves first. Sofia turns her head back my way as she speaks softly.

"At least that damned chair is gone."

I'm still panting when she leaves, my breath leaving me in short gasps. I catch a brief glimpse of Cadmus outside, his mouth wide open as the door slams shut, and then Axel is in my face, bringing me towards the bed.

"Breathe, little warrior. Breathe with me."

I'm trying to. I wish I could say to him. I'm trying to break free of this cage.

It seems impossible.

I'm panicking slightly now.

He can't think I did not love our little fish? I did. I swear I did.

A whimper leaves my chapped lips as heavy hands push me down, and then my mate is staring into my eyes as he nods his head sadly.

"I know you loved Oliver, my little mate. You were his fiercest protector, my love."

I can see the heartbreak in his eyes. I hate that I can't do more to comfort him.

I open my lips, my voice raspy from disuse and screaming.

"*I'm...try-trying...*"

A tear trails my face as Axel pulls me close, burying my head into his chest. His hands stroke my hair while he whispers sweet nothings to me. My body relaxes into his familiar scent and hold. I look out the window, my head resting on his shoulder. I look to the left, catching sight of the hill. The hill that holds my son's grave.

My son's body.

And then the nothingness returns to me tenfold.

34
Elaudia

One month later

It's been weeks now, and I still can't feel my body.

"She needs to come. We need to get her away from all of this. She will not return to us while she is surrounded by all of his things. His memory."

Sofia's voice reaches my ears from where I lie in bed. I have taken to a curled-up position in the center for about a month and have not left it except to use the bathroom. Kettuna lies by my side in her fox form, her coat dull and her eyes as devoid of life as mine.

"You are not taking my mate away from these walls. We still have no idea of Neem's whereabouts—let alone if he has given his armies orders to finally attempt to retake Lashforn."

My mate's voice leaves no room for argument, but she continues on.

"We have sent Bristol's scouts ahead and placed one at every quarter mile around the castle walls. If anyone should approach, we will hear of it immediately! She needs this, *please*! If we do not do something soon, we will also lose her. I beg you, Axel. She is a daughter to me, and I cannot bear to sit by another day while she withers away into nothing."

Sofia's voice breaks as she begs my husband. I almost muster enough strength to feel sorry for her. Feel sorry for them all for what I have become.

Almost.

A heavy sigh leaves Axel's chest, but he says nothing more to Sofia. I hear the door open and shut. His booted footsteps sound across the floor, scuffing gently along the stone. A moment later, I feel his weight settle beside me on the bed. His hand reaches out, brushing tangled hair away from my face softly.

He puts me in the large bathtub every single night—sending our servants away as he tends to me with his own hands.

He washes my skin, brushes my hair, and lowly hums Fae songs that have been long forgotten.

But my hair always becomes tangled once more after restless hours of fitful night terrors.

"Is she right?" He muses mournfully. "Will I lose you, too?"

I don't respond. Because I don't even know the answer myself.

I stare straight ahead—my knees tucked to my chest. He is quiet for a moment, and then I hear the door open again. Axel's voice is muffled, but a clear chime answers him.

"Yes, Your Majesty?" Nelly. She sounds...sad.

"Prepare Elaudia's things. She is leaving tonight to visit Lashforn with Sofia and Henry. Tell Cadmus to prepare as well."

"At once, Your Majesty. Shall Bria and I join them?"

I hear a hopeful note in her tone.

Axel shakes his head.

"I need you both here for now. I shall leave on another scouting mission before joining her in Lashforn."

I can hear Nelly's skirts brush the stone floor beneath her as she curtseys to Axel and gets to work, packing my clothes and bathing necessities. Her eyes glance over at me every few moments, and I can see the sorrow that takes over her eyes at the sight of me. I'm sure I am quite the sight.

I'm sure my skin has lost all color, being locked away inside for so many months.

I'm paler than I've ever been before.

Not as pale as my son's face, though.

Axel waits until she has finished before nodding at her to depart. His body angles closer to mine as he lays down next to me, his masculine scent hitting my nose. I inhale it softly. We are about to be separated. For the first time since he died. For the first time ever, really.

"I know it seems scary...I'm just as nervous about this as you are. But I think Sofia is right. You need to get away from home...just for a little while. You can't heal while surrounded by all of these things. All of the memories we shared here with him."

Axel places a soft kiss on my bare shoulder, tightening his grip around my midsection.

I turn his way softly, the first movement I have made in days. I look up, my milky white eyes meeting his golden speckled black ones.

"Help...me." I manage.

His jaw clenches as I speak, and he shudders. His eyes close tightly for a brief moment, and then they open once more, shining with an undying love for me that makes my bottom lip tremble.

"I'm going to sweetheart. I'm going to make it better for you, I promise. But this is the first step."

I don't want to leave him. I don't want to leave my little fish.

It's raining outside.

It's cold, the summer is gone, and fall is coming steadfast.

What if he's cold?

"He's not cold baby." Axel's voice breaks. "He's not cold, I promise. He is part Fae. The earth welcomed him with warm, open arms. I swear to you, he's being taken care of right now by my ancestors."

A keening whimper escapes me, and I close my eyes.

I should be the one taking care of him.

He should be in my arms. I sniffle slightly and burrow my face back into the pillows, gripping Kettuna closer.

He should be here.

And it's my fault that he's not.

***

Cadmus whispers lowly, attempting to keep the conversation quiet.

He forgets that I am more than human, even more so since my son's death. My powers have emerged with a vengeance.

"Are you sure this is going to work?"

Sofia sits by Cadmus—with Henry by me—in the large royal carriage. I sit on the bench, unmoving. I stare blankly out the window, not seeing the countryside as it passes us by.

"It has to. He needs to pay for what he has taken from this family. She needs a reason to live. Right now, revenge against General Neem is the only thing we have to offer her."

Cadmus nods and sits back, glancing over at me before sighing. He hasn't been the same either. There is a certain gleam of evil in his eyes now. Rage towards our enemies. Oliver and Cadmus spent every free moment together, playing soldiers and trolls. Oliver begged him for a new story of us as children every night before bed. I know a piece of his heart is gone now, too.

Trumpets sound from outside the carriage, raising an alarm as we approach.

My eyes widen as the once flourishing countryside slowly turns to burned trees and ashy air. I can hear Sofia gasp as she looks out the window. Our carriage comes to a halt.

"On your guard!" Men shout.

The door opens, and a somber-faced Yumin stands in front of us.

"Your Majesties..." He trails off with a broken note as Sofia pushes him to the side, exiting the carriage with haste. She pulls up the skirts of her gown as she steps down, almost missing the last step in her panic.

"No...." She whispers.

I follow after her, taking in the scene before us.

Lashforn is *gone.*

It's been burned to the ground. Dark gray smoke rises high into the sky above, turning it black.

For the first time since Oliver died, I can feel myself. I can feel who I was before it all went to hell. My fight returns slightly as I turn abruptly and head back to the carriage, gathering my Labrys from underneath the seat. I shuck my heavy coat, leaving it where I just sat, before exiting again.

Henry holds Sofia close as she cries, and my heart aches for her at the sight of her home reduced to rubble. At the sight of what was once *my home*, reduced to rubble. I'm still angry with her for her cruel words, but I hate to see her in pain. I stalk forward, continuing down the hill to Lashforn's charred gates.

"Laudi..." Cadmus warns.

I ignore him, letting some of the rage inside me fuel my desire for justice. I enter the gates first as everyone follows me slowly, looking around at the damage.

Substantial damage.

Bodies litter the ground as we walk on. Men, women, and children. I halt in my tracks, squeezing my eyes shut as the body of a little boy comes into sight. His body is held tight in the arms of a woman my age, her mouth open in terror, her eyes now forever unseeing. She is the closest to the gate, meaning she was among the first to fall. A civilian from the town's square. Perhaps a seamstress, or the wife of a baker.

I take a breath.

You can do this, Elaudia. Do it for them.

I shudder once more and open my eyes, keeping my head held high. The earth crackles beneath my steps as I work through charred homes and bodies, looking for survivors.

There won't be any.

Sofia's sobs continue, and I come to life even more. My eyes whip back and forth as we approach the castle, the great doors on the ground broken. The dark rebels took a battering ram to it, meaning the servants attempted to barricade the doors shut.

Yumin growls low, barking orders.

"Search the palace grounds! Look for any survivors."

It was General Neem. I know it was. He has finally made his second move.

The first was killing my little boy.

I look over my shoulder, my Bellator nature taking over as my fingers spark with blue static—my new powers begging to come out and play.

"Cadmus, stay with Sofia and Henry. I'm going to check the royal rooms."

Cadmus opens his mouth, but I snarl and lift my labrys over my shoulder, shaking my head. He nods and steps back, letting me go alone.

I can only hope I won't be leaving here the same way.

35
Elaudia

Every flag hanging has been torn to the ground and lies on the bloodied marble, Lashforn's sigil desecrated. My ears perk up as I walk, listening for the tell-tale signs of feet scuffling or un-even breath. I pass by more bodies as I go—bodies I recognize.

The cook.

The stable man's daughter.

The maids.

Not one soul was spared in this slaughter. I breathe through my nose, even though the smell that hits it causes my eyes to burn. I want to feel it all. Every single bit of this massacre.

I will feel *everything*.

I hit the landing at the top of the stairs and clear out each room as I go until I hit my old bedroom. I halt there, almost ignoring it. It was abandoned when I left, save for when we would visit. It's where Oliver would stay.

I push the door open softly, listening to the wood creak as it goes. The room is in the same state as the castle, upturned and destroyed. I step back to leave when a glint of light catches my eye on the desk in the corner. My brows furrow as I walk over and look down.

A knife is embedded into the desk, keeping a letter in place. I remove it, letting my eyes skim over the words.

You took my daughter from me.

I took your son from you.

Did you think I would let it be?

I will take them all from you.

I can feel my body shaking as I digest the threat he has left for me. General Neem continues to threaten the people I love. It will never stop. My rage surges forward, and I welcome it like a long-lost friend. At the same time, screams bellow out below that have my heart freezing to stone inside my chest.

No.

I race for the door and rush down the stairs, my heart thumping in my ears. I hear the sound of blades meeting and realize the castle wasn't abandoned. They were lying in wait.

To kill us.

To take the rest of my family away from me.

How did I not see this coming? How did I not sense them?

But I already know the answer—*black magic.*

A shriek leaves my throat as I jump the railing, slashing my labrys through the neck of a man attacking Henry. His head rolls to the ground, and his black armored body drops.

"Run!!" I order him, fighting off another soldier. His panicked eyes meet my own, but he doesn't turn to leave.

"They have Sofia!"

Something inside me breaks at his words as another man comes up behind him. He looks into my eyes, his choice made.

"Save my wife." He begs me, just as the tip of a blade appears in front of me, right through his stomach from behind.

"No!!" I scream, spinning to the left.

I deliver the same blow to the man who just killed my uncle, slicing my labrys through his neck. His blood coats my arm as my blade leaves his severed head, and I thrust it into the man behind me. I don't have time to mourn.

Not yet.

I spin around, clearing the room. My chest heaves as I close my eyes, listening for Cadmus and Sofia. It's only a moment before I can make out her frantic heartbeat, and then I'm rushing for the ballroom. The sight that greets me stops the blood in my veins.

Sofia has been restrained by one of Neem's guards, her arms behind her back and her face wet with tears. Cadmus lies on the ground, his torso bloody. I focus on his chest and breathe a sigh of relief when I can make out his heartbeat. It's slow.

But it's there.

"He told us you would come. He's always right."

The man that speaks has blonde hair and cruel eyes, with crowfeet wrinkles surrounding them. A contradiction in itself. How can someone so evil laugh so much?

I twirl my labrys, walking towards the man holding Sofia by the neck. Three other guards watch me closely, their weapons raised. I hiss at the threat, allowing my blue fire to take over my weapon. I enjoy watching their eyes widen with a well-deserved wariness. I will kill them all for this.

Sofia's face is wet with tears, but she keeps her composure. The blade held angled up towards her heart is steady.

"Cadmus has lost too much blood. I'm so sorry." Her lip wobbles, causing me to stop walking as the guard tightens his hold on her hair. She winces, and I snarl.

"You two are children to me. Both of you. You saved me, Elaudia...please never forget what you are to me."

My own eyes sting with tears at her confession.

A daughter.

I am a daughter to her, as she was a mother to me. I shake my head, knowing where there is going.

"Henry is dead." She states.

It's not a question. She knows. When I don't answer her, she closes her eyes. When they reopen again, the choice she has made stops my heart.

"Save Cadmus. *Now!*"

And then she throws herself forward and down onto the blade resting against her stomach. The tip pierces up through her ribcage, impaling her.

And I break. Once again.

"No!"

I scream until my voice is raw as my power erupts and completely engulfs my body. I launch my labrys into the face of the man who just killed my aunt, watching as they both drop to the floor. I'm panting and out of control as I turn to face the last three men surrounding my cousin, and I embrace this new extent of my power, watching as two battle axes made of blue fire appear in my hands.

Something...*otherworldly*...is flowing through my body now. I exhale a breath as the weight of its power threatens to consume me.

I sprint to them, ready to end their miserable lives. The first two go down easy, my blades leaving their corpses as cleanly as they entered, but I have no time to study these new weapons.

Not when the last man alive holds his sword over Cadmus's unconscious form.

"Let me go, and he lives. Please just let me leave!"

He's younger than the rest, probably conscripted within the past two years.

I don't care.

I conjure a dagger in my left hand, letting the axe disappear, but just as soon as I raise it to strike, an arrow flies through the air and embeds itself into the eye of the guard. His mouth is open in disbelief as he falls dead to the ground. I look up, finding a figure standing with one foot propped up on the railing above, her arms raised with her bow.

Clarice stands there, partly cloaked in the shadows, her form still. I look back to Cadmus and run forward, immediately kneeling over his unconscious form. A thud from behind tells me Clarice has jumped down and landed nearby. Her hand touches my shoulder a moment later as she looks around at the damage. A whimper escapes her throat when she catches sight of Sofia's still body behind us.

"Oh, gods." She whispers.

"You need to get him back to Atarah. Now."

My voice is cold, but my body is on fire. Something is happening to me, but I don't know what.

"Laudi..." She's confused.

So am I.

But I won't risk them. Something inside of me is about to break free, and I don't want them anywhere near me when it does.

"Get him out of here now!!" I roar.

She listens this time, tucking her bow on her arm and gripping the charm Axel had gifted her last summer solstice.

A warping stone.

It can only be used five times, but with a hold on the stone and a destination in mind, she is gone within a few seconds—Cadmus with her. As soon as I'm sure that they are gone, the tears finally break loose, and my body slumps to the floor.

Pain racks my body as I hold my forehead to the floor, my black hair acting like a curtain as it surrounds me.

"Lau-di..." A voice rasps. I look up instantly at my aunt, who lies there, her hand reaching for me.

"Aunt Sofia!" I sob. I scramble over to her on my knees, taking her limp form into my arms. I brush soft brown hair away from her face, cradling her close.

This is my fault.

Again.

Someone I love is dying once more because of me and *my* failure to act. I moan desperately through the pressure caving in on my chest. It's unspeakably painful.

"I'm s– so sorry." I cry.

The tears leave me freely, and I swear I can feel the organ in my chest physically aching. Sofia smiles up at me softly, her lips coated in blood.

"I should be apologizing. Not you...I didn't mean the t–things I said. I just...just needed you to fight."

I sob harder at her words, my breath hiccup-ping.

"No...it's my fault. It's all my fault." My aunt struggles to place a hand on mine, squeezing it softly. She doesn't have much strength left.

Or time.

"Life loses its meaning when you choose to let the evil of it wi–win." Her body shudders as she coughs up more blood. I'm rocking her back and forth now, my sorrow consuming me.

"You saved me, child. But now, I will rest. You need to find a–another reason to live. Find it...and live well. *Love* deeply and without re-straint."

Her bloody hand cups my cheeks as she speaks her last words.

"Just as I did...when I found you." I cry hard-er at her words and watch as the life leaves her eyes. The panic hits me hard as I clutch her closer.

"NO! Please! Please don't leave me too! Please..."

I gasp, shutting my eyes as I murmur into her ear. Words she will never receive again.

"I'm sorry...I love you...I'm so sorry."

But she's gone.

Henry is gone.

Oliver is gone.

Cadmus might be dying right now.

My body attempts to fight back the ancient power rising inside me, filling so quickly that it overflows. I cannot stop it, I don't know if I even *want* to.

So, I let the welling power inside overflow—unleashing it once more as it leaves my body like a tsunami—ravaging everything within its reach.

36
Elaudia

I'm sitting on the cool dirt, and for once, my mind isn't blank.

It's plotting all of the ways I can kill General Neem and his black witch. I don't know how long it has been, but I know the midday sun has already reached its peak and has begun its slow descent towards the horizon. My mind is clearer than it has been in months as I think. I will hunt the General to the ends of this continent and I will kill him for everything he has done.

He's fucking dead.

The area around me is nothing but an open sky now. My power disintegrated everything in Lashforn until nothing was left but a giant black hole.

The trees are gone.

The buildings are gone.

The bodies are gone.

Hopefully, in some way, I have set their spirits free from this now-tormented land. My eyes have finally dried, the well of my tears empty.

"My Queen."

I whirl on the intruder, raising my labrys, the only thing remaining after my destruction. The man before me steps out from the shadows slowly, and I know if this land were occupied by any living beings, their eyes would all be drawn to the electrifying male.

His face is no different than the last time I saw him, with a vicious scar ripping down the left side of his face. A result of his last battle, a thousand years ago. His icy blonde hair has grown slightly since the funeral and is brushed away from his face. Eyes the color of glaciers stare down at me on the ground with a pity that I resent.

"Graven." I hoarsely whisper.

The stoic dragon shifter offers me a scarred hand, and I take it, allowing him to haul me up and away from the scorched earth.

"Clarice told me where I could find you. I'm sorry for your loss."

I close my eyes and breathe through my nose, fighting off the demons that attempt to rise.

"Have you heard from Axel? He was supposed to meet me here."

I look up and around, truly seeing the damage for the first time. When he doesn't answer, I look him in the eyes.

"He never showed," I state.

Why hasn't he arrived yet? Graven's jaw clenches as he looks down at me.

"The King has been captured by the black witch, Karisma. He left on a scouting mission West of Aland, where they were lying in wait. Karisma moved in with a smaller group of soldiers and overwhelmed him with black magic."

I look up, baring my teeth at the ancient dragon.

"When?" My heart races as I think of my husband, my mate, trapped within the clutches of that vile whore.

"An hour ago. I left Atarah immediately in search of you, but Clarice intercepted me. I'm here to bring you to the west wall, where we are currently rallying our troops."

I sheath my labrys on my back and nod.

"Let us go then."

Graven arches an eyebrow at me, looking around as if making sure no one can hear us.

"Have you ever ridden a dragon before, my Queen?"

I blanch at him—mouth open—and my worries are forgotten for a nano-second.

"No...I assumed Kettuna was close behind you."

He shakes his head, grimacing. No such luck, then. I look him up and down, wondering how big he truly is in his other form at such a close distance.

My question is quickly answered.

"You might want to get out of this crater you have created first."

It does seem like the most logical thing to do, so I turn and start jogging, waiting until I hit the wall to jump out, using my gifts to propel me forward. I turn around to face the crater once more, watching with slightly widened eyes as a glow begins to emanate from within Graven.

I don't wait long before I watch as an honest-to-God *dragon* transforms before my very eyes, for the first time in my life. Graven's body is engulfed with a bright light for almost three seconds before a giant white and red scaled dragon stands before me; his jaw opening wide to accommodate the pillar-sized teeth in his mouth. His white scales blend to a fiery red color around what I assume to be his ankles.

The ground shakes as he walks towards me, his wings tucked close to his sides. The crater he is in is not even large enough to contain his size. I look into the beast's eyes, trying to see if I can recognize Graven in them. He approaches me at the edge, where grass still grows, and lowers his back and wing slightly so I might climb on.

I hurry, carefully climbing up the membrane that runs between his bones. I settle myself between two raised scales at the center of his back, and he graciously waits for me to get settled as his head turns, watching my every move.

I reassure him that I'm ready with a nod, and then his wings expand, covering the entire length of the crater as he flaps them once. We're airborne immediately as the wind rushes against me, blowing my hair back from my face. My heart stutters in my chest at the movement, and I tighten my grip on his spikes, hunching over. My mind is on killing Karisma and freeing my mate. I close my eyes, reaching out through our bond.

"Axel..?"

No reply. I huff out a breath of panic, refusing to let this beat me.

He's okay. He has to be okay.

The General wants him alive to taunt me. I try again.

"Axel!"

"Laudi..." His voice is like a whisper across my skin, and I can tell our bond is weaker than ever. It has to be Karima's magic causing such a strain on our mate bond. There can be no other reason.

"I'm coming, my love. I promise I'll get you out of there."

He doesn't reply, and it fuels my rage. Sofia wanted me to fight. She wanted me to take vengeance for Oliver.

I'm going to fight. I'm going to watch the life drain out of their eyes as I strangle them with my bare hands. The wind whips around my face freely, causing my waist-length hair to unravel from its already loose braid. Graven flies faster than anything I have ever seen before, and I watch as the landscape changes, switching from grassy fields to the wide-open ocean.

He flies by the countryside as I admire the waves crashing against the cliff-side below. A sudden splash further away from the land catches my eye, and I lean over in an attempt to look down, studying the way the waves break apart whenever a sparkling tail makes way.

Mermaids.

Small creatures who used to walk on our lands, but escaped to the sea when the creatures of lore were slaughtered. They've only made themselves known on the shores of Atarah, where they know they are safe, yet not a single one has come back onto land. From what I have seen of them, their slanted eyes and fragile frames say they are not made for fighting.

They seem like delicate creatures.

I break away from their glittering tails and look at Graven, who watches them as closely as I do.

No...Not *them.*

His eye is on the form at the back, the slowest of the bunch.

And the smallest.

He keeps his pace with it for a moment, slowing down slightly. I'm not even sure if he realizes what he's doing. I watch as the mermaids disappear from our sight, but not before a rumbling growl escapes the great dragon's chest.

I arch an eyebrow but say nothing.

We're only flying for another twenty minutes before I see the army ahead, armored and ready for battle. My heart beats faster at the thought of confronting them, a dark eagerness taking over. Axel was a true mate to me throughout my grieving, never leaving my side and yet—somehow—still maintaining order in our Kingdom.

He put his responsibility to me before his responsibility to our citizens, all so I could grieve.

My eyes sting with tears at the thought of it. He went through it alone...without me. Because I was too far gone to be helped, yet still did all he could to bring me back. We land about fifty feet from the chunk of soldiers—all who look up—waiting for their orders. I wait until Graven has settled behind me before I turn to face my army, who all watch me with varying degrees of wariness.

Oliver was the kingdom's pride and joy, loved by all. These men have not seen me since the funeral.

I take a deep breath and step forward.

"I must apologize," I say loudly enough so they may all hear me.

"I lost myself to grief I have never experienced before. Grief I would not wish upon any of you, though I know many of you have experienced because of this war. I was not the Queen you needed, and I will never forgive myself. Queen Sofia and King Henry were murdered today at the hands of the general's men. My royal guard, Cadmus, is at home—fighting for his life."

My lip trembles, but I am determined to be strong now.

I walk closer to my soldiers until I am making my way through the prong of men who stand ready to die for our home.

"But I swear to you before every God to ever exist, I will never fail you again. General Neem has run out of options, and I have run out of patience! Neem will die before the snow arrives this winter. This I vow to you!"

Roars erupt around me as my army lifts their weapons in their hands, shouting their accord as they steady their mounts. One roar explodes over the others, and I look over, catching sight of Kettuna in her fully shifted form. Her eyes are darker now—filled with rage—and I know she will never be the same again.

Neither will I.

But I can be better for Ollie—for his memory. I *will* be better. I stalk over to the large Chimera, allowing her to nudge her forehead against mine.

"Hello, my friend." I whisper gently as I place my hand upon her mane as she whips her scorpion tail back and forth with anticipation.

"Hello, small Queen." She trills in my head.

The sound of metal greets me as the soldiers ready their swords and begin making their way down the trail Karisma walked. I gently clutch Kettuna's mane between my fingers and look into her eyes. My lower lip trembles as I recall the last moments she had with Ollie.

"It wasn't your fault," I whisper. A keening sound escapes her chest, and I can tell she did not expect me to do this here. But it cannot wait any longer.

"It wasn't." I urge her, my jaw clenched tight. I move slightly to the right so that our eyes can connect once more.

"I am the only one able to fight off and destroy the black magic. *Me.* Not you. I know that you did everything you could to protect him! As you always did. It wasn't your fault."

Tears leak from my eyes as I speak to the gentle beast, and they threaten to fall as I watch the agony once again take over her facial features.

"My cub...." She rumbles softly.

I whimper at her broken trill and pull her closer, burying my hands into her thick fur.

"I know, Kettuna. I know. But we must honor his memory. And it starts now."

I pull away and wipe my eyes, nodding to-wards Graven, who has stayed behind.

"I'll ride with Kettuna. You go ahead of the troops and scout them out. I need to know how many guards are watching Axel."

Graven nods his enormous head and takes to the sky, causing my hair to fly in all directions as his wings lift him into the sky. I make sure my labrys is steady in its sheath before Kettuna kneels before me, allowing me to mount her back. This is the most riding I have done in months, and I know I will feel it later.

Good.

I want to feel.

I need to.

I promised Sofia I would live, and I intend to keep that promise until my dying breath. Kettuna's scaled back shimmers in the after-noon light as we take the sky, and for the first time since I buried my son, I come alive at the thought of finally killing Karisma.

My son will have his justice.

37
Elaudia

The sound of the battle reaches my ears first, and I know it means we have finally caught up to Karisma's small party.

The only question is, who is attacking them if my men are still almost a half mile away? Kettuna and Graven circle each other in the sky as I try to make out the fighting underneath the canopy of trees below. I can make out the red shields and black armor of the General's men, but the men they are fighting off wear no such armor. Their skin is bare, and they only wear trousers to cover themselves. They wield long staffs in their hands, and to my surprise, they are holding off the enemy.

That's when I catch sight of Axel.

"Over there Kettuna!"

I lean to the left, and she follows my lead, having spotted my mate. His hands and mouth are bound with a rope that seeps with black magic, and I can see the skin around his mouth graying.

My lips curl into a snarl, and I hiss, pulling my labrys out. I have yet to spot the black witch. Kettuna lands with a heavy thud, and I watch my mate's heavy eyes lift at the sound. I pull the static electricity from the air, allowing it to spark all over my body and weapon as I jump from Kettuna's back. She lunges for a soldier who rushes us, tearing his head from his body—her favored way of killing.

I'm starting to agree with her.

It is quite efficient.

"Axel!" My mate's eyes widen, and he shakes his head frantically. I ignore him, rushing over to the cage that confines him.

"It's a trap!"

His voice is not as weak as it was before, but it's still too quiet in my mind. The black magic is draining him, slowly leeching him of his Fae lifeforce. I ignore his warning and slash my labrys through the bars, allowing my power to feed off the magic. Just as I break the bars, a net of solid silver chains drops over my body and drags me to the ground. Axel is still trapped, tied down, and unable to move, though I can tell by his thrashing that he is doing everything he can to escape.

"So...you're the one that all of this fuss is about." A soft voice drawls.

I look up through the heavy chains to the voice that speaks, surprise flooding me when I realize it's not an old woman like I had previously imagined. The girl before me is young—younger than me—though her eyes tell me she has ancient power.

"It is true...yes. When I slaughtered my sisters and my mothers, I gained access to all of their power and knowledge. They were useless anyway."

Her hair is black like mine, but her eyes are soulless.

Shit.

She can read my mind.

"Not all of it..." She purrs, stepping closer.

She studies me as if I am an experiment that has all of her attention. I growl at her form, struggling underneath the heavy silver.

"You're quite an extravagant-looking thing, aren't you?"

Her head tilts, and I can feel something poking at my head from the inside. She's trying to gain further access. I imagine a metal claw snapping at her probing fingers, and she jerks back with a hiss, blinking fast.

"Stay the fuck out of my mind, you cunt." Her lip curls, and she sniffs in irritation.

"Vulgar as well, it seems."

Okay...I've had about enough of this bullshit. I draw on the well inside of me, allowing my eyes to take on a bright blue sheen as I lash out with my free hand, breaking the chains with a sharp blue whip of fire. Her eyes widen in disbelief as she steps back towards my husband's cage.

"That spell was an *ancient* one—you should not be able to break free of it so easily." She says, her words showing awe instead of irritation. "I see I will need to infuse more spells together to truly hold you at bay."

I don't want to waste any more time as I pick up my labrys and launch it at her. She looks back at Axel once more, and I can see dread take over her eyes for a brief moment as she watches her small battalion lose this fight before she raises her hand and is swallowed whole by a black mist, disappearing from our sight.

God dammit.

I look over at my mate, who still struggles, his black eyes on me. I can tell his beast is on the surface and in control right now, so I hurry to free him, breaking the black magic apart as if it were made of cotton. His straining biceps wrap around me the moment he is out of the cage, and I relax into his hold, breathing in his unique scent of sandalwood and leather.

Kettuna stands guard, biting off the head of any remaining soldier stupid enough to get too close, and I smile as she spins, her bladed wings slashing through a man's stomach. She trills with pleasure as his innards spill to the ground.

Bloodthirsty creature.

The sound of battle has dwindled, and I finally look up to see our men arriving, looking miffed that they have missed out on the action. Graven approaches the strange men slowly, watching their every move. I smirk as they warily watch the large beast. I pull away from my husband's arms and turn, taking in the men who walk towards us. I've never seen them before—and that's saying something considering this is technically still the land of Atarah.

"King Axel. Queen Elaudia."

The man at the front bows his head slightly, showing respect but maintaining his own among his people. Axel's beast is still in control, his eyes watching every move with a calculation that makes even me shiver.

With lust.

But still.

"I am Prince Roarke of Protisteria—the siren kingdom. I have come to aid you in your war against General Neem. His soldiers have sullied our waters with oil, intending to draw us out of our homes."

By The Gods.

Neem wants to rule even the *ocean*. Prince Roarke smoothes light blue hair away from his face, stepping closer. Axel growls, standing closer to me. Roarke notices the movement and stops, his hands releasing the hold he still has on his weapon. I look at the man who claims to be a Siren, the companions to the mermaids.

Creatures we haven't seen in *so* long.

I walk slowly to the cluster of bare-chested men, ignoring Axel's hand on my wrist. He steps with me.

"How did you know where they were taking my husband? How did you know to intercept them? How did you know they were even here?"

Prince Roarke swallows and looks down, his jaw clenched.

"I can't tell you."

I raise my eyebrow at the refusal, tilting my head.

"Spy?" Kettuna chirps in my mind.

No...I don't think so.

"I'm not going to ask again. My family has lost too much these past few months. Give me one reason to trust you, and we will accept your help with open arms. How did you know my mate had been captured?"

I wait for him to answer, but when he doesn't, I turn away. My movement is immediately halted when a shrill voice rings out from the water bank on the river to my right.

"I told them!"

Prince Roarke's eyes flare with anger, and he shifts, blocking my vision from the voice that spoke. I don't have to move him, though, for the young girl pushes him aside with a shove, standing before me in a see-through shimmering silver dress, her light-colored hair wet.

"I told my brother that King Axel had been captured, Your Majesty."

I look between the two ocean creatures before me. They look to be siblings, though the girl's hair is closer to white than blue. She's slightly thinner than I—which I did not think could be possible—with bright blue eyes and cheekbones that glisten with purple scales every time she turns to the light. She trips on her too-large dress and almost falls into me when Roarke wraps his hand around her wrist and pulls her back, watching me with a wariness that disturbs me.

I would never hurt a child.

And that's exactly what this girl is, no older than sixteen.

"Forgive Princess Nalah, My Queen. She is only sixteen summers, not accustomed to the lands and the *clothing* they require."

He won't look her way, and it's obvious that he is uncomfortable with her attire.

They are surely siblings. Axel looks down at her, and I can see his beast retreat in the presence of such an innocent being. She only smiles up at him brightly, her naivety shining through to even Graven, who shifts into his human form, his eyes never leaving her face.

Oh...no. I recognize that *look.*

"I sneak away sometimes to watch the people. I've never seen the king before, but his crown kind of gave him away."

She twists her small toes into the dirt sheepishly. She's fucking adorable.

"I called for my brother as soon as I realized what was happening, but I did not know he was already on his way to speak with you both."

Her voice is soft as she addresses me, and she never loses her smile. A smile that reminds me of Ollie. A pang of distress lashes throughout

me, and I put a fake smile on my face and nod,
gesturing over to the trail we came from.

"Allow us go back to Atarah, and we will
speak more about aligning with the sirens and
mermaids. Anyone who wishes to help us defeat the general is welcome within our home
and at our table."

38
Elaudia

Nalah grins up at her brother brightly, bouncing with excitement.

Her childlike enthusiasm is precious. Until her brother shoots a stern look her way and tosses his head back towards the riverbank from which she came. The excitement leaves her body, and her smile drops into a frown for the first time.

"No, no...please! I'll be good, I swear! The other girls are still too fast, and they left me behind."

Roarke growls in annoyance, but nods to one of the males on his left.

"Krino will take you home."

Her bright pink lower lip trembles with disappointment, but she nods her head, casting a forlorn glance my way before looking at her feet. My heart squeezes painfully in my chest as she turns to walk away.

"Actually...I'd like for Princess Nalah to join us. I have some more questions for her. I assure you—she will be perfectly safe in my home."

Nalah's head flies my way, and she glances at me with a sort of reverence that I'm uncomfortable with. Graven is still silent, watching her every move. Roarke opens his mouth to disagree, but Axel finally speaks up, raising a hand to silence him.

"My mate has made her wishes known. Either agree to them or go back to the sea, young prince."

He's not going to leave. This means too much to him; I can see it in his eyes. He nods with a huff, pulling Nalah closer as Graven approaches. Graven takes a cloak from the closest horse and offers it to her, waiting for her to accept it. She does so with a bright smile, pulling on the fabric and immediately drowning in it. Graven's body relaxes slightly, invisible to anyone else's eye but mine, seeing as I'm the only one who has recognized the look in his eye.

Possessive.

Frantic.

Needy.

Graven has found his mate. His *young* mate. I'll need to talk with him soon.

The Sirens follow closely behind our soldiers on the trail, and I nod at Kettuna when she tilts her head, silently asking for permission to fly ahead. Axel and I wait until the last of them are out of earshot before we link hands, allowing the mist to surround us. The magic that comes with his fae powers engulfs us, and then a moment later, we appear in our rooms back home in Atarah. I look around, truly seeing everything for the first time since Ollie died. My husband's hand strokes down my spine. His gruff voice echoes in the quiet room as he speaks.

"I'm so sorry about Henry and Sofia, my love."

My nose twitches at his words as I feel the oncoming sting of tears. Before long, those tears are overflowing, and my body begins to shake with my uncontrollable sobs.

"I was so horrible to her," I say softly.

My husband turns me to face him, his eyes gentle.

"You were grieving our *child*, little warrior. She knew that. The things she said to you, they were only said to bring you back. She loved you more than anything."

I cry harder as he speaks, burying my face into the warmth of his chest. He soothes me quietly as he picks me up, forcing me to wrap my arms around his shoulders as he carries us to our bed. His hands stay where they are around my lower back as he settles us into the plush blankets. I wait for him to say something else, but he doesn't. He holds me and lets me cry while whispering sweet nothings into my ear. I cry until I can't anymore, and when I look up with sore, red-rimmed eyes, Axel presses a kiss to my temple.

"Henry sacrificed himself—they both did. For Cadmus and I." I whimper.

Axel nods. "I know my love. I saw everything that transpired."

In my mind—he means. It's honestly a relief not having to recount to him everything that took place in Lashforn. I sit back, still resting on his lap, but far enough away so that I can see his face.

His *beautiful* face.

My mate's usually clean–shaven face has been taken over with a coarse beard, but his eyes are still the same familiar color of honey. My voice shakes as I try to get out a sentence, giving out halfway through.

"I will never forgive myself for letting you go through h–his death alone."

He opens his mouth to stop me, but I shake my head frantically.

"No, I need to say this."

Axel clenches his jaw but lets me speak. I know he hates what I'm saying because he doesn't want me to blame myself for anything. But I do. I am at fault here.

"Even through my grief, I should have been there for you. The same way you were there for me. *Every. Single. Day.* You continued to rule Atarah and take care of me, all while you had to grieve *your* son. He was yours as much as mine, and I forgot that in my despair. But I will never forget what you gave me during that time. The chance to escape from this reality, all while you had to bear it tenfold."

My cheeks are wet with tears as I look at my mate. A part of me—the shameful part—wants to look away, but I refuse. He deserves more than this.

He deserves more than me.

"So...I am *so* sorry, Axel. I can only hope one day you can forgive me."

He doesn't wait for me to finish my sentence. He just swoops down and kisses me until I am panting for breath. His hands rise from my hips to cradle my face before sliding to my chin, tilting my head up so that his eyes meet mine.

"There is nothing to forgive, little mate. You carried our son for nine months. You felt him move within your belly. You brought him into this world. You had a connection with our little one that no one in this world could ever have. It only makes sense that you felt his death in such a severe way."

I'm crying again, and Axel rocks me gently, his words a warm whisper in my ear.

"I was *never* angry with you for how you needed to grieve. I only worried for you, my love. It's why I agreed to let Sofia take you to Lashforn. I feared I was losing you, as well."

I look up, my eyes wide.

"Never! Never again. I will always be by your side. I swear it."

One of his hands smoothes the wild strands of my hair away, while the fingers of his other tighten their hold on me. He lies back so that I rest on his chest, and he begins to run his fingers up and down my spine softly.

"Bador will greet the Sirens. Nelly and Bria will ensure they have comfortable accommodations. Rest, little warrior. I will be here when you wake."

I do as he says, not that it's difficult at all. Between the fighting and the loss of my aunt and uncle...and the tears I have shed, it's only a moment before I know nothing but the howling wind and peaceful bliss.

***

"She doesn't want to see us yet, Nelly. Let her first awake."

A soft voice hisses to my right, and I peek open one eye to see my oldest friends—aside from Cadmus—placing a tray of food by our bedside.

Cadmus!

I sit up in a panic and try to leave the bed, but Axel's arms band around me and pull me back. Nelly and Bria look at me as if I am a wounded animal, their eyes wide. Bria does not look like she has just lost the man she loves, so that must be a good sign. She speaks up at the look of hysteria on my face, her hands raised.

"Cadmus is just fine. I had Yarlon called to the castle to patch him up. He needed a bit more magic than a normal healer could provide. He is good as new, if not slightly sore."

A wave of relief sweeps through me, causing me to slump over, pressing a hand to my stomach.

"He's alive because of you. Clarice told us that you ordered her away with him...without you. Thank you, My Queen."

Bria's eyes shine with unshed tears, and she bows low before me. I choke at her words—and her *formality*. I did this. I pushed them all so far away. I stand with a kiss on Axel's lips before facing the girls, opening my arms wide.

"Please forgive me," I say softly, looking at both of them.

Their lips tremble for a second before they're both racing forward and into my arms, hugging me tight. I step back slightly from the force of them, but hold strong, inhaling their familiar scents of cookies and jasmine.

"We're so sorry."

"We should have done more."

"I thought we had lost you, too."

Their words jumble over each other, and I tighten my hold as much as possible with extremely short arms. They both place a kiss on my cheek, and I pull back, looking up at them. I take one of their hands in each of my own and hold them tight.

"It is I who should be apologizing. Thank you both for being there for me when I needed you most. I—I heard *every* word."

They spent endless nights by my chair, stroking my forehead with such tenderness and running warm clothes over my neck. Trying to coax me to the land of the living. A place my son would never be again. They grieved for the little nephew they loved more than life. Axel relaxes in bed, watching us closely. This is the first time his beast has retreated so much since Ollie's death, and I am relieved. I sit on the soft fox rug by the fire with the girls, their hands linked in my own, while we soak in each other's presence and enjoy the quiet of the early night. My husband stays awake, watching us diligently.

And for the first time since I lost my son, I feel like everything is going to be alright.

It will never be the same again...not without my Ollie.

But life will continue, and I will do everything I can to ensure I live this life for him.

Just like Sofia wanted me to.

39
Elaudia

His eyes are closed, though if the movement behind his eyelids is any tell, it looks like he is dreaming.

With the smile that gently stretches his lips, he is probably dreaming of Bria. I place a hand on his thick forearm, shaking him slightly. His eyes fly open, and he reaches for the sword by his bed, stopping when he sees me.

"Laudi..." He croaks.

I smile softly at him and sit on his bed, grinning wider when he attempts to scoot over to make room for me.

"You are a headstrong, stubborn mule." He rasps, clearing his throat this time around before he speaks. I let out a laugh of my own that sounds more like a sob. I shake my head slowly.

"It was the only way to save you. Henry was already gone, and Sofia left me no choice. She sacrificed herself for both of us."

He closes his eyes, breathing through his nose.

"I know." He whispers.

Axel must have seen him before I did to prepare him. He doesn't want me to get too upset too soon. Cadmus reaches a hand towards me, clasping mine within his, his eyes searching my own.

"I'm okay..." I say quietly. I look down and then back up, blinking furiously.

"Or at least, I will be. I want to think the worst of it is over now. Some people still need me, I have realized. And it was unfair of me to leave you all the way I did."

"You were grieving your child." He says, sitting up.

I choke a bit before shaking my head. "*Axel* was grieving his child. *Sofia and Henry* were grieving their grandchild. *You* were grieving your nephew. Everyone who loved Ollie was grieving his loss, and everyone in this kingdom felt his death. It wasn't just me. But I will never be able to thank you enough for the time you all gave me to mourn him. I won't leave you again. I will never go back to that."

Cadmus swipes a thumb over the back of my hand before pulling me down into a hug. I relax into his hold, soaking in the feeling of an old and well-known bond. I nudge my chin over his shoulder to speak without sounding too muffled.

"Bria told me," I whisper.

His frame stiffens as he sighs, pulling away.

"She was supposed to wait until you were better." He grumbles.

"I am as good as I can be at the moment. The girls and I had a bit of a heart-to-heart last night." I smile down at him encouragingly.

Cadmus arches an eyebrow as he pulls away and smiles.

"Congratulations, dear cousin. I mean that. A child is a cause for celebration. Not distress. She will be kept here, safe from the war to come. No one other than Axel and I know, and it will stay that way. We will give general Neem no upper hand on us."

His eyes harden as he thinks of the general getting his hands on his unborn child. A child they conceived just before Oliver's death.

"She has already been clucking about it to the entirety of the servants, but...thank you, My Queen."

"Oh, hush with *that*. I have been Laudi to you for almost a decade. That won't stop now."

His lips pull up into a grin, and he nods as Bria enters, knocking hesitantly.

"Thank you, Laudi." I nod at him and gesture with my head for her to take my place. She clasps my hand softly as we pass, and I head for the door.

"Axel and I will meet with the sirens and the council to discuss our next plan of attack. Rest easy, cousin."

He opens his mouth, most likely to argue that his presence by my side is required. I shake my head, stopping his argument.

"I will keep you informed of what is happening. I promise."

He sighs but nods, slouching into his bed once more as Bria climbs on to the bedframe to snuggle him. I smile at the sight, feeling a warmth build in my chest. I did not think I could feel pure happiness at the thought of another child coming so soon—but strangely—pure happiness is all I feel.

I nod at the guards waiting for me outside, and they follow me as we approach the war room. I changed this morning into something comfortable, but still wear my Nahirian armor under my black dress. The council stands promptly as I enter—the sirens entering shortly after—and I glance around, noticing Roarke, but not Nalah.

He clears his throat from his position, clearly picking up on my unasked question.

"I did not think it was appropriate for her to be present in the discussion of war, your Majesty."

Ah, yes...of course. I smile at him gently and nod.

"I will call her for tea later on in the afternoon."

His body relaxes, relief sweeping through him. It seems he wishes to protect his sister from everything in this world. Axel appears by my side the next instant, black smoke swirling around his body as he takes my hand. A few gasps from the sirens ring out as they look at him with awe.

Thankfully, Lynola speaks up, saving us from having to explain.

"King Axel, son of King Aeacus and Queen Cheche, the last Fae rulers before the war of Shamonhide."

We both nod our gratitude and go to our seats at the front. Everyone else follows suit and looks around the table, prepped to explain what territories General Neem currently holds. He holds almost everything. With Lashforn now gone, and Aland still in his clutches as a base camp, Atarah is the last standing kingdom in this war. The smaller cities never stood a chance.

"He has to be planning a large-scale attack. There is no other way to take Atarah than by brute force, especially with the number of free city civilians." I say, taking the lead.

The others nod, and the sirens sit forward, soaking in every bit of information we can offer.

"Why did the black witch capture King Axel, though? It makes no sense if they were going to just outright attack Atarah. Him being here would make no difference in the grand scheme of things." Prince Roarke has a point.

"Because they weren't focused on King Axel. They wanted Queen Elaudia lured away, where she would be easier to slaughter. She is the last of the Syraxes line, and the only one capable of destroying black magic."

Bristol swaggers in as if he owns the place, an arrogant look on his face as he speaks. He pops a grape into his mouth before swinging down to plant a kiss on my cheek, ignoring Axel's eyeroll. He plops down next to us, legs spread wide open. I have to admit, even though he is the cockiest son of a bitch I have ever met, he grows on you. I flash him a small smile and nod, coming to the same conclusion.

"You intercepted them, which they were not expecting at all," I explain. "And I arrived quickly, which was most definitely not their plan. They would have wanted to get as close as possible to their home base, but she could not take them all away with her magic since she was so close to the walls of the kingdom. The mages we have on guard would have sense the disturbance. How she infiltrated our castle—"

My eyes sting, but I clear my throat and continue.

"How she managed to infiltrate the castle the first time around is still a mystery, and if her magic was the reason, then it is strong magic indeed."

I look over at Axel, who sits quietly, drumming a thick finger on the table before us.

"I am now wondering how she managed to get on my lands at all. The mages would have felt it and told Bador immediately of any disturbance."

We only caught them in the woods because of the number of soldiers traveling with her. Not even her magic can transport so many at once. Bristol leans forward, his elbows on the table, and flashes my husband a wicked grin that promises *someone* pain.

"You, sexy King, have a traitor in your midst...or holes in the walls."

There are a few grumbles at that, and more than one male siren looks at Bristol with confusion. Most likely because he just referred to the great Fae King as *sexy*. I sigh and shake my head, letting my braid fall from my shoulders. It's getting hot in here. Axel notices my discomfort, and a moment later, I can feel the whisper of a cool breeze along the back of my neck. I toss him a grateful smile—to which he responds by squeezing my thigh gently.

Niho bangs a heavy-handed fist on the table, causing it to rattle. The troll shifter is thick, taking up the space of two chairs.

"So let us go hunting then, eh? It's been too long since I have enjoyed some good ole bloodshed."

Axel raises an eyebrow and tilts his head, studying Niho.

"We have only one true secret left in our arsenal that could be useful to us in the war against Neem, and that is the council's true identity. We cannot risk it over a traitor—if there truly is one. I will take care of it."

Opanic and Miranon—our tiger and wolf shifters, nod solemnly. Ballon only grunts his approval, ever the stoic old dragon, though I use the term *old very* loosely. Hydrandra blinks

her slanted eyes once before nodding her agreement. My mate leans back, staring at the druid
across from him.

"Tysla?"

The soothsayer stays quiet, her long brown
hair falling like a waterfall down her front.
She looks around the table with wise eyes before resting on me. I hold her gaze unflinching.
A moment later, she nods, her eyes falling shut.

"If a traitor walks amongst us, he will die."
She whispers.

It is a heavy burden to carry—to sentence a
life to death. But there is no room for traitors
in this war. The continent's survival depends
on it. Our people's survival depends on it, and
they are innocent. The council stands to leave,
our business with them concluded, but I motion for Prince Roarke and his men to stay.
Once the door has fallen shut, I turn to address
him.

"You know this war will mean lives lost on
both sides, correct?" Roarke studies me for a
moment before replying.

"The poison Neem is spreading reached our
home without warning, and my father tried to

get everyone out in time. Nalah was injured by a leviathan when she was just four years old, so she swims slower than everyone else. She would have been lost to us had my father not sacrificed himself for her. She had to watch him die. It's only been two weeks."

Oh god...the poor thing. My sympathy must reflect on my face.

"Our father, King Bulgoth, was a good leader. Now that he is gone, our people's survival falls to me. I take that responsibility with the utmost seriousness." He vows.

"So, you're not a prince then...you're now the Siren King." Axel drawls.

Roarke nods and sighs. "It does not yet feel right to officially take his throne. It's too soon."

The siren on his left nudges him with brotherly affection before looking at my husband, speaking softly, but sternly.

"That is what will make him a good king. He cares for his people. *Truly cares*. He only wants peace."

I look up at my husband, letting him inside my mind.

"We could use the reinforcements they will bring. Having a force of attack from the water could give us an upper hand."

Axel does not break eye contact with the sirens when he replies to me, his gaze steady.

"Neem will look for other ways to draw you out now that his first plan has failed. We need to go on lockdown. Wait for them to come to us. We can send the citizens to the bunkers in small parties of forty. It will take the next three weeks to move them without detection, but with our scouts watching, it should work. We can use that time to train the newcomers in human fighting techniques. Neem has twice as many fighters as we do."

"Would you two quit that telepathy shit! Some of us are eager to get in on the plans." Bristol sits back, whining to the ceiling, and I laugh softly. The sirens watch us curiously, having never encountered the abilities of a full-blooded fae male and his mate.

I address Roarke first.

"Your people will be welcomed into the Kingdom of Atarah with open arms. We will begin training tomorrow, while we let our informants gather new information on Neem's whereabouts to ensure the safety of our citizens before we move them." I can see the tension visibly exit his body as he slouches and nods, a grateful look in his eyes.

"Thank you, Queen Elaudia." His gaze flashes to Axel, nodding once more. "My King."

"Well, whoopee doo, we have more fighters." Bristol rolls his eyes and leans forward with an evil grin.

"Now, can we discuss the dead traitor walking? I'm sure I could convince Yarlon to come have a little fun with me."

I roll my eyes and stand to leave, putting a hand on Axel's shoulder.

"My husband can discuss the traitor's death with you. I have an afternoon tea to attend."

I place a chaste kiss on Axel's lips and moan when he pulls me back to take my mouth dominantly, thrusting his hot tongue past my lips. I sigh into his mouth, kissing him back just as passionately, when Bristol coughs and fakes a gag.

"Should we come back?" I smile and huff out a laugh, pulling away.

"You talk. I will see you back in our bedchambers." Axel's eyes promise me an orgasm, and I shiver in anticipation as I think of taking my husband to bed.

I smile softly at the guards waiting to escort me to my tearoom—which doubles as a small library—breathing in the smell of ink and freshly baked lemon tarts. I enter the grand room surrounded by limitless shelves of books. I spent countless hours here with Ollie, reading every book he could get his hands on. A flash of yellow catches my eye, and I glance at the book left in disarray.

The tales of a Pirate's son.

Oliver's favorite book. The last book I read to him. It still sits where I left it, lying open on chapter twenty-two.

We never got to finish it.

Tears burn my eyes as I breathe through my nose, lost in the memory of my son's kicking feet and giggling laughter. The Pirate's son had just tried on his father's hook and left a gash in the bedding. A smile escapes my lips briefly with a small sob.

"My Queen?"

I startle at the voice and turn to my left, finally noticing Princess Nalah as she slowly stands from her chair. She shuts the book she was reading and looks at me with concern.

"Are you alright, My Queen?" She steps forward, and I hurry to wipe my eyes, running my damp fingers over my dress.

"Yes...I'm quite alright." I fake a smile.

She keeps walking until she stands before me, her beautiful white hair hanging loosely to her waist. She looks at the book that had caught my eye, and her brows furrow in confusion.

"Is that a very sad book?" She questions softly.

Oh...such a sweet thing.

I look at her and can't muster anything other than gentle affection.

"No, sweet girl. Please, let us sit." She nods hastily and follows me, settling back into the chair she had taken over. Her wide, expressive eyes never leave my frame as she waits for me to speak.

"That book..." I sigh, taking a breath. "That book was the last book I read to my son before General Neem and Karisma murdered him."

Nalah gasps as she gently falls to the floor before me, reaching for my shaking hands.

"My Queen...I am so sorry! I should not have pried." Nalah's eyes shine brightly with tears and shame, and I shake my head, holding her hands with my own.

"It's alright, my sweet girl. It's only been a few months. To be completely honest, this is the first time I have managed to speak about my son at all. Ollie is—*was,* five. He was Atarah's pride and joy. He *is* my pride and joy. And I miss him every day that I draw breath."

Nalah watches me speak, not saying a word, but tears fall down her face. She stays kneeling by my feet and nods, looking down.

"The general has taken far too much from us all." She whispers.

I glance down, pulling her chin up so that her eyes meet mine.

"I am so sorry that you have lost your father to this war. Prince Roarke told us what happened."

Her lip trembles, but she straightens her spine. She's attempting to be tough, with determination in her bright blue eyes.

"Roarke is all I have now. My mother died giving birth to me. I've been begging Roarke to teach me how to fight for years, but he refuses. I think he is afraid of losing me as well. I could have escaped the leviathan if I had known how to fight."

I don't bother correcting that no one on this continent could single-handedly face a *leviathan,* let alone a mermaid as young as she.

"We have all lost in this war. But now is not the time to bow down. Now is the time to fight back, harder and stronger than ever."

Nalah looks up at me and smiles a hesitant smile.

"Is it true that you are the last Syraxes Bellator? I've heard legends of the Bellator's skills in weaponry and the art of battle. It always sounded like a bedtime story to put you to sleep." She murmurs sheepishly.

I laugh lightly at that and sit forward, nodding. Her eyes light up with excitement.

"Could you teach me how to fight, Queen Elaudia? Please?! Nothing too extreme that would give Roarke a heart attack, but I would love to know how to defend myself. The girls back home aren't always so nice. Weakness is seen as a fault of our kind. And I am most *definitely* the weakest." She drawls out, looking down at the floor.

I sit back, studying the small mermaid shifter. My heart aches for her, orphaned and left out. She is subject to distaste and apprehension because she is frailer than the others. She reminds me of myself. I stand slowly, allowing her to scoot back.

"The first lesson in battle is never to hide your eyes. You keep your chin held high. Let them look and judge, for you will be the last one standing."

She glances up with shock as I make my way to the door. I glance back and smile, taking notice of her still kneeling position.

"Come on then, young princess. It's time you learn how to defend yourself."

Her shriek of joy is so heart-warming that I don't even think to look back down at the little yellow book on my way out.

40

Elaudia

"Parry left! Back! Switch the blade into your left hand and strike!"

Nalah follows everything I say with precise movements, never once questioning me. I can see the slight tremble in her arm progress as we go on, but she doesn't complain.

Her eyes are bright with determination.

The training grounds are barren, most likely because everyone knows the true training begins tomorrow. The sun has dimmed slightly in the afternoon, and I welcome the cool breeze that comes with it.

Wearing the trousers and a loose shirt that I provided for her, the memory of her giggling with excitement when I laced the corset over her slight form brings a smile to my face. It was the only way to keep the clothing on her frame, as she is much smaller than I am.

***

"I've never worn a corset before! Some of the older girls back home would talk about them as if they were the key to getting a land man into bed!"

She giggles. "As if we don't roam the sea pretty much topless."

I roll my eyes at her and fake my shock, but she can see right through me. She told me tales of her home while I braided her white-blue hair into pigtails, her eyes never once leaving my face. I can tell she loves her home, but the people treated her far less than well anytime she went without Roarke's protection.

"They blame me..." She whispers, her eyes misting with tears. "For my father's death."

I clench my jaw and tie off the end of the second braid, turning her to face me.

"Your father did what every parent should do for their child. Protect them from harm until *their last breath. Do not ever think for one second that what happened was your fault."*

She sniffles but nods. I bite my lip before speaking softly.

"I wish every single day that I could go back. That I could take his place. I wanted my little fish to have a life...he hadn't even begun to live yet. And neither have you. Your father knew that. He sacrificed himself so that you could live on, carrying his memory. And that's what you need to do now. That's what we both need to do now. We need to carry their memories."

I wasn't expecting her to throw her arms around me, but she did. Squeezing me tightly, as if she were afraid to let go. So I squeezed her back, letting out a deep sigh.

"In times like these—of war and danger—we are only left with the family we choose. Remember that, little princess."

She pulls away and nods, her face serious.

"I will."

***

I look over to the fence that now hosts three figures and continues to grow by the second.

I should have known someone would spot us soon enough. I have not entered these grounds in quite some time. I continue to circle Nalah, instructing her on how to disarm a sword from someone's grip. My own swings up as I twist slowly, letting it fall into her waiting stance. She does exactly as I say, rushing forward to grip the handle of my sword before deflecting the blow and disarming me, pointing her sword at my neck. She drops it as quickly as it is raised, looking at me with hesitation.

I can see why.

I am the Queen, after all.

Clapping rings out from the posts, and I glance over at Bristol and Nelly, the former who straddles the wooden poles as if he owns them. Nelly's soft hair frames her face in loose curls, and I am surprised at how close she stands to the redheaded playboy. My husband's large form is the last one that my eyes find, and I grin as our mate bond sings between us. He smiles at me softly, a look of relief on his face.

"This is the first time in months that I have seen something other than despair in your eyes."

God, how I have missed the deep timbre of his voice in my head.

"It is hard to know despair in the presence of someone so innocent and full of life."

My mate nods, and his smile widens. I return to Nalah and continue our practice, determined to fit in as much practice as possible before I am pulled away for the call of war. My Bellator nature allows me to go for hours without tiring, but I can see the fatigue set in on her as the sun falls.

She's panting softly, her temples shining with sweat.

"We should call it for the night, sweet one."

We have been at this for five hours straight—her body showing signs of discomfort from pushing herself so hard—but she does not so much as wince. She has done better today than most soldiers in their first week here. She uses the size of her frame to her advantage, and she is remarkably quick despite the scarring on her two legs. The attack in her other form must have been brutal for it to show on her human body.

"No, please! I can go longer, My Queen." She steps forward, her chest heaving.

I reach over and push sweat-soaked hair from her face.

"You may call me Laudi. And you have *more* than proven your ability to learn the ways of self-defense and battle. But it is now time to rest and eat."

She opens her mouth to say something else, but a hard voice takes over, cutting her off.

"You heard Queen Elaudia, Nalah. Go and bathe before dinner." Roarke's tone leaves no room for argument, and I listen to my instincts when the hair on the back of my neck rises.

He has just stalked out of the castle's back entrance, and I find I do not care for the way he glares down at her. Nalah huffs but nods, flashing me one last smile before she leaves, her head held high. I smile at her confidence, no matter how new it may be.

Graven stands in the corner—not far from Axel—his arms crossed over his chest. Nalah briefly glances at him before she flushes and looks away, hurrying for the path to the foyer. I pick up the two wooden staffs we left discarded on the ground earlier, ignoring the look in Roarke's eyes as I turn away to shelve them.

"Just who do you think you are?"

A few gasps ring out from our spectators, and I stop, my body falling still. A ferocious growl rips from Axel's chest, but he stays where he is, waiting to see if I will handle this myself. He knows me well enough. Graven's icy eyes have zeroed in on Roarke, watching him closely as I turn around with a small smirk.

"I am Queen Elaudia of Atarah. I am *Queen* of the Syraxes bloodline, and mate to High Fae, King Axel." My head is held high as I speak, and I note that more than one spectator is watching with eyes widened in disbelief—shocked that someone would speak to me this way. Especially in my kingdom.

My home.

Roarke's jaw clenches as he regards me silently.

"She is not a soldier to train for battle. She is weak. Her body is not made to fight our enemies. The mermaids are to look at. They are not to be heard. They do not fight. They are not to be used for anything but breeding and alliances. That is our way. I offer you my men freely for this war, and the first thing you think to do is put my young sister in the fighting pits! You will cease teaching her immediately."

I scoff at that.

"You did not offer your men freely, young prince. Do not forget what my mate and I provide to your people while this war wages. As for Nalah, she is not *weak*. Your incompetence blinds you to the truth—and the truth is—Nalah has the heart of *twenty* Bellator warriors! Do you think I took it easy on her? Do you think I allow just *anyone* to know what makes *me* who I am?"

The crowd is even larger now, and Roarke swallows before he replies. "Everything I have done has been to protect her."

I approach him, waiting until he looks me in the eye.

"You're not protecting her by coddling her. This world is not for the weak. It is not for the soft-hearted. Not anymore. Your father is gone, and now you are all that remains between her and ten *thousand* dark rebels, along with their General, who wants to slaughter us all. One single defense could save her life in the weeks to come. So, I am not asking for your permission. I was too soft before, too naive to the threat he brings to us. And it cost me my son's life. I will not make the same mistake twice. At her request, I will train her twice as hard. I will teach her to be twice as ruthless. I will teach her to be a thousand times better than the warriors who stand amongst us now, if it will *protect* her."

My voice is hard as I speak, my eyes showing no forgiveness.

"I am Queen Elaudia of Atarah, blessed blood of the Syraxes line, and I take no orders from *you.*"

I don't wait for him to reply, stalking past him and over to my husband, who watches me with prideful eyes. Axel's hand reaches toward mine, intertwining his thick fingers with my slim ones. I nod slightly as we pass Graven, who returns with his own. The look in his eyes tells me he is not impressed with what he has seen of the new siren king so far.

That makes two of us.

The crowd disperses as we leave, and soon, only Prince Roarke stands, his body still in the middle of the training grounds. Axel reads the look on my face easily enough and sighs, kissing my temple as we walk.

"I understand his fear; I do. But you are right, little warrior. This is no time or place for the weak."

I sigh and lean into his embrace, grateful that he understands me so well—as he always has. I stand on the tips of my toes, pressing my lips into his, moaning as he grips my hips tight and pushes me against the wall behind us as he transports us to our room. My fingers slide to the nape of his neck, pulling at the grown-out strands of hair there. His chest rumbles, and I can feel his hard length pressing into me harder with each swipe of his tongue. I reach down to grip his cock through his pants, eager to feel the steely length between my palms—when he stops me, grabbing my wrist lightly before I can hit my target.

"My sweet little mate...there is nothing I would rather do at this moment than take you to bed and spread those creamy thighs. Your sweet cunt is a feast I have missed dining upon."

I shiver at the lustful words, nuzzling my face into his chest.

"Then what is stopping you, mate?" My sigh is breathy as I look up at him.

His sigh is heavy as he looks out the window to our left, his gaze falling upon a hill. It's like a bucket of cold water had been thrown over my head as my mind registers what I'm looking at. I look up at Axel, whose gaze is filled with sympathy.

"There is something you need to do first."

41

Elaudia

"Hello, little fish," I whisper.

The wind blows loose strands of my hair away from my face as I kneel in front of the grand tombstone, setting down pale yellow flowers in the place of the wilting ones. My lip trembles as I look around, taking notice of how the grass has grown back completely, the area no longer brown with dirt.

It's been that long.

I look over, catching sight of the two slightly bigger tombstones on either side of Oliver's. Something that Axel must have just done while I was training Nalah. My eyes drift over Sofia and Henry's names before returning to my son's.

"I've failed you all." My voice cracks as I say it, but I push through, clearing it.

"I don't think I ever knew the responsibility that had fallen upon my shoulders. Not until I lost you, Ollie."

A tear leaves my eye.

"What I am...it's a heavy burden. One that I no longer wish to bear."

My lips are trembling now, and I look down at my hands, clenching my knuckles tight until they are pale from lack of blood.

"But I will. I will bear it until my last breath, for all of you. I will kill him, and I will make this world what it once was again. I will live for all of you."

My eyes stray to Sofia's name.

"I promise," I whisper.

The clouds above me rumble as a storm moves in rapidly, and I almost breathe a sigh of relief as the calm rain washes the tears from my face, hiding my pain. The light rain trails down my son's tombstone, cleaning the specks of dirt that have drifted upon it. I place a hand on it as I close my eyes, breathing out.

"These past years have changed me from who I used to be. I will never be the same." I whisper, my mind flashing to the young, care-free girl I once was.

"You are a mother now."

I whirl around, catching sight of Graven. The dragon shifter regards me silently from a few yards away, his shirt soaked through.

"You *have* changed. Just because you no longer have a child, does not mean you are no longer a mother. That doesn't just vanish. I saw you today with Nalah; you treated her no differently than you would have Ollie if he were training for the first time. She was looking at you as if you hung the moon."

He snorts, smirking slightly, and I laugh with him as I wipe my sorrow from my face.

My tender friendship with Graven has been strange over the years, but I will never overlook the fact that he gifted me his skin. Skin that kept me alive in battle.

"Change is not bad, little Queen, though it can be painful. We only have the ability to move forward and protect the ones we love the best we can. Oliver knew nothing but love from his mother. He knew nothing but love from his father. Hell...this entire Kingdom. Remember that."

His pep talk must be over because he turns to walk away, only stopping when I hastily stand and call out for him.

"Is she your mate, Graven?"

His body tenses, and he looks at me from the corner of his eye. The drizzle has stopped, and the sun peeks out from behind a black cloud.

"Are you asking as my Queen?" He rumbles.

I snort and look away, shaking my head.

"I'm asking as your friend," I say softly.

He nods slowly, looking at the castle. I think for a moment that he's going to answer, but he doesn't. He just walks away, leaving me to my thoughts. Some people change. But others will stay the same. I can't say I expected much change from a centuries-old dragon. I stand up slowly, brushing the grass from my damp skirt.

"I'll see you soon, my love." I gently kiss the tip of the marble, then move on, doing the same to Sofia and Henry's.

I leave my son resting between two people who loved him more than anything, and I can feel my heart lighten just a bit, knowing that wherever he is—he is not alone.

I've only reached the entrance to the castle when my husband's voice brushes against my consciousness.

"Come find me, little warrior."

I smile and open the door, taking the staircase one at a time. Our large bedroom door comes into sight, and I almost moan when I catch the scent of freshly baked lemon tarts. My mouth waters as I open the door and halt in my tracks. The light in the room has been turned off, but hundreds of candles lie around the room, casting a soft glow as far as they can reach. Steam comes from the bathroom, and I walk over, letting my fingers trail along the soft bedding still rumpled from this morning.

"Axel?" I call out.

He doesn't answer, but as soon as I enter the bathroom, I catch sight of my stunning mate. He stands with his back to me in front of our in-ground bathtub, though I use the term loosely. It's big enough to fit ten people, with a natural warm water spring from below the mountain. Axel has stripped off his armor and clothing, leaving behind his body's sinewy muscles and sharp edges. I walk towards him slowly and reach out, smoothing the tips of my fingers over his spine. I kiss him gently under his shoulder blade, delighting in the shiver that takes over his body.

"Thank you," I whisper.

He knows I'm not thanking him for the bath he has prepared, though I am happy about it. My wet clothes cling to me like a second skin.

"You always know what I need before I do," I admit.

And he does. He knew I needed to see my son. Axel turns around, and I have to pull my eyes up and away from his long length, already half-hard.

"Little mate..." He murmurs, gripping my hair tight in his fist.

He presses a small kiss to my collarbone and then nips my neck, causing a yelp to escape my mouth.

"I will always give you what you need." He growls. His hands reach down, and I hear a slight ripping sound before he tears the blouse from my shoulders, causing my breasts to spill out from their binding. He feasts on my neck and then the swell of my breast, lapping at anything he can touch. I toss my head back, moaning into him as his fangs nip at my tender skin.

"And right now...you need to cum around my cock while I fuck you raw." He rasps.

I nod hastily, helping him get me out of my boots and pants. His hand grips my hips tightly as he forces me to turn around, bending me over the counter beside the bath. His fingers reach under, teasing my already wet pussy, and I moan as the tip of his forefinger circles my clit, making me arch my back into him further. He presses against me while his other hand pinches a taut nipple, making me whimper.

"Axel, please." I breathe out. The steam from the water hits my face, and I can feel a flush of red as it breaks out across my skin.

"Please, what, little warrior?" He growls.

I arch my back into his hard stomach, feeling the granite press of his abdomen. He switches to my other breast, pinching my nipple as his fingers work against my clit, bringing me closer to my release with every strum of his finger.

"Fuck me now!" I beg him.

He doesn't wait for me to beg again, thrusting in just as I shatter into a thousand pieces, my orgasm wracking my body violently. I cry out at the intrusion, wiggling my hips in an attempt to adjust to the sheer thickness of him. I moan as he impales me on his cock, fucking me into the marble.

"Oh...gods, it's been so long..." I moan.

Axel growls in response, but does not slow, fucking me as if I were about to leave him forever. His large hand is positioned on the middle of my back, holding me down as he takes what he wants from me. I give it to him freely. His cock slides against my walls, pushing them apart to make room for his large shaft. I cry out as he kicks my legs apart, causing me to arch my back further. This new angle causes the tip of his cock to hit my cervix with every thrust, and the pain mixes with the pleasure.

"Axel!" I yelp out, wiggling away from the severity of his fucking.

It's too much.

I can't think of anything else other than the warmth and steel of his cock.

"That's a good girl...cry my name." He snarls.

I sob against the marble, letting myself feel it all.

The pleasure.

The pain.

The connection with my husband that I was afraid had been severed. He must be in my head because he roars out, pulling me upright until my hands are secured behind my back, and I'm watching us in the mirror. My skin is flushed red, his eyes black with lust.

"Never! You and I will be together even in the depths of death. Hell will rip us apart by force and thrust me into the pits of damnation before this bond is ever severed."

Tears spill from my eyes at his proclamation, and I fall over the edge once more, feeling the warm release of his seed shoot inside me as he growls into my neck, biting the tender flesh with his sharp teeth. I'm panting softly as we stand there, soaking in the pleasure and magic of what just occurred. That wasn't just love-making.

That was fucking. It was raw and visceral, and it was exactly what I needed. I must have said the last part out loud because Axel huffs, brushing my hair from my neck.

"I told you that I will always give you what you need, little mate. You are now all that matters to me in this world."

I fall into him, my legs giving out, but his hands are there before I can crumple. He swoops me up and into his arms as if I weigh nothing, holding me close to his chest as he walks us into the still-warm water.

I moan as it laps against my skin, and he settles me gently between his thick thighs. My eyes are half closed as I try to recover from our passion, but I don't need to. Axel washes me, wiping the sweat from my brow with an orange-scented towel before rinsing my face with water. I let my eyes fall shut, soaking in the feeling of my strong mate and his scent.

"I'm sorry," I whisper. Axel's body tenses as he continues to wash me.

"*You do not bow before anyone.* You do not apologize. It is time you remembered who you are, little warrior. The Laudi I know does not make excuses, nor ask for forgiveness for things she could not control. Pull yourself out of this eternal agony you have created, and act like the queen you were born to be."

I snort at his hard tone, my lips twitching into an almost smile.

He's right.

"We have both changed, little mate. Before Oliver, I did not know I could love someone as fiercely as I love you. Now, I know that my heart is vulnerable in more ways than one. I thought you were it...and then your belly swelled...and I saw a greater life than I could have imagined." His breath is a whisper against my neck as he speaks, and a shiver goes down my spine.

"I *still* see that life, Elaudia."

I look up through my lashes at my husband, turning my face so that he can see my eyes completely. His thumb strokes my cheekbone softly, trailing down to my lips.

"You do?" I whisper, trying to put some strength into my voice. He nods and kisses me gently.

"It will never be the same as when we had Ollie, but it can still be good. We need to find our way back to it, little warrior. And I know that with you by my side, we can. Just remember Sofia's words."

I snuggle closer into him and close my eyes, thinking back to the last time I saw her before we left Atarah.

Get up and fight, she had said. I lower my head into the water, my mind flashing to her bloodied body in Lashforn.

Find another reason to live.

Her voice echoes in my mind

I open my eyes and turn to my mate, my heart aching at her memory, but my mind is set on my decision.

"I will live for the innocent," I say softly. I sit up and face my mate as the water gently ripples around us.

"I will live for those who cannot defend themselves against the evil of this world. I will fight for them...the men, women, and children."

Axel smiles as I speak, and he gently kisses my forehead.

"And I will fight by your side, little warrior."

42

Elaudia

The sound of metal striking and heavy breathing hits my ears, and I smile as my feet hit the dirt, noticing that Cadmus and Graven have already rallied the first round of rebels for training.

They need to learn our ways of fighting so that we might have an upper hand against the dark rebels. Their fighting styles are very similar. It is mostly men strewn about the grounds—with some women from Atarah—but I catch sight of Nalah quickly, standing at the front and centered closest to Graven.

My crown reflects the light, and more than one subject bow as I pass, breaking their formation. This one is slightly larger than the one I wear most often, featuring dark blue jewels embedded in the center. A gift from my husband early this morning. A black corset holds my white blouse close to my body, and my black leather pants cling to my skin.

"I was wondering when I would see your face again." A playful voice calls out.

I reach Cadmus in no time and allow his arms to fall around me, holding me tight. His arm moves up and down my back, moving my loose hair around.

"I'm so happy you're healed," I murmur. He hugs me tight before pulling away and smiling down at me.

"You didn't think I was down for the count? Come on...I'm much tougher than that." He jokes lightly, and I breathe a sigh of relief at the sight of my cousin standing tall and strong.

"Only because of that hard head of yours." I snort.

He huffs and rolls his eyes, standing back with me to look out at the grounds. Graven has everyone doing one-on-one combat, walking around them in circles, and correcting them as he goes. His eyes flicker between the combat and Nalah every other second, and I have to restrain myself from sighing.

"What do you think? The change of technique might be jarring, but the dark rebels won't expect fighting like this from people who lived underground in a bunker. Do you think it will work?"

He arches an eyebrow as he questions me softly, waiting for my answer. I look over the bodies in front of us, noting the determined looks on their faces. The camaraderie between them is strong.

"It has to."

"It will." A voice from behind says. We both turn to a sauntering Bristol, who smiles as if he has just been told a secret. I nod a greeting to him as he pats Cadmus on the back.

"Hey, tiny queen."

I roll my eyes, but say nothing, focusing on the fighting forms before us. Not everyone can be an obnoxiously tall giant like the company of men who frequent Atarah.

"Strike with the left, not the right. Once his arm is deflected, bring your foot down on the kneecap and snap it backward."

Graven's voice is loud as he speaks, and I note more than one female rebel eyeing him with lust. I can't say I blame them. The dragon shifter is covered in ancient tattoos from neck to ankle and has biceps the size of my head.

A female voice cries out, and my head snaps to the front corner, where Nalah is on the ground, hand to her nose. Prince Roarke stands over her, a look of regret on his face. I run over, pushing through the crowd of people, Bristol and Cadmus at my back. Graven beats us there by a second, his face curled into a dangerous snarl. Bright red blood gushes from Nalah's pale nose, soaking her beige training clothes.

"I'm okay..." She winces as she reassures us, and I kneel before her, using her shirt to wipe away the mess on her face.

"Look at me," Graven commands her, his voice like ice. I let go as she slowly lifts her head towards him. I note how gentle his hands are as he lifts her chin, inspecting the button arch of her nose. She whimpers softly as he prods the side of it, checking for a break. His frame is so large that her body is almost completely hidden by his.

"*Shhhh mihi minima saltator.* Let me see it." He rumbles gently.

My eyes widen in shock at the softness of his tone, and I stand up, letting him see to her. I turn to face Roarke, whose body is still as he looks down at his little sister.

"We are not working on combat today, only technique. There should be no physical striking." My tone is hard as I address the siren, and his jaw clenches.

"She needs to know what she is getting into by asking to fight."

I hear Graven snarl at his words as he stands, heat rolling off his body in waves. Scales emerge from the deepest recesses of his skin, and I can see more than one rebel back away, their eyes locked onto the very pissed-off dragon shifter.

I step between them and raise my hands.

"Stand down, Graven," I order.

He doesn't listen, lost in his rage. Graven almost bowls me over in his attempt to get to Roarke, but suddenly, I'm framed by both Cadmus and Bristol.

"Your Queen gave you an order, Graven," Bristol says, his voice hard.

Cadmus is eyeing Roarke with the same distaste I feel for him, and Graven snarls, his eyes black. I almost think I'm going to have to fight him to get him to calm down, when a small hand wraps around his wrist and gives a gentle tug. He turns and snarls, stopping immediately when he catches sight of who is holding onto him.

"I'm alright. I promise. Please listen to Queen Elaudia." Nalah coaxes him back, and I watch with shock as he follows her back a few feet. His skin slowly shifts back from scales to human skin, and every single person in eyesight is watching, mouth hanging open wide. I look at Roarke, who has a constipated look on his face at the sight of his little sister murmuring softly to the ancient dragon.

"In. The. Ring." I command Roarke softly.

Eyes whirl my way—Graven's rage forgotten—as I stalk to the fighting grounds. For a moment, I think he's going to ignore my order, but then he follows, a frown on his lips.

The crowd gathers in anticipation. Whether it be from watching the Queen of Bellators fight, or watching Roarke get his ass handed to him, I couldn't tell you.

"I don't wish to fight you, My Queen." His stance is relaxed, and I'm almost offended. I raise an eyebrow at him and circle him slowly.

"And why is that, Prince Roarke?" I drawl, my eyes roaming up and down his figure with distaste.

His lips are pursed together as he eyes my small stature. "Women should not be fighting."

A loud laugh rings out at the wooden posts, and I can see Bristol bent over on his knees, cackling so loud I'm sure Axel can hear him from his study. Cadmus murmurs to an approaching Bria, who nods and hurries away to the castle with a hand on her swelling belly. I can see now why Roarke did not wish for Nalah to learn self-defense. It is not because of some need to protect her out of love. He does not believe women should know how to fight. An archaic notion of a world that once was. But we are no longer in that world.

"You will fight me. Or you will fall."

He shakes his head, but I don't give him more time to contemplate or get out of it, rushing forward and striking with my labrys. His eyes widen as he unsheathes his sword at the last second, deflecting my blow. The tip of his blade still rests in its sheath.

He didn't think I was serious.

I whirl and lash to the side—aiming my hilt at his stomach—and he swings up, backing away from my strike.

"This war is not just about how well someone can fight their enemies physically," I say, striking again. We circle each other, taking turns deflecting blows. Every eye is on us, the crowd silent. I can see my mate walking towards us slowly, followed by slightly panting Bria. She should not be running in her condition. She's only human. I tell Axel that through our bond, but he only raises an eyebrow at me, saying nothing in return.

I turn back to my fight.

"This war will be won by courage and determination to defeat an evil that has taken everything from us."

I strike again, waiting until his sword deflects mine before kicking him in the stomach. He flies back, flipping over his head and losing the grip on his sword. I toss my labrys to the side, waiting for him to get up.

"It is not about weapons!" I say loudly. Roarke stands with a growl, the bloodlust of battle taking over. He's not enjoying getting his ass kicked by a girl, that much is *certain*.

He runs forward, swinging a fist wide and aiming for my head. I duck and spin, punching his kidney. He growls and turns towards me, his fist striking up for my chin. I lean to the right so quickly that he does not see me move, and I slap his hand away like an annoying insect.

Cadmus snorts, and Axel grins ear to ear as he leans forward on the post.

"*Such disrespect.*" His voice coos in my mind.

I ignore him, focusing on the important lesson at hand. Roarke is panting as we go about, and I keep in mind that about ten minutes have passed. I'm not even breathing heavily. I jump up, using my thighs to flip him, and I watch with satisfaction as he crashes to the ground, the breath knocked out of him. I leave him there, walking the length of the ring.

"This war will be won *together!* It will be won by intelligence and *faith* in each other. It will be won, standing side by side. Brothers and sisters united as one!"

The onlookers nod their heads, looking at each other. Nalah hasn't taken her eyes off me since I entered the ring—her nose no longer bleeding—and Graven hasn't taken his eyes off her. Standing next to the giant dragon, she looks minuscule, but I know the truth now.

She is his mate.

He won't say anything yet, and I can only assume it is because she is two years away from being a grown woman. At least his cock is not interfering with his ability to think rationally, though his possessive nature might be a problem in the future. I hear a scuffle from behind me, and my ears perk up just as Roarke shouts and stands, sprinting toward me. A few people call out—attempting to warn me—but I am already spinning, a rope of blue appearing in my hands.

I lash out, wrapping it around his ankle as I spin and pull, making him crash to the ground. His face smacks into the hard earth, and I can hear a crack as his nose breaks. I stand up straight and pull my power in, letting the whip hang from my hand in a blaze of blue sizzling fire.

"Stay down," I order him.

He groans and sits up, using his knees and hands to hold himself upright.

"Any young man or woman who wishes to fight may fight. I will never restrict you on account of your status, gender, or age. I know many of you have lost brothers, sisters, mothers, fathers, and *children* to this war. I will not take that justice from you. You will have what you desire if you wish to take vengeance upon General Neem and his army. I swear it."

The crowds shout, rallying together as I promise them something they have longed for.

The chance to exact revenge on a tyrant. I walk over to Axel, who watches me with a proud smile. Roarke is now standing, his eyes on me. His face is bloody as I stare him down. I wait for another dispute—but he only nods—letting it go. He glances over at his sister, who still stands protected by Graven, before stalking off, his siren guards at his side. Graven's eyes follow him until he disappears, and I watch him closely, willing him to look my way.

When he finally does, I shake my head at him. He knows what I'm asking.

Let it go.

His eyes narrow before he nods, looking down at the small mermaid at his side.

"Go find Nelly." He says softly. "She will help you clean up."

Nalah tilts her head up to look at Graven, smiling gently and wincing at the pain in her face.

"Okay." She whispers. I face the crowds, nodding at Cadmus and Bristol.

"Take an hour and then return for more lessons."

The people disperse like a flock, scattering about in groups. I notice more than one person patting each other on the back and laughing. Axel props a foot on the post and leans back, watching them go.

"They needed that." He says softly.

I look up, my brows lifting. "They needed to watch me kick someone's ass?"

My husband snorts and shakes his head.

"They needed to be reminded of why we are fighting as we are. Together. So many blood-lines united for the first time in a thousand years."

I nod and lean back next to him, letting out a sigh.

"My power is manifesting into something I'm not sure I can control," I murmur, ensuring no one else is around. Axel glances down at me, letting me speak.

"Sometimes I feel as if *I* will explode com-pletely, eviscerating everything and everyone in my path." The sun is high, and I squint through its brightness.

"You won't." That's all he offers me as he twines a hand through mine, and pulls me to-wards him, leaning down to devour my mouth.

"You need to eat. Then you can go check on Nalah. I know you're itching to."

I grin at my mate and laugh softly.

He knows me all too well.

43

Elaudia

I watch from the doorway as Nalah attempts to be tough, her lips pushed into a firm line.

"Do not fear feeling weak while in pain," I say softly to the disgruntled shifter. Nalah grimaces as Nelly pats her face, using warm water to wash away the drying and flaking blood.

"I don't want to be weak." She grimaces, looking down at her hands.

Nelly clucks her tongue at Nalah, tilting her chin back up with a smile.

"Stay still, little princess." She orders.

I walk over slowly, taking a seat on the cushioned chair beside her vanity. I had Nelly and Bria put Nalah in my old room, wanting to be close to the girl in case of an emergency. Axel had the door changed out after we mated and I moved into his bedrooms though, switching it so we could lock it from our side.

Bria enters in haste, carrying a yellow cream I've grown used to applying to my bruises and cuts over the years. She sets it next to Nelly and takes a seat, waiting to put it to use. The women of the castle have been fawning over Nalah, and I can see why. The poor thing is so gentle and innocent, with a smile that shines like a thousand suns. It is hard not to be enamored by her.

"I should have gotten up and continued through the pain! I disrupted the entire training lesson!" She insists. I roll my eyes and open my mouth to speak, but I'm cut off by a coy and feminine voice.

"You think you are the first to let pain overtake your lessons? Laudi couldn't make it through a single training session without moaning like a little babe her entire first month."

We turn to the newcomer, and I huff at Clarice, who leans against the doorway with crossed arms. Nelly and Bria giggle and continue treating Nalah, but the latter stares wide-eyed at my fellow Bellator sister. Clarice has at least a foot and a half on the girl.

"She couldn't?" She whispers. I snort and look at Clarice with pointed eyes. She just blows me a kiss and ignores me. I purse my lips, speaking up before she can cut me off.

"If I remember correctly, by month two, I was kicking your ass." My red-headed friend saunters in—hips swaying—as she takes a seat on the edge of the bed. She lifts a hand, preparing to whisper to Nalah.

"The first day of training, she cried because she twisted her ankle incorrectly."

Giggles burst out from my oldest friends, and I roll my eyes, feigning annoyance.

"Okay, I think she gets it," I laugh lightly.

Clarice smirks at me and leans back on her hands, relaxing.

"What Clarice is trying to say, Nalah, is that even The Queen of Bellators had to start somewhere. Everything I am now—my power—and the knowledge at my employ, were all earned over time. It has taken me years to get where I am, and you will get there as well. You need time, as you already have the dedication."

Nalah smiles softly and nods, tossing a grateful look at us all.

"Thank you for telling me that," She glances up at Nelly and Bria.

"And thank you for tending to my wound."

Nelly smiles, and Bria scoffs as if offended that it might even be implied that they would *not* care for an injured guest. Nelly pats her hand after she sets down the bloody towel.

"We are here to serve Our Queen. Whatever she may need, we will always provide."

I raise an eyebrow.

"So, if I told you that I believe Bristol has suffered long enough, and I think you should give him a second chance?"

Bria snorts her laughter before quickly muffling it and looking down. Clarice is cackling, and Nalah is looking around at all of us in a state of confusion.

"Bristol has been begging to court Nelly for quite some time, but while he was waiting for her answer, he got caught red-handed with his trousers around his ankles, and the stable boy on his knees."

Nalah gasps, bringing a delicate hand up to cover her mouth. Nelly grimaces and stands up, cleaning up the area.

"That promiscuous playboy has enough maids drooling after him; I'm not going to make another." Her huff is half-hearted, and I nudge her as she walks by.

"You could always use the situation to your advantage," I smirk. Clarice claps her hands and leans in close, her eyes alight with mischief. I was well-known back in Lashforn for my ways of plotting.

"Do tell us your plans, Laudi." The rest of the girls turn their bodies towards me completely, gasping in shock as I explain the plan to them. Nalah's bright blue eyes are alight with joy at being included, and a piece of my heart mends together gently as I look around at this close group of girls. My best friends, and a little princess who looks like a dream of a daughter, and second chances.

I tug Nelly's hand until she is sitting beside me in the large chair and glance toward the door, ensuring no one is eavesdropping.

"So, here's what you're going to do."

"You're sure it will work?" Nelly whispers.

I shrug and smile.

"He owes me a favor for a little secret I'm keeping for him."

***

I'm sitting at the dining table in the small lunchroom with Axel, his hand on my thigh as his fingers trace patterns around my knee.

I glance up discreetly at Clarice and Nalah, who pretend to be enraptured by the food on their plate. Bristol is eating fast, glancing up and around the room every few seconds. Cadmus and Bria are in their own world, smiling and whispering to each other. I peek to my left and nod at Graven, who stands stoically by the kitchen door. I can tell this is torture for him, as he continues to cast forlorn glances at Nalah, but the Princess is none the wiser, only excited for the scene that is about to happen.

I'm fairly sure her excitement for this is the only reason he agreed to it. Just as we planned,

Nelly rushes through the dining room doors, her face flustered.

"I'm so sorry I'm late! Some of our new girls got confused between the rooms and I–Oh!" She gasps as liquid drenches her front, her white shirt sticking to her breasts. Graven steps back, a grimace on his face.

"My apologies...let me help you." His voice is as stiff as his fingers as he dabs her shirt with a cloth. What makes it even better is that she did as I said and left her bindings off so that her breasts are now in plain sight through the thin white cloth of her blouse. I look over—watching Bristol's face turn as red as his hair—and then his chair shrieks as he throws it back, stalking over to the pair.

Nelly is giving Graven the come-hither eyes that I told her to give, which is only making Graven *more* uncomfortable. Clarice and Nalah snort into their food and cover their mouths, trying not to laugh. Cadmus is confused, but Bria and Axel smile my way. Bristol shoves the dragon shifter aside, his chest puffed up.

"I've got this." He growls.

If it were a real situation, I'm sure Graven would have planted him on his ass, but he only rolls his eyes and stalks off—but not without a pointed look at me. I toss him a wink and sit back, watching as Bristol fawns all over Nelly, his eyes glued to her nipples. Bristol mutters about clumsy dragons and pulls Nelly towards the exit, covering her see-through shirt with his coat. She tosses an excited grin back at us as they leave, and I wait until they have cleared the room completely before laughing, my eyes falling closed. Clarice and Nalah exchange a high-five before continuing their meal.

"So, you've moved on from war strategy to love plots? What can't my little mate do?"

I smile at Axel and shrug.

"I don't know what you're talking about." I smile coyly.

He hums at my answer before glancing at Bria, who can't keep a secret to save her life.

"It was *absolutely* perfect, you have to admit." She squeals.

It was.

Nalah finishes her lunch with a happy sigh before leaning back and looking around the table. Her cheeks warm, and then she speaks.

"Thank you for allowing me to dine with your family, Your Majesties."

I smile at her gently, not expecting Axel to speak.

"You are welcome at this table any time you wish, young one."

She grins at him brightly as she moves to clear her plate. I motion for her to set it down.

"Leave that. The staff will get it. You should hurry back to the training grounds; they will be picking back up on lessons very soon."

Nalah nods her head vigorously and rushes around the table. And then she does something completely unexpected. She throws her arms around me, squeezing me tight. I fall still, my breathing slow. And then I wrap my arms around her thin frame, hugging her back.

"Thank you." She whispers.

Tears sting my eyes, and I nod, pulling away and clearing my throat.

"Of course. Run along now." She turns and hugs Axel quickly, before running out of the dining room in an excited jog. I look at my mate whose eyes follow the young girl.

"She yearns for parental figures." He says in my mind. I nod, taking a gulp of my water. I know she does.

Axel sighs and nods.

"Whatever you wish, my little warrior. As long as you know it won't replace what you lost."

My cup slams onto the table, water sloshing out. The table grows silent, and I can feel three pairs of eyes on me. They know us well enough to know we are having an entire conversation in our heads.

"Nothing with ever fill the hole that Ollie's death left us with. But I still have love to give. So, I will give it. To whoever needs it."

I leave it at that and stand, throwing my napkin down.

"Excuse me."

The room is silent as I walk out, and I can hear Axel sigh before standing to follow me. I walk throughout the castle—through the back kitchen doors—not stopping until I reach the cliff. The cliff where it all truly started. Where Axel and I came together for the first time.

"I did not mean it like that, Laudi." His voice is loud enough to hear over the roaring of the wind of the day, and I breathe through my nose as my long hair whips around my frame like a raging waterfall.

I whirl around, facing my husband.

"You think I don't know it will never be the same? Do you truly think I do not fully comprehend it? Because I do! I promise you that I do!"

Axel sighs and stalks closer, his jaw hard.

"I can't see you like that again. Don't you understand?! Watching you like that? A shell of who you were? I had to watch you wither away into nothing for *months*! I will not let you recede into that ever again!" He's pointing at me as he speaks, as if will make what he is saying soak into the very core of my bones.

"Then don't! Don't watch me do anything! *Be there with me*! Through every step, as you always have! I promised you that I would never leave you again as I did, and I will keep to that promise until my last breath. I swear it! But don't ask me not to love a child who needs a mother's love. Because she *does*. She needs me, I can feel it."

I can hear the begging tone of my voice, but I don't let up. Axel looks at the sea briefly before he looks back at me.

"You barely grieved Sofia and Henry." I stop in my tracks at his words.

"It's as if you haven't let yourself feel the true severity of their deaths."

I close my mouth and slump forward. Axel continues to walk until he is in front of me, close enough that I can touch him, if I want. My mate's wide shoulders strain against his black shirt, and his spicy scent hits my nose, making my body relax slightly.

"It is not that I do not grieve them, Axel. With Ollie..." My breath hitches, but I ignore it.

"With Ollie, it was different. He didn't have the chance to live a *full life*...he did not learn the ways of battle from his father...he did not get to meet girls and sneak out of the castle to have late nights with his friends. He did not get to experience *life*. But Sofia and Henry? They did. They knew what they were doing when they sacrificed themselves, and while I miss them *every single day*—while I mourn them—it doesn't feel as severe as when we lost our son. Because they got to live, and he did not."

I shake my head back and forth, praying to God he understands what I am saying, what I have kept to myself since they died in fear of being judged. My arms wrap around my stomach as if that will stop my ache.

"And I know it's wrong. I know there should not be levels of severity to someone's grief—but for me, there are. And I can't change it." I grasp for the breath I can't seem to take as tears fill my eyes.

"Believe me, I've tried."

Axel's body flies into mine as he pulls me close, letting me cry into his chest. I'm so tired of crying. It's all I've done for so long now.

"*Shhh*, little warrior...I'm sorry. I'm sorry. I should have known."

I shake my head into his chest as he speaks and I pull back, sniffling softly.

"No matter our bond, you can't know everything inside my head. Not even the great King of Fae can be attuned to everything."

Axel's chest expands with a deep sigh, and I snuggle into his arms, relishing his tight hold.

"So talk to me." He says, pulling us to sit on the cliff's edge. He settles me into his lap and holds me close, his chin resting on my head, before he pulls back and presses a tender kiss to my forehead. His dark eyes stare into my light ones as he strokes my back.

"Tell me everything."

So, I do.

From the last words I spoke to Sofia, to the blooming feeling of tender love I feel for Nalah. I tell it all. And my mate sits and listens to me until the sun sets over the sea's horizon, and night swallows us whole.

44
Axel

"**Y**ou know, I thank the Gods every day that she found you."

I turn to look at Cadmus as he approaches me slowly. Elaudia has gone down to send off the first wave of our subjects—and to see Jaharis and Nyreen, who will accompany every group until the last. I move from my stagnant position on the balcony and nod at Cadmus.

"I'm the lucky one...to find my true mate in times such as these, it should be labeled a miracle."

Cadmus snorts and leans against the wall, still favoring his left side. He studies me closely as if trying to read my mind.

"I never thanked you for everything you did for her after Ollie."

I close my eyes and sigh at his words. I never thought there would even be an *after* when it came to my son. The first fae-blood to be born in hundreds of years. I should have been here. My guilt is strong inside of me—a living, breathing furnace of guilt and shame.

But I can't show it.

Not when Elaudia is still healing. I have to be the rock right now. I can bear it, though.

I *will* bear it.

For her.

"Never thank me for taking care of my mate. It is what should be done. She gave me the greatest gift of my life by bringing Ollie into this world. That gift is not now void just because he no longer lives."

Elaudia's closest friend nods before looking down, as if he is weighing the options of saying what he truly desires.

"Speak freely," I command him.

He sighs and pushes golden blonde hair away from his face.

"With Bria pregnant...I see so many things differently now. I have so many forces pulling me in every direction, and I can't tell what is right or wrong anymore. The decisions I have to make, decisions that have the power to change the lives of the people I love most. How do I leave her pregnant with my child? How can I abandon Elaudia to this war?"

He sighs and clears his throat, standing straight.

I study him for a brief moment before crossing my arms over my leather armor.

"You're here because you want me to tell you what to do."

It's not a question, but a statement. Cadmus clenches his jaw and stares into my eyes.

"I cannot tell you what to do. You made a lifelong vow to stand by Elaudia through all of the trials in her life. You made that vow before you knew love...true love. It is an impossible situation."

I walk over to him, placing a hand on his shoulder.

"But know this. Elaudia and Bria are two of the most kind-hearted and understanding women I have ever met. They will support you, as will I, no matter your decision."

His shoulders slump forward, and he nods. Bador knocks on the door and pokes his head in, his eyes falling on Cadmus, who straightens and claps a hand on my shoulder.

"I'll leave you to it."

Bador nods at Cadmus as he leaves and I lift my glass, sipping the fae wine I so rarely indulge in.

"How did it go?" I rasp after swallowing the last bit.

Bador clasps his arms together and smiles.

"It was a successful send-off, My King. They should arrive before dusk, and we will send the next group to arrive before tomorrow's sunrise."

I relax at that and nod, thanking him. Bador takes his leave, and silence returns. Alone with my thoughts, I stare over my great kingdom. A kingdom that has not been infiltrated in a thousand years because of its high walls and my discretion. These people rely on me to keep them safe; before now, they always were. The people of the Free Cities agreed to hunt and provide fresh and dried meat to the tenants of the bunker until this war is over, and I trust their abilities to do so discreetly.

I pick up the soft orange cloth that rests beside my bed in a drawer, breathing in the scent of my son. I've kept his favorite blanket with me every night. A reminder of what my failure to protect once caused. His powers were just starting to show, orange flames of fire telling me that he was going to take after my great grandmother's side of the family, with earth and fire elemental abilities.

My eyes blacken, my claws lengthening on my fingers.

I wasn't here when I was needed the most.

I will never make the same mistake again.

A horn sounds from the west wall, and I stand immediately, stalking over to the window. A horn sounding is a warning of approach at the wall. I set Oliver's blanket down on the bed, and then I'm gone in a cloud of black shadows. My guard startles as I appear, and he immediately points to an approaching party. A group of women who look badly beaten. A snarl escapes my lips, and I look at the guard to my right.

"Send for Queen Elaudia immediately."

He nods and begins to run for the stairs. I stalk to the edge of the wall and breathe in, searching for their scent.

Motherfucker.

They smell slightly like my wife.

Bellators.

A guard a few stories below converses with them, but I ignore it, appearing on the ground outside the wall. They stay where they are, not looking away from me. They are covered in blood, their clothes torn to shreds. There are seven of them in total, and they lean on each other as if seeking support to keep themselves upright.

"Elaudia." The dark-skinned one whispers from the arms of another woman. She and one other Bellator look to be in better shape than the others, but that mostly means they don't look to be dancing with death.

I study them, looking for signs of black magic. I see nothing. Moments later, the gates open.

"Zemira!" My wife appears through the gates, rushing towards the group with a look of disbelief, Clarice hot on her tail. They reach the girls and pull the most severely injured ones away, taking their weight. Elaudia looks up at me, her eyes wide. She glances at the two guards who followed her.

"Take them to the healing bay."

I look over the group once more before helping the brown-haired one who has blood dripping from her ears. She's moments from collapsing. I lift her into my arms easily enough and follow after my wife, nodding at my guards to close the gates behind us.

"Oh my god...how is this possible? There was no trace of them on the borders of Lashforn. Jaharis and I searched for days!"

Clarice is frantic as she looks over the women who are like sisters to them. My mate shakes her head, muttering to herself.

"We just need to get them to the healers. We can ask our questions later once we know they'll be alright."

A path is cleared for us as we walk, and we have to slow down more than once to keep pace with the only two Bellators who can stand on their own, though they moan through their wounds. One has a severe scar lashing through her mouth and neck, and the other one has gray hair, shorn at her shoulders in a ragged manner. We burst into the hallway in a frenzy, and Bria and Nelly are already standing there, clearing the way with wide eyes. The healers rush towards us, helping the injured onto beds and rushing for medical supplies.

"What happened?" Nelly gasps.

Before the two women still standing can respond, Kaleen hurries forward, pushing the healers aside gently.

"They were tortured." She says severely, waving a hand over the group. A flush of magic sweeps out, and Elaudia and Clarice both choke as we all look down at the seven women who now lie there unconscious.

"They should not feel what is about to be done to them. They should remain unconscious for the next few days while we work on them."

Elaudia nods at Kaleen, trusting her explicitly as the other two are urged into beds on the far side of the medical room and immediately fussed over. The healer from the bunkers is a quarter-blood spirit. She can see every working of the body, inside and out.

"This has to be Karisma's work! Only she would want to keep them alive for this long. General Neem would have just ordered them dead." Clarice paces back and forth before settling beside the woman called Zemira, tears filling her eyes. My mate looks over the lot of them, her eyes trailing them slowly.

"Juniper." She caresses the cheek of the one with bleeding ears. She moves over, naming them softly.

"Azylia, Desiora, Sage..." She ends at the honey-eyed blonde, her eyes sad. "Miyana and Vina." She gestures over to the other women before she looks up at me, her lip trembling.

"How long did we leave them to this torture? It's been five *years*, Axel." She shakes her head frantically as Clarice openly sobs. I pull her to my chest, looking over the injured. Kaleen chants above them, calling on her magic, and I watch as wounds slowly close, bones mending together.

"We know who is to blame, little warrior. Let us focus on that rage and aim it where it needs to go."

Elaudia nods and pulls away, gesturing for Clarice to follow.

"We are no good to them here, sister. Let us make our plans to avenge them."

Clarice frowns but nods, her tears drying as she kisses each forehead of the women lying in the medical beds. We leave quietly and head for the war room in silence. Cadmus and Graven are already present, waiting for us.

"He has to have a secret camp close to Atarah. There is no way they could have traveled too far in that condition."

Elaudia looks at the map as she speaks, moving pieces to the side slowly as her eyes peruse every territory. Her fingers trace the river's length to the east, landing on the ocean it leads to.

Clarice is the first to speak, her face still stained with tears. "Could it be Misit? Lord Krevosh had many plans, plans that could have been carried out even after his death."

I ponder Clarice's idea before shaking my head.

"We cleared the traitors out after his death; the implants we have there would have sent word if anything was out of order. No...they have a bunker somewhere nearby."

I watch my mate closely, her white eyes scanning the map with precise movement. I can see the wheels turning in her head as she draws on her power, her mind far more advanced than any other in this room when it comes to battle strategy.

"They've kept the route from Hilgonsfort to Aland to supply food for the dark rebels. Our archers continue to take out anyone who wanders too close to the borders." Her finger trails up, passing a cluster of trees and landing on the waterfall right after them.

"There! They wouldn't want to risk exposure to the elements if they've been ordered to stay for so long. They would have sought cover from us as well. There has to be a cave big enough to host thirty men."

"And five Bellator warriors in cages." Clarice sneers. My mate looks up at me.

"Have you ever traveled to Jioni?" She says gently, her brows furrowed with confusion.

I shake my head as my eyes roam over the map.

"Bador handled the outer cities; for the most part, they were small, too small to cause any problems. But if you're right and General Neem somehow overturned it secretly, we have a serious problem."

"And why is that? Other than the obvious?" Cadmus says. I sigh and let my beast come forward, drawing on my other senses.

"Because a century ago, my father created a tunnel system from the kitchens to Jioni so that refugees could safely enter Atarah as the war of Shamonhide began."

Elaudia curses by my side as I reveal this information, and she grabs her labrys from its resting position by her legs.

"Motherfucker! Clarice, secure the medical wing and then meet me in the kitchens!"

Clarice runs off to secure the wounded as my mate heads downstairs. I'm right behind her, scenting for anyone in the castle that I have been too busy to recognize.

"Someone would have seen a new face. Wouldn't they?" Elaudia half-jogs as we keep pace, and I shake my head.

"With the fall fest approaching, we hire new civilians every year. Sarabeth becomes over-run too quickly, and fresh hands help the parties go smoothly." Elaudia groans and turns left, taking the staircase towards the kitchen maid's quarters.

"You and Graven cut off the grand entrance; I'll take the back. Where exactly was it sealed shut?"

"Behind the ovens, a brick floor will be solidly built to come apart as a door. It should be sealed with steel." I growl.

My mate nods and jogs down the steps, her hair flying as she goes.

"I know you're already blaming yourself for this, Axel, but it's not your fault." I snort at Graven's comment as he catches up to me.

"I'm their King. It's my job to ensure this castle is secure."

Graven halts at the doorway and stands to the left while I take the right. I look at the guards on their posts and nod towards the side door.

"Do not let anyone in or out," I command. They hurry into position, raising their swords.

Clarice skids around the corner, barely panting as she nocks an arrow. I listen for my mate as she commands everyone to evacuate softly, not wanting to alarm anyone listening in from the tunnels. I open the door quietly and peek in, watching as she stalks to the back of the ovens and pushes them aside gently. Her eyes harden as she takes in the flooring below her, and her eyes flash to mine as she nods in confirmation.

Son of a bitch.

I nod at everyone else, and they tense as we wait for Elaudia to open it. I walk in and over to the other side, waiting for someone to lunge out as soon as she opens the door.

And they do.

As soon as she lifts it and flips it over, a man lunges out, sword drawn. Elaudia deflects the blow easily, causing the man to growl as he aims to tackle her. Elaudia smirks as he rushes forward, spinning so that he misses her. She takes the blunt edge of her sword and whips him in the back, watching with glee as he yelps in pain and falls forward. I stand watch at the door—ensuring no one else attempts to enter—as my mate plays with the enemy, letting out aggression that she has kept bottled inside for months. When she chooses to unleash her true rage on General Neem, I fear the damage will be catastrophic.

But she is *glorious.*

Just as she was when I first saw her, hair as black as coal, and lips so pink.

Her spirit is unbreakable.

My wife parries back and forth as I guard the trap door, using my power to seal it. She kicks the man in the chest, and I watch as he flies back into the doors, causing them to fly open. His head smacks the brick floor as he falls, but she ignores his groans. Using her foot, she rolls him onto his side. Elaudia leans down as he lunges, labrys at his neck, drawing blood.

"Move, and you're dead."

The hall is silent as we all watch my mate. Her lip is curled with disgust as she stares into his eyes.

"Now...You'll tell us everything we want to know, and if your information is useful, I'll make your death quick." She hisses.

I finish sealing the door with my magic and stalk over to them, nodding for Cadmus and

Graven to secure the man. He yelps as his arms are pulled behind his back, and I nod.

"Take him to the interrogation room."

The others follow after them as backup, and I take the weapon from my wife's hand.

"I can do this on my own if it is too much. Say the word, little warrior." She only shakes her head and twines her small fingers into my own.

"I told you I will never leave you again, and I meant it. We do this together."

45
Elaudia

The male I bested stands in the middle of the dark room, his hands restrained above his head.

Blood already gushes from his nose and split eyebrow, courtesy of Cadmus. My cousin backs up, and then Graven lunges forward, kicking his steel-covered boot into the man's kneecap, watching as it snaps back. Clarice has gone back to rest by our fellow sister's bedsides, waiting for them to wake up.

"That's enough," I say softly.

Graven and Cadmus immediately back up, giving Axel and I room to walk over. Our prisoner still wears the armor of General Neem, and my lip curls with rage at the insignia of the man who murdered my son. My power trembles beneath the surface, and I can feel my hair lift lightly with static as I watch the man who has pledged his life to a tyrant with no morals.

"I won't talk." The prisoner grumbles through his bloody mouth. I laugh lightly at that, getting into his face.

"Are you so sure about that?" I trail my finger lightly up his armored stomach, infusing electricity into the metal. His body bows backward as I electrocute him, and I can see all of the eyes around me widen at the sight of my power, which they have never seen. I pull away, cutting off the power circuit, watching with cold indifference as he slumps forward, groaning. Axel stays close behind me, watching me with keen eyes. I smack the man's face as his eyes roll back into his head, attempting to keep him conscious.

"Stay with me." I coo.

"Please...I don't know anything." He growls pathetically.

That makes me laugh.

"Yes, you do. Someone removed the seal from that door, and you know who did it. General Neem trusted you enough to guard the door alone."

I wiggle my thin fingers once more as he tries to scurry back from them.

"Tell me," I say, this time harder. I think of my sisters in arms, lying in those beds from *years* of torture. I think of my family, dead from this war...*my son*...dead. I push my hand back onto his body, this time lower. He cries out in fear, begging me to stop, but it's too late. His body shakes back and forth once more as I push my power into him a little harder.

A hand touches my shoulder lightly, and I withdraw my power immediately, fearing that I might hurt my mate. Groaning continues behind us as we stare into each other's eyes, mine with rage, and Axel's with worry.

"I will get the truth," I hiss into his mind.

My husband looks uneasy, and I sigh. He's never treated me as fragile, and he sure as shit better not start now. He shakes his head as he reads my mind.

"I'm not worried about that waste of space behind you. I'm worried about you pushing yourself too hard. When did this gift surface? How far have you ever gone with it? The static

ignited your fire, but you've never used pure electricity."

I bite my lip and look down.

"Lashforn," I whisper hoarsely. Axel's eyes narrow as he nods, stepping back.

"I'll support whatever you wish to do, however you wish to do it." I toss a grateful look his way and then glance back at Cadmus and Graven.

"You two should leave. We will handle this."

They both shake their heads. I look at Graven first with an arched brow.

"Prince Roarke was probably at the training sessions this afternoon." Graven's jaw clenches, not at the thought of the siren prince's presence, but at his proximity to a shimmering little mermaid. We would both prefer to be there to shield her from her brother's menace, but one of us will have to do. Graven nods and stalks to the door, leaving in haste.

I look over to Cadmus, but he shakes his head before I can speak.

"Don't even think about it. I don't know what you have on Graven, but nothing will work for me. We're getting answers today."

I huff, ignoring him. Cadmus steps up, waving a vial of herbs and toxic bluegrass under the prisoner's nose. He wakes with a shout, looking around before his eyes settle on me. He whimpers, a most undignified sound coming from a man.

"Please..." He sobs. "Please stop!"

I walk closer, grinning manically as he cries out.

"You know how to make it stop." I lean in, moving my hand to his neck this time. I'm an inch away when he cries out loud and piercingly.

"Bador Humar! Bador Humar!" He screams.

My heart stops in my chest, and I can hear Axel's breath stall in his chest as we stare at our prisoner. He cries harder, his eyes pleading for mercy.

"The man who helped us infiltrate the castle is named Bador Humar." He whimpers again.

Bador.

Our closest advisor.

Axel's hand for nearly five decades.

How did we miss this?

I look at Cadmus and nod, knowing he understands what I command. He sprints out of the room, sword in hand, and begins shouting orders.

I look at the man before me, a pitiful excuse of flesh. I glance back at Axel, waiting for him to recover from the treachery that was just discovered. I walk past the hanging man to the door and look over my shoulder just as Axel swipes his blades through the man, cutting him in half as if it were nothing. For my full-blooded fae husband, it isn't.

We leave together, passing by Yumin and his first guard.

"Seal all exits to Atarah immediately; no one gets in or out."

The castle is in a frenzy, with soldiers hurrying about in every direction I can think of. We reach the second floor, and I see Nalah hurrying up the steps, her face soaked with sweat from training and a beaming smile. My blood goes cold. I rush over to her, gripping her shoulders.

"Listen to me, my little wave; a traitor to the kingdom walks these halls. Go to your room now and lock the door!"

Nalah's smile falls as she glances between Axel and me.

"But I can help!" She protests as I shake my head.

"No. You are not ready. Please, do as I say!" I catch sight of a jogging Nelly and wave her over.

"Laudi, what has happened? Guards are searching the servants' staff rooms."

"Bador is the traitor. He's been working with Neem this entire time. Take Nalah immediately and hide in her room. Do not open the door for anyone but me or Axel. Promise me!" My eyes are shifting back and forth, watching our surroundings. Nalah has a look of fear on her face that I've yet to see. My hands leave her shoulders to cup her angular face.

"Do not fear, my sweet. You will be safe."

I won't lose another child.

She bites her lip and looks up at me through her eyelashes.

"It's not me I'm worried about." She whispers. I want to reassure her, but I can't say anything else because Axel nods at Nelly, ordering her to take Nalah. She struggles for a moment before I silence her with a look.

"I will come to you once we have captured Bador. I promise."

The girls hurry down the hallway, taking the back way to avoid the frenzy of guards. Axel and I keep pace next to each other as we stalk through the castle, eyes peeled for a certain redhead.

"Could he already have left the castle?" I glance up, questioning my husband.

He shakes his head with a snarl. Black bleeds from his eyes as he reels from this betrayal. Bador was playing the long game.

"I have no idea, it depends entirely on how many tricks he has up his traitorous sleeves. And to deceive me for so long...he had to have had many secrets. His mind never once stayed to thoughts of treachery." I say nothing more, knowing my husband is blaming himself harshly. We reach the back entrance to the training grounds when Graven rushes in, a tight and slightly panicked look in his eyes.

"*Where is Nalah*?!"

He almost bowls me over, and Axel's arms slide around my lower back, keeping me upright as he growls at the large dragon shifter. Graven growls back, his scales shimmering alive on his skin. Axel's eyes grow completely black as he pushes me behind him, his long black hair shifting over his shoulders as his form grows larger.

"Remember who you *challenge*, dragon."

I roll my eyes and shove Axel to the side, getting in between them.

"He's not *challenging* you, Axel. He's panicking for his *mate*."

Axel chokes at my words and looks at Graven with astonishment. I turn to Graven, offering him a tight smile.

"I sent her with Nelly to hide. Nalah is fin—" I can't even finish my sentence because a piercing scream echoes throughout the castle, stopping my heart.

Nalah.

"Nalah!!!" Graven roars, startling us out of our frozen state.

And then we're running. So fast, I fear my heart will burst from my chest at the panic that is taking over me. We race up the steps toward the second story of the castle, my blue fire alight on my hands. We have no idea exactly where her scream came from, so Axel can't shift us there with his magic. Graven has partially shifted, his serpentine eyes glowing in the dark halls.

Nelly lies on the floor just outside of Nalah's bedroom, her body unmoving.

"Axel..." I whimper.

"She's alive, just knocked unconscious." My mate confirms.

We get to the open door, stopping suddenly as we catch sight of a sweaty Bador with a knife at Nalah's throat. My little wave doesn't flinch or cry. Her eyes are hard as she struggles against the traitor, and I feel so much pride for her. Graven roars at the sight and stalks over to him, not realizing the threat present in his rage. Bador backs away and presses the knife in, causing light red blood to spill from her neck. Nalah whimpers once but then gets angry again. Graven halts in his tracks, his body shifting even more until he's larger than the doorway he just entered.

"I don't want her! I just need Queen Elaudia!" He's panicking at the sight of being cornered as soldiers flood in, Clarice and Cadmus front and center. A portal opens behind him, the black of its magic seeping into the room with a decaying scent of rot. I raise my hands, letting my fire fall away. I take my labrys and throw it to the left of me.

"Everyone, back up."

"Elaudia...?" Clarice questions.

"That's an order from your Queen. Back up, *now*."

I hear feet shuffling on the brick as everyone lines the room's wall.

"Graven...I'm going to walk to Bador. Bador will let Nalah come to you, and you will shield her from this mess. Do you understand?"

The dragon shifter growls, his claws flexing. I can only hope he reads the true intentions of what I just said. I look at Bador, my eyes searching.

"You watched me bury my son." I hiss. Bador swallows and glances back.

"Oliver was a gentle kid. But we're at war. You decided to bring him into a world of chaos and control. We need to wipe the world of creatures such as *you* so that we will truly be safe! Humans are superior—our numbers are vast, and Atarah's fall is how we will finally win this war."

I nod slowly, hands still raised. But my mind is thrashing as an evil and dark rage is slithering to the front of my mind at the thought of this bastard working with the man and the witch who murdered my son in cold blood. And now he threatens my little wave?

I look up at Axel and smile a watery smile, feigning despair at the thought of surrendering to Bador. I walk to Bador slowly, stopping halfway for him to release Nalah.

And he does.

He instantly throws her across the room and into Graven, whose thick biceps wrap around her slender frame, pulling her against the wall. Her eyes peek at me from under his arm, her face terrified for me. He put that look into her eyes.

I'm going to burn them *all.*

That look of fear.

I'm going to burn them *all.*

Burn the rot.

A foreign voice hisses in my mind.

Burn it!

I walk to him again, my hair lifting from the portal's whirl. He reaches out with the hand that is not holding the knife, pulling me into his chest. And then...I let it out. I scream as I twist, digging my nails into each side of his face as I let my electricity pulse out of my body like a tsunami, lighting his body on fire. I direct one hand straight into the portal, feeling a blissful sense of happiness when a blood-curdling shriek echoes from the other side.

The lights in the room burst as glass flies in every direction. My white eyes flicker like the dying sun as my power surges into Bador until nothing is left but bone. The portal closes, and I let Bador fall, his charred corpse hitting the floor with a thud. I'm panting softly as small shocks slither around my body.

And then I look up and into the shattered mirror hanging distorted on the wall.

To the sight of white eyes streaked with electric blue.

46

Elaudia

My mate's voice rings out, vicious—and leaving no room for argument.

"Clear the room."

Axel's order is sharp, and I look from the mirror to his eyes, noting the concern. Everyone exits in haste, though Nalah struggles briefly against Graven before giving up shortly after, realizing it is futile to try to escape the grip of a full-blooded dragon. Especially one who just witnessed a knife held to his mate's throat.

Not that she knows that.

The door shuts softly, and Axel walks to me slowly as electric shocks roll over my body in small waves.

"Elaudia?" His hand is raised as if to touch me, but he makes no move to make contact

with my skin. I look down at my hands, checking for any damage.

There is none.

I've never done such a thing directly.

"Lashforn..." I whisper, looking up at my
mate. It's hard to admit to him when I first
experienced the rush of this power, mostly because I'm terrified that he'll start to see me as
some kind of monster.

"I was too blind with my grief to see what
truly happened, but this must have been the
extent of it. I created a *crater*, Axel."

I realize then that he is trying to touch me,
and I close my eyes, willing my gift to retreat.
When I open them again, my eyes are their
normal hazy white hue, my gift gone for the
moment.

I feel stronger than I ever have, though.

"It's not supposed to be possible. That
gift—the *power* you just displayed—was exiled
from the world centuries before I was born.
My father said that the Goddess of Rage wanted to bestow her power upon the witches. But
her first experiment resulted in chaos and the
loss of thousands of lives. The God of Justice

deemed it too uncontrollable before he struck the witch down."

I look up at my husband as he speaks.

"Is anything truly not possible when it comes to me? I have defied all odds to this day. Maybe the Goddess of Rage is tired of General Neem's conquest. Maybe she is just as angry as the rest of us."

Axel shakes his head.

"She can't be. The Gods took a vote and destroyed her. The Goddess of Rage no longer exists."

My eyes widened, and I looked down at my hands again.

Burn the rot.

A voice had whispered in my mind. A voice I had never heard.

"Axel..." I whisper warily. His eyebrows raise alarmingly, and he pulls me into his arms, tilting my chin up so he can look into my eyes.

"I don't think they destroyed her...I think she's inside me."

His breathing stops as his body falls so still, I fear he is paralyzed, though his grip remains tight.

"Axel...?" I whisper with uncertainty.

My mate doesn't move. He doesn't speak. I purse my lips and raise a finger gently, wincing as I press it into his chest and release the most minuscule amount of my power. It does exactly as I wish, shocking him out of his stupor.

"Axel." I scold. "I'm right here, and I'm fine. There must be someone who has the answers for us. Even if she is somehow *inside* of me, she's never harmed me before. She has only influenced my gift to be even stronger. I'm sure we don't have much to worry over."

Axel releases a worried breath. "Until you are the one who makes her angry. We must go to Yarlon at once."

I raise my eyebrow at the mention of the mage who married us.

"Yarlon is one of the ancients. He was gifted _The Accounting_ before my father was even off the breast. The Gods deem one soul in each lifetime worthy of such an honor. The book has every account of The Gods and Goddesses' actions, but only if they interfered with humans and specific creatures of lore."

Axel grabs my hand lightly as he pulls me toward the door. I look down and clear my throat.

"Ahem."

He stops in his tracks and follows my gaze to the burned hemline of my dress.

"Go on and change then. I'll have Cadmus and Yumin dispose of the body."

I kiss him once before pulling away from his embrace. I head to the door and throw one last comment over my shoulder.

"Toss him off a cliff."

Axel's chuckle warms my heart, and I smile slightly. No matter what has happened or is *happening* to me, my mate and I will stand side by side, as we always have. It's not until I'm in my room that my mind brings Nalah to the forefront. I ring the rope on the bell, signaling for one of our servants. Bria rushes in a few moments later as I attempt to lace a new corset over my blouse.

"How often do we have to tell you that we are here for a reason?"

Her voice is light and playful, and I turn around, catching sight of her bulging belly. With the commotion of the castle only just dying down, I panic at the sight of her anywhere but resting in bed.

"And how many times do *I* have to tell *you* that you are absolutely *not* working in such a condition! Not to mention you haven't been my personal ladies in half a decade."

Bria only rolls her eyes at my irritation as she turns me around gently, her hands immediately fastening my corset with expertise I can only dream of.

"I'm pregnant, not disabled. I swear, you're almost as bad as Cadmus." A grin tilts my lips as she mocks the very words I said when I was pregnant with Ollie, and I toss another snarky comment at her over my shoulder.

"I'm sure I cannot give you the gift he has so willingly bestowed upon you." Bria giggles lightly and taps my ass.

"Harlot!" She scolds with a bright grin.

We laugh together for a moment before she finishes, and then she leans forward from behind, resting her chin on my shoulder.

"I've missed you dearly, my friend." Tears shine in her wide eyes.

I smile at our reflection in the mirror and grasp both her hands. The events that have just transpired weigh heavily on my mind, but I will not pass that on to my closest friends. I believe in Axel and Yarlon finding an answer if one is to be found.

"I've missed you too." I turn slowly, keeping hold of her hands.

"So, tell me...has Kaleen told you the sex of the little one yet?" Bria bites her lips and nods.

"We know the sex and the name." She whispers.

My eyes widen, and I lean in.

"Well, tell me!"

Bria shakes her head and laughs. "I promised Cadmus we would make the announcement together at the fall fest celebration." I huff lightly and smile.

"As long as you're not working the celebration...has Nelly found your replacement?" Bria shakes her head with a wince.

"Turns out our shoes are harder to fill than we thought. But we have some promising candidates!"

I smile at that.

"I trust you two avidly, I'm sure you will pick the best one." She goes to answer me, but her eyes widen as she hunches over slightly.

"Bria!" My heart races in my chest as I pull her to me, my mind a whirl of worry.

"I'm okay...I think the baby just kicked!" Her face spreads into a wide grin, and she laughs heartily as she pulls my hand to her belly, settling in on the lower right side.

"Feel...right here."

And she's right. A powerful punch knocks into the palm of my hand, and the joy that overtakes me is almost indescribable. I did not think I could ever have this joy again...these moments. Tears fill my eyes. Bria's own eyes widen with alarm, and she shakes her head.

"I'm so sorry, Laudi...I didn't think!" I silence her with a smile.

"Do not ever apologize for such a gift. I'm not upset." I laugh lightly with a sob.

"I'm just so happy for you and Cadmus. This is truly a blessing."

Bria bites her lip warily. "Really...? You're not upset?"

I pull her into a gentle hug.

"You and Nelly have been my closest friends throughout my life. My most loyal companions and ladies. I could only ever feel happiness for your joy."

I sigh and squeeze her tight once more before wiping my tears. She wipes a few from her own and smiles brightly as she rests her hands on her stomach.

"I hope you know that Nelly and I could not have imagined a kinder and generous queen to serve. We have loved every moment with you. We will be your faithful servants until death."

My eyes crinkle as I smile, and I shake my head.

"I only need your friendship."

Bria nods. "You have it. Forever."

A knock at the door startles us both, and Nelly enters with Nalah trailing behind her closely.

"Well, how come I'm always missing these little get-togethers? I'm fine, by the way. Just a bump to the head."

We both roll our eyes at Nelly, and I reach my hand out for her, grateful that she's feeling well enough to joke.

"I brought a certain Princess to see you. I thought she would claw Graven's eyes out if he kept her from you one more second. Not that I wouldn't pay to see it happen, it would be most entertaining...to think, the only creature on this continent able to put that grumpy old dragon in his place, and she is no bigger than a thumb."

Nelly smirks when Nalah elbows her stomach. As soon as she elbows her, she returns to nervously fidgeting with her fingers.

"She was frightened," Nelly whispers lowly. I sigh at the nervous mermaid and open my arms.

"Come here, my little wave." Nalah doesn't waste a second, flying across the foyer and into my arms. I step back an inch from the force before wrapping my arms around her slender frame. Sobs rack her body as she clings to me.

"I thought I was going to lose you, too!" She whimpers softly. My eyes widen as I recall the death of her mother and father, and I sigh, smoothing my hand over her silken hair.

"You're not going to lose me. That was *nothing*."

Her body continues to shake with her terror. Nelly and Bria look at her with soft eyes before Bria locks arms with Nelly.

"We'll go gather some tea for the young Princess."

I nod my head at them and smile gratefully. I wait until the door is shut before I pull away from her and lead her to the small couch at the end of the bed. We sit slowly, and I wipe the tears from her eyes gently. She sniffles slightly, and I look into her bright blue eyes, almost purple from the salt of her tears. She has partially shifted from fear, and I look over her shimmering purple cheekbones to her sharply pointed ears.

"Do you know what it means to be a Bellator, my love?"

She shakes her head gently, eyes wide.

"It means that my entire life must be sacrificed to others. I was made stronger, faster, and able to endure more than you could imagine. I was *made* that way so that others might be safe from the evil of this world. But to be a *Syraxes Bellator*, to be able to vanquish the power of black magic at every corner of this world, means that my life could be forfeit at any moment."

She whimpers softly from her chest and looks down. I lift her chin with my fingers.

"But it also means that I am *very* hard to kill," I say severely.

I smile at her gently and clasp our hands together.

"I'm not going anywhere anytime soon, my little wave. I swear to you."

Nalah smiles softly and nods, pulling one hand away to wipe her nose.

"I have to leave the castle with Axel, but I'll be back for the fall fest supper tomorrow night. Promise me you will listen to Graven if any danger should come about. He will keep you safe." Nalah nods and looks at me.

"Why does he care so much about my safety?" She questions, obviously confused.

I bite my lip as I look at the mermaid shifter, a girl who is barely of mating age.

"Because I have ordered it so," I say softly, keeping Graven's secret. She'll know the truth one day. But today is not that day. She nods and smiles as we stand, pulling me into one more tight hug.

"Go, my little wave. I will see you at dinner tomorrow."

I walk to the door and almost reach it when Nalah calls out softly.

"Why do you call me little Wave?" My heart clenches as I turn gently, a sad smile on my bow-shaped lips.

"My son, Oliver, was just learning to swim. He was a bit of a disaster at it...he would flop all over the place." I smile softly at the memory. "He was my little fish...but you...I saw you swimming with the others on my way back to Atarah just before we met. I didn't realize it at the time. It wasn't until you mentioned how far behind you would fall because of your injured tail that I put the pieces together."

She winces and looks down with shame.

"But I did not see a Princess who could not live up to her title. I saw a mermaid who was once gravely injured and only had to make shorter strokes than the rest. Who glided through the waves with sharp precision and determination that the others could never dream of making. Small—but fierce. A little wave."

Nalah looks up at me slowly, seeing herself through my eyes for the first time.

"You are delicate and may have to work against a few odds that others like you do not, but you will always come out stronger because of it. Never forget that."

Nalah nods, her smile this time as bright as the sun, and I can already tell she's going to head to the training grounds immediately. I exit my room and twine my fingers through Axel's, who has been listening for ten minutes.

I arch my eyebrow up at him, but he only smirks.

"Let's go find Yarlon, little warrior."

47
Elaudia

The streets are just as lively as they were on my first day here, and I look around at all of the innocent and smiling faces.

Fall fest will come tomorrow as we place a hold on sending citizens to the bunker. The ones still here were adamant that they do not miss the century-old tradition and feast. Vendors remain open for one more night, and then, before they leave—they will seal their stalls until the war has been won. People stop in their tracks, bowing as we pass by. I return their smiles and happy gestures, soaking in this night of peace.

"You know I'm going to do whatever is necessary to preserve the happiness of our people?" I murmur the words softly, hoping to keep them between us. Axel smiles and looks down at me as he bumps my shoulder.

"And I'm not?" He raises an eyebrow.

I snort and look around at the children running throughout the kingdom streets.

"I'm just making sure you don't attempt to run off and be the hero."

Axel grins down at me with a devious smile, leaning down to whisper in my ear.

"Don't worry, little warrior. I know my dark side is what gets that tight pussy of yours wet."

I gasp at his words as warmth pools in my lower belly, my abs clenching with a need for my mate. He pulls me out of the way of a rushing carriage, and we smile at the apologetic father attempting to wrangle the horse and two children.

"No..." I say softly with a smile. I look up at the night sky that seems to offer nothing but peace to us, and then I gaze into my husband's caramel eyes so filled with love, and I sigh.

"We'll do this together. Just like it should be."

Axel's smile is so bright, I feel he is competing with the stars as he pulls me close, kissing me soundly as we approach the alley that leads to Yarlon's home. Axel's lips are warm against my own, and I moan as his tongue invades my mouth, sweeping in before I can comprehend what's happening. He pushes me into the dark alcove off the main street before throwing out a shield to protect us from onlookers.

"Axel..." I whisper.

He continues to feast on my mouth before trailing down to my chin and then my neck.

"What is it, little warrior?" I can hear the cocky grin on his lips as one large hand tightens around my waist and the other around my neck.

Heat is building slowly in my core, and I can feel the walls of my pussy clench down as if seeking something to fill it. I let my head fall back gently as he devours me slowly, his teeth scraping the sensitive skin along my jaw.

"Yarlon..." I moan. Axel tenses, and I open my lust-filled eyes to find his beast staring back at me.

Shit.

"I was saying we needed to hurry up and get to Yarlon." I pant with apology. Axel's beast bares his fangs, sharp and deadly as his grip tightens around my throat.

"Saying another man's name while your mate's mouth is on your skin...such a naughty girl."

His growl is fierce as he whirls me around and pushes me roughly into the brick wall behind us. I glance up to see if he is maintaining the shield, but the pedestrians seem none the wiser. Axel yanks the belt of my pants off so hard that I fear he has torn it in two as he throws it to the ground below us.

"I'm going to remind you who this body belongs to, little warrior." His claws have lengthened as he drags them down my skin, but his beast is gentle, only scoring my skin lightly enough to bring a shiver of pleasure to the surface.

"Axel has been soft on you, mate. He's been *so* gentle with you. I think it's time you remembered your place." His snarl is severe, and I smile genuinely as I recall how often his beast and I have played together. He's such a dominant creature.

"My place is above you, is it not?" I taunt him.

His already hard body grows still like granite as he releases a deadly hiss. And then his teeth are in my neck as he bites down. I almost scream from the pain and pleasure, but then his hard cock is thrusting inside my wet cunt, cutting off any sound trying to escape. I moan as he begins to move inside me fast and hard, his pace punishing.

"Say my name, little mate. Who's fucking you?" His hand holds my face to the wall, and I can feel the brick abrading my flesh.

I fucking love it.

"What was your name...?" I pant with a grin.

Gods, he is fucking me so good. His dick pushes my walls apart with every thrust, and I can feel my slick running down my thighs. My fingers curl into claws on the wall, and he pounds into me with a fury at my response. His hand leaves my hip briefly, and I almost moan at the loss of contact when a sharp sting lands on my left ass cheek, quick and brutal. I cry out as he does it again, this time to the other one.

"Elaudia..." His warning is guttural, and I close my eyes as my orgasm builds, my pussy tightening with the promise of release. His hands grip my hair and yank it hard so that my neck is once again bared to his mouth as he licks the tiny amount of blood still there.

"Daemon was it...?" I push the limits of my teasing.

His answering roar is loud, and I can feel him begin to withdraw from my slick heat. I giggle and look back, my eyes half-closed with pleasure.

"Axel..." I moan.

He growls and thrusts back in, so hard that I can feel the first inch of his dick ram into my cervix. I cry out loudly at that, and I can see his lips curl into a grin.

"Axel!" He does it again. Over and over again at an unforgiving pace. His body is larger in this state, and I can feel my feet lift slightly off the ground as he fucks me hard.

"Say my name, little mate. Who is fucking this perfect little cunt?"

I whimper as he punctuates each thrust with every word.

"Axel!" I cry out.

The crest of release builds so high that I feel like I would kill anyone who tried to take it away from me. His pace becomes relentless, and I cry out as I come around his cock, my walls fluttering quickly and violently. Axel roars his as his orgasm hits him, and I whimper as his hot release coats my insides. I fall limply against the wall just as Axel's arms shoot out to hold me up. I sigh at the feeling of his large body closing in around mine as he pulls my pants up and straightens the corset around my blouse. His hand runs gently through my hair as I turn around and gaze at him with a dopey grin that would call for years of teasing from Nelly and Bria.

His chest expands as he inhales sharply, offering me a feral grin.

"I love the idea of you being in the presence of other men with my seed running down your thighs, little mate."

I giggle and let my head fall against his chest softly. His eyes have gone back to their original warm color as his beast retreats, and he presses a kiss to my scraped cheek.

"He was too rough with you." He growls. I smile up at him and roll my eyes.

"It was perfect." I sigh, placing a deep kiss on his lips as I stand on my tiptoes. He waits until we have both straightened our clothes to drop the shield. As soon as it has fallen, a voice from the left muses softly.

"It's about time. I was beginning to grow cataracts from staring at the door."

I laugh at Yarlon, who stands at the entrance to his home, his arms crossed, and a fake look of irritation dawns on his face. Axel huffs out a laugh and claps him on the back as we pass by, entering his home.

"Hello to you as well, old friend." Yarlon's lips tilt up into a grin as he ushers us inside, shutting the door with a grumble.

His hair has grayed over the past five years, and I can see that time is catching up with the mage. He shuts the door softly, securing it with a wave of his hand and yellow magic. In the years that creatures of the lore have become known once more to us, I have learned of four different types of magic, all gifted by the Gods.

Yellow magic is gifted by the God of integrity. Pure and true magic, only to be used for the safety of others.

Green magic, gifted by the God of Envy. Trickster mages and witches use this gift for their own gain, and we have had to kick more than one out of the gaming saloons in Atarah.

Red magic was gifted by the Goddess of Beauty, and those who possess it use it to enchant others. Not so harmful unless they are forcing another to love them for all eternity. We've been watching those closely over the years as they emerge.

And Black magic, gifted so sparingly by the God of death, that only one witch in the world is left with access to it. Karisma.

Yarlon gestures us over to his living area, and I take note of the new furniture. I raise an eyebrow his way. Yarlon loves his antique finds, and he hardly ever changes the scenery of his home. He rolls his eyes and nods to the back room, which I know leads to an even larger home that hosts his two daughters.

"Some showy mage has taken an interest in Gelda. He insists on only providing the very best for his future father-in-law. And well..." He trails off, a forlorn look on his face as he stares in the direction of his daughters.

"If you saw the look of utter love on Gelda's face, you wouldn't have been able to say no either. The hope of the girls finding mates was lost for so long, but now, with the crossways on the sea open once more...that hope is larger than ever." He waves a hand and sits in front of us.

"Never mind me, though. My King and Queen have need of me, so how might I serve you?"

I bite my lip and look down, wondering if I should take the lead on this or if Axel will. My mate only raises an eyebrow at me, and I sigh like a petulant child, and not the twenty-three-year-old Queen I am. I look back at Yarlon, who waits patiently, before I raise my hand and stare into my palm, watching as static sparks over my limb before lighting into a raging blue fire.

Yarlon's eyes widen, and he slowly leaves his perch on the cushion to fall before me. I let the fire fall away slightly before lighting it even harder and we all watch as electricity comes to life between my two hands. His mouth falls open, and he stares at me as if I am a deity in his presence.

"The Goddess of Rage..." He whispers. Axel tenses, and he cuts a look at Yarlon.

"So, you know what this is?" He says sharply.

Yarlon nods but never takes his eyes off my gift.

"Axel says it isn't supposed to be possible. He says that the Goddess of Rage was destroyed."

Yarlon nods, his face serious.

"She was. But what most don't know about Gods and Goddesses is that they can never truly be destroyed unless their very essence is ferried to the underworld by Thanatos himself. If not, their essence lives on. But it has only ever happened two times in our history. With the Goddess of Rage, and the God of Greed. They wander without a host until they reincarnate. Into whom...we have never known or heard of. Until *now*. The Goddess has chosen you, Queen Elaudia."

Axel stands and begins to pace, his frown severe.

"What does this mean for Elaudia?"

Yarlon's grin is bright as he stands slowly.

"It means she will win this war. The Goddess would have already corrupted her mind by this time if our queen were weak-minded. But she is not. She is a Syraxes Bellator..." He trails off and grips my hands gently.

"My Queen, have you ever heard her speak to you?"

I glance at Axel warily before sighing. He's not going to find joy in this news.

"Twice only. Recently. In Lashforn, and when I destroyed Bador. He put Nalah in danger—he put the entire Kingdom in danger, and I was so angry."

Yarlon nods as Axel swears viciously.

"Fear not, My King. Don't you understand? The Goddess has not taken control of Elaudia—because she *cannot*. Her will and her mind are too strong. Think of her as an extension of her powers, only truly coming to light when they are at their peak."

Axel walks over to me and cups my face in his palms, his eyes panicked.

"Are you positive, Yarlon?"

The ancient mage nods.

"My King, this is only good news, I vow it to you. Against General Neem, with access to this kind of power—she will be unstoppable. He stands no chance."

I can feel Axel's relief to my core as he rests his forehead on my own.

"I'm sorry I didn't tell you. It was all so new...and it happened so fast."

My mate shakes his head, pressing a kiss to my hand.

"I do not care...as long as you are safe. That is all that matters to me, my little warrior."

I frown, realizing the fear that must have been overtaking him. The thought of losing me, after we lost our son...it must have been crippling him. I wrap my arms around his thick form, inhaling his scent.

"My mind will never be broken. I will never leave you." I whisper softly.

I hope for his sake, you're right, little Queen.

My body tenses at the gentle whisper, but I fix it rapidly, praying that Axel didn't sense it. When he continues to hold me gently, I breathe a soft sigh of relief before replying to the voice in my head, my tone like a whip as it cracks against a stone.

I will never submit...to you or anyone else.

48
General Neem

I lean against the wall, my body failing me.

"I can't withdraw them from Lashforn. I must hold that land to succeed."

"You must. Rally them together in one place...you know where she is. It would be best if you killed her."

"I don't want to leave. I can't...there's too much danger."

"If you don't leave, she will come for you and take me away. Then you'll be alone once again. You don't truly think Karisma cares for you? She's only here because you forced her hand."

"No! Karisma loves me. They all love me. I must take back the lands and kill those wretched mystical creatures."

"You know what you have to do to complete that mission..."

"She has to die."

"You have to kill her."

"Kill Queen Elaudia, General Neem. Rip her apart piece by piece, and watch that bastard of a Fae wither away into nothing but dust!"

"Arghh!!"

The glass I throw shatters as I smash it into the chair, watching as the shards gather together on the floor in front of it, along with my haggard reflection. It's not real...

"You are not real!!" I'm screaming as I shout, my face purple with rage.

"Who is not real?"

I turn rapidly, catching sight of my little witch, the one who has never left me.

"Karisma..." I breathe, rushing forward. I place my hands on her soft, pale cheeks, forcing her to look at me.

"You must give me more, my dear one. He has returned, and he won't stop. Give me another dose now!"

I shake her body violently as her head whips back and forth, rattling her. She looks at me with a face full of confusion and pain.

"Who won't stop?" I grit my teeth and shake her once more. The young girl grimaces in pain, but I don't care.

"He won't stop." I hiss. "He says I have to bring all the soldiers here...he says that we must attack Atarah!"

Karisma places thin fingers around my wrist, and I can see that look enter her eyes, the one right before she tries to coax me down from this edge—as she attempts to convince me that there is no voice in my head. My chest heaves in anger at the thought, and I grip both her wrists and toss her away from me viciously. Her small form flies back, landing on the pile of glass I left on the floor. Blood spills from cuts along her arms and cheek, but I do not care.

"Give me more!!!" I roar at her.

Her lower lip firms as she shakes her head.

"I cannot! It took too much of me to go into the castle to take the child. And restraining King Axel took even more. I have not yet recovered...I'm losing my magic."

I cut her off with a snarl, my mind crazed.

She hisses in response as she stands.

"If I lose too much more, I will be useless in the coming battle! You know black magic is not limitless like the others!"

I roar into her face at the rejection and toss her to the floor, watching as she cowers away before her hand lashes out and a black mist leaves her body, trailing to mine. I relax and groan in pleasure at the feeling of the black magic entering me, smiling as the voice fades away into nothing.

"You can't keep me at bay much longer..." The voice taunts me.

My smile fades slowly into a frown as I look down at my hands, and then at Karisma, who is still shaking on the ground. My hands twist into my tangled hair, pulling at the roots, but I don't feel it.

I don't feel anything anymore.

49
Elaudia

The hallways are bustling with energy like never before, and I have to wonder if it is because this may be our last festival before the war hits.

Axel and I were torn apart from each other early in the morning to go about our duties, which mainly consisted of ensuring that everyone in the castle who was walking around actually belonged there. The tunnel has been sealed off permanently, but Axel continues to scour for any other secret passages he might have missed.

Once I've checked over the servants with Nelly, I head to the kitchens where Nalah has been learning every one of Sarabeth's recipes. My regular armor is in place for now, though I will be expected to dress for the occasion tonight. I push open the wooden door to a sight I did not expect.

"You don't think they care for you, do you? I am the only one left who cares! No one else would do as I have done, taking the cripple of the pack under my wing, as I have done with you."

I enter further to discover Prince Roarke standing over Nalah, who is wrapped in the embrace of Sarabeth. The old woman has a fierce look on her face, and it looks like she is about to tear him a new asshole. I'm about to step in when Nalah steps forward, pushing her finger into her brother's chest with a force I haven't seen from her yet.

"They do care! Just because you're an arrogant asshole who doesn't think I'm worthy of anything, does not mean that everyone else thinks like you! I *am* worthy. I am worthy of love and affection, and I will be ten times the warrior you could ever hope to be!"

Her pale cheeks are bright pink, and her blue eyes shine with unshed tears.

The pride I feel for her holding them back is enormous. Roarke stands with his mouth open wide, and I know from that look that this is the first time she has spoken back to him. His mouth curls with rage as he lifts his hand and strikes her viciously before anyone else can make a move. Her head whips to the side violently, and her body would have fallen if not for Sarabeth's embrace.

I slam the door open, causing more than one kitchen staff member to startle as it hits the wall, and I stalk over to him.

But I'm too late.

Because Graven has appeared out of nowhere, rushing Prince Roarke. Graven's large hands wrap around Roarke's neck as he slams him into the wall, his feet hanging off the ground. Graven has partially shifted, and I wince as his dragon scales come to the surface.

"You dare to strike my mate!?" Graven's roar causes plates to tumble from the counters, and I place my hands on Nalah's face, eyeing her reddened cheek.

Roarke says nothing.

He can't say anything because the hold around his throat is so tight that his face is slowly turning blue as he claws at Graven's rough, scaled hands. Nalah faces them both, her eyes wide as Graven's words sink in.

Motherfucker.

"I will send your rotting soul to the underworld myself." Graven hisses with serpentine eyes.

Nalah leaves the comfort of mine and Sarabeth's arms to approach the two men slowly, her arms outstretched. Her hand rests gently on Graven's shoulder, and he snarls, turning bright yellow eyes her way. His hiss cuts off at the sight of her, and she shakes her head solemnly.

"Let him go."

To my shock, he listens, immediately releasing the siren prince. They both step back as Roarke sinks to the ground below, hacking and gasping for air. Nalah's soft green gown gathers on the floor as she kneels in front of her brother, her eyes devoid of emotion.

"Meet me at the training grounds in twenty minutes. If you do not show, I will take that as you being the coward I now know you are."

She leans in closer, whispering to him so softly that I know only those of us with enhanced abilities can hear her.

"And we both know you are too proud to lose to a girl."

She stands slowly as Roarke glares at her back, and I bare my teeth at him in warning. I wait until she has left the room before ordering everyone back to work.

"My love...I need you here."

My voice is quiet but firm as I reach out to Axel's mind. I don't wait a minute before he appears by my side, his face confused. I sigh softly as Roarke stalks out of the kitchen, face filled with rage as he shoulders Graven to the side.

"It seems my little wave has something to prove today," I murmur.

Axel raises an eyebrow at my comment before pulling me close, pressing a warm kiss to my temple.

"What would fall fest be without a bit of family drama?" He winks as he says this, and I giggle, thinking back to the first year we celebrated the event together.

Cadmus and Bria had their first lovers' spat at the dinner table, resulting in an honest-to-God *food fight*. I sigh happily as the memory hits me before following Axel to the training grounds.

"Unfortunately, this family drama will be a call for blood, not flying boiled potatoes." I huff at the thought, my worry for Nalah rearing an ugly head.

Axel shrugs his thick shoulders as we walk, and I gaze up at him, eyes narrowed.

He only grins.

"Nalah has been working with the Queen of Bellators for weeks now. She has improved greatly. She and Cadmus even tied in their duel a few nights ago."

My eyebrows raise in shock. Even though Cadmus is human, he has been training in the art of battle since he was a young boy. To tie against him means she must have been extremely clever whilst dueling him.

Graven's heavy footsteps pound behind us as we emerge on the training grounds, and I sigh when I see that they are heavily occupied already. Word spreads fast in this castle, and almost everyone not on mandatory festival preparations is here. I peek around Axel's large form, spotting my fellow Bellator sisters standing around Clarice like a beacon.

I rush over at the sight of them healed and standing tall. They bow as I approach, and I snort.

"I can count on one hand the number of times I've seen you bow to someone, Desiora. And you grew up in a castle."

My beautiful friend smirks before rising, her long black braids falling over her shoulder as she lifts her head and hugs me close to her chest. The others follow suit, bringing me into their arms one by one with soft murmurs of gratitude. I pull away and make a face.

"Do not ever thank me for such a thing. I should be the one on my knees, begging for forgiveness. We had no idea you lived. If we had known, we would never have stopped searching for you. The border of Lashforn and Aland—it was nothing but ash and blood."

I wince at the memory, and Juniper shakes her head, noting my misery.

"The black witch made sure you could not trace us. We always knew, and we never placed the blame on you...or Clarice. The witch showed us visions of you here, with King Axel. She believed seeing you happy and safe would turn us against you. But she underestimated our bonds to you."

Her voice is soft, probably because of the new deafness in one of her ears.

Sage steps forward, her blonde hair swishing against the tops of her shoulders.

"Nothing could ever turn a sister against a sister. We saw your son...Oliver." She trails off, biting her lip.

"We are so sorry, Laudi." Desiora's voice wobbles as tears fill her brown eyes. Sage nods as she echoes Desiora's sentiments.

I smile softly as Zemira picks up where Sage leaves off.

"We fought so hard to try and warn you—but her magic was too strong."

I shake my head fiercely as tears well in my eyes, and I look around at the five women who made me into the warrior I am today.

"You endured unspeakable things...because of me. Because I was naive to this war."

Azylia opens her mouth to speak, the scar across her face stretching wide, but I cut her off.

"I was. But I won't be ever again. General Neem has reached the end of his life, and I will kill him for everything he has done to us. I promise you, they will both pay for the suffering they inflicted upon you."

"We know you will. And we will be by your side to help you." I smile at Azylia before turning my gaze to the training ring. Sage turns, smirking as Nalah steps out into the ring, her face twisted into a severe frown. She wears the new armor I gifted her for training, pausing briefly as she passes by Axel and me.

"My Queen, My King..."

I can tell she is uncertain if we approve of what is about to transpire, but as I glimpse the fading blow on her cheek, a savage smile tilts the corners of my lips.

"Do not go easy on him," I say. Nalah's lips abandon the downward tilt as she sighs her relief and turns to face Prince Roarke.

"It seems you will have another sister in this war," Desiora says softly. I shake my head, gripping Axel's hand tightly.

"Not a sister," I murmur.

Their heads turn my way, watching me watch my little wave.

"A daughter."

A few eyes widen, but they quickly harden and nod, turning to the duel about to begin. They will now forever protect Nalah as fiercely as they would have Ollie. Right before Roarke lashes out with the first strike, Zemira speaks loud enough for those around to hear, proving my inner thought correct.

"Then we will protect her with our lives, My Queen."

I can only nod as the battle begins, and Nalah dips left to avoid Roarke's strike. She twirls around and crouches, kicking his legs out from beneath him. But he does not go down. He lands on his left arm and flips backward, standing to face her once again. She strikes first, this time landing a punishing combination of blows to his kidneys before bouncing away on the balls of her feet. Roarke growls and swings his right arm out, trying to catch her throat.

"She's quick." Axel murmurs. I smile lightly as she dances around the ring, evading when necessary and attacking when he is unbalanced.

"Just like I taught her. To be small is to be quick."

I grin as Axel huffs and pulls me into his chest, his heavy arm banding around my chest. Cadmus whistles in appreciation as Nalah backflips off a wooden post, using the momentum to strike Roarke across the face with her booted foot. Blood spurts from his nose as he growls in anger, and he rushes her again. He grips her collarbone, and I watch him expand his claws, drawing blood. It's not until she smirks that I realize she *let* him get a hold of her.

Juniper and Sage exchange a wide-eyed look before Clarice says,

"Is she going to...?"

Yep, she is.

A loud cracking fills the air as she head-butts him and flips around, using her thighs to strangle her brother as she flips him forward, breaking his arm as soon as he is on the ground. She releases him immediately, scrambling to her feet and backing up a respectable distance. Roarke stays on the ground, a keening sound leaving his bloody lips.

"I don't think the boy has ever broken a bone." Axel muses in my mind. I snicker and look up.

"I think his fragile ego is what was just damaged."

I nod towards the siren soldiers, who continue to watch the events unfold closely. Nalah slows her breathing before approaching her older brother and offering her hand to him. My chest swells with pride at the act of honor—and I smile—but it's quickly wiped away as Roarke's lips tilt down in a vengeful snarl.

He's quick, but I'm quicker.

I am already hopping the wooden fence, using my gifts to propel me forward and into the middle of the siblings. I catch the clawed hand that was meant for Nalah's stomach and twist it away, breaking that arm as well. Roarke screams through the pain, but that sound is quickly cut off as I kick him in the chest, forcing him into the wooden post behind him.

"You dishonor your people with such a show of disrespect. Only a true coward would attack after he has so clearly been given a peace offering."

Murmurs ripple through the crowds as everyone watches me with wide eyes, including the sirens. I can see the males letting their eyes roam between the siblings, confused. Honor holds the highest esteem among the sirens, as Nalah has told me. From the looks on all of their faces, it seemed she was right.

"Get out of My Kingdom." My voice is hard as I speak, and a gasp ripples across the crowd, but no one dares to question my decision.

Roarke looks up at me with a bloody sneer and attempts to rush me, but he's stopped in his tracks as his body locks up, freezing in place by an unknown force.

"My mate gave you an order, young princeling."

Axel's voice is dark as he addresses the siren who just tried to attack me. Roarke's body cracks in a few more places, and I hold back my wince, noting Axel's anger. Just as quickly as he stopped him, he released him, letting him fall into a heap on the ground. Axel nods to our Royal Guard, and I watch as they rush forward, picking Roarke up and dragging him away.

I turn slightly, waiting for the other sirens to follow. But they don't. They all share a look, almost so brief I barely catch it. And then they enter the ring, one by one, until they all stand in a line before Nalah, who stands tall with wide eyes.

"You bring honor to our people, Princess. Allow us to serve you."

The world around us is completely silent for a few moments before the crowd cheers, and I catch a proud look on Graven's face as Nalah smiles softly and continues to do so, even though the raging screams of her banished brother echo all around.

50
Elaudia

Nalah winces as I clean more blood away from her face before quickly correcting herself and sitting tall.

I snort and look at our reflection in the mirror.

"You don't have to act tough all the time now, little wave. There are times when being allowed to be vulnerable is scarce. You must take the reprieve when you can."

Nalah sighs as her shoulders slump down in defeat.

"Did I do the right thing?"

Her bright blue eyes meet my white ones as she continues to frown. I move onto her hair, pulling it away from her face as I begin weaving it into a braid. She is silent for a few moments before she speaks again.

"He was right about one thing. He saved me when no one else wanted to. He took me into his care."

I tie off the end of her hair, fluffing the braid I wove together as I purse my lips.

"Your brother was never going to change, and while he did help you in a time of need, that does not mean you owe him the rest of your life. You will never fit into the mold he crafted because you are meant for much more."

Her eyes shine with tears before she closes them and nods. I reach around and lift her chin, stepping slightly to the left to stand by her side at the vanity she sits at.

"I am so proud of you. What you did today was not easy; I know it. But it is what needed to be done."

Nalah sniffles softly before falling into my embrace. I hold her gently as she cries, soothing her with whispered words of hope for a better future. I pull away and wipe at her eyes, smiling as her cheeks shimmer purple in the fading light of day.

"Mourn for what is lost. But do not dwell on it. Tonight is a cause for celebration, perhaps one of our last for a while. Let us enjoy it."

Nalah nods, helping me to wipe her tears.

"You're right...I'm sorry." She sniffles.

I shake my head, hushing her.

"Do not apologize for how you feel. But you might need to apologize when Nelly realizes you haven't made it in time to act as a buffer between her and Bristol."

Nalah snorts, adjusting her skirts as she stands.

"What has he done this time?"

I grin as we walk to the door, nudging it with my shoulder so it opens.

"He decided that Nelly needed the most beautiful flower of all, for none other compared to her beauty."

I flip my hand with a flare as I mock the foolish red-headed male. Nalah's eyes furrow in confusion.

"A Kelpaif flower is treasured for its beautiful violet colors that fade into a bloody orange—it rivals the brightest sunsets on the continent. It is native to Atarah, unfortunately for Bristol and Nelly."

"Why is it unfortunate?" Nalah inquires. I smile widely as I recall Nelly's bright red face, filled with anger.

"Because the Kelpaif flower is poisonous, its pollen is known to inflame the skin and cause terrible boils to those who hold it."

Nalah's breath leaves her in a whoosh as she covers her mouth with her hands, her eyes wide.

"No!"

I snort at the memory of my two friends in the infirmary early this morning as the healers worked their magic on them. I've never heard a male apologize so much, but Bristol intended to earn a puffy-faced Nelly's forgiveness before the supper we are about to attend. I don't think he'll be successful if I know Nelly at all.

"Should I hurry then?" Nalah questions with a giggle.

I glance out of the corner of my eyes to Nalah, her face still glowing with laughter and disbelief. I nod.

"Run."

***

Nalah barely made it in time, slickly sliding into the seat next to Nelly just as Bristol entered, his face still peeling.

They look much better, and I grin as Nelly covers her face, attempting to hide from the love-sick fool. His face falls comically when he sees that both seats on Nelly's side have been occupied, and I watch as his chest puffs up before he stalks over. The look of false bravado quickly leaves him as Graven shakes his head severely, warning the rebel away from Nalah.

He perks back up, reaching out a hand to prod Bria's shoulder. That hand is quickly tossed aside by a smirking Cadmus, who tuts his finger at Bristol like he is a naughty child. I try to smother my laugh with my hand, but the entire scene is just *too* hilarious.

"I would laugh too if I didn't feel so bad for the poor sap." I whirl around, my eyes dancing with delight at the sight of my mate.

"How bad can you feel bad though? We had classes for those who settled with us from the bunkers. Bristol just didn't pay any attention."

Axel smirks before shrugging.

"I know what it's like to feel that tug. It starts here...in your heart." His thick hand caresses my left breast in the shallow light of the alcove, and I sigh.

"Then it continues further down, planting itself here, so fierce you feel as if you cannot breathe without just one touch." His hands tweak my nipple through my dress before trailing down to my core. My stomach heats as my mate continues to touch me softly, whispering in my ear.

"Then it ends here..." His hand grips my pussy tightly, causing me to grind my pelvic bone into his wrist as I attempt to relieve the pressure. I'm panting softly as I look around, ensuring no one has spotted us yet.

"And then it goes up, just to start all over again in an endless cycle of torture—well, until they put us out of our misery."

He whirls me around, and his lips crash down onto mine. I moan as his tongue swipes along the length of mine as we battle for dominance. He wins, as he always does. I nip at his bottom lip, drawing him down so that I don't have to stand on the tips of my toes.

"Ahem!"

I startle out of my daze and twirl around, blushing as a dozen sets of eyes meet mine. I clear my throat and adjust my dress, stepping away from Axel. Cadmus, who broke us out of our lust-induced stupor, stands as we approach. The rest follow suit, waiting until we sit at the head of the table, before falling into their seats again. I elbow Axel, who only grins arrogantly.

His power over my ovaries is concerning sometimes. I look around as everyone continues coming to the table, taking their seats and softly chatting. All six of my Bellator sisters have joined us, and they mingle with the siren guards warmly. Food is served promptly, and I roll my eyes as the men dig in eagerly.

Sarabeth's cooking is other-worldly. Chatter lights up around the table, and I smile softly at the sight, breathing in this moment of peace. Music plays softly, the strings of the violin calming my heart. I moan around a bite of buttered lamb, and Axel growls lowly.

"Careful with those sounds, little warrior...I am famished for a taste."

I chew slowly and take a sip of my wine before coyly responding.

"I'm quite famished as well...Nalah! Sweet thing, pass the sausages if you could."

Nalah smiles brightly and passes the platter of hog sausage to me, never the wiser to mine and Axel's foreplay of words. But Bria is, and she snorts into her glass, attempting to ignore us. A hand curls completely around my thigh in a possessive grip as I take two sausages from the platter and pass them down.

"I'll give you the meat you crave just as soon as this supper ends, little mate." Axel purrs softly into my ear, his nose nuzzling my cheek gently.

My belly clenches in anticipation as I pretend to be unaffected by his lustful words.

"Now, darling, you know I am not a fan of turkey." I look away and take another sip, only spluttering when the grip on my thigh moves up through the thigh-high slit in my gown, dipping under and into my panties.

"You and I both know I wasn't talking about turkey." His voice is husky as he teases my clit gently, and I thank the Gods for our high festival table and rambunctious company.

"Axel..." I warn, my cheeks flushing.

"Hush and come around my fingers like the good little slut you are."

A peek into his black rimmed eyes tells me that his beast is ready to play, and I grip his coat sleeve tightly as he works the bundle of nerves between my legs with expert flicks and pinches. The thought of someone catching us only fuels me further—as he knew it would—and it isn't another minute before my core is clenching down in release as it searches for something hard and hot to clamp down on.

I hide my face in his neck as my orgasm crashes into me, and to anyone else, it would look like two lovers whispering words of affection to each other. I whimper softly as he draws his two fingers out of my wet and sticky pussy, lifting them to his lips.

He inhales softly before opening his lips, licking my release from the thick digits. His eyes flash completely black at my taste, and I open my mouth to scold him for such an act of voyeurism. Before I can even get the words out, a glass clinking draws my attention away from my smug mate. I turn and look at Cadmus and Bria as they both stand, the latter holding onto her bulging stomach gently.

Her cheeks are flushed pink with joy, and her golden locks trail down her back gently. Her pregnancy has only furthered her beauty, and I smile at the sight of true love and joy in their eyes. Jaharis and Nyreen look up at their son with all of the love and affection in the world for him. A hush falls across the large crowd, and the five tables in line across from ours all go silent as they watch my Royal Protector.

"As many of you know, Bria and I came to Atarah nearly six years ago to serve our one true Queen, Elaudia Sonella Syraxes."

Glasses rise all around as people toast our health.

"Long live the King and Queen!"

I'll drink to that. Cadmus waits until they have spoken to continue.

"What you may not know, though, is that no other monarch in this world has existed, or ever will, with a heart and soul as pure and kind as Our Queen's is. By her side, I have known pure affection and joy, and I have been given the gift of finding what many of us yearn for...true love."

He looks down at Bria and pulls her close with one hand, his other still holding his glass.

"So now, here at our sacred and long-held tradition of the celebration of fall, a coming of new times and bonds, I wanted to announce that the healers have confirmed our babe to be a little girl, and she shall be called Sonella—in dedication to her godmother and Our Queen."

Cadmus raises his glass to my tearful face, and the room cheers. I look up at Axel, who smiles at Cadmus, and I know he is grateful to my cousin for this gift he has given to me.

I stand quickly, reaching my two friends and embracing them hard, my grip so tight I begin to fear I will hurt them. My face is wet with tears as I pull away. I gaze up at both of them as Bria takes my hand.

"We owe you everything." She says softly, her eyes bright with love. I shake my head, looking between the two of them.

"Family owes me nothing. I am delighted for you both, and cannot *wait* to meet her."

Cadmus smiles down at Bria before replying softly.

"Me either."

With the crowd's roar—and the toasting that continues, I don't catch the exact meaning of his words as I hug them again.

Not until it's too late to change it.

51

Elaudia

The sun is streaming through the gossamer curtains, and I smile softly as the warmth of it hits my exposed skin.

I twist in our bedsheets so that I'm facing my mate, giggling as he pulls me close to his chest and places a kiss on my lips.

"Good morning, husband." I purr.

"Good morning, wife."

His lips trail down my jawline as he speaks, licking the spot where my neck meets my jaw. I soak in the silence of the dawn and Axel's scent, preparing myself for the difficult day ahead. Axel's fingers run through my hair softly, and I groan as he massages my scalp.

"We have to go see off the last group."

Axel sighs against my skin as I murmur to him, and he growls.

"But I still have so many things I wish to do with this delicious little body of yours."

His claws lengthen slightly, and he scrapes them against the swell of my hips until I'm arching my back under his touch. His fingers trace up until they are circling my pebbled nipples, and I whimper softly as he pinches and pulls them until they are taut points.

"You have magnificent breasts, little mate." He growls lowly before his mouth descends upon them, biting and sucking viciously.

My mouth falls open as he pleasures me, but no sound comes out. His tongue flicks against my hard nubs, and he rolls over so that he is on top of me completely, settled between my thighs. The muscles there burn as his large body stretches me wide, and I can't help but run my fingers all over his muscled body. I can feel his hard cock nudging my entrance gently, and I reach down, desperate for the feel of his thick length.

My fingers have barely touched it before he swats my hand away and thrusts inside me without warning, forcing my walls apart in the most spectacular way. My wet cunt is pulsing from the work he's done on my nipples, and I know my womb is aching for another round of his seed.

Axel thrusts in and out viciously like the beast who lives under his skin, growling as my pussy attempts to suck him in with every thrust. He's fucking my body deeper into the bed with every movement, and I love every second of it.

"I want to feel those tight little walls clench around my cock, Elaudia. Be a good girl and let me have all your release."

I groan at his words, feeling my belly clench, and I reach my finger down, rubbing my clit gently. The additional stimulation sets me off as Axel's lips crash down onto mine, as I come apart, crying out as my orgasm soaks his cock. He shudders hard, and his hand tightens in my hair, pulling so hard that tears sting my eyes but only further my violent orgasm.

"Little mate..." He growls, shooting his seed inside my belly. I can feel the hot jets of his release as they pulse inside the walls of my pussy, and I sigh blissfully as Axel relaxes on top of me gently, holding his weight off of me with his thick arms.

"I love you, Elaudia...more than life itself."

I smile at his hoarse confession and meet him halfway, kissing him languidly as we bask in the aftermath of our lovemaking. I look down at the simple but expensive band that adorns my ring finger, the ring that once belonged to his mother, before looking back up at him.

"And I love you. More than my own life."

***

Axel holds my hand tightly as we exit the archway that leads to the stables, where the last wave of our people waits to say good-bye to us—Including Cadmus and Bria. Nelly is back at the castle training with my sisters-in-arms, her decision to stay and fight firm. She's been training over the years in her spare time, but she's no bloodthirsty warrior. Still, I could not change her mind.

My eyes water with sorrow as we walk around the horses, moving out of the way as the stable boys move them around and saddle them for the journey. I quickly find Cadmus's honey-blond hair standing tall amongst the rest as he stands, embracing Bria tightly. Before I can reach them, she pulls away, her face streaked with tears as she tries to offer him a watery smile.

No.

No, no, no.

My heart thuds harder in my chest as I stalk over to them, my eyes wide.

"You can't do this!" I hiss, my heart aching.

He sighs and turns to me as Bria cries in earnest now. But it's not Cadmus who speaks, telling me I'm wrong. It's Bria, her hand resting gently on her bulging belly. She's at the tail end of five months along, and her bump has begun swelling beautifully.

"It is not your choice, Laudi. It is ours. Cadmus made a vow to stand by you in war, and he is a man of his word. Don't ask him to abandon you in this time of need."

I sputter at her words; frantically look between two of the people whom I love dearly.

"So, you're asking me to let him abandon *you*!? His pregnant wife!"

Axel squeezes my hand, but it doesn't look like he is learning anything new. He must have known.

And he said nothing.

Cadmus clears his throat and lays a hand on my shoulder.

"We are not asking anything of you, Laudi. Bria and I made this decision together—as one. We both agree that I am needed here with you more than I am needed down in the bunker. Bria will have all of the supplies and help she needs. She and Sonella will be safe—and I will be here, watching your back, as I have done my entire life. It is my *sworn duty*."

Cadmus speaks firmly, leaving no room for discussion. I look into his eyes once more before switching to Bria's. My friend offers me a watery smile and nods before pulling me close and embracing me tightly.

"You watch his back, too, okay? I need both of you to come out of this alive. Sonella will need both her father and godmother."

My eyes sting, but I nod into her neck before whispering.

"I swear, we will win this war."

Axel clears his throat and arches an eyebrow at Bria, who laughs. She leaves my arms and walks into my husband's gentle embrace.

"She'll need her godfather too, so don't do anything stupid." Bria punches him lightly in the stomach.

Axel chuckles as he releases her.

"I'm offended at your lack of faith in my abilities."

Bria rolls her eyes and walks back into Cadmus's arms.

"Not a lack of faith in your fighting abilities, just a lack of faith in your ability to focus when Laudi is involved."

My mate snorts but doesn't answer, only nodding to them both before turning to help the others prepare for departure. I sigh and look up at my cousin, searching his eyes for any chance I might have to change his mind.

There is none.

"I'll let you two say your goodbyes," I murmur, turning away. Cadmus gives me a grateful smile before pulling Bria back into his chest again, hugging her tight. I turn the corner and bump into Axel, who is lifting a child onto the back of a horse with her mother. The men will walk, protecting the women and children on horseback. Axel pats the horse's hind, and it trots forward, getting into formation.

"You knew," I say softly. It's not a question.

My mate clenches his jaw lightly before sighing his confirmation.

"Cadmus came to me a few weeks ago, and I suspected his decision, but he never directly told me."

My eyes widen.

"Why did you keep it from me? I could have changed his mind!"

Axel cups my cheek in his hand and shakes his head.

"There was no changing his mind, little warrior. He is a man of honor, and I admire that about him. It is one of the reasons I like him so much. But he is also your family—family you grew up with. Those two things combined ensured that there was no decision to be made. The only option was to stay and fight by your side."

I close my eyes and soak in his words, knowing he is right.

"And if he dies, he won't see his daughter come into this world." I sigh.

"Perhaps. Perhaps not. A few months is only the estimation of what we have before General Neem makes his move on Atarah, but it is not confirmation. He could come sooner. Kettuna has been patrolling the camps from the sky and will report to us tonight. We will go from there."

"And if he comes much sooner than that?" I question.

I'm not sure our fighters are ready for the coming war. Axel reads my mind easily enough because he turns me to face the courtyard. I look past the courtyard to the training grounds, taking note of the hundreds of bodies hard at work. Perfecting their movements and skills. My Bellator sisters walk the grounds, showing them new moves—showing them how to end the enemy permanently.

"We will be ready." He murmurs.

I sigh and nod, returning to his embrace so that I can lean my forehead against his stomach. A scuffle behind us makes us both look, and Cadmus stands behind us, his face grim.

"It's time for the last wave."

My heart constricts painfully when I realize he's completely serious. He's not going with the group. I bite my lip and nod, moving away from Axel and tossing myself into Cadmus's arms. He steps back one step from the force of my body, but quickly returns my embrace, squeezing me tightly.

"It's going to be alright, Laudi. We will win this war, and then we will all be together again, one family united."

I nod my head on his shoulder and let go, waiting for him to lower me to the ground. He smiles softly—ruffling my hair—and I grumble, swatting him away. But then I smile.

"I am the luckiest cousin in the world," I whisper.

Cadmus grins and walks by us as we return to the front.

"I don't know; once Sonella hears all of the stories about Oliver, she might have you beat."

My lip wobbles, as I had not even thought about Sonella, one day hearing stories of my son. But the idea does not make me cry. It only fills me with a new sense of hope.

My smile is genuine as we wave our goodbyes to the last of our citizens. And my determination is absolute.

General Neem will die by my hand.

"*Ooh*...how *fun*..." A voice croons lowly.

My breath hitches at the whisper of a voice in my head, and I close my eyes.

Son of a bitch.

52
Elaudia

"He wants to meet you..."

I shudder as the sly voice speaks out in my mind as I make my way to the catacombs. I was going to rest, but that whispered voice quickly had me changing my direction.

Alex has left to welcome new blacksmiths from across the sea, and my heart calms, knowing our plea for help is being heard from so far away. These blacksmiths are known for forging weapons that end great battles, and I know we will need them with how many citizens we have who have chosen to fight in this war.

But if he knew what I was doing right now, he would kill me. Like, really kill me.

"You know it would be much less creepy if you stopped whispering like that," I say out loud.

To anyone else, I'd look as if I were talking to myself, but the good thing about the catacombs is that they have essentially been empty for decades. The lack of fae means there have been no new bodies to bury here. Still, as I pass by King Aecus and Queen Cheche's statues, I bow low, whispering words of respect before continuing.

"Not whispering...you are...too strong. I cannot break through more than this. General Neem did not fare so well..."

A smug sense of satisfaction rolls through me before I stop in my tracks, the meaning of her words hitting me. The torches cast a warm flicker on my face as I look down.

"Do you mean what I *think* you mean?"

I wait what seems like a lifetime for the Goddess to answer me, her voice a light chuckle.

"My brother...the God of Greed. He always chose the worst options. It was something to taunt him with when things were...harmonious in our home. Now...it is just pathetic."

My eyebrows scrunch together at her words as confusion ripples through me.

"I thought that if the host succumbed easily enough, it was a testament to the strength of the God or Goddess?"

Another chuckle inside my head.

"Even Gods have rules, little queen. If we are cast out by our brethren and destroyed, we only have one chance at a host on Earth. The quicker the host is overwhelmed by the strength of a God, the sooner it will die. But...my brother...the God of Greed...sees nothing but his glory. And it is why he will always fail."

My footsteps are quiet as I continue, and my mind races over this new information.

"That's why you chose me?"

A slight hum of confirmation.

"I want vengeance against my brother. I knew this war would come; I knew I would have my chance. So, I waited an additional twenty years for you to be born, knowing the Last of The Syraxes Bellators was my chance."

I lift my hands, trailing them along the brick walls. The light dims the further I walk, but I fear nothing.

"And after this war is over?"

She stays silent for so long that I almost think she won't answer me—but then, just as my foot leaves the final step, her voice rings out.

"I am tired of my existence. Give me my revenge, and I will let you be."

My heart almost stops at her words, and I close my eyes, feeling her sorrow and anger.

"What did he do to you?"

"He framed me for the witches. He knew I would stand in his way to conquer the creatures of Earth...our creations. And when I caught his plans before the others, he made it look like I was the one who was experimenting with the witches. He drained me of my gifts briefly so that I was weak, and then he struck like the vile serpent he is."

"They did not hear your words? They didn't allow you to defend yourself?"

I feel outrage on her behalf. How could they not see it? They are *Gods*, for Hell's sake.

"I could barely stand, let alone speak. They assumed it was from the experiment. But once I was gone, and the experiment continued, they knew the mistake they had made. They de-

stroyed him painfully, and I'm sure my sisters and brothers know sorrow for what was done to me, but once a God or Goddess is destroyed and cast out, you may never speak to those on the throne again."

I'm quiet for a few moments, tossing this around in my head. As I reach the doorway, my hand placed on the handle, I make my decision.

"I will help you get your revenge; I swear it."

A delighted chuckle trembles across my mind as I twist the knob, prepared to meet him.

Finally.

"Then you will have the full extent of my power, little Queen."

And then I open the door to a sight I never thought I'd see. A sight I've been waiting to come face to face with for *years*.

***

The light is dim in this room, so dim that a normal human would not be able to see a thing.

Luckily for me, I am not a human. The body against the wall is taller than me, though not as tall as Axel. He is of average height for human males, with black hair that hangs limp around his ears. His face is wrinkled, more so than it should be at his supposed age of fifty. His eyes watch me with a calculating gleam, and I know from that look that I am not staring at General Neem, but the God of Greed.

His eyes rake over my body, seemingly unimpressed. A grin tilts the corners of his chapped lips, and I grimace at the sight of yellowed teeth.

This is nothing like the strong General I had imagined over the years. A man strong enough to command thousands of dark rebels. This man...he is dying.

"Hello Lytta..." He croons.

The Goddess prods my mind gently, asking for permission. Permission that, a few days ago, I might not have granted. But now...things are so different now. I close my eyes, accepting her, and she comes forward quickly. But I'm still there. It is the strangest thing I have ever experienced in my life. I thought I would be thrown into the dark abyss of my mind, but I can still hear, smell, and see everything she does.

"Plutos...you're looking worse for wear...you could use some sun."

My voice rings out in my ears as the Goddess speaks, her eyes cold. Plutos furrows his eyebrows as a sneer graces his lips.

"Keep taunting me, sister. This time around, I will make sure you are destroyed permanently."

My lips open with a chuckle, and I can see the anger in his eyes at my disregard for his threats.

"Let's take a good look between us, brother. Who looks better? You and your human General...or me and my Syraxes Queen?"

A growl of rage escapes his lips, and he steps forward, lifting a finger my way.

"Your host may be stronger than mine, but I have a black witch on my side. I will not fail."

As soon as he mentions the witch, I catch a glimpse of her, standing behind him as if he is protecting her. He's not, though. Her hand is lifted against his back and placed on his spine.

"She's fueling this meeting. Plutos fused his power with hers; it is how they are here now."

Lytta whispers gently to me. I watch the small witch; her face pale and brows furrowed in concentration. It won't last long. He's been draining her dry, and a witch's well only goes so deep.

Lytta purses her lips through me and chuckles.

"You will fail...make no mistake about that. I think it is time for you to go now. Your energy source looks like she is about to faint on these grounds. Not a smart choice considering the lands you now stand in."

We walk forward, grinning menacingly.

"But go ahead and push it...as you push everything in this life. Let us see what happens without your young witch's shield and her magic. Let us see how quickly you will truly lose this war."

Plutos snarls but looks back, his eyes growing dark at the sight of the witch about to fall.

"I will see you on the battlefield, sister. And this time, I will ensure your demise. Forever."

With a flash, they are gone. No smoke, no dust...just gone. I look around the room, ensuring nothing of their essence is left as Lytta withdraws.

"He's coming soon, little queen. Prepare your people."

And with that, she is gone.

And I'm once again left pondering if the God of Greed is General Neem's weak spot...or if the young witch is.

53
Axel

My boots are silent as I stalk throughout the halls—a feat for someone of my size, but a perk of being a full-blooded Fae.

I nod at the few servants who bow my way as they clean. We kept only twenty women, including Sarabeth, to stay during the war. All volunteers who stayed will be locked in the catacombs when General Neem finally strikes. My halls have not been this empty in so long, and it makes me think about the joy and love that my mate has brought into this kingdom these past six years.

I'm so lost in my thoughts that I don't see the tiny body in front of me until I crash into it. The girl goes sprawling to the floor in a heap, and I internally wince, putting my hands under her arms and lifting her.

"I'm so sorry, My King! I wasn't looking where I was going." Nalah's panicked grimace causes me to chuckle as I set her right.

"I was lost in my head, my apologies, little one."

The once frail mermaid looks up at me with a timid smile as she straightens her fighting clothes, and I take note of the new muscles that have formed on her arms. She looks sturdier now with all of the training, and I feel a sense of pride for her.

"You're working hard." A statement, not a question.

Her face lights up with a smile, and she nods enthusiastically.

"Azylia says I'll be the fiercest mermaid that the world has ever seen!"

Glimmers of hope swim in her eyes and I smile softly, remembering what she said the very first day we met her.

The others would always leave her behind because she was weaker.

"You'll be a sight to see; that is an absolute fact."

She grins once more before looking down and biting her lip.

"I am really glad I ran into you, King Axel. There was something I wanted to talk to you about...it's about Queen Elaudia and Oliver."

My heart squeezes at my son's name, and I furrow my brows. Nalah did not know my son, so what she could have to say about him was lost to me. She reaches into her bag and pulls out a small yellow book.

And then it hits me.

The Tales of a Pirate's Son.

My heart squeezes painfully in my chest at the sight of my son's favorite book, and I reach out slowly to take it from her.

"I saw Her Majesty looking at it, and she told me it was his favorite. I thought, maybe since she did not get to finish it with him...maybe *you* could finish it with her?"

I sigh as she finishes speaking and I close my eyes, my fingers gripping the book. My son...my precious little boy.

"My King...?"

I open my eyes, blinking away my sorrow as I smile gently at Nalah.

"It is a wonderful idea, little one." I pull her forward and place a kiss on her forehead.

"Thank you. Run along now and get to the training fields. You don't want to be late."

Nalah nods, offering me a curtsy before hurrying away. I look after her until she turns the corner, and then I look down at the book in my hand. I tuck it into my coat before continuing to the back of the castle, where Kettuna waits. As I exit the castle, I catch sight of my mate walking towards me, her face unreadable.

I twine my fingers with her smaller ones as we walk, and I look down at her, concern furrowing my eyebrows.

"What has happened?"

My mate grimaces but doesn't say anything. I almost stop her in her tracks, but then a light trill meets my ears, and I glance up, seeing a fully transformed Kettuna. The large Chimera shakes her mane as she approaches us, immediately nudging her nose against Elaudia's chest affectionately. My wife smiles and returns her hug, pulling her close.

"I missed you too, my dear one," Elaudia murmurs.

"Were you spotted by anyone, Kettuna?" I question softly. Her lion head shakes as if offended by my question.

"I am an assassin. Unknown until I do not wish to be."

Elaudia laughs outright at that and pulls away before returning to my side.

"Of course you are. I cannot believe my mate would ever doubt you."

Elaudia looks up with mischievous eyes as Kettuna huffs, looking away.

"It is why I prefer his female counterpart." She trills obnoxiously.

I roll my eyes as the girls make fun of me before looking at Kettuna seriously. She knows immediately what I am asking for.

"The General orders his camps to be packed; they will move within the next week. I'm sure of it."

"Did you catch sight of General Neem?" I ask.

Kettuna shakes her head, and I glance at Elaudia, wondering what to do about the tyrant we know almost nothing about. I stop, though, because of the guilty look on her face. My mate bites her lips softly and glances at me through her eyelashes.

"I may have...just had a...*slight*...meeting with him."

Silence sounds out around us, and I swear I hear swords clatter to the ground in disbelief in the distance. The Bellators would have heard us, as well as Graven.

"What *the fuck* do you mean you just had a meeting with him?!"

My temper flares as I look down at my wife in outrage. I can only think of everything that could have gone wrong in this supposed meeting. How easily I could have just lost her in this past hour...and I had no idea. My blood sings in my veins as my beast roars his rage and attempts to take over.

Hide her.

Bind her.

Punish her.

Put our mate on her knees and spank her round ass raw until she never thinks to do something so stupid again.

"I was going to tell you as soon as we met with Kettuna!" Elaudia protests, but I turn away, pacing the grounds beneath my feet as I try to control the beast who wishes to break free from within.

My wife reaches out a hand with a frown, pulling me to a stop.

"Axel! I am fine!"

I growl savagely, whirling around on her as I flash my fangs. Kettuna hisses a warning, attempting to step between me and my mate. Elaudia puts her hands up towards both of us, rolling her eyes.

"I am fine! Now, if you calm down for five *seconds*, I can explain everything!"

She looks at me as if she is dealing with a child throwing a tantrum, and not a full-blooded Fae male on the edge of a deadly, territorial display. I frown at her, but recall my beast, looking my mate up and down to ensure she is safe. Once I'm sure she is fine, I toss a pointed look at Kettuna, who only chuffs and backs away a few steps.

Elaudia sighs, planting her hands on her small waist as she blows a piece of loose hair out of her face.

"The Goddess of Rage, *Lytta*, was innocent of the crimes she was accused of."

I look at her, waiting for her to finish and get to the part where she meets with General Neem.

"The God of Greed framed her. She was never experimenting with the witches. *Plutos* was. He stole some of her power and made it look like she was doing it. Soon after she was destroyed, Plutos's nature compelled him to continue on his quest to ravage the humans and enslave them all. He was discovered and cast out as well."

I look at her expectantly, wondering how she now knows all of this. And then it hits me.

"She is speaking to you even more now." I breathe my disbelief.

Elaudia nods solemnly.

"But she does not wish to take over my body. She only wishes for one thing—vengeance against her brother, Plutos. Then...she has promised me she will rest. Forever."

I sigh and look up at the sky, taking note of the gathering storm clouds.

"How are we to find the God of Greed...he was cast out centuries ago."

"That's why I had to go to this meeting." She smiles softly, and I know she's asking for my forgiveness.

My brows furrow as my mate clasps my hands with her own as she looks up at me with a grin.

"Plutos took his host almost three decades ago. His host is General Neem."

54
Elaudia

I wait by the docks to receive the last group of fighters for our war against General Neem, and if it wasn't for Axel's...enthusiastic wake-up call this morning, I'm sure I would be on the tips of my toes with excitement.

Because this last round is not just any old group of fighters, but mercenaries who fought a usurper across the sea in Queen Cheche's Homeland, Soundra. Including the great-grandson of the blacksmith who created the sword that won the war.

Rumors say he has the blood of a God and can weld *Orichalcum*, the strongest metal in the history of this world.

And I have an immediate need for his services. I close my eyes as the breeze hits my face, inhaling the scent of the salt water and the sound of horns as ships arrive and depart. The last call of the port, coming and going.

"If I knew My Queen would be here to receive me, I might have worn my good breeches."

My eyes fly open at the drawl of the familiar voice before me, and I gasp with a delighted laugh.

"Natonak!"

I run to the tall man before me, embracing him as he chuckles and catches me. His blonde hair has grown long since we last sat behind the stables with Cadmus and stolen wine, mocking the guests of Aland's glamorous parties. But the warmth and love he radiates is still the same as when we were ten.

"What on earth are you doing here?? Did Cadmus know you were coming?"

My cousin used to tell me of all the letters he would receive from Natonak, but I know they lost contact over the years.

Natonak smiles down at me as he sets his bag down. He blows out a breath with squinted eyebrows.

"Well, let's see...I was making my way through the streets of Fa Vanneth, boozing away my troubles and enjoying quite a few Jimini women..." I snort at that. That's one way to say he wasn't studying an ancient technique of fighting—like he was *supposed* to be. He grins with delight before continuing.

"Then one night, as I was lying in bed...resting."

I cough into my hand and grumble, "Recovering."

Natonak smiles before continuing.

"Recovering...this Jimini woman tells me of a tale that has reached her ears, of the Bellator Queen across the sea, Elaudia Syraxes *Volith*, who is taking the Kingdom of Atarah to war against the tyrant General Neem. You know, I was always fond of storybook tales, but this? This seemed too good to pass up on."

I sigh and nod.

"It is true. The God of Greed has possessed General Neem for nearly thirty years and has amassed an army greater than I have ever seen. We are preparing and expecting him to attack before the snow comes."

Natonak rocks back on the balls of his feet and shrugs.

"So let us give him hell, cousin."

I smile at the old nickname before pulling him into a hug again.

"You're more Cadmus's cousin than mine."

He only frowns down at me.

"If I recall, you two were the only ones who didn't treat me like the peasant I was when the maid brought me in from the orphanage."

I reach out to help him with his bags, but he only swats my hand away.

"Well, you did have a certain appeal as my grand duke. You made the best lemon pies." I laugh lightly, remembering all the times I made a young Natonak serve me fake delicacies.

"Still a fan of anything lemon flavored?" He questions.

I step aside and nod, looking over the crowd as they exit the ship. My gaze lingers on a boy who can be no older than twelve summers. His arrival must be a mistake. The poor thing will have to brave another long journey across the seas, back to where he came from.

"You have *no* idea. Hey, did you happen to meet the blacksmith named Gryffin on your voyage over? I've been eager to speak to him."

Natonak grins and tips his chin.

"You're looking right at him."

My eyes widen as I look the boy over, and as if he heard us, he begins to make his way through the crowd. I whirl on Natonak with panicked eyes.

"It can't be. He's too young!"

Natonak only shrugs.

"That's him. Nearly every male on the ride here boasted about his fine edges and quality work."

My heart aches at seeing his dark black hair and wide brown eyes. My mind freezes as the child approaches me, bowing as low as he can, an ultimate bow of respect.

"My Queen, it is my honor to serve you."

His voice has not even matured, the lilt of his voice still light and childish. All I can think of is my son. I bite my lip and attempt to control the crack in my voice.

"I appreciate the journey you have made for me more than you will ever know. But I'm afraid I must reject your services at this time. You must leave."

His bow falters, and he straightens with con-fused eyes.

"Please, My Queen, allow me to serve you. I swear I will not disappoint you or the king!"

Natonak places a hand on my trembling shoulder.

"Elaudia...he's not going to fight. Only pro-duce more weapons."

His brow is furrowed, but I shake his hand off and stalk away.

"Send him home." My voice is cold and ab-solute, but I don't spare a glance back as I leave the docks, trying to hold on to the pieces of my trembling heart.

***

"Bristol has not made a failed attempt on Nelly's heart for the past week at least, and Sarabeth has a fresh batch of lemon tarts waiting at the dining table. I see no reason that a frown should be upon your face, little warrior."

I glance up and away from the window with teary eyes, sighing at my mate as he enters our room.

"There was a boy today...the blacksmith."

I shake my head in exasperation. He's only a child, supposedly renowned for his skills with metal, with the blood of a God running through his veins.

"I met him," Axel says softly. I stand from my chair faster than he can blink.

"You what!?" I stalk over to him, the skirt of my dinner dress brushing against the floor.

"I met Natonak as well...he is interesting. And he thinks the world of you and Cadmus. They are catching up over dinner as we speak. A dinner, I mind you, that we are currently supposed to be at." His lips tip up into a smile as he speaks, but I know he's watching me closely, always trying to read my emotions.

"That child was supposed to be on the last ship out of the harbor! He is not to be here for this war! He is a child!" As I speak, I throw my hands from my sides, pacing back and forth. Axel walks closer.

"He is not Oliver."

That stops me in my tracks. I face Axel and ignore the tears stinging my eyes.

"He is not our son Elaudia. I can see the resemblances as well as you can, but he is *not* Oliver, my little mate. He is well respected in his field, and we need his help. There are not enough blades for the rebels who came to help, and we cannot leave them defenseless. You know this as well as I do."

My lip trembles because I know he is right. But it hurts.

To just look at him, it hurts.

Axel sighs as he reaches into his coat pocket, pulling out a tiny yellow book. A sob escapes me at the sight of Oliver's favorite book.

"I think it is time we finish this. Don't you agree?"

My body is frozen as I try to control the whirlwind of emotion going through my body and mind.

"We will do it together, Elaudia. We will finish his favorite book as a family, set it down, and go on stronger than before. Because that is what we must do. For this Kingdom. For our family. The family who is *still* here, with warm breath in their lungs, and a future to fight for."

Tears escape my eyes and slowly trail down my cheeks as I nod and whisper my answer.

"Okay."

Axel strips himself of his coat before turning me around and walking us back over the window, its fading light accompanied by the candles I had lit to keep warm while lost in my thoughts. His arms reach to wrap around me before opening the book to page fifty-seven, chapter twenty-four. And then his melodic voice fills the space around us.

"If only ye could trap the fish with my father's hook, we shall eat well for the next three days. Perhaps then, he will forgive me for tearing up the bedding."

I close my eyes as he reads the chapter, and I swear as he reads, I can hear Ollie's laughter ringing out around us, an echo of a life that once was—but shall never be again.

55

Elaudia

"You may stay and produce as many weapons as you possibly can. Any resources you need, my husband and I will provide. Any men you need to help you, are yours."

I have to bite my tongue as I finish, wishing I could take all of these words I have just spoken back, but the young boy in front of me only sighs in relief before bowing low.

"Thank you, My Queen, My King! I swear on my life, you will not regret this decision."

Axel takes charge in my stead as he smiles down at the boy.

"We have a week at most, go on and get to work. I look forward to seeing the results."

Gryffin bows once more before stalking off in a manor strange for one so young. His hands stay behind his back until he leaves my sight entirely, and I glance to my right where

Axel sits on a throne identical to mine. His first-anniversary gift to me as he proclaimed that his mate would never sit lower than any male in this realm.

Including himself.

I stand slowly, the skirts of my gown swaying softly as I approach him.

I waste no time plopping onto his lap as I lean into his familiar embrace. His thick arms wind around my lower stomach as he pulls me close so that the heat of his chest melds with the heat of my back.

"I'm proud of you." He whispers softly.

I shiver as his hot breath washes against my neck, and I tilt my head to the side, welcoming him even closer.

"I fear I will regret this decision," I admit softly. Axel only sighs and presses a warm kiss to my jawline as we watch our citizens enjoying their last days before war together. Human rebels and lore-blood, dining and laughing as one. A united front that has not been achieved since the rule of King Aecus.

"He will be safe in the catacombs, Laudi." Axel reminds me with a soft murmur.

I close my eyes as he speaks, knowing he is right. I look out at the smiling faces of our people, all of the fighters who have stayed to end this war once and for all, a war that we did not understand has been waging for so long. Nalah sits at Natonak and Cadmus's sides, her face lit up with joy as the two men make her giggle with stories of our youth. Her bright eyes meet mine across the room, and she grins my way. I smile back at her gently before catching sight of her Dragon mate—who stands in the corner, his face hidden by the shadows. I can see it though...the way his eyes never leave her frame, ensuring she is always safe.

"I don't see Nelly..." I murmur to my mate.

He lets out a sound that's a mix between a growl and a snort, gliding a calloused hand through my braided hair.

"I believe I caught sight of Bristol proclaiming his undying love for her by the library entrance. It was...slightly dramatic. But it must have worked in his favor."

I arch an eyebrow and look up.

"How do you know?" I grin.

Axel smirks, nodding his head toward the guarded doorway, where a flustered Nelly and Bristol enter, hand in hand. I smother a laugh with my palm at the sight of her unruly hair and flushed cheeks.

"Oh my." I snicker.

Axel's deep chuckles follow after me as we watch the pair make their way to the table closest to us, where our friends dine. Kettuna lifts her large frame off the floor by our sides and stalks down the throne steps, her long, scaled tail flicking side to side. I watch as her lion's mane shakes once before she jumps up, licking away at Bristol's face. Nelly pulls away, laughing with delight at Kettuna's display of affection.

Bristol shakes his head with bewilderment as he falls to the floor under her heavy weight.

"Down, Lion-lamb-snake beast! *Down*!"

The room erupts in laughter at the sight, and even I cannot stop my laughter. Kettuna finally recedes from Bristol, licking him one last time before turning away and heading back for Axel and me.

"What on earth was that about Kettuna?"

"The red furred male finally asserted his dominance on small female's friend. I show him pride."

Kettuna's trill reaches my mind, and I chuckle, stroking her mane as she sits beside us again. Her chest rumbles in contentment, and I close my eyes, listening to this sound.

The sound of peace.

"Yarlon and I are leaving in the morning." My mate whispers in my ear.

I narrow my eyes and glance up at him.

"What for?"

"He believes that there are scrolls in a library that boarders Atarah that speak of the events of *Lytta* and *Plutos*. We leave at first light."

I open my mouth to argue, but he kisses me.

"I know you trust Lytta to keep her word, but I need to know if anything else out there could help us destroy Plutos permanently."

I cross my legs as I sigh, knowing he's right.

"Promise me you'll be safe?" I whisper.

Axel grins devilishly at me, his eyes darkening with lust as his hand drifts lower, spreading my legs open gently as he throws up a shield to hide us away from the crowd.

"Nothing in this world could keep me from this beautiful cunt, mate. Not even the Gods."

I gasp as his thumbs press against my clit, causing a fire to erupt in my belly.

"Take me to bed."

I don't have to say more than that. Axel stands immediately, swooping me up with him as he stalks down the stairs. I ignore the hoots and hollers from our friends as we depart the great room. As soon as we exit, our mouths clash in a frenzy of passion and haste. His tongue pushes my mouth open, an act I greedily accept as I moan into his mouth. I feel the air shift, and then my back meets our bed as he shoves me onto the covers. The balcony doors are open, causing the night air to breeze in, and shivers to erupt along my flesh. My lips stay connected to his as he works on the buttons of my dress, pulling it down from my shoulders.

I tremble at the cool contact, but then his mouth is there, sucking one pebbled nipple into his warm mouth.

"This life was eternal damnation without you, Elaudia."

His voice is hard and husky as he speaks, licking a path from one breast to the other. I cry out as he bites down gently, my legs spreading as wide as the skirts of my dress will allow. He notices my struggle, and quickly relieves me of the fabric, tearing it away with his bare hands. I'm left in nothing but my garters and silk panties, my bra having been torn away with my gown.

I decide to return the favor in my haste to feel his bare skin on top of my own, shredding the cotton of his shirt with my Bellator strength. His heavy weight is pressing against my core most deliciously, and I move my hips closer, trying to alleviate the pressure.

"Axel, please!" He only chuckles as he works his mouth down my body.

"Please, what, little warrior?" I whine against his warm tongue that teases the crevice where my thighs meet my pussy.

I hate this game.

"You know what," I growl.

It doesn't work. A slight stinging erupts on my inner thigh where he has just smacked it, and I yelp, my lust intensifying.

"Use that filthy little mouth, and I might give you what you want."

I tremble as his beard scratches against my sensitive skin.

"Please...lick my pussy, Axel."

He chuckles and hesitates, and I briefly wonder if he will deny me the pleasure I am begging for.

He doesn't.

My panties are suddenly torn from my skin, and then his mouth is on my cunt, licking and sucking at it like it is the most delicious dessert he has ever tasted. I cry out as his thick tongue presses into my entrance. I can feel the walls of my pussy fluttering down, trying to grasp at anything they can.

"Such a sweet little cunt..." He murmurs. His jaw shines with my cum as he works my clit with his tongue, faster and faster until the slight vibrations work a tempo into my belly...higher and higher. My hands claw for purchase, landing in his thick black hair as I use his face for my pleasure.

"Axel...I'm going to come!" He growls at my words and works me harder until that cresting wave turns into a blast of pleasure.

"Oh god!"

My body shakes as my back bows off the bed, but I'm quickly flipped over. Lost in my release, I don't realize that Axel has shoved his way inside my cunt until my walls stretch, trying to make room for his thick length.

I whimper and moan as my release calms, but then my mate's large hands are on my hips, and he's fucking into my body with every bit of his fae strength.

"I'll ensure you feel this for the coming days, little mate. I'll ensure your tight little cunt knows just who she belongs to every time she's grasping for my cock."

I moan into the silk pillows at his words, feeling his cock touching the deepest parts of my womb. His fingers yank my long hair until my face is no longer smothered in our bedding.

"Oh no, little mate...you're not going to hide those noises from me. Let this entire castle know who you belong to."

Axel snarls, but I can hear the hint of his beast in his voice as claws dig into my waist. I open my mouth to say *anything*, but the words are lost on my tongue.

All I can focus on is the pleasure my mate is giving me. His growls are unhinged as he uses me as his own sex doll, and I can feel the slick of my heat dripping down my thighs and his balls. The substantial weight of them crashes against my clit with every thrust, and it's not long after that I can feel my walls fluttering with the anticipation of another orgasm.

This is what we both like.

Dirty, feral, fucking.

"Oh...there it is...good girl...let me feel that little pussy come around my cock."

I whimper at his words as they only fuel me further into my lust-induced haze, and my stomach clenches down violently. I come hard around his cock as I cry out, the feeling so intense I know he did exactly as he said he would.

I'll be feeling him for days.

Axel growls viciously as he slams into me once, twice, three more times—before his hot seed pulses inside my cunt, shooting into my womb as we come together.

I collapse onto the bedding below us, the sheets damp from our sweat and release. I moan as his weight blankets me, feeling so comfortable that I feel as if I could live this way for the rest of my days. I wait for a moment, wondering if he will withdraw from my cunt, but he doesn't. He tilts my hips up slightly and stays inside me, his cock pulsing with every movement. I sigh in pleasure, reaching my hand over so that it rests on top of his larger one. He presses a gentle kiss to my spine, then my temple, and finally, my lips as I twist to the side to accept him.

"It's not just this life," I murmur.

Axel pets damp hair away from my temple as his brows furrow.

"What isn't?" He asks.

"Eternal damnation...it's not just a life without you. This life, or death, or reincarnation...*anything* without you is eternal damnation."

My eyes flutter shut as I speak, the exhaustion from the day's events taking hold of me.

His voice reaches my ears right before I'm lost to sleep, a lulling and comforting sound to my tired mind.

"Then I will find you, little mate. In life—in death—and a new world of souls unknown. *I will find you.*"

56
Elaudia

The Kingdom has had its moments where the morning starts slow and quiet, the streets are empty, and the citizens of Atarah are safely tucked away in their beds.

Hearts content.

Bellies full.

A Kingdom that knew not of war, but happiness and prosperity. As my eyes flutter open and I twist in my cool bedsheets, that stillness reaches my ears. But it's not the same as it used to be. Because this stillness is an anticipation of the war to come. Their hearts are not content, but ready to avenge those lost to General Neem's tyranny.

Their bellies do not overindulge.

The streets are filled with weapon-making, and armor is being sized for those smaller than the soldiers who guard this kingdom.

I move my hand, reaching for my mate, but I come up empty. I sit up slowly, glancing around our bedroom before finally resting back to where my mate usually sleeps, a note in his place. His thin cursive is spread across the paper, and I pick it up, cursing him silently for not waking me up before he left.

Elaudia

Yarlon insisted we leave before the sun reaches the cliffsides. I fear he is all too eager to find the answers we seek. I'll see you tonight, little warrior.

Forever Yours, Axel

I sigh softly, flopping back onto our bed. It is moments like this when I wish, only for a moment, that Axel and I were not the monarchy of a great kingdom. That we were not about to go to war. That we could have this slow life, in another world...with our son.

I groan and push the sad thoughts away, forcing myself to focus on the here and now.

I stand slowly; my hair still wound in a loose braid. I catch sight of my reflection in the full mirror leaning against the far wall, taking in my flushed cheeks and bright eyes. It took weeks, but I am finally gaining back some of the weight I lost after Ollie. My skin is no longer ghostly pale, but tinged with a slight pink color from my days on the training grounds. I walk closer, examining my figure. After Oliver was born, I wondered if my frame would fill out more in the hips and bust.

It didn't. I was made to be a warrior of an ancient bloodline, and my body returned to its previous figure, my stomach and hips thin, my breasts staying small. We can't have it all, I suppose. I move away from the mirror and walk into our closet, reaching for a clean pair of training clothes. As I reach for them, I hesitate, looking at my leathers and Nahirian armor.

It's almost as if my instincts are telling me that with the war looming on the horizon, I would be foolish not to be ready at all times. Those instincts have never failed me before. I'm finishing with the laces of my chest plate when a knock sounds at my door. I glance up before tying off my armor.

"Enter."

The door is pushed open to reveal Nalah and Nelly, their faces bursting with excitement as they rush to me.

"It's happened!"

"He did it!"

They shout over each other, and I turn so that I can face them fully, my hands on my hips as I laugh.

"Woah, there. Calm down...what has happened?"

Nalah glances up at Nelly and nudges her forward with shooing hands. Nelly stumbles slightly before correcting herself and throwing her hand into my face.

"Bristol asked for my hand!" She screeches.

My eyes widen at the gold band wrapped around her ring finger, and I quickly join them in their delight. I pull Nelly into my arms as we jump up and down.

"I'm so happy for you! How did he do it? When?"

Nelly smooths her hair down as we part, pulling Nalah and me to the sitting area.

"This morning, when I woke up, he was waiting by my side on his knee! He confessed that while I was the most infuriating female ever to walk this planet, he could not imagine a life without my—and I quote—antagonizing presence, and that he wishes to spend the rest of his days worshipping my—ah, you know, my heart." She quiets down as she trails off, and I smirk at Nalah's reddened face.

I arch an eyebrow.

Not the most romantic proposal. I think to myself.

"No kidding."

Lytta's voice only slightly surprises me, but I ignore it.

I pull Nelly's hand into my own and grin.

"I am so happy for you. For both of you. You have become one of my dearest friends, and I have only ever wanted you to know the same joy Axel and I know together."

Nelly bites her lip.

"So, you approve?" She questions me timidly.

As her queen, I know it is a centuries-old tradition that the queen must approve of any marriages of her handmaidens. I smile at her.

"Of course, I approve, Nelly. I only want for your happiness."

She squeals and launches forward, hugging me tight. I grin over her shoulder at a still-beaming Nalah.

"I helped him pick out the ring." She mouths. I giggle and roll my eyes. Nelly pulls away and looks around the room.

"Where is King Axel? I had hoped to receive both of your blessings."

I shrug and walk over to the marble stands in the corner of our room, gathering my crown. Nalah stands and comes over, urging my hands away as she places it on my head and secures a new, tighter braid around it.

I will give it to the mermaids; they know how to make the most gorgeous hairstyles I have ever seen.

"He left the kingdom walls with Yarlon to search for some scrolls. There could be an answer to defeating Plutos without the necessity of Lytta's presence."

Though I'm certain Lytta can hear every word I speak, she stays silent.

Nelly's eyes trail over to the windows that overtake the entire west side of our rooms.

"I hope they are swift; the weather mages predict a storm of great magnitude to approach before the sun sets tonight." I shrug softly, my eyes on Nalah's deft fingers in my hair.

"Axel will be able to sense anything that gets too close; if need be, he can bring them back before it gets too bad."

Knowing I'm right, the girls move on to the subject of true matter, Nelly's wedding. I listen with half an ear as she speaks of color schemes and the length of her veil, but soon enough, Nalah is tying off my hair, proclaiming herself finished.

I don't bother containing my shock at how beautifully she has done my hair, and I turn to her, cupping her cheek.

"Thank you, my little wave."

Nalah grins at me with uncontained happiness before dipping into a slight curtsy.

"I should head to training. I was late yesterday, and Graven almost went all dragon on me. He's been so...broody, lately."

I arch an eyebrow at Nelly, but she only lifts her hands and backs away. She mouths to me over Nalah's shoulder.

"Not touching that."

"Why would Graven get mad at you for being late?"

Nalah bites her lip.

"He may have seen Natonak and me on a morning walk." She winces.

I huff out a breath and shake my head.

"Uh uh. Nope. Not in a million years. Natonak is a wonderful man and a dear friend, little wave. But he has also seen more naked women in his life than a well-run brothel."

Nelly snorts into her hand, and Nalah's delicate cheeks flare with blood.

"It wasn't like that. I was curious...I have never been out of the water, at least not before coming here. And he has seen so many places. I was only curious to hear the stories he had to share—the many places he's been." While Nalah pleads her case, Nelly coughs into her hand, a cough that sounds suspiciously like—

"The many *pussies*."

I glare at her lack of decor, and she stands quickly, excusing herself. I sigh and close my eyes, praying to whoever is listening for the patience to explain this to Nalah.

"Do you know what it means, my love? To be the fated mate of a *dragon*?" Nalah glances away, and her shoulders slump.

"I know that Graven and I are connected in a way that I shall never be with anyone else." She whispers.

I grimace, wishing Graven had contained himself slightly more when Roarke had struck Nalah. Then, she might still be in the dark about things she is too young to be burdened with.

"Yes, that is true. But it is more than that. Have you...have you ever had feelings...for a male?"

As I speak, I try to remember what it was like when Helena spoke to me about sexual encounters with the male species. My mind comes up with a stilted conversation about keeping my legs shut until I was wed. I sigh. I don't want to scar Nalah in the same manner.

"Mermaids are a bit different." She murmurs.

"Oh."

Oh.

I clear my throat and motion for her to sit once more.

"Well, soon enough, I'm sure...you will begin to find males attractive. More so in the sense that if you catch sight of a male who...pleases your eye...feelings will erupt inside you. These feelings will seem warm and pleasant—"

"My Queen!" Nalah shrieks.

I startle and stop, looking over at her.

She clears her throat and glances up at me through her eyelashes.

"Nelly and Bria have already beaten you to the sex talk. Excuse my language."

I laugh softly, relieved.

"Oh, thank goodness." I breathe deeply. "I was afraid I would scar you for life...my adoptive mother, Helena, made me so frightened of the male appendage I was terrified that it would bite." We both break out into laughter together at that.

"Graven will be battling his urges and instincts because he knows you are not quite ready for the commitment of what being his fated mate entails. You must be patient with him; I cannot imagine it would be easy. He is centuries old." I trail off when it hits me.

"Does the age difference bother you, little wave?"

Nalah shakes her head vehemently.

"No, no...it's not that. He's just so...intense. I'm sure I must seem so naive and uncultured compared to him. He's a bit intimidating." She murmurs, looking down at her twined fingers. I purse my lips and blow out a breath.

"When I first arrived in Lashforn, I was only a year older than you. I had not only just learned that the people who raised me were not my true family, but that I was the last member of the greatest warrior bloodline to ever exist. I knew no one outside of Cadmus...and I was afraid. But I realized that in that fear, there was determination. Determination to find happiness, and family, and love. *True Love*. The kind that never fades."

"And you did." She whispers.

I smile softly.

"And I did. I found my mate. I found Sofia and Henry. Nelly and Bria. I came to know a kingdom full of love and joy...I came to have a son. I came to know you. All these things...they are why I have been fighting so hard...for so long. They are why I will not give up, not even in the face of death. I lost much...but I gained even more. Trust your heart as I did, little wave. It will not lead you astray."

Her lower lip trembles, and her bright pastel purple eyes shine as tears sting them.

We both stand, and she walks into my embrace, squeezing me tight.

"Thank you...if it hadn't been for you...I never would have known the person I can be—the warrior, I can be." I smooth her soft bangs away from her face.

"You would have. Do not doubt your character. I never have. Now go on. Graven should be in a better mood today since you were late because of me, and not Natonak."

She giggles lightly and nods, grabbing her short sword from its resting place by the door as she exits. That act reminds me of one very important thing I must do today.

57
Elaudia

The heat of the room explodes against my face as I enter the large hut, and I grimace.

I thank the Gods I was never blessed with the ability of metal work. It's too damn hot. Metal crashes against metal, and more than one soldier at work bows as I walk by. I offer them nods, keeping my eyes peeled for the God's blessed blacksmith. Rows and rows of newly fortified steel meet my eyes, and I have to admit, I am impressed.

For Gryffin to have made so many new weapons in such a short period is a true gift. His back finally catches my eyes, and I watch as he pounds the fiery metal into a blade so sharp that it rivals my blades of magic. His strength impresses me, as does the determination etched across his brows.

"Gryffin," I say.

The young boy stiffens immediately and whirls around, his body standing tall.

"My Queen." His chest is heaving with every breath he takes, sweat pouring down his face. My motherly instincts take over before I can stop them.

"Have you eaten? Or slept?"

I wait for him to answer, but the Breadmaker who stayed to help us fight calls out from beside a water trough.

"He hasn't, Your Majesty. That boy has been hammering away at the metal for the past sixteen hours. Ain't even seen him piss, pardon my language."

I roll my eyes at the hefty man, known for his crude sense of humor to the locals, before turning back to a wide-eyed Gryffin.

"Is that true?" I question.

He swallows and licks his lips.

"I have only reached three hundred and four swords, Your Grace. I have another four hundred to complete before the week is up. I will be allotted much time to eat and rest once this war has started."

"Three hundred and four! So many over the night?" How is that even possible?

A couple of the men surrounding him grin and ruffle his sweat-soaked hair.

"This boy is special, that's for sure."

Gryffin shuffles uncomfortably at all the attention, but nods, confirming the count of weapons.

"You need to eat and rest."

He opens his mouth to protest, but I cut him off.

"That is an order. While you eat, I need to discuss something with you." I toss my head to the side, gesturing toward a table.

Gryffin slumps but nods. This is the first time since I ordered him off this land that I've seen him show disgruntlement with me.

"Anything you wish, My Queen."

Gryffin sets his tools down gently before making his way to the small table in the back corner that holds bowls of leftover stew. He wastes no time devouring it, his eyes flickering from me to the bowl as he eats.

"I need you to make something special for Nalah. She is determined to fight in this war, and I will not have her without the best of the best. This weapon should have dual heads, and the sharpest blade you have ever created. She needs every advantage she can get."

"That's the small mermaid shifter, right? The one with the glittery hair?"

His face flushes, and I smirk.

"The one and only. Can it be done?"

Gryffin looks up and nods heartily.

"I'll start now."

He stands quickly, the bowl of stew forgotten. I almost make him sit back down, but I stop myself. He's already back to work, heading straight for a boiling metal pot. I stand and leave the hut, breathing in the cool air—a welcome relief.

Thunder rolls in the distance, causing me to glance to my left. Dark black clouds begin to gather miles and miles away. But I can see them as clearly as they were right over us. It seems the weather mage was on to something. I close my eyes and reach out to my mate.

Have you made any progress with the scrolls?

He responds quickly, his voice gentle.

Not in the slightest. I fear Yarlon's hope was misled, but fear not, little warrior. With or without these scrolls, Plutos stands no chance.

I huff and frown.

Or he is right, and Lytta is not strong enough to defeat her brother.

"I can hear you, you know?"

"Well, it is a valid concern...you were without a host much longer than he was. What if you're not strong enough?"

"I am."

It's all she says as I focus back in on Axel's voice.

Laudi...Elaudia!

Sorry, I'm here. Don't worry about the scrolls; just come home. There is a violent storm coming.

I'll be back before dinner.

I love you.

There's a warm caress against my mind as he responds.

I love you more, little mate.

I focus back in on the world around me, startling when I find Cadmus's stern face staring down at me. He is dressed like me, fully armed and prepared for battle. His golden blonde hair is tied at the nape of his neck, and I grimace, prepared for the lecture.

"You shouldn't be—"

"I know." I drawl.

He snorts and looks around.

"The outer walls are no place for you, not with General Neem's plans unknown." I arch my eyebrow. at his words.

"You do know I am stronger than you, right?"

Cadmus grins and gives me a slight shove.

"If I had magical blood running through my veins, I'd give you a run for your money."

I only hum, letting him think he's right. We both start down the road back to the inner walls, where almost every bit of our army remains. Lightning strikes in the distance, and I look up, letting the static of the coming storm touch my skin. I breathe deeply, almost feeling as if the electricity running through the particles in the air is somehow fueling me.

"Did you hear that Bristol finally grew a pair?"

I snort at Cadmus's remark and shake my head.

"I can't believe he said he wanted to worship her lady bits more than her."

Cadmus looks down at me with wide eyes, his eyebrows arching as if asking me if I am joking. I purse my lips and nod.

"Sometimes I wonder if that boy was dropped on his head as an infant. No one can be that daft in some areas but so intelligent in others."

I giggle, knowing he's right.

"I have to admit, I did not just come looking for you to ensure your safety," Cadmus speaks lowly, his voice carrying a rasp. He slows to a walk on the cobblestone entrance of the castle, and I blink, hardly believing we have already arrived home. I turn to face him, waiting for him to speak. When he finally does, my heart clenches in my chest at the look in his eyes.

"I have never been more proud to know someone...to call someone my family. You have grown so much in these past years, and you have been kicked to the ground more times than I care to remember. But every single time, you have stood your ground and fought back.

And after losing Ollie—" His voice breaks, and he looks down as he tries to clear his throat.

"I thought I had lost you as well as him, *truly* lost you. But you fought for us, all of us. And I am so *fucking* proud of you, Elaudia. I—" I don't let him finish. I throw myself into his arms, tears streaming down my cheeks and his. His arms squeeze me as if he's afraid I will disappear.

"I love you, cousin." He whispers.

I tighten my hold around his neck and squeeze my eyes shut.

"I love you, my brother," I whisper.

He slowly releases me, and I slide to the ground gently, my hands resting on his shoulders. He wipes the tears from my eyes gently, smiling down at me. I open my mouth to speak when Axel's voice suddenly rushes into my mind, causing a wave of dizziness to strike me.

"My love...please don't panic."

I suck in a breath at the hard tone of his voice, focusing in on his presence. When has telling your wife *not* to panic ever made her not panic?

"What is it? Did you find the scrolls?"

"No."

His voice is grim as he answers, and I can feel my heart speed up in my chest as Cadmus watches me with worried eyes.

"What is it, Axel?"

"It's General Neem. His armies have just crested our borders. I will hold them off, but you must prepare the troops immediately; I won't last against them all."

"How many are there?"

My feet are already moving as I sprint for the castle entrance.

"Ten thousand dark rebels, including the God of Greed. I will hold them off...but Elaudia—"

"NO!"

I wince as I screech into our minds but ignore the pain.

"You will not be saying any form of goodbye, mate. I will be there in time. I swear it!"

Silence greets me.

"Axel??"

Nothing.

"Axel!"

I'm crying out loud for him now, but I don't care; my only focus is getting to Kettuna. Cadmus sprints by my side, waiting for me to speak.

"Rally the troops now!! General Neem has just ambushed Axel. I'm going ahead for him! Prepare them and meet us at the borders! Send for Gryffin immediately. He has Nalah's weapons! Do not put her in the first wave!"

My breath skips as I shout orders swiftly, knowing he will remember every single one.

We reach the crest where we need to split up, and I vaguely spot Nelly rushing out from the castle, her brows furrowed with worry. But I can't focus on her or anyone else. My only thought is my mate. My fae mate has a fierce power, but he won't stand a chance against *ten thousand soldiers.*

I rush past them, climbing the outer steps of the East tower.

"Kettuna!!" My voice comes out as a hoarse screech, but I don't care.

Axel.

I need to get to Axel.

My thighs lift high as I sprint up the steps, and I only climb ten more before a powerful beat of wings appears at my side instantly. My chimera friend is fully transformed; her lion's snout lifted into a gruesome snarl. Axel must have reached out to her as well. She lands on the steps, her claws digging into the stone and shaking the foundation as she lowers her wings, allowing me to climb onto her back. A great honor for a Chimera to bestow.

I slide my hands into her mane, holding on tightly as she takes off. She instantly takes to the sky, and I look down, seeing Graven shouting orders at our scrambling fighters. I close my eyes, knowing I must trust my friends to prepare them all. My belly warms with rage as we fly at a speed we've never flown before, the thick muscles in Kettuna's back working fiercely as her wings pump, carrying us toward the blackened clouds miles ahead.

We won't make it.

A voice whispers in my mind, slowly spilling a seed of doubt until it overflows, causing my chest to constrict with terror. I was too late with Oliver. I didn't make it in time. And now history is repeating—only this time—with *my mate*. General Neem has been a step ahead of us in this war for so long, having concocted his plans before I was born.

I'm supposed to be better than him.

I *have* to be better than him.

"And so you will be, young queen."

Lytta whispers across my mind gently, almost sounding like a grandmother who would soothe her beloved young.

The wind beats against my face, and the thunder rolls viciously, getting louder and louder the closer we get. I can see them now, just on the horizon. A sea of black to match the storm clouds—their swords lifted high—and at the very back, a steed of pure midnight carries General Neem, his body swaying as if he can hardly hold himself up.

"No human is meant to carry the essence of a God...it is time for us to rest...both of us," Lytta says softly.

My eyebrows furrow as she speaks, trying to decipher what she means, when my eyes finally catch Axel's form. He looks minuscule from our height in the sky, but I would know him anywhere. He has fully transformed; his Fae nature taking over. Pure muscle ripples across his body, his arms loosely holding the two ancient broadswords he always wears.

He is ready.

I can tell from his stance as the army closes in on him. My breath stutters, and my lips lift into an involuntary snarl. How dare they think to attack him? How dare they try to take my mate from me? An ugly beast rises inside me as the first wave reaches him, and I don't even notice that Kettuna has begun to nosedive straight into the ground. A sword is raised, pointing straight, and its destination? My mate's chest.

His heart.

They took my little fish.

Blue eyes.

They took Sofia and Henry. I begin scream-ing.

Blue eyes.

They will *not* take my mate.

"It is time," Lytta whispers.

A flush of power soaks my skin as I scream out my rage, a glow of blue shimmering across my body as my white eyes focus on the soldiers below. Kettuna bellows out, a roar that echoes to the mountains miles away. She viciously lands in front of Axel as my power explodes out of me in a tidal wave, just as the first line of dark rebels reaches us. Fiery waves of blue burst out of the clouds ruthlessly, hopping from soldier to soldier as if they were all connected by the same current of life. My power shakes the ground beneath us, my hands raised as if commanding the electric flames to each destination.

The Earth beneath their feet breaks open, tiny cracks slowly departing from each other until craters form around us. I don't see their panicked faces. I don't see their bodies fall to the ground, dead. I don't see the second wave, a mile behind, stop abruptly, their mouths agape in fear.

Kettuna turns to the side, and I immediately search for Axel's eyes, my mind wanting to ensure his safety—to ensure he is alive.

He is.

My mate stands behind us, his swords lowered as he looks up at me with reverence. The power surge from Lytta's fades slowly, leaving me with my previous power. It's not as strong as Lytta's, but it will be enough to defeat the last two waves. I can hear the pounding hoofbeats of our army approaching.

We can win this.

"My beautiful mate...I cannot wait to feast upon you coated in the blood of our enemies." Axel purrs, his black eyes watching me with love and lust. At that look, I can finally breathe again. Kettuna suddenly snarls beneath my fingertips and twists, lunging for the soldier aiming for my back. Her jowls open wide as she rips into his neck, tearing his head from his body.

"Let us fight, small female. I yearn to taste the blood of my cub's murderers."

Her trill is savage, and I quickly slide from her back, permitting her free rein to focus on the kill and not worry about me. Kettuna swipes left and right, taking our enemy down without remorse, and I rush to Axel, letting his forehead fall to mine.

"I love you," I state with untamed emotion. His thick hand tilts my head up as he places a kiss on my lips.

"I'll say it back once this is done, little warrior. Stay alive."

I nod and let my arms fall, my blue swords slowly materializing from thin air.

"You too."

I step back as he smiles, and then he lunges from the ground and launches himself into the middle of the second wave, taking them down from the inside out. I spin out as the sound of metal slicing through the air reaches my ears, and I thrust backward, letting my sword slice the soldier behind me in half. My blood sings in my veins as I twist and turn, taking them down individually.

I can tell they think I am the bigger threat, so they swarm me first, not realizing it gives Kettuna and Axel the biggest advantage to take them down from behind. Blood sprays my face as they fall, one by one, soon leaving me with red-soaked skin. Only ten minutes pass before the ground thunders again, but this time, it's not from the rumble of mine or Lytta's powers.

Our troops are here.

Horses gallop towards us, men and women alike bellowing out in anticipation of their long-overdue vengeance. Clarice sits forefront with my Bellator sisters, their weapons aimed, though they cannot kill on this land. They're here to give our weaker warriors an upper hand. I spin to avoid a flying arrow before turning one of my swords into a shield of luminescent blue, blocking a flurry of fast-approaching archers.

A sword reaches me from behind, and I cry out as the skin on my back opens swiftly. Axel's eyes reach my pain-filled ones from across the battlefield, and he snarls with a deadly rage, disappearing from his spot, causing the two soldiers attacking him to impale themselves on the other's weapons. He reappears behind me, and his arm reaches out, breaking my attacker's neck mercilessly.

"Elaudia—"

"I'm okay! Watch out!"

I shove him to the side and let my power burst out of me, forcing the three soldiers back a few feet before swinging my sword and decapitating them. I turn back to him to urge him to keep going when an ear–splitting screech echoes around us. Our troops have started on the second wave, standing half a mile away from where we stand in the midst of the third.

I can no longer see General Neem, but I can feel him.

He's close.

Cadmus and Natonak fight side by side on the ground, abandoning their horses. I follow the screeching sounds and see Graven—his body fully transformed into the great beast that lives in the other half of his soul. His scales are wet from the rain beginning to fall, but that is not what stops me in my tracks.

Nalah sits on his back, holding on for dear life. He swoops low, his spiked tail batting away flying arrows before he opens his large snout and breathes fire. The screams of our enemy sound like a lullaby to my eardrums, and I can see Nalah pointing out areas, most likely the most heavily populated groups, where the dark rebels have yet to split up.

Fire and rain rage all around us, along with screams and cries of anger.

A familiar grunt to my left catches my attention, and I see Bristol taken to the ground by a dark rebel. They roll a few feet, the dark rebel struggling to keep the upper hand. My eyes widen as the man pins Bristol from behind, but my promiscuous friend only laughs.

"If I tilt my ass up just a hair, would it make you more comfortable?"

The man pinning him snarls and goes to cut his throat, but Bristol's hand is already wrapping around the hilt of his hidden dagger. He thrusts up, piercing the rebel's kidney before rolling and pushing him off. Bristol attacks once more, stabbing him in the heart before tossing his dagger into his left hand and putting his sword back in his right. He catches my eyes before tossing me a devious smile.

"Worried about me, little lady?"

I roll my eyes and turn my glowing sword into a whip, swinging it around him and lashing out at the ankles of the two approaching rebels behind him. I pull hard, watching them fall and scramble as Bristol turns to kill them.

"Stay alive!" I call to him before turning away to take on my enemies.

The rain turns into a full–blown storm, and mud splashes up as I sprint through the soldiers, killing anyone in my way. My body feels as if it's taken an eternity to clear a path, but I finally catch sight of the General. His face slowly lowers until he is no longer staring into the clouds, and his eyes lock onto mine. Slowly, a grin lifts the corners of his lips, the sinister smile shaking me to my core.

That is all the warning I have before a shudder leaves his body and blue flames sweep down from the sky, striking targets all around the battlefield. I look up at the sky, my gaze homed in on Nalah and Graven. Graven screeches as a flame goes straight through his left wing, and the breath leaves my lungs as his enormous form folds, plummeting out of the sky. My breath shudders as I realize what is happening.

He can replicate power.

58
Elaudia

My throat closes, and I cannot breathe as I do nothing but watch the great beast fall from the sky.

Nalah clings tightly to his spikes, her newly forged weapons strapped to her back. The wind rushes against them—and I can see her lips moving, though I cannot make out the words.

"Graven!!!" I bellow out, my voice straining as I scream, imploring him to save them both.

This is not how they die, goddammit! He falls another hundred feet before roaring a deadly bellow and straightening himself in the sky. His great head shakes back and forth as he shrieks his anger and unleashes a flurry of flames bigger than ever before, immediately disintegrating a hundred soldiers at once. He lands on the piles of ash below him, ultimately disrespecting the dead.

Good.

His wing twitches, and I grimace at the large red-ringed hole there, knowing that it must be an unimaginable pain. Nalah's lips are moving as she climbs down, and I want to run to her, but I know that will just turn General Neem's attention to her. Plutos wanted the dragon out of the sky, which he got.

Now, I must finish him before he redirects his sight to my little wave or the others. I launch onto the lowest point of the mountain, using my power to propel me from ledge to ledge. I can feel my strength waning as I go, but I push forward. Lytta's initial display drained me more than I care to admit. Just as I reach the crest where he stands, power slams into me, tilting me off the ledge. I quickly right myself and send back my wave of power, blasting him just as fiercely.

His chest rumbles with laughter that is not his own.

"So...we finally meet where the sky touches the earth. A fitting end for you, sister. Though you would think dying would grow old. I figured once was enough."

Lytta ignores his jabs, so I do as well, and I can tell it infuriates him.

He stalks back and forth, watching me with keen eyes.

"Where is Karisma?" I ask him softly, wondering about the whereabouts of the young black witch.

His nose twitches, and he tilts his head.

"She was irritating me a bit too much, groaning on and on about how weak she was becoming. So, I killed her."

He shrugs as if it's nothing, but I know it must have been Plutos who swung the sword. Karisma was way too valuable to General Neem. He steps closer, a look of malice in his eyes.

"You know, it didn't have to be this way. I only needed your help. If you had only agreed and hadn't gone to Zeus and Hera...we could have ruled in their stead! We could have had everything!"

He's speaking through me to Lytta, and I watch the veins in his neck bulge as he continues to pace back and forth. Slowly, it falls into place, and I have an epiphany.

A very *gross* epiphany.

"You love her," I whisper.

General Neem stops pacing as I speak. His mouth clenches shut as he watches me, and Lytta neither confirms nor denies it. She just...waits.

"Yes..." He says darkly. "I *loved* her. I wanted her, and only her! But she betrayed me. Just as General Neem loved Queen Fridella, but she betrayed him for her *beloved* Griffin." He snarls.

My eyes widen as he speaks my parents' names, but before I can say anything, Lytta takes over for the first time since our meeting—her words guiding my tongue.

"We are creators first and foremost. You only seek to destroy. You only seek death. The same can be said for the General. Even *Thanatos* had a better sense of life than you, Plutos."

Those words enrage the being in front of us, and he roars his rage, rushing us. And I know why. Lytta loved Thanatos. And Plutos loved Lytta. It was a fucking God filled love triangle.

My head is still spinning at this new information surrounding General Neem and my mother, but I can no longer think about it. Not when General Neem and Plutos come for us, attacking brutally with everything they have. I summon my weapons and cross them over my face just as he lands in front of me and pummels his fists forward.

But his fists aren't the weapon; the unknown force field he's projecting is. I meet his power head-on, standing my ground as we trade blows back and forth. He's working me to the edge, but I let my arms flow with fire, allowing my gift to engulf my weapons. I strike him in the kidney, and he bellows out, clearly not used to being struck.

A dark laugh leaves my lips.

"You're so weak." I mock.

That only makes him angrier, which is what I was aiming for. We dance around each other, and rocks fall from the ledge as we go, reminding me of the cliff we fight on. The sounds of battle reach my ears once more as I focus on the fighters below.

I search for Axel as I fight the general—or Plutos—striking once before looking down. I can't see him. I can't see Nalah either. She no longer stands with Graven. The battlefield flows red with blood. General Neem's sword slices through my ribcage, and my vision blurs from the splattering of blood. I curse my distraction.

I thought I would be used to it by now.

The bloodshed.

The cries of sorrow and the rage of their screams.

Maybe I am.

Maybe I have split myself into two—to survive what was wrought upon me unwillingly.

The younger version of myself who was carefree and happy. Truly happy. Before the truth. Before the training. Before the heartache and death.

My swords strike out, returning a wound to my opponent.

I can't see him.

My heart beats faster in my chest as I look down and around at the hills of bodies before deflecting another of the general's blows. I reach out for Axel's mind, but touch nothing.

I can't see him. That's the only reason I am still breathing.

I steel my spine and calm myself. I'll find him.

But I can't see or feel him.

I can't see him or her.

I focus back in on my fight, but just as quickly, a fist clashes into the side of my head with a brutal force of power, and suddenly, I am lost.

59
Elaudia

"Mama...mama, wake up."

His voice is just as I remember it, that childish lilt so soft and innocent. My eyes slowly flutter open, and I sit upright, realizing I am no longer on the bloody battlefield. White flowers and the yellow silk gown I now wear surround me. No blood touches my skin, no crown upon my head. And sitting in front of me, perched on his knees, is my *son*.

"Oliver...?" I whisper, my voice breaking his name into three syllables slowly.

My beautiful little boy smiles brilliantly as he falls into me, his little arms wrapping tight- ly around my neck.

"I missed you, Mama." He says softly.

Tears flow freely from my eyes as I inhale the soft scent of the salty ocean and cotton. A scent I thought I would never smell again.

"Oh, my baby." I cry. Oliver pulls away gently, using his tiny hands to wipe my warm tears.

"Don't cry, Mama...everything is going to be okay."

I shake my head fiercely.

"It's not okay...you're not with me. You're not where you belong. You're alone."

I sob deeply as my fingers brush through his black curls as I try to memorize every detail of his little face. He sits in my lap as I cradle him, soaking in the feel of my son once again in my arms. Where he should have been for as long as possible. But I failed him.

My *little fish.*

"But Mama...I'm not alone."

His tiny voice breaks through my sorrow, and I turn to follow his gaze. My heart breaks into a thousand pieces at the sight that greets me, and I'm suddenly sobbing harder than before.

Sofia stands between two men, both taller than her. They all stand there peacefully, gentle smiles on their faces. Henry...and...

Oh my God.

Claude.

The strong man cradles a little girl close to his chest as he looks down at me with warm eyes. The little girl has brown hair the same shade as Sofia's.

Odette.

My mind whispers. Sofia's daughter.

They all smile at me, and I sob harder, tightening my hold on my son. Two more figures step out from behind them, a petite woman with full curves and hair as black night. She clings to a sturdily built man; his face covered in a full beard.

"It is not your time yet, my beautiful miracle."

The woman speaks softly, her eyes carrying a fierce love, and my breath catches. It is the same way I look at my son.

"Mother...?" I whisper.

Fridella flashes me a breathtaking smile before looking up at the man she holds on to. A tiny hand redirects my face, and I glance down at my son, who wears a solemn look.

"I'm right where I'm supposed to be, Mama. It's all gonna be okay. But they need you still."

My son speaks with wisdom beyond his years, and I look up at Sofia.

"He's right, my love. Your fight is not over yet. Now wake up."

I shake my head. I can't.

I must say it out loud because their eyes turn sad. Something shakes my foundation at my refusal.

"Mama...please...wake up!"

I glance down at Ollie, but it's not him speaking. He only looks at me with a small smile.

"Go on, Mama. I'm okay...I promise. I'll be right here waiting for you when it's time. Tell Papa I love him more than anything." He whispers.

Everything around me shakes again, threatening this perfect illusion around me.

"Please, Mama...please don't leave me here alone."

I can hear the sobs echoing throughout the peaceful field I sit in, the sound wrenching my gut as I stare down at my son...my son who's already dead.

Am I dead?

I furrow my brows and close my eyes, listening to that voice.

I know that voice.

Nalah!

"Nalah...?"

I glance down at my son, who no longer sits in my lap. He stands in front of Sofia, who has gentle hands placed on top of his shoulders. Fridella smiles down at her grandchild with pride before looking back at me. They all smile at me, but I focus only on my little fish's face.

His is the last face I see before I'm thrown out of this illusion and back into a world of bloodshed and violence, where a small mermaid shifter kneels in front of me, shaking my body in an attempt to wake me up. Sobs wrack her delicate body, and I glance to my left, noting the ground I lie on. I'm no longer at the top of the cliff. General Neem knocked me off, and I wince as the soreness comes to my body.

"Please wake up." Nalah moans through her cries, her eyes closed.

I must make a noise because her eyes open, and she cries out with relief, her arms wrapping around my frame.

"Shhh...it's okay, little wave."

She cries harder at that, her arms tightening. We cling to each other for one more moment before she sits back, her lips wobbling.

"We saw you fall from the cliff...I t–thought..."

I cut her off, pushing hair from her face as we stand.

"I won't go down so easily."

My eyes scan the area for General Neem, catching sight of him just as he appears above us, his face grim with determination. He launches himself from the cliff, but before I can move, Nalah shoves me to the side and meets his sword with her new weapons. She grunts as the force of the impact hits her, but pushes on, swinging with the hand of a mad woman. I watch momentarily as the weeks of training take hold of her, and she fights him with the heart of a lion. Blood spills from my temple, and I groan as I flex my arm, almost positive it's broken.

He snarls at Nalah, taking the force of her blows and returning them tenfold. Pride settles into my chest as I watch her become the warrior I always knew she could be, but I'm done playing games with him. I open the lock inside my mind, allowing my power to wash over me. Static sparks along my skin, and the surrounding air no longer escaped Neem's notice.

"Lytta..." I trail off, knowing she will know what I'm asking of her.

It is time to end this.

"Stand strong, young queen. This will hurt."

I breathe deeply, coming to terms with what's about to happen. I don't know how I know...but I do. Lytta's power unfurls inside me for a second time, but an ache spreads across my bones this time.

Nalah continues to push him back away from me, and I glance to my left, where Graven fights his way through the hordes of rebels on the ground in his human form. He was much too big of a target in his dragon form on the ground. Blood soaks his arm, and the entire limb is singed black, but his eyes are locked onto Nalah. I meet his eyes when he turns, slicing his sword through the stomach of a rebel.

I nod softly and watch as the realization reaches his mind. He sprints for Nalah, determined to get her out of the way. The air around me is thick, and my hair begins to lift away from my face—the locks loose, having fallen from the tight braid around my head.

Nalah cries out as General Neem catches her sword and twists her arm, but she only kicks back, snapping her booted foot into his kneecap. He snarls and throws her to the ground, but then Graven is there, partly shifted as he blocks a killing blow to Nalah and picks her up. Blood trickles from her nose where her face hit the ground, and I get angrier, the rage fueling me.

"Run," Graven grumbles fiercely to Nalah as they move away, her panicked eyes looking back at me. They calm when she catches sight of me, standing with power oozing from my every pore.

"Lytta...don't." Plutos has surfaced again, his eyes holding a warning and the tiniest bit of fear.

She doesn't listen or respond. Only fuels my body with more. The pain is beginning to sink in, but I hold on, my son's words echoing through my mind.

"It's not your time yet."

"Lytta!"

The wind picks up around us, swirling dirt and blood together until I can no longer tell the difference. An ancient tongue reaches my ears, but I slowly realize I'm not hearing it out loud. It comes from within me, inside my mind. Plutos stalks forward, his face ashen.

"Don't!"

"Thanatos!"

Plutos roars his rage, his face turning purple with blood as he screams out his anger. But the sound is drowned out as lightning cracks through the sky and splits the earth before us. The power rushes through my body, and I cry out as the power inside me flows out like a tidal wave, the force encircling us until another figure appears.

A man steps out of the portal I just made, his frame bigger than life. Horns protrude from his forehead, with curls of black hair falling around his face. A sneer lifts his lips as he looks around at the bloodshed, an almost frantic look in his eyes before they finally settle on me.

"Lytta." He mouths the words but doesn't speak.

How is this possible?

I just created a portal for a *God.*

"It is your power...the strongest that still walks this earth."

Thanatos still stares at me with an uncomfortable look, but I remind myself that he is seeing Lytta's essence, not my own.

"My love."

The words come from my right, and I startle as Axel appears by my side, his skin red and chest heaving. Nobody moves or speaks for what seems like an eternity when, finally, Thanatos glances around.

"I have seen the bloodshed you have wreaked upon our creations, Plutos. We have all watched and decided that only one punishment fits such a crime."

Plutos snarls and lifts his sword toward me.

"Raise your finger at me, death sorcerer, and I will have my sword plunged into the neck of your beloved before you can get the words out.

Zeus may have cast me out of the Heavens, but he cannot remove me from the earth. My essence is to do with as I please."

Thanatos raises a brow as Axel steps slightly to the right, his body acting as a shield to me. Plutos's eyes shift back and forth, and even I can read their panic.

"You'll need to distract Plutos so Thanatos may successfully extract his essence."

A smirk reaches my lips at Lytta's words. I can most certainly do that.

"So..." I say towards Plutos. "I heard you were in love with my mother Fridella."

His eyes flicker at her name, and I watch as the struggle inside his mind ensues as General Neem fights for control. His body twitches, his thin frame swaying to the side before his eyes flicker and General Neem appears, his essence surfacing briefly.

"Fridella..." He gasps.

I nod. "Yes...Fridella. I can see why she chose my father...he's much better looking."

Axel snorts from behind me, and Neem's face darkens with rage.

"I was her closest friend for decades—her most loyal general and advisor—and she chose a fae blood over *me*."

My heart stops at that information, but I keep him distracted as Thanatos quietly moves away from his line of sight, a black mist taking over his eyes.

I grin and glance back at my mate.

"Can you blame her? They are *such* good lovers."

Axel flashes me a wicked grin, and we watch Neem's eyes flicker as Plutos attempts to take control again, his arm moving to spear me with his sword. I twist away as it flies towards me, letting my weapons transform into a bow and arrow. The sword flies by my head, the metal cutting a few locks of my hair off. I pull back and let the arrow fly, hitting my mark.

The tip pierces Neem's neck, and his eyes widen as Thanatos places his large hands on his head from behind, words falling from his tongue.

"Veni ad me anima, portae inferi."

"What does it mean?" I ask Lytta in my mind.

"This language is for the ears of a deity alone, but he is pulling the soul of Plutos, his very essence, from the general, where he will escort him to the gates of hell. Where he belongs."

"Sounds rough."

She doesn't answer.

The cries of war around us begin silencing as an orb of glowing red leaves Neem's body and stays nestled firmly in the hands of Thanatos. General Neem's body drops to the ground, dead, the arrow still in his neck. Thanatos looks up, his eyes disinterested, until they rest on me. I catch a brief longing gaze before he closes his eyes and turns away, walking slowly to the portal that brought him into our realm.

"He cannot speak to me. My essence, though disgraced, shall live on. He could speak to Plutos because he was here to take his soul for eternal damnation. It is forbidden for him to speak to the disgraced."

Her voice is small and sad as she speaks.

Thanatos turns, his large body causing the ground to tremble with each step. I don't know why, but I step forward, closing the distance between us.

"She loved you too." I declare.

Lytta helped us win this war...I can't let their story go without closure. His entire body freezes, standing so still, I fear I broke him. He doesn't turn back to face us, nor does he make a move to speak.

"She forgives you for not believing her. She forgives you, and she loves you."

Thanatos still doesn't say anything, though I swear on my life; I watch as his shoulders droop in what looks like relief. And then he is gone, stepping through the portal that diminishes from our sight within seconds. As does Lytta's essence.

A featherlight touch reaches my cheek as I breathe out, and I'm left only with whispered words and pain from the battle.

"Be well, young queen."

And then my world goes dark.

60
Epilogue

Laughter greets me as I slowly wake, the air around me clean and fresh.

It has been a few weeks since the battle of the Gods—as Cadmus and Natonak so intelligently named it—and our citizens have been returning in clusters. I roll onto my side, humming softly at the sight that greets me. My mate lies on his back, his thick chest cradling one arm, the other behind my head. The morning sun shines into our room, hitting his sharp cheekbones gently, and I smile, reaching out to stroke his hair away from his forehead.

He shifts at my touch, his eyes slowly opening. His lips pull into a smile when he sees me, and he turns, rolling my body into his. His hands roam everywhere, and I sigh into his chest, breathing in his scent.

"My beautiful miracle." He murmurs.

The words strike me through my chest, and I sit up abruptly. Axel's brows furrow with concern, and he follows me into a sitting position.

"Laudi...?" I glance up into his eyes and whisper hoarsely.

"I forgot...after everything happened. It was real." I say softly. Axel runs a hand through my hair before using his fingers to move my face up.

"What was real, little warrior?" A gentle sob escapes my lips before I can stop it.

"I saw Ollie."

Axel's eyes widen as I speak, and he sits back; his eyes locked onto mine.

"When I fell from the cliff, I woke up—but I didn't wake up here. I was in a field of flowers." I murmur.

Axel nods at me, encouraging me to continue.

"Oliver was there...with Sofia and Henry and Odette and Claude. And my parents. They were all there, smiling at me. And O-Ollie—"" I choke on his name, tears dripping softly down my cheeks.

"Ollie was in my lap. He was touching my face."

Axel chokes, and I watch as his eyes burn red with unshed tears.

"He told me it wasn't my time."

Axel closes his eyes, and I watch as one single tear leaves his eyes as his forehead touches mine. I reach up to cup his cheeks.

"He told me to tell you that you were the best Papa in the world." I tremble as I speak, and then Axel is crushing me to his chest as his own shudders with barely contained sobs.

"He's okay." He murmurs roughly. I nod into his neck.

"He's okay," I murmur back.

And then we're both smiling at each other at the knowledge that even though our little fish isn't here with us, he's safe and happy.

He's *loved*.

And one day, we will see him again.

A frantic knock bursts through our intimate moment together, and I startle, looking at the door.

"Come in!"

Nelly bursts through the doors, her face panicked, but happy.

"It's happening!"

My heart drops as I stumble out of bed to stand, grabbing my silk robe.

"Bria?! It's still too early!"

Nelly trembles with excitement as she backs away, gesturing for us to come quickly.

"I guess the little one is eager to come into this world."

Axel and I dress quickly, my mate throwing on a loose shirt and breeches as Nelly respectfully turns away. We hurry out the door and rush down the stairs to the labor room. Cries reach my ears as we enter, and my eyes widen at how many people take up the space amongst us. Cadmus and Bria did approve for our chosen family to be present—but still—it shocks me that they're all here.

Natonak stands close to Graven and Nalah, and Bristol wipes sweat from Bria's forehead gently as Cadmus holds her hand, coaxing her with gentle words.

"Come on then, you knew what was gonna happen when you let him come in—"

"Bristol!!" I scold him as I rush over, smacking him on the head.

He grins at me sheepishly before backing away with his hands raised. He offers Bria a wink before striding over to the other three by the wall.

Bria's face is red as she looks up at me, searching for a better comfort than Bristol could provide.

Dumbass.

"Laudi..." She sobs.

I hush her softly and shake my head.

"Do you see the people surrounding you? The people who already love this child as if she were their own?"

Bria nods frantically, looking around. I step to the side as our castle doctor appears with Yarlon, Kaleen, and two healers. They begin preparing for the child.

"Nothing bad will happen with them here, I swear it. She's going to be fine."

I don't let any doubt cross my face as I speak, and Cadmus shoots me a grateful look as Bria finally begins to calm down, relaxing her body as much as a woman in labor can.

"You and this little girl will have a long, *happy* life together."

I'm speaking to both of them, and tears prick Cadmus's eyes. Bria moans as another contraction hits, but she nods her head. The doctor places himself at the end of the bed as the healers take hold of her legs. Nalah looks at the scene as if it's the most beautiful sight in the world, her fingers digging into Graven's large bicep. Graven looks like he would rather be anywhere else, but he stands still, never leaving Nalah's side.

"Push." The doctor commands.

I nod at Bria, and determination sweeps across her brow as she closes her eyes and pushes.

Her labor goes on for a short time, her body slowly draining from the exertion until—finally—a piercing cry echoes throughout the room all around us. Cadmus looks down with wonder, his face alight with a joy I've never seen from him before.

The healers begin working on the girl immediately as I kiss Bria's sweaty forehead. She looks up at me with hazy eyes and a tired smile.

"You did it," I whisper.

She smiles back, tears falling from her eyes. Cadmus follows the healers, not letting his daughter out of sight for one moment. Nalah smiles up at Graven, and I watch him smile softly back at her. Bristol high-fives Natonak, and I roll my eyes before looking at Axel. His eyes are warm and alight with love.

"Look around you, my little warrior, at this family you have created."

His voice whispers across my mind gently, and I smile back at him, the pain that once held a place in my heart soothed for the first time since it arrived. Cadmus takes the little bundle of pink into his arms, rocking her gently as he brings the baby to Bria, who eagerly holds her arms out. The smile she shines on the baby is brighter than the sun, and then she looks up at me.

"Meet your Goddaughter, Sonella."

I cry softly as she hands me her newborn baby, a true honor and privilege. I cradle the baby gently, cooing down at her softly. Her eyes look up sightlessly, and I grin, kissing her fore-head. As I hand Sonella back to her parents a few moments later, laughter surrounds me. An echo of my son's laughter, a joy that once was—and will one day—be once more.

***

A few months later

"Word has reached across the sea of your success on the battlefield. Many people who once called this land their home are eager to return."

Lynola smiles gently at me from across the council table, and I breathe a sigh of relief. We were uncertain about word traveling across the seas, but it seems Natonak was successful on his voyage. A voyage that Bristol and Nelly joined him on.

Axel sits back lazily, his arm resting on the back of my chair.

"Keep scouts at the docks. Let them pass along the message. Anyone who wishes to help us rebuild this land and the surrounding kingdoms to their former glory is welcome. But there will be no fighting—no bloodshed—else they deal with me."

The council all nod, agreeing with this.

As do I.

These people will be their own; it will be up to them to handle each bloodline. They stand as one and bow to us, and I grin as Niho places a heavy hand on my shoulder, squeezing lightly. I breathe deeply as they leave, and then it's only my mate and I left in the room.

"Cadmus wants to take Sonella and Bria to Aland. He's eager to join with Jaharis and Nyreen in rebuilding what Helena broke."

Axel arches his eyebrows.

"Have you made your decision?" He questions softly.

I smile and twine my fingers through his, nodding.

"Jaharis and Nyreen will ascend to the throne of Aland, with Cadmus and Bria as their successors."

"And Lashforn?"

I wince at the mention of my aunt and uncle's kingdom.

"Well...it's nothing but a crater in the earth now. Can we expand our walls? Nalah has received word that Roarke has returned to the sea and is content to stay there, ruling the sirens and mermaids in Prosteria in her absence. That might one day prove to be a problem."

"He's an untried youngling with a temper that will get him into trouble." Axel comments dryly.

"Yes, but Nalah wishes to stay here with Graven. She turns seventeen soon, and the mating effect will slowly begin. She'll want to be close, whether she knows it yet or not. And Graven won't want her out of his sight."

Axel chuckles, stroking my hair away from my face.

"I know the feeling all too well." He murmurs.

He leans forward and kisses me softly, his tongue coaxing my mouth open. I moan into him, imprinting the feeling of my mate's skin on mine.

I glance over at the door, wondering if Tylsa closed it behind her.

She did.

Devious thoughts fill my mind, and then I stand, moving to straddle my husband. His legs widen to accommodate me, letting me settle into his lap comfortably. I lean down, peppering kisses along his jawline as his head falls back.

"Little warrior...do you want something?" He murmurs huskily. I nod into his neck as I grind my center against his hard length.

His rough hands caress my hips gently before latching on, his hold tight and unforgiving as he begins to work my center, grinding it down until a warmth flutters through my lower belly.

"I was thinking..." I pant softly as he moves my dress up until my legs are bare, spread, and waiting for him. I don't even see his fingers as he unbuttons his pants, and then I'm being impaled on his cock, the thickness of him stretching me open deliciously.

I hum softly in pleasure, letting him know that I'm listening to his words.

"I haven't left the walls of Our Kingdom in so long...and we never did take an official honeymoon."

He lifts me up and down, impaling me onto his cock, faster and faster. His lips reach my breast, and he pulls a hard nipple into his mouth, biting down gently. I cry out.

"Once the refugees and our citizens are settled, I'm taking you away for a week."

My eyes are half closed with pleasure, but I'm aware enough to sit back, still grinding my clit against him in a way that makes my toes curl.

"Oh, are you?" I say breathlessly. He growls against my neck, flexing his cock into me until I'm whimpering for my release.

"Yes...I'm going to take you away where no one will disturb us, and then I'm going to fuck you raw until your belly is swollen with our child."

I cry out at his words as my release crashes into me violently, hitting me out of nowhere.

"There you go..." He murmurs. "Such a good girl." He groans deeply as his own release hits, and then he's coming inside me, his seed taking root in my womb. He holds me tight to his body, his cock flexing inside my walls. Strong hands whisper up and down my back, and I snuggle into my mate, thinking about what he said.

The thought of having another child should terrify me, and it does slightly. But it also does something more.

It excites me.

So, I look into my mate's eyes, the male who saved me in every way possible, and nod.

"Okay."

Made in the USA
Middletown, DE
16 November 2025

20776470R00378